ON PAIN OF DEATH

On Pain of Death

A SUMACH MYSTERY BY

Jan Rehner

SUMACH
PRESS

LIBRARY AND ARCHIVES CANADA CATALOGUING IN PUBLICATION

Rehner, Jan
On pain of death : a Sumach mystery / Jan Rehner.

ISBN 978-1-894549-66-0

I. Title.

PS8585.E4473O6 2007   C813'.6   C2007-903672-4

Edited by Jennifer Day
Copy-edited by Emmanuelle Allison
Cover and design by Elizabeth Martin

*Sumach Press acknowledges the support of the Canada Council
for the Arts and the Ontario Arts Council for our publishing program.
We acknowledge the financial support of the Government of Canada
through the Book Publishing Industry Development Program
(BPIDP) for our publishing activities.*

ONTARIO ARTS COUNCIL
CONSEIL DES ARTS DE L'ONTARIO

Printed and bound in Canada

Published by
SUMACH PRESS
1415 Bathurst Street #202
Toronto Canada
M5R 3H8
info@sumachpress.com
www.sumachpress.com

To my sisters
Betty, Nancy and Shirley

ACKNOWLEDGEMENTS

I wish to thank Fran Cohen and Alan Davies, first readers and fast friends; Dominique O'Neill, *mon amie*, for guiding me through 1940s French; and the women of Sumach for their advice and continual support. I am indebted to Jennifer Day, a dream of an editor. And, as ever, Arthur Haberman: map reader, driver, researcher and listener, from first word to last.

"Asking yourself a question, that's how resistance begins. And then ask that very question to someone else."

— REMCO CAMPERT, Dutch poet, from "Someone Asks a Question"as featured in the Museum of Resistance in Amsterdam, the Netherlands.

"If you save one life, it is as if you have saved the whole world."

TRADITIONAL JEWISH SAYING

JULIETTE BENOIT

JUNE 1940 – JULY 1942

June 18, 1940

Paris has disappeared.

A week ago, as the steady boom of artillery drew closer, I watched the desperate flight of citizens from a window overlooking the Gare d'Austerlitz. By the time the Germans marched into the city on June 14, their triumph watched only by stragglers or the most stubborn of Parisians, the narrow, winding streets and grand boulevards lined with chestnut trees were eerily quiet. Now, as I write these pages, the Germans seem almost festive. They are taking photos of each other and visiting famous landmarks. They don't realize that Paris is missing. I am documenting its memory.

My name is Juliette Benoit. In a few days, weeks or months, I may be dead. In the meantime, I cling to words, to the here and now. My words ground me, shelter me. They may survive me when all else melts into air. Perhaps some unknown hand in some unknown future may find this document, turn its pages and hear one woman's voice whispering from the darkness. This is my story, my testimony.

I fell in love with the real Paris before the world went mad. I came to study French literature at the Sorbonne and to discover what lay beyond my little town of Chapleau in northern Ontario. Europe was darkening even then, but the skies still seemed bright in Canada and I heeded no warnings.

The Paris that welcomed me was generous and gay. My fellow students teased me about my French, street French they called it, rough-edged and nasal. But I didn't mind. I told them the bare facts about Chapleau, a tough little railroad town of only a few thousand. Its only claim to fame is that Louis Hémon, who wrote *Marie Chapdelaine*, the bible of schoolgirls in Quebec, was struck by a train there and killed outright in the summer of 1913. Of course, no one in Paris had ever heard of Chapleau, but since they'd not heard of Toronto either, I was secretly pleased. In their eyes, I was even exotic. Over wine or endless coffees in the student cafés, I could cast a spell over my friends by describing the thick forests of ancient trees and granite, the deep green lakes and the dancing lights of the Aurora Borealis that sweep across the huge night skies of my home.

Gradually, my French improved, tutored by passionate discussions of Hugo, Zola, Flaubert and Malraux. My friends and I talked about everything from philosophy to art to who sold the best baguettes. I discovered that I held my knife and fork differently than they did. I learned to smoke Gitanes. We went dancing and listened to music in smoky little jazz clubs. We took long walks that started on the Île-Saint Louis and traced all the bridges of Paris. We even talked about Hitler and the Nazis. We laughed about them, God help us.

My friends opened up the city for me. It was as if, all my life, I had been looking at Paris in a black and white picture book. Then suddenly I was seeing it with depth and undertones, as if I had turned a page in the book and come unexpectedly upon a colour plate. I'd always thought that the City of Light meant that the city never slept, but now I understood the meaning behind the name. Here the light is fluid, shifting, filled with surprise. Sometimes, when the sky is overcast, it looks bruised and the light is purplish blue. Sometimes, on sunny afternoons, the light is pale champagne, almost liquid. Most often, the light is pink, a soft rose. Street musicians play Edith Piaf's song "La Vie en Rose" for the tourists. It means seeing life through rose-coloured glasses. But the tune is haunting, and I've seen even the most sophisticated Parisians look dreamy when they hear it. Only in Paris, where the light is pink, would it move them.

My first studio apartment was far from romantic. It was cramped and a long climb up from the heart of the city in the Montmartre district. The hallway usually smelled of sweaty bodies and stale urine, and I learned to take a scrub brush with me when I went to wash in the shared bathroom. I also brought along a chair to jam under the doorknob to discourage unwanted visitors.

If I arrived late at night, I had to fend off amorous drunks, and artists who couldn't draw to save their lives, begging me to pose for them in the nude. The prostitutes taught me a trick or two. "You're not much to look at," they remarked, not unkindly. "But you're ripe." Later, I realized that they meant I looked vulnerable. I looked like the naïf I was. Twice I resorted to the knee-in-the-groin evasion tactic. I stayed for two months because I was overwhelmed by everything new, and because I had a small casement window opening onto slate roofs, the white dome of Sacré-Coeur and the sporadic flights of pigeons.

I was rescued by my circle of students at the Sorbonne who were horrified, first by the distance I had to travel to attend classes, and later by the apartment itself. Céleste Touvier, Henri Dumais, Pierre Rousseau. But mostly Luc Garnier. These are my friends, my family in a new life. Céleste and I became roommates in a third-floor flat on the rue Jacob in the 6th arrondissement, spacious by my Montmartre standards. We each had tables to do our writing at on opposite sides of the front room, and big, overstuffed chairs facing the windows. With the money my parents sent me for my twenty-first birthday last year, we splurged on colourful swaths of printed Indian silk, which we used to cover the chairs and beds. Besides the living space and the bedroom, there was a little kitchen with a working oven and a small icebox. We shared a bathroom one floor down with a group of other girls, but they smelled much nicer than my old Montmartre mates.

Céleste is several months older than I — several *years* older to hear her talk — and she took me under her wing.

"*Mon amie,*" she said, lifting up my lank, dead-straight hair. "We must do something, *non?*" She stood in front of me, holding me by my shoulders at arms' length. "Let's see. Long legs, good bone structure, good teeth. Big brown eyes. But the hair? *Non,* it must go."

I was neither so vain nor so rash to object, and I must say she did improve the style with a pair of scissors, a fist full of pin curlers and a lot of French swear words. I wouldn't let her do anything about the colour — dark blonde she called it, but it's really just plain brown. I was a tomboy in Chapleau — *garçon manque* — so most days, I still wear my hair in braids. Céleste sighs when she sees me, as if the world is resting on her exquisite shoulders.

All of this, all of this strange new beauty, camaraderie and sense of discovery is what kept me in Paris when it was clear that I should have left. I can't pretend I didn't know what was happening. Our group spent hours reading newspapers and listening to the radio. Hitler and the Fascists had a death grip on Germany. We heard bits of Hitler's speeches, the frenzied tone and emphatic shouts. Almost worse than his singular staccato voice was the responding roar of the German crowds.

I lingered when I should have run. I told myself I couldn't abandon my studies, but the truth is I couldn't abandon my friends. I didn't want to be safe and tucked in bed in Chapleau. I wanted to be here, where I'd never tasted so much excitement.

Then the Nazis marched into Austria. They overran Czechoslovakia. Chamberlain flew back and forth across the Channel. Then it was too late. On September 1, Germany invaded Poland. *1939* Two days later, crowded around a radio with my friends, I listened to Britain and France declare war. Exactly one week later, Canada declared war. If the Germans entered Paris, I would become an enemy alien.

Luc held my hand and said there was still time, I should go. But I was stubborn, and a little in love. He has dark unruly hair that spills over his forehead, dark eyes and dark skin, like a suntan that never fades. Most of all, he has a quietness about him that makes others feel calm in his presence. He likes to walk with me in the rain. During long evenings of mist and drizzle along the banks of the Seine, Luc stole my heart. He made a present to me of the real Paris, his words evoking its smells and textures.

I made my choice. In any case, no one really believed that Paris would fall. There were all those brave French soldiers. We were entrenched behind the Maginot Line, built after the Great War to keep the Germans out.

All that fall and winter and into the spring, it seemed I'd made the right decision. The rhythm of my life remained unchanged, except that I spent more and more time with Luc, away from the rest of our group. We wandered the labyrinth of narrow winding streets on the Left Bank, and kissed on our favourite bridge, the Pont St-Louis, with its breathtaking view of Notre-Dame. In the

Place du Parvis Notre-Dame, at the west end of the cathedral, Luc showed me the bronze star that marks the official centre of Paris, from where all the distances on French roads are measured. While the chestnuts bloomed, it seemed impossible that those roads would not remain free. The war seemed to have melted away like the winter frost.

The Phony War, the papers called it. But Luc found the lull unnerving. Perhaps Hitler is satisfied now, I argued. Luc only shrugged, the elegant Gallic shrug which I'd come to understand was eloquent shorthand that could be interpreted several different ways, depending on the context.

When the attacks began, they took our breath away. Blitzkrieg, they called it. Lightning-fast strikes. Norway fell. Then the Netherlands, Luxembourg and Belgium. The Maginot Line couldn't cope with highly mobile warfare — the Germans simply flew over it and it crumpled like a dyke made of loose sand. The German army was on the doorstep of Paris, edging ever closer like a cloud of poisonous gas.

Our response was to get drunk. Céleste bought a bottle of wine for each country overrun by the Germans, and Pierre solemnly intoned each country's name as he drew out the corks. For Paris, there was champagne and a farewell toast from Henri that made Céleste cry. Luc and I, like many wartime lovers, had resolved to sleep together that night for the first time. In the end, that's exactly what we did, too woozy to attempt even the removal of our clothes.

On June 14, our exuberance and illusions died. Luc and I stood on the Champs-Élysées and watched, stony-faced, as the Germans entered Paris in perfectly straight lines, like arrows pointed at our hearts. There were thousands of them: young, disciplined, standing four abreast in the backs of trucks or marching in polished boots. Their uniforms were impeccable, their tanks gleamed. They wore none of the fatigue or grime of a hard-fought campaign. It had been so easy for them, that was part of the shock. They seemed invincible.

Two old ladies with bulging shopping baskets watched with us. One of them began to weep and Luc put his arm around her. In childish defiance, I had tied a red, blue and white scarf, an imitation of the tricolour, around my neck in the morning. I reached up and pulled it off, crumpling it in my hand. I felt a fluttering in my stomach that I recognized instantly as fear.

Within hours a new city was constructed in place of the old. The buildings and the monuments were still there, but they seemed to shrink and flatten, as if transmuted into two-dimensional facades, or *trompe l'oeil* paintings. Faux Paris was draped in huge, ugly swastikas. Tanks patrolled the streets, and men in jeeps with loudspeakers trolled along, warning people not to panic. Within hours, posters appeared that read "Abandoned French People, Put Your Trust in the German Soldier."

But there was no panic. Those with wit enough to foresee the reality of Occupation had already chosen to be part of the exodus to the South that I'd witnessed only days ago. Those of us left behind were numb, suffering a vacancy of spirit. The Germans were broadcasting to people temporarily deaf, with eyes turned inward.

The next few days passed in a blur. The French government fled to Bordeaux. Reynaud, the Minister of National Defence, resigned, and old Maréchal Pétain, hero of the last war, succeeded him. Almost immediately, he called for an armistice. Classes at the Sorbonne were temporarily suspended as everyone, not least the professors, tried to understand what was happening. Some railed at the government's betrayal, calling it cowardice. Others believed that Pétain was trying to save lives, trying to save the dignity of France. Céleste and Pierre snorted at that. If a temper tantrum could have had any impact, Céleste's would have made the Germans run for cover. Yet beneath her flair for drama, I knew her well enough to see that her anger was cold and steely.

Henri emerged as the realist in our group. He is tall and lanky, with sandy hair and a boyish face made serious by the steel-rimmed glasses he wears. Uncharacteristically withdrawn, he absorbed everything with a degree of calmness and tried to counter Céleste's emotion with logic.

"Perhaps it's for the best," he sighed. "The war is over for France. Pétain will make the Occupation bearable."

"No. I refuse to accept that," Luc insisted.

"You're a romantic," Henri shrugged. "It's time to stop living in the clouds. The Germans are here whether we like it or not, and we have to go on living our lives as best we can."

"Some of us can't," Luc countered, and everyone turned and looked at me.

His words shook me, a foreign student from a country at war with the Germans. There were records, documents at the Sorbonne that would give me away in an instant. I tried to smile bravely, but I was close to tears. Luc put his arms around me and must have felt my trembling.

"Don't worry. We'll think of something."

But we sat up all night, in our room that smelled of smoke and wine and Céleste's perfume, and could think of nothing.

August 6

In the end, it was practical Henri who discovered a way to hide my identity. His father is a banker who knows many important people, and though Monsieur Dumais disapproves of me, he agreed to help. He has iron-grey hair and a thin mouth and eyes that glower at me because I'm a foolish woman. Still, he has a heart and I'm grateful to him.

Henri shepherded all of us to his family's home in the 16th arrondissement, and we concocted a plan. Monsieur Dumais has a friend in the Swiss embassy who agreed to provide me with a passport and set of identity papers, but of course there were still the records at the Sorbonne, and classmates and professors there who knew me as a Canadian. So I had to go underground for a few weeks. Céleste, Henri, Pierre and Luc made a point of telling everyone that I'd left for Canada, and in the initial shock of the Occupation, we hoped no one would notice or remember exactly when they'd last seen me. I am now Renée Benoit, a distant cousin of Henri, and the Swiss identity helps to explain my still slightly accented French. We kept the last name because it's a common one here, and will be easier for me to remember. Céleste, though, has had her way. I am now the blonde she always wanted me to be.

When we were all together, it was much easier to pretend to be brave, but those weeks living with the Dumais family were lonely and difficult. Madame Dumais cautioned me that Juliette was gone now, and I must learn not to react to the name. *Juliette est perdue*, she said. Lost. So now I am one of a sea of refugees, *émigrés* and fugitives washed up at the end of Europe, but so much luckier because Henri's family is rich.

The 16th arrondissement is a world away from the flat on the rue Jacob. Before he left, Luc whispered to me that it was a velvet prison. The Dumais home on the rue de l'Assomption stands high above the Bois de Boulogne, with dramatic views. There are thick green meadows and riding paths with lovely old plane and oak trees. I often stood at the window watching the shifting patterns of light and shadow, and the shine of wet slate on the rooftops after a summer rain. There's a marble foyer with black and white tiles, straight from a Vermeer painting, and delicate furniture, elaborately carved, upholstered in pale rose satin. I was afraid to touch anything.

Mostly, I was afraid to say anything. Madame Dumais is devoutly Catholic. What this means in practical terms is an acceptance of Pétain and everything he believes in. There was no whisper in her house of Général de Gaulle's radio broadcast from London just one night after Pétain surrendered France. I missed hearing his words first-hand, but Luc told me the student area was buzzing with the news of his speech the next day: his call for resistance spread hope like wildfire.

But in sedate rue de l'Assomption there was a different story, a different France. On June 22, Pétain signed the armistice with Hitler and moved the government to Vichy. France was divided into two zones, with the North and West occupied by the German army, and the South administered from Vichy. "Peace with honour," Pétain said. Who would believe that?

Madame Dumais and thousands like her believed. I learned to be silent. I learned to recognize the Pétain creed from the slightest inflection or glance. It goes like this: France *deserved* to be conquered by Germany because it had lost its hold on the old, true values of family and country. Its national character had grown weak, corrupted by alcohol, by promiscuity, by idleness, by socialism, by communism. It's ironic that the Dumais sense of family is finally what motivated them to help me. It was loyalty to their son, who invented a load of rubbish about my destitute family unable to scrape up the funds to get me out of France.

So for weeks I was silent, and I smiled a lot and blessed them for their intervention. They fed me and were kind, but I couldn't help but be shocked by their sense of *laissez-faire*. They did not welcome the Germans, but neither did they seem unduly alarmed. *C'est la guerre. C'est la vie.* Life goes on, that was their creed. Just another *débâcle*, the lost war. *The Métro has shut down again*, they complained. *There are queues at all the shops, butter is scarce. Merde.*

Then one day, Monsieur Dumais brought home a paper someone had left in his office. *Aujourd'hui*, it was called. I opened it and read a contemporary reworking of the Lord's prayer, glorifying Pétain:

Our Father,
Who art our leader,
Hallowed be thy name.
Thy kingdom come.
Thy will be done …
Give us each day our daily bread.
Give France back her life …

I shuddered. Not long after this, I returned to the 6th arrondissement as Renée, but I couldn't get the mangled prayer out of my head. I never told any of the others about it. Henri would have been ashamed, and I owed him too much to embarrass him.

Moving back to the Left Bank was like leaving a protective bubble. Returning to the same flat on the rue Jacob would have been reckless, so Céleste and Luc found a new place on the rue des Beaux-Arts, smaller, but with its own bathroom. On the first night, the *gardien* of the building rapped sharply on the door to the flat.

"Ah, Mademoiselle Touvier. You will introduce me to your new flatmate?" He peered over Céleste's shoulder to where I was sitting at my old desk, writing these pages. He is pompous and short, and wears an eight-inch heel on built-up shoes to compensate for a stature that doesn't match his imagination. Céleste finds him repulsive and swears he can smell money from a block away. I could feel his curious greedy eyes boring into my back.

My heart hammering, I rose to greet him. Maybe it was the

blonde hair, or the accent, but he seemed to accept me easily enough as Renée Benoit.

"*Enchanté*," he said, eyeing me up and down.

I shook his hand, and lowered my eyes demurely. Céleste, after all, has not tutored me in vain.

He nodded and began to stride away, duty done. But he turned back at the last moment. "That young man, Luc. He'll be sniffing around, you can be sure. Two young girls on their own cause trouble. You mind the curfews, you hear?"

Céleste closed the door and the two of us fell into each other's arms, smothering our laughter.

It wasn't always so easy to become Renée, though. Far, far worse, was the first time I was questioned on the street, coming from a long wait at the shops for food. I was tired and hungry, and I hurried by a pair of soldiers without even noticing that they were stopping people to check their papers.

"You, halt!" a voice shouted.

My heart jumped, and I had to fight the urge to run. I had adopted the habit of many Parisians not to look directly at the Germans. Now here was a soldier directly in my face, annoyed and shouting at me. The strap of his helmet under his chin made his small mouth seem predatory.

"Name!"

I almost said it, my lips moved to form the "jay" sound of Juliette. I stuttered, and felt my face flush.

"What's this? You can't remember your name? *Papiers.*"

He held his hand out, snapping his fingers with impatience. I dropped one of the shopping bags of vegetables, fumbled in my purse.

"My name is Benoit. Renée Benoit." I studied the ground.

"A Swiss miss, eh? Here, look at me."

We held each other's gaze for a second or two, no longer. But it felt as if I were pinned under a searchlight. Then, suddenly, something in his eyes changed. I don't know for certain what he read in my expression — fear certainly, maybe resentment — but a kind of weariness seemed to come over him.

"What are you doing here? You should go home." He handed me back my papers and walked away without another word.

I was left alone on the sidewalk with my spilled vegetables, realizing how easily I could have been caught. It was only then that I finally admitted to myself that I might have made a terrible mistake in staying.

September 18

Fear is like a slow poison spreading through my veins. I seldom sleep through the night.

The Germans have ordered a census of the Jews.

Henri says it will be best for them to obey the ordinance, not to draw attention to themselves. But Pierre and Luc are worried about their favourite professor, Bernard Levy, who says he will refuse. I remember him from the days when I could still attend classes. Tall and dark, soft-spoken and gentle. Will a generous Swiss official give *him* a new passport and a new identity to hide behind? Between the pillars on the front of the Palais Berlitz, the Germans have hung an enormous four-storey-high poster of an old Jewish man with a long nose, digging claws into a distorted globe with France drawn in the centre. His skin is yellow, ghastly. It's meant to whip up hatred of the Jews, to make them seem threatening and as foreign as possible. I wonder how French-born Jews feel when they see it. No one could be kinder or more benign than Bernard Levy.

October 27

Pierre and Céleste are part of a student group at the Sorbonne planning a demonstration to pay tribute to veterans of the Great War. They want to march to the Arc de Triomphe on November 11, Remembrance Day, and place flowers on the grave of the Unknown Soldier. A clash is unavoidable since the Germans stage a military parade down the Champs-Élysées every day.

The strain of the Occupation has caused a split in our group. Henri has become more and more withdrawn. Sometimes we don't see him for days on end, and when he does join us, he and Pierre quarrel bitterly about the communists. Henri taunts that Stalin is in bed with Hitler, and Pierre counters by charging that Henri is flirting with the Nazis. Luc and I agree that I mustn't be involved in the student demonstration, yet I can see he's restless, and we've begun to bicker over trivial things. Since I was stopped for my papers, he seems to feel I shouldn't go out alone. He has appointed himself my protector, a role that doesn't suit either of us.

That leaves me to cope with Céleste alone, and I'm frightened by her rashness. She is too beautiful, dangerously so. With her chestnut hair, black eyes and stylish clothes, she draws eyes wherever she goes. It would be so much better if she could fade into the background like me. Blonde hair doesn't suit me and often I just look washed out and too thin, scarcely worth an inquiring glance.

"Please, Céleste. Don't do this. The Germans will never allow a demonstration."

"Nonsense. They can't stop a group of us from walking up the Champs-Élysées. We're only paying our respects to the past."

"You know that's not true."

She made a *moue* with her lips, which only made her look lovelier than ever, and her eyes flashed.

"It's for morale. The French have become so dreary. Dreary food, dreary clothes, dreary men who talk politics all night. Pierre mopes about the communists. Henri wastes his time trying to make the *boches* seem palatable. Even Luc has become a rabbit, too cautious. His nose is beginning to twitch. We're all too scared to act naturally."

"Not you."

"Yes, me. But I'm going to try. It might work." And she spread her hands to end the conversation.

November 13

The afternoon before the demonstration, Céleste decided we should all be together later that night for courage. She phoned up Luc, Henri and Pierre and made them promise to come by. Then she took my hand and flew with me down the stairs of our building.

"Where are we going?" I laughed.

"*Tais-toi!*" She put a finger to her lips and then whispered. "I know a place. Black market."

Almost everything has been rationed since the arrival of the Germans. They eat chicken and cream while the rest of us use our coupons for bread, rice, pasta, vegetables, a little salt and margarine instead of butter. Pierre tells us there have been BOF men almost from the beginning of the Occupation, BOF standing for *beurre*, *œufs* and *fromage*. Black marketeers can still, somehow, get their hands on butter, eggs and cheese.

The café was ordinary looking, a hole in the wall with red-checked tablecloths and sawdust on the floor just off the Place St-Michel. Céleste and I ordered watered-down brandy, and when the bill came, she slipped the proprietor some extra francs and a knowing glance.

"Behind the bar," he whispered.

We went down a narrow hallway to a small storeroom lit by a single dangling light bulb. There were tins of salmon and sardines, sacks of sugar and flour, real coffee, a wheel of cheese: things I hadn't seen or tasted since leaving the Dumais home. Céleste bought some sardines, five perfect oranges and a very expensive small square of chocolate.

"How ..."

"Don't ask any questions," she said.

Suddenly we felt light-hearted again, walking arm-in-arm and clutching our sack of treasures. As we rounded the corner into the rue des Beaux-Arts, a young boy, maybe sixteen, swerved on his bicycle to avoid running into us. His school bag skittered across the pavement, spilling out a sheaf of papers. I knelt down, began picking up the scattered pages.

"Mademoiselle," the boy said. His voice was urgent.

He looked directly into my eyes, an intimate, searching look.

I glanced at the paper I was holding in my hand. It was a broadsheet, a one-page newspaper. *Résistance*, it was called. "We Must Fight Back," the headline asserted.

The boy reached down, gently removed the page from my hand, and smiled at me. Then he was back on his bicycle and flying away.

Céleste had witnessed everything. "They're called butterflies, those Resistance papers. It's an omen. Tomorrow will go well, you'll see."

The men joined us at the apartment around eight, and for once we let the war ebb away from us. We sat cross-legged on the floor with a platter between us and ate the sardines greedily, licking the salty oil from our fingers. The fruit and slivers of chocolate we savoured, letting taste and smell transport us to gentler times. Around midnight, it began to rain, clouds swallowing up the moon. We listened to music on the radio in the dark: "Mood Indigo," "Body and Soul," "Time on My Hands." Celeste leaned her head on Henri's shoulder, Luc stretched out with his head in my lap, Pierre tapped his fingers to the cadence of the melodies. As we drifted toward dawn, I wondered aloud how the choices we'd each made in our lives had brought us to this place. It was a mystery nobody could explain, and nobody tried.

In the morning, Luc and I left the apartment first. When the door closed behind us, Henri was again trying to dissuade Céleste and Pierre from marching. I knew they wouldn't be budged from their decision.

It was a chilly day, and I wore a thick knitted sweater under my trench coat. We walked briskly, trying to warm up and wake up after the night's vigil. Luc was quiet. The streets were empty. The sound of our footsteps grew monotonous. When we came to the Pont Neuf, I slowed up, hoping that Luc would want to kiss me on our favourite bridge, but he strode on, scarcely noticing I was there. I looked away quickly to hide my disappointment.

It was then I saw the black Citroëns — there were six of them, parked one behind the other on the Quai de la Mégisserie that ran along the banks of the Seine. Only high-ranking officers and Gestapo rode in those cars. The sight of them was alarming. The sight of them meant somebody rousted, probably arrested, dragged off to the rue des Saussaies and beaten. It was rare to see so many at once. They must be — I went cold. They were waiting.

"Luc. Look! Go back. Tell the organizers to stop. Something dreadful's going to happen."

He turned, but it was too late. We stood rigid on our bridge, staring up the Seine at the marchers crossing the Pont des Arts to the north of us. They were laughing and singing, oblivious to the line of cars. *La jeunesse folle*, I thought, the madness of youth. Surely the Germans would see it for what it was? There was nothing for us to do but finish crossing the bridge. We walked steadily toward the cars, crossed the Quai and slipped into one of the side streets.

The students marched on. I waited, praying. I could just see Céleste in a jaunty beret up among the leaders at the front of the group.

Then the cars slowly began to trail them, low to the ground and sleek, like blind reptiles that could smell a nest of young.

We ran through a maze of little streets, trying to get ahead of the students to warn them. But soon we reached the broad boulevards designed by Baron Haussmann a century earlier. Too wide, too open. No one ran in the boulevards in Nazi Paris. If you did, you ran for your life.

What we saw ahead of us made me cry out. The students had reached the Place de la Concorde at the foot of the Champs-Élysées. Hundreds of German soldiers encircled them. Machine guns had been set up at strategic points.

Suddenly, as if to a signal, a shout went up, *Raus! Raus!* The scene exploded with the juddering of the guns, the whine of bullets, screaming. Chaos. The students were running in all directions — leaping up, twisting in the air, jumping out of range, trying to get away from the bullets aimed low into the crowd. Two men, hit in their legs, were crawling over the ground until their friends grabbed them under the arms, dragging them from the maelstrom.

I leapt forward but the force of Luc's arm clamping across my waist swung me off the ground. I struggled from his grasp, running to the edge of the dispersing crowd. Some instinct led me to Céleste, who stood like a stone in the whirlwind. She was in shock, her legs covered in blood. I shook her. She looked at me as if I were a stranger. Luc thrust me aside and picked her up in his arms.

"Now. Juliette, move!"

We scrambled away. The Germans were not giving chase, concentrating instead on those who could not or would not move.

At the edge of the Jardin des Tuileries, I looked back. The black Citroëns were taking on passengers. I saw Pierre with his hands in the air, a gun pressed to the back of his head.

My mouth went dry and I couldn't swallow. There was nothing we could do. Almost worse than seeing Pierre arrested, his dark head drooping forward, his body already so thin, was the certainty that there was nothing we could do.

Luc half-carried Céleste back to the rue des Beaux-Arts. She was badly shaken and had a flesh wound in her left calf that bled profusely. She was lucky, Luc said, that the bullet had not shattered a bone.

But when I helped her off with her clothes and into a warm bath, I didn't think she was lucky. Worse than her wound was her mute obedience. She was like a small child, behaving as if the punishment she'd just received was deserved. I bandaged her up with an old scarf as best I could and she fell into bed and faded out.

Luc had slipped out to the university to see if he could find out what was happening, but he returned quickly.

"They've shut it down," he told me. "There are Germans in the classrooms and patrolling the streets. We'll have to wait."

Waiting and waiting. It seemed the French people had adopted *attentisme*, the strategy of waiting. But after the bloody suppression of my friends, I could hardly bear it. What was there to do? We paced, looked at each other, looked out the window, looked at the telephone, willing it to ring. And in the midst of this nothingness, in our minds, again and again, seeing Pierre shoved into a car, imagining the rue des Saussaies, the headquarters of the Gestapo, and what might be happening there.

I thought of the boy I'd seen on his bicycle with a sheaf of butterflies and remembered the way he'd smiled at me. I counted all the little acts of resistance that people had sometimes indulged in and soothed themselves with — giving Germans misleading street directions, sneaking out after curfew to deface posters or raid the railway yards to steal provisions from German trains. Not enough, not nearly. The press talked about how restrained the occupying forces were, how polite. I knew now that brutality was only a misstep away, that students could be shot, that a boy on a bicycle with a satchel full of "butterflies" could be arrested, maybe worse. But doing nothing, and *accepting* that I was doing nothing, was suffocating me.

Luc seemed to read my thoughts.

"Not yet, Jules." He hadn't used his nickname for me for months. "The time will come, but not yet."

Dusk comes early in November, and I went to check on Céleste as the light was beginning to fade. She was sitting on the bed in the darkened room, the blackout curtains already pulled.

I reached for her, put an arm around her shoulder. "Are you all right? You should keep your leg up."

"It's fine. I'm fine," she said, but she'd been crying. "What happened to the others? Have you talked to Pierre?"

There was no point trying to keep the news from her. Delay wouldn't make it any easier to bear. I thought she would crumble, but I had underestimated her.

"Quick — we must call Henri. Old Dumais, perhaps he can do something. Help me get dressed. I must go out."

I was flabbergasted. "*Tu es folle!* You aren't going anywhere."

She grabbed my hand.

"Then you must go for me." Her voice was urgent, pleading.

"What are you talking about? The Gestapo have him. Don't you understand?"

"Not Pierre. Professor Levy. He must be warned. Pierre knows about the printing press. The Gestapo will be after any information they can get."

"What printing press?"

"Juliette, listen to me. That boy we saw with the flyers. He wasn't wary of us, because he recognized me. Pierre and I have been helping Professor Levy print them. You must get to him. Tell him to hide everything. Bring him back here if you can. He can stay for a few days until we find a safer place for him. If that's too dangerous, perhaps he already has a bolthole where he might go."

"But surely we could call instead?"

"No phone. He's Jewish. He didn't register. He doesn't want a public record. He doesn't want to be traced. What's the matter with you, Juliette? Haven't you been paying attention? What do you think will happen to him if he's caught?"

"You really believe Pierre would tell them?"

"You really believe you wouldn't, if the Gestapo arrested you?"

I flinched. "All right. Give me the directions. What will we do about Luc? He won't like my going."

"I'll distract him until you're gone. It's better that you do this than him. A woman will seem less threatening to the Germans. Take the side streets. Say you're lost if they stop you." She hugged me. "Thank God you're Swiss. They won't expect you to know the streets."

There was no time to think about what I was doing. I slipped into the bathroom with my coat and my bag under my arm. Céleste called out to Luc and then I was down the stairs, six flights, a quick glance to be sure the *gardien* wasn't creeping about, and out the door.

The cold sobered me. Cold outside, cold inside. I walked quickly, but not too quickly. It was an hour, maybe an hour and a half to curfew, but as usual these days, there was hardly anyone on the streets. I crossed the Seine, a black stripe in the dying light. In my head, I repeated the directions Céleste had given me. I stopped for a moment, looked behind me, rummaged in my bag. I found a much creased pocket map, and carried it ostentatiously in my hand.

Finally, I reached the Marais — the old Jewish quarter with cobbled lanes and alleys, silence and deep shadow. There were Hebrew letters chalked on some of the storefronts, everything shut up now for the night. Between two leaning tenements, I found the address. It wasn't a residence, as I'd expected, but a small bookshop. A spill of yellow light came from beneath the shuttered door.

I knocked. Once, twice — the second time more loudly. I thought I could hear footsteps and the scraping of chair legs across a wooden floor.

Then the light went out.

This time I hammered on the door. "Please. It's urgent."

The door opened suddenly, and an old man pulled me across the threshold. "What, are you crazy? Do you want to alert the whole neighbourhood?"

He had white hair, a face lined with a lifetime of worry. There was no one else in the shop, as far as I could see. I felt weak in the knees. I didn't know if I could trust him. I'd come all this way. What if it were for nothing?

He was staring at me, trying to read my expression.

"Are you in trouble?" he asked, more gently.

"Not me. I've come for — I've come from Céleste."

I paused in case I said too much, hoping he might recognize the name, hoping he might leap to the right conclusion.

A shadow stirred at the back of the shop. Professor Levy.

I rushed forward.

"Hurry. They arrested Pierre at the student demonstration. Gestapo. Céleste has been injured. I've come to take you back with me. But we've got to hurry."

The professor read my expression, heard the desperation in my voice. He turned to the old man and nodded.

"Go now. Warn the others." Then he turned to me. "Céleste is hurt?"

"Not badly. A bullet graze on her leg."

Without another word, he disappeared into the gloom, re-emerged with an overcoat, a scarf wound around his neck and a hat with a brim that shadowed his face. "Come with me," he said.

I turned toward the door, but his voice stopped me.

"No, no. It's too dangerous. Curfew will have started. This way."

I didn't argue. The thought of retracing my route in the dark frightened me so much I was relieved to follow him almost anywhere.

We went through a back door into a little alley, then crossed through a maze of twisting streets. I could smell onions frying in chicken fat. Somewhere a child laughed. Above us someone slammed pots and pans around in a kitchen. We came into a narrow lane behind a row of shops, and were just approaching another cross street when we saw somebody run past the top of the lane. Then there was shouting and more footsteps in pursuit. Boots. Soldiers.

The professor grabbed my arm and we pressed ourselves against a wall, holding our breath.

We heard a scuffle, a man cried out.

"A Jew," one of the soldiers shouted. "A stinking Jew."

Faint beams of light from the soldiers' flashlights cast distorting shadows across the mouth of the alley, making everything seem more unreal and more brutal. They began hitting and kicking him. It was sickening. The sound of it.

We stood rigid until the soldiers' laughter faded away.

Professor Levy looked into the street, walked toward the fallen man, then turned sharply away.

"Don't look," he hissed.

We ran in the opposite direction. Finally we came to a doorway, went up a staircase. The stairs seemed endless. The muscles in my legs burned. At last, we entered an attic, untidy with bits of furniture, dust and cobwebs. Professor Levy adjusted a blanket nailed over a small casement window, and lit a candle.

Then he looked at me and smiled. His face was wet with tears.

"We'll be safe here for the night. In the morning, I'll write you directions to get home. You can sleep over there."

I followed the direction of his gaze and saw a mattress on the floor in one corner of the room.

"You won't be coming back with me? Where will you go?"

"Somewhere, anywhere. It's better you don't know."

"Yes, I see that. I'm sorry." Sorry I couldn't do more, sorry for what was happening to him, sorry for the man beaten to death in the street. "You knew him, didn't you." It wasn't a question.

He turned away from me, wiped his face with his scarf and sat down on the floor, his eyes closed, his head leaning back and resting against the door. I realized how young he was, probably in his early or mid-thirties, though his black hair was beginning to grey. I wondered if he had a family. Did he have a wife, and maybe children? He opened his eyes and caught me staring at him.

"I remember you, from the Sorbonne. You're the Canadian girl — Juliette, isn't it? You should try to rest."

"I feel wide awake."

"That's the adrenalin. In a few moments you'll be exhausted."

I didn't believe him, but I could see that he needed to think, so I settled down on the mattress and tried to be quiet. When I next heard his voice, it seemed to come from a long distance away.

"Tell me, Juliette. If you had the chance to leave now, would you go?"

I was still thinking about my answer when I fell asleep.

In the morning, he was gone, but I followed the directions he'd left for me and made my way back to the rue des Beaux-Arts without anyone paying me the slightest notice. The queues were growing outside of the shops and I felt ravenous.

Céleste was waiting for me, and she hugged me fiercely.

"Pierre?" I asked.

"There's hope. Luc and Henri are at the Dumais house now. Monsieur Dumais has a car and he knows someone who knows someone and so on. They've already released some of the students with a stern warning."

"A car? I thought the Germans had requisitioned private cars."

Céleste shrugged. Privilege was a bad sign in Paris. It usually meant rubbing shoulders with high-ranking officers.

"And you?"

I knew she meant Professor Levy. "Safe. For now."

"Bless you. By the way, Luc isn't speaking to me. Probably not to you either."

We were in the kitchen eating nuts for breakfast when Luc and Henri knocked on the door. Céleste was still limping, but her leg was properly bandaged now, and she insisted on riding in the car to the *gendarmerie* where Pierre had been transferred and was awaiting release.

Soon we would all be together again, but for now Luc and I were alone.

"I thought I would die when I learned where you'd gone," he said softly.

"I'd like to take a bath," I replied.

I'd already checked myself in the mirror. I'd splashed my face with water and run my fingers through my hair, done the best I could. But I knew I looked exhausted, and probably smelled of sweat from running and sleeping in my clothes.

His eyes smiled and he took my hand. We undressed slowly. The bath was only tepid, but I didn't mind. I felt warmer than I had in months.

Later, we met somewhere on the bed, clumsy and shameless and quick to laugh. I felt too dizzy at getting what I wanted to be seductive or graceful. We were like little children again, playing.

Breathing hard and fast. Then something else, something better.

Afterwards, I snuggled against his chest and breathed in his smell. So, I thought, there is still love in the barricaded city.

April 26, 1941

This winter was the coldest of the century. The limbs of the plane trees were stiff with ice. Swirling snow blackened the Seine and the wind howled through the arches of the bridges. The price of coal soared. At night, we went to bed wearing every scrap of wool we owned. I swear the winter tried to kill us.

A cruel winter, then a reluctant spring, with the sky a hundred shades of grey, and thick, brooding clouds. The yoke of the Occupation rests more heavily on our shoulders. Pierre has drifted away from our group since his release from the rue des Saussaies. His body has healed, but he's still bruised inside. We asked no questions. Since he was ashamed to look at us those first few weeks, we knew the Gestapo had broken him. Céleste tried to comfort him by telling him that Bernard Levy had escaped, but he gripped her arm, made her swear to tell him nothing unless it could be safely heard by German ears. He continues to punish himself for being human, and has become sullen and embittered. Henri told us Pierre's been seen running with a rough crowd, the FTP, he suspects. The *Francs-tireurs et partisans*, the clandestine action group of the French Communist Party. Pierre tells us nothing — secrecy for him is now like water in the desert.

In the meantime, daily life grinds on. The French have a word for the grey light of Paris — *grisaille*, they call it, when it seems like dusk from morning until night. Now I think *grisaille* describes not the light so much as the people. A greyness has descended upon us.

My friends have stopped going to classes. Many of the professors have been dismissed, the Jews the first to disappear. It's common now to pass empty shops with "Enterprise Juive" scrawled in peeling white paint on the boarded up windows. In the Luxembourg Gardens, benches are marked "No Jews Allowed." I often wonder about Bernard Levy, but no one speaks his name. Over the winter, he vanished into the cold air.

Céleste, Luc and I have pooled our resources. I took all the money I had out of the bank before "Juliette" disappeared, but, without any way to contact my family, it has dwindled to a handful of francs. We had no choice but to search for jobs, anything that could keep the *gardien,* who is fierce about collecting the rents, from our door. It is even harder to find decent food. Luc is working as a hospital aid, an odd choice for him but he doesn't seem to mind, and Céleste, less surprisingly, is a waitress in a black-market restaurant. Sometimes, when we're lucky, she's able to bring home scraps of meat, leftover vegetables and bread.

I'm thin enough now to wear her clothes, and managed to look presentable enough to get a place as a salesclerk in the Galeries Lafayette, the huge department store just north of the Opéra district. Underneath its glittering glass dome, which seals out the real world, I sell hats with veils and bows and little clusters of fake cherries and silk flowers. Many of the customers are German officers, buying up the luxuries of a mythical Paris to send home to their wives, or more often to sweeten up their French girlfriends who sometimes accompany them. My boss, a quarrelsome woman with orange-coloured hair piled on top of her head, rebukes me for staring, but I can't help being amazed by the girlfriends. Occasionally, they are elegant and dignified, and they shy away from my gaze. Others wear too much makeup on their sad pinched faces, painted like kewpie dolls, and still others are brazen and haughty. Once, I saw Madame Dumais, who looked through me as if I were a pane of glass.

I smile at them all because I want to eat. Outside the Galeries Lafayette, with its rows of evening gowns, expensive perfumes and ropes of pearls, I see the very old, the very poor and the very tired standing in queues and queues and queues. The women wear long black coats and kerchiefs, and their faces are chapped from cold winds and rough soaps. There are two classes in Paris now, and it's no longer a simple matter of economics. Poor is poor, but wealth is suspect. Wealth could mean a noble family history, or just as easily a factory owner raking in German marks by making German weapons. Or a black marketeer. Or a German's mistress. Or a *prefecture* trading information for francs. Once we used our eyes to look away from the Germans, as a small sign of resistance.

Now we use our eyes to look sidewise at each other. *Where did she get that stylish coat? He looks well fed, has he always worn such fine suits? I saw him sitting in a café, whispering into the ear of a German soldier.* Suspicion and denunciations are everywhere.

Today, provisional administrators — French, according to the terms of the armistice — were given the authority to sell Jewish properties to Aryans or to liquidate them. More money for the state, more spoils for those who ask no questions. More poor among the victims.

June 22

Germany has invaded Russia. The news flashed through the city like an electric shock.

Pierre was drunk with joy, strutting like a rooster again.

"You'll see," he crowed. "Stalin will get the Nazis. They've got a real war on their hands now. We'll fight them here, too."

"We?" Henri asked. "You mean the FTP, I suppose. Be careful, Pierre. The Gestapo have a record of your arrest. Do you imagine they've stopped watching you? My father can do nothing if they pick you up again. Stay away from that crowd."

"That crowd," Pierre countered, "is going to make the Germans sit up and take notice for once, instead of sitting on their fat asses drinking Dumais wine."

The gibe was a cruel one — Monsieur Dumais owns a small vineyard in Burgundy, just north of Beaune. Henri was now working in his father's bank and had a travel pass, an *Ausweis*. Often he went out to the countryside, bringing us back food and Dumais wine that Pierre had enjoyed as much as any of us. But Henri ignored the insult, as he so often does when attacked by Pierre.

"*Non, mon ami.* The Germans will only notice you. What can you hope to achieve, anyway? The FTP will explode a few bombs, fire a few bullets. The Gestapo will crush you. And what of the reprisals, have you thought of that? You'll bring terror to the streets of Paris, with innocent people rounded up for your brief and pointless moment of glory."

He was right, of course. Though Pierre had distanced himself lately, anyone watching would easily connect us with him. Since we'd never considered Pierre dangerous, it was difficult to believe that he could put *us* in danger. Pierre grasped the truth at once. His eyes widened and he looked around at us, his gaze lingering for a moment on Céleste. He seemed momentarily confused, even bereft. Then his expression hardened and he rose to leave.

Henri intercepted him at the door. "Please," he said softly. "Don't choose this. There are other ways. Stay with us."

They stood facing each other, the tall, serious man in the banker's suit looking down at the shorter, dark-haired man in his rumpled clothes.

"It's too late, Henri. I hate them so much it's eating me alive. There's not room for anything else. *Bonne chance, mon ami. Au revoir.*"

The two men embraced and then the door closed.

July 27

Henri invited us to accompany him to the countryside. Family business, he said, and the travel permits had all been arranged. I thought we'd be crushed into one of the trains that make almost daily runs into the country for food — potato trains, the Germans call them — but we rode first class, where the obligatory checkpoints for identity papers are conducted with more politeness. We were only rousted once, ordered off the train to stand on the platform under the hot sun while the soldiers searched the compartments. Henri joked and laughed with them, and offered one guard a cigarette. Céleste pursed her lips at this, but said nothing. She had told me she has seen Henri two or three times in the restaurant where she works, dining with a *petit fonctionnaire* known to be a collaborator.

Despite my worry about Henri, I was enchanted by the journey. I'd never been outside the city, had never seen the deep green fields of *la France profonde*, its tiny villages strung along one after the other or nestled in gentle valleys. Cows dotted the pastures under painters' clouds. The occasional bright yellow patches of sunflowers or streaks of scarlet poppies brightened the fields, edged by the darker green of forests. An old farmer on a horse cart waved at me, the reins held loosely in his hand as he watched the train go past. I felt a flash of homesickness, for the farmer was so natural, carved from his own landscape. I closed my eyes and imagined the train chugging into the old wooden station house in Chapleau, followed the tiny dirt road that runs alongside the tracks and then curves away into the muskeg and stands of timber so vast that they could swallow France whole. So vivid was that memory of spaciousness and horizons that stretched forever, that some part of my mind believed that I would reach home again, as long as I stayed on the train.

But the dream lasted only a moment and soon we were pulling into the station at Beaune, the inner part of the town still encircled by stone ramparts. Marcel, who manages the vineyard for the Dumais family, met us in a white van. He has thick grey hair and blue eyes deeply set into a face so creased with wrinkles that it resembles a dried grape. We sat on the floor in the back of the van, leaning against the wine crates and jostling into each other whenever we hit a bump in the road.

We were all laughing and excited to be out of Paris for a weekend, but I caught Henri with his head down a few times as if he were bracing himself for something unpleasant, probably Céleste's reproaches for his behaviour with the soldiers. I raised my eyebrows at Luc, wondering if I should intervene, but he shook his head and raised a finger to his lips.

The Château Dumais was the first surprise. It sits atop a small hill and vines fill the landscape, growing right up to the house so as not to waste a handful of precious soil. Though not so grand as the word "château" might imply, it is made of lovely fifteenth-century pale stone, its square shape softened by two turrets and a polychrome roof of black and yellow tiles. Henri proudly opened the wrought iron gates and Marcel's wife came rushing out to greet us, wrapping Henri up in her arms and then kissing each of us in turn. She smelled of lavender and wine, her gap-toothed smile irresistible.

"So," she began, "Henri's friends. *M'sieur* and *m'dame* don't approve of you, you know? Bad influence, they say. But Lucette knows. Henri is a good boy, *hein?*"

She winked at us, and from behind our circle we heard Marcel growl at her to be careful.

"*Eh bien*," she shrugged. "It's my fate to be married to a quarrel-some old man. You two watch out. Mind you don't fall for the first silver tongue whispering in your ear. Marcel here thinks I've gone deaf. Does nothing but shout at me now. Off with you. I've cooking to do."

We settled into our rooms, Céleste and I on the second floor at the back of the house, Luc and Henri on the third floor in what used to be Henri's nursery. Lucette had her rules, after all. We spent the afternoon touring the small property and the *caves*, a network of underground tunnels and rooms where the wines were aged in huge barrels, or bottled and stored by year.

"Some of the cellars closer to Beaune interconnect," Henri explained. "You can enter a cellar in one house and come up in another half a kilometre away. C'mon, let's choose a wine for dinner. The Germans have requisitioned the *grands crus*, but I suspect Marcel has managed to tuck something away."

"Requisitioned?" Céleste asked. "I thought ..."

"I know what you thought," Henri whispered. "I know what you're thinking." He shook his head sadly, and pulled a bottle from the racks. We followed him back to the château without another word, unspoken doubts dogging our footsteps.

Dinner was in the courtyard, with candles everywhere, white linen and the sweetness of the night air. When Lucette lifted the lid off the huge copper pot, releasing the heady aroma of meat roasted with thyme and garlic, I thought I would faint.

"Henri's favourite," she said. "Navarin of Lamb."

She ladled tiny potatoes and onions and chunks of lamb onto my plate, and then let some of the thick brown sauce flow over it. I felt a rumble of pleasure from deep within.

Lucette stood back and watched our first bites. No, that's much too polite. We didn't bite, we gobbled.

"Ach, peasants," she said, well pleased. "So much for Parisian manners."

When we felt we could stop eating long enough to make room for words, Céleste started reminiscing about French films and we all understood why. The night was like that — a weekend in the country with four friends, two of them lovers, gauzy light from the candles, ruby-coloured wine silky on the tongue, a glance here, hands touching there. We floated in Céleste's radiance. Hours passed.

Then Henri stood up. "Are you ready, Luc? It's time."

More than the words, there was something in his voice, something in his face that alarmed me. He looked determined, his face almost stony in the moonlight, but there was a trace of something else too, some emotion he was fighting to control.

"What are you two doing? A song, perhaps?" Céleste teased, oblivious to the shift in mood.

Neither of the men smiled, and I touched her shoulder.

"Shh. What is it, Luc?"

He turned to Henri for the answer.

"We're going back to the *cave*, all of us. But you must be very quiet and there'll be no light. You'll have to follow me closely."

"Henri?"

"*Tais-toi*, Céleste. This isn't a game. Are you coming or not?"

She instantly sobered and the three of us fell mutely into line behind Henri. He led us out the door at the back of the courtyard, then slowly across the field in the narrow lanes of dirt between the rows of vines. The soft, rustling sounds we made were absorbed into the earth like rain. When we reached the entrance of the *cave*, he took a key from his pocket and turned it soundlessly in the padlock. We ducked our heads and followed the stairs down into the cool dark space that smelled of damp walls, raspberries and vinegar.

Then a shadow moved at the mouth of one of the tunnels, separating itself from the deeper blackness stretching behind it.

I couldn't see clearly enough, I didn't know what it was.

Then the figure took a step closer. A long robe, tied loosely at the waist, a cowl. *A monk?*

I rubbed my eyes, and the figure moved again, slipping the hood away from the face.

Henri turned on a flashlight and Céleste gasped.

She ran into the arms of the monk who kissed her mouth, her cheeks, her forehead, buried his face in her hair, holding her against him as if he could not bear to let her go.

Then he raised his face and smiled at me. "Hello, Juliette."

"Professor Levy?" I stammered.

"No more. You must call me Frère Jean-Claude. A good disguise for a Jew, don't you think? Thanks to Henri."

I turned and stared at my friend, and in that moment read plainly the expression on his face that had puzzled me earlier. Pain. It was the pain of seeing Céleste in the arms of another man. Poor Henri, I thought, and all of us too stupid to have realized, most of all Céleste.

She turned then and walked toward him, taking both of his hands in hers. "Forgive me, *mon cher?* I should never have suspected you would collaborate."

"Of course." He brushed a strand of hair away from her face. The gesture was so tender, it broke my heart to see it.

"But now, you must tell us everything," she continued, her eyes too filled with joy to see anything else. "How did you manage this? How long has Bernard been here? How long must he stay?"

"There's an abbey in the Morvan, some distance from here. Abbaye de la Pierre-qui-Vire. It's linked to a local resistance group. Bernard has been helping them."

I turned to look at Luc who had been silent too long, silent and noticeably unsurprised by the appearance of the Jewish monk.

"And you and Henri have been helping, too. Helping how?"

"Transporting people, usually away from Paris into the Unoccupied Zone. But not this time. Tomorrow we need to get someone into Paris. Bernard?"

At Luc's signal, Frère Jean-Claude disappeared into the tunnel and emerged a few minutes later with another man, dark-haired, dark-eyed, about Luc's height.

"Meet Max," he said. "He parachuted into the Morvan forest two nights ago."

I guessed their plan in an instant and protested. "His skin is fair. His clothes don't look French. What are you, English?"

"Yes, miss. Pleased to meet you."

I groaned. His French was heavily accented, a comma after every word.

"It'll never work."

"Yes, it might," Céleste interrupted. "A little makeup to darken the skin. Luc's clothes will just about fit. But what happened to your own identity papers? Surely they didn't send you over here without any."

"We ran into a bit of bother, miss. The Brother and me, we had to duck into a stream with a fast current. I lost them."

A bit of bother. The scene flashed across my eyes. Two men running, armed Germans combing the woods, maybe with dogs.

"*Incroyable.* So the Germans are looking for you, and if they find the papers, they'll know exactly whose face they're looking for. Perfect."

"Please, Jules," Luc urged. "Four people travelled down together. Four people will travel back together. Henri will distract the guards. In a few days, Marcel will drive me back to Paris in the van. We'll just be two workers delivering a shipment of wine."

"Don't blame me for being in shock. You might have trusted Céleste and me a little earlier, you know. Of course I'll do it, provided Max doesn't try to speak French again."

"I'm a fast learner, mademoiselle, a natural mimic."

I rolled my eyes and Luc laughed. "Oh, and there's one more thing."

"Naturally."

Luc pointed to a square case, about the size of a small suitcase. "The radio."

I closed my eyes and took a deep breath. Max was an agent. He would be useless in Paris without some way to transmit messages back to London. There wasn't anything to say.

That night in the wine cellar, we all faced a fork in the road — Bernard and Céleste silhouetted in the dim light, Henri standing forlornly to the side with his head bowed, Luc and I exchanging glances in a way that only lovers can. I had thought that if ever I became an active part of the Resistance, the moment would be remarkable in some way, the decision carefully weighed and minutely planned. It wasn't. I just picked up the case and followed Henri back to the house, leaving Luc and Max to exchange clothes, and Céleste and Bernard to the few precious hours remaining to them. I just put one foot in front of the other, breathing in and out as I crossed a French vineyard in the moonlight.

The train slowed to a crawl thirty kilometres from the outskirts of Paris. Sabotage on the tracks ahead, according to the conductor.

The earlier checkpoints had gone easily, the guards remembering Henri's bonhomie and cigarettes. What now?

I leaned my head against the window and saw passengers being pulled off the train, lined up on the cinder banks that edged the tracks. The uniforms of the soldiers were black, silver bolts of lightning on the tight collars.

"SS. They're looking for something, or someone ..."

My words hung in the air.

Céleste casually removed her shawl, draped it over her arm so that it just covered the radio case wedged between her body and the edge of her seat. She crossed her legs, inched up the hem of her skirt.

Henri tossed Max the book he'd been reading and lit up a cigarette, leaving the pack open on the seat beside him.

I closed my eyes and leaned my head on Max's shoulder, pretending to wake up when the officer entered the compartment.

He was in his thirties, with short hair parted on the side, clean-shaven, small cunning eyes that widened slightly when he saw Céleste. She looked at him resentfully, pulled her skirt down so that it covered her knees.

It worked. He seemed embarrassed to have been caught staring, turned away from her. Henri blew smoke at him. The officer looked at Max and me.

Max smiled.

A mistake. No one smiled at Gestapo officers.

The officer now scrutinized him more closely, then lazily inclined his head toward the luggage rack.

"*Valise,*" he said softly.

Max stood up to get his — Luc's — case, and the book he was holding slid to the floor. He reached for it, but the officer picked it up quickly.

He held it by the spine in his gloved fingers and shook it. Next he prodded the front and back covers, riffled the pages, worked a finger down between the spine and the binding and ripped if off, then tossed the book back onto the seat. He opened the suitcase, the popping of the snaps sounding like gunshots in the breath-held quiet. He poked around beneath the folded shirts, a razor and shaving soap, socks and shorts. His fingers closed around the neck of a bottle of Dumais wine and he withdrew it slowly.

"*Was ist los?*"

"Please," Henri intervened, holding out his papers. "From my family's vineyard. Help yourself."

The officer checked the papers, checked the name on the wine label.

"*Ja. Danke.*"

He clipped his heels together, bowed slightly to Céleste, and left.

We all stared at each other. *What would they have done to us?*

November 15

The wind was wicked today, lashing the Seine. I shivered my way to the Maubert market in the 5th arrondissement, staring at baskets of eels. No matter how hungry I get, I can't bring myself to eat them. Instead, I bought some tired leeks for soup and queued up for bread. People were talking about the headlines, passing a newspaper down the line. The *Paris-Soir:*

> Terrorist Attack On the Métro!
> *Jews and communists were shot after gunning down a German officer. Bolshevik criminals, they do not care if they bring down heavy reprisals on the French people. Beware these slaves of the Communist Party!*

People murmured and grumbled. One well-dressed lady with a fur collar on her thick coat complained aloud. "Fools. They say a thousand Frenchmen killed for every German."

Most of us ignored her. It was dangerous to have opinions in the queues. You never knew who might be listening, or where your words might be repeated.

On my way home, crossing the Place Maubert, I was approached by an older woman. "*Pardon*, mademoiselle, I believe you dropped this." She handed me a piece of paper.

A butterfly.

Citizens of Paris! Last night three militants of the FTP were martyred on behalf of the French people. Eva Kohn, Leon Casson and Pierre Rousseau died as heroes in a strike against Gestapo brutality. Follow their example! Vive la France!

I felt an iron band close around my throat. Almost a year to the day from his release from the rue des Saussaies, Pierre was dead. My friend. He didn't die for the Communist cause. He didn't die for France. He died because the Gestapo had hollowed him out and filled him up with hate. He was twenty-three years old.

December 18

It's a week before Christmas and the winter is not giving out presents. It promises to be as bitter as last year's icy grip. Already the willows along the Seine are white with frost, and the river is sluggish and black. The Germans have set the coal ration at fifty-five pounds per family per month, enough to heat one room for two hours a day. In their need for food, many Parisians have taken to raising ducks or rabbits on their balconies. Yesterday morning when we were walking, Luc and I found a chicken that had wandered away from its coop. It had frozen to death overnight.

I find myself thinking about Chapleau again and again. Perhaps it's the season, or the weather. I remember great white storms, and snow banks taller than I was as a child. My friends say I've no right, as a tough Canadian, to be cold here. But in my memory I was always warm there. Not like this. Not shivering under a thin coat, feeling damp icy fingers insinuating themselves under my clothes. Luc found a patient at the hospital where he works who was travelling to Lisbon and promised to mail a letter to my parents for me. Perhaps he will. It says very little that is true, but will give them comfort.

The truth is that the city is edgy. The Americans, having been bombed by the Japanese at Pearl Harbour, have entered the war, finally. Late starters. Luc says it will take a year, maybe more, before they will make a difference. In the meantime, the Russian winter has joined the Allied forces. The headlines in the collaborationist newspapers, *Aujourd'hui* and *Le Matin*, are less boisterous as the list of German triumphs grows thinner. There are frequent reports of sabotage — power stations, the railroads, the telephones and the telegraph shut down, then repaired, then shut down again. A tool and die works in a northern suburb was blown up. The soldiers patrolling the streets are silent, speculative, watchful.

I think of Max occasionally, and Max's radio, and wonder when I will see him next, though I know better than to ask. Occasionally, though, I pass information to Max and we linger together over coffee. I did him a disservice when we first met, for his French has improved rapidly. I feel sorry for the lonely life he must lead, always scurrying from one shadow to the next, one safe house to another, never able to settle. We lost him once for over a week and feared he'd been arrested, but he'd simply burrowed more deeply underground. Sometimes his hands shake and I pretend not to notice.

Intelligence is vital now — information gathered from photographs, maps, gossip. Céleste is studying German, her voice choking on the guttural sounds. But she is getting quite good at it, and at night in the restaurant she lingers by the German diners and later passes on what she hears. Henri says the vintners of Burgundy can predict troop movements from the wine shipments — a thousand cases to the Eastern Front, a thousand more to Normandy. Workers in the French arms factories leak increases in production figures. The air around us is heavy with a vast network of coded signals.

German signal detection units — vans with rotating antennas — cruise the streets now, listening for transmissions, working up and down the scale of wireless frequencies. Céleste and I witnessed an arrest a month ago. Gestapo men in suits watched as the French police led two men and a woman out of an apartment building. A long chain encircled their waists, and they were handcuffed. We hurried away, both thinking of Max. Operatives like him are called pianists, their fingers flying across the keys of the radio sets. Their survival odds are low.

I've forgotten how to walk in a normal fashion, without my eyes darting everywhere, without the sound of following footsteps washing the whole world away in a wave of panic. I am a courier, delivering messages and papers for Henri. Most of the people I meet remain strangers to me — it is safer that way in case we are caught. No names to betray. Always different meeting places, different times.

I've taken to hiding these pages when I'm not actually writing them. It's too dangerous to carry them with me, and I'm suspicious of the prying eyes of the *gardien*. I think he sometimes enters our apartment when Céleste and I are out working or performing "errands" for Henri. I've found a clever hiding place in the hallway. When people are arrested, their rooms are searched, but not necessarily the hallways leading to them. Suffice it to say that the spot is too high up for the stumpy *gardien* to notice.

June 7, 1942

Almost overnight, thousands of people have become visible, separated from everyone else by a single piece of yellow cloth, a six-pointed star the size of the palm of the hand on which the word *Juif* is inscribed in black. Every Jew over the age of six has been ordered to wear them, affixed to the left side of the chest, securely attached.

During the first months of the Occupation, Luc and I once leaned over a bridge to see the Seine reflecting a drift of stars. With Paris under a blackout, the night sky had returned. Those stars were an accidental gift, lifting our spirits. These strident yellow stars are meant to crush spirits. They bring with them a different kind of night.

Often I pass the Café Dupont with its sign, "No Jews or dogs."

Jews must ride only in the last car of the *Métro*.

Jews are forbidden to go into libraries and museums.

Jews are forbidden to use public telephones.

Jews are forbidden in many shops altogether, and can only shop between four and five o'clock, by which time most of the food is gone.

Everywhere I go, I memorize faces, memorize reactions. Some Parisians wear yellow scarves or yellow flowers in their lapels in a mute gesture of solidarity. Too many others do nothing, looking away quickly when they pass a Jew on the street, pretending not to see. The worst of them sneer or swear, their faces distorted with hate.

This is how I met Mathilde, more French than I am.

I was walking down the rue St-Sulpice, not far from home, just a few steps behind her when a thickset man deliberately stepped into her path, bumping her roughly with his shoulder as she tried to duck out of his way. She lost her balance and I reached out my arms instinctively to break her fall. Her elbow hit the pavement and she cried out in pain, but the man didn't turn around.

Apparently stunned more by the casual meanness of the attack than by the fall itself, she rose to her feet, one hand cushioning her elbow, and stared at me in a kind of daze. Her eyes were large and dark with faint shadows under them like bruises. I was angry at the man, and my scowl must have frightened her because she tried to pull away.

"It's all right," I reassured her. "My name's Renée Benoit; I live not far from here. C'mon. Your elbow's bleeding."

I tucked my arm around her waist and ushered her along. She glanced up at me from beneath her black tousled hair and I tried to smile encouragingly.

We reached the building, but as we passed through the door, the *gardien* materialized at the foot of the stairs. His eyes narrowed when he saw the yellow star. He stretched his neck forward as if about to object when I took a firm step toward him. My look of fury paralyzed him, and I have no doubt he looked upon the face of Medusa in that moment.

I stared him down and he scurried away.

Later, over an infusion of hot water and chicory, I learned that Mathilde Kovar used to be a student too, before Jews were barred from the Sorbonne. Her father had fought for France in the Great War, and had a modest jewellery shop in the Place Vendôme. Once. Their business was liquidated, and now they survive by selling off the remnants of their former life. A bit of furniture here, a carpet or a piece of jewellery there. Mathilde tried to warn her parents that worse was to come, but they were born in France and refused to believe they would be abandoned by the state, left without a bulwark against Hitler's cruelty.

"I'll tell you something I've discovered," Mathilde said, her hands folded and resting in the lap of her pale blue dress. "You can be scared for only so long; then you don't care anymore. You must survive. I have a little sister. Sophie. She is only seven years old."

She looked deep into my eyes and I read a question on her face she was too cautious to ask.

"I'd like to meet your Sophie," I responded. "May I walk you home?"

We crossed the Seine, winding our way to the 11th arrondissement and a modest flat. The child, curled up on a sofa with a storybook, glanced up at me and smiled with all the trust of someone born into a loving family. Madame Kovar, round and welcoming, insisted I stay for tea, so I sat down beside Sophie who immediately began explaining that her book was about a mischievous dog that stole bones from the butcher.

"If we move to the country," she confided, "Mathilde has promised me a puppy. Why don't people in Paris like dogs?"

"Of course they do. What makes you think they don't?"

"The signs say no Jews or dogs. What's wrong with dogs?"

"Nothing, Sophie. Nothing at all."

My eyes met Mathilde's. Then I crossed the room and picked up the phone to call Henri. We must try to get them out. It is what we do.

July 30

This is what happened.

Luc finally told me why he was working in the hospital, Hôtel-Dieu near Notre-Dame. I always found it odd that he chose to scrub floors and transport bodies to the morgue, such grim work for anyone, but especially for someone with his background. His mother died when he was ten, after lingering for months in that very same hospital. I can picture him in short pants, trudging down the long corridors, clutching a nosegay of violets in his small fist for a mother who was already lost to him behind a veil of pain. But when Henri asked him to do this work, he did not even murmur.

The hospital is at the centre of the network. There are several sympathetic nurses and a doctor who help in the deception. Death certificates are signed, sheets pulled up over bodies, and Luc pushes the gurneys down to the morgue where people are reborn with new identities and passed on to Henri.

This time, it is Mathilde and Sophie who must be reborn.

Luc and I have spent many hours in the Kovar home. Monsieur Kovar, as thin as his wife is round, is grave and dignified. The old couple welcome us and share what little food they have, nodding as, day after day, Luc gives them yet another reason why they should attempt an escape. But the answer is always the same. "Take the children," they say, "but we will stay."

I've watched Luc playing with little Sophie, lifting her onto his back for a piggyback ride, or lying on his side on the floor reading to her from picture books, and I've sensed he was thinking of another child growing up without a mother, but I can only guess at what he's feeling. He keeps his sadness hidden from others, even from me. Some part of him has always been withheld from me, buried deep inside where I can't reach. I wonder if all men have this little room they can't unlock, can't open to anyone. Only in the dark, when I am tracing the vertebrae down the length of his back and feeling his breath against my cheek, do I come close to knowing him fully. My need is no longer physical, or at least not purely physical. It is the desire to be known; the desire to know and be known by the one other.

On the night when everything changed, Mathilde and Sophie said goodbye to their parents. Luc was to lead Mathilde to a secret flat in the Marais where Max would meet them with the identity documents. I volunteered to keep Sophie safe with me. I don't think she realized what was happening, that she wouldn't see her parents for a long time. She is such a serious little girl, with dark glossy hair, deep eyes and a face at times filled with wonder. I wanted her to have a treat, so I made a picnic and we sat in the Luxembourg Gardens and watched the water from the fountains turn to golden spray as the sun set. She was tired afterwards, so I tucked her into my bed and slept on the floor in the living room.

We were to meet Mathilde and Luc first thing in the morning at a café in the Marais before the journey into Burgundy. I slept badly, restless and uncomfortable. Very early, before six, I roused Sophie and we began the walk across the Seine to the Place des Vosges. I remember the air was soft against my skin.

As we approached the rue des Rosiers, I knew at once something terrible was unfolding. I saw barricades and police swarming everywhere — *gendarmes*, SS and members of the fascist PPF, *Parti populaire français*, with their armbands and pinched, angry faces.

In the distance, glimpsed between the shoulders of the police and the forest of rifles, people, hundreds of people, were being boarded onto green buses and into furniture vans.

I ran along the line of spectators, dragging Sophie behind me. "What's going on? What's happening?"

"A *rafle*," someone growled. "They're rounding up the Jews."

A cacophony of voices:

It started at dawn.

The Yids are done for now.

Where are they taking them?

You. Get out of the way.

Serves them right.

I saw old people, pregnant women, children.

I felt dizzy, nauseous. I pressed Sophie to me, turned her face away. Where were they, where were Luc and Mathilde? People were calling out names, searching for each other. *Hélène! Sarah! Over here! Have you seen Moishie?* The police were beginning to push back the crowd, but the buses were pulling away. Behind the guards, the arrondissement was emptying quickly.

I sat Sophie down on the curb of a side street.

"Don't move!"

She looked up at me, her eyes huge and glassy, her arms hugging a rag doll to her chest.

I pressed forward, close to the front of the line now. I saw a gap between soldiers, and slipped through it.

A *gendarme* grabbed me by the arm.

"Please. I have to find —"

He shook me, hard. "Get away. Hurry. Before they see you."

I followed the direction of his gaze, saw the Gestapo officers beginning to turn around as if in slow motion, their eyes like pieces of flint.

I turned away, stumbled back to Sophie.

Rafle. It means a raid. It means a violent and greedy taking. It means smashing through doors in the hour before dawn. It means whole families roused, police snapping like dogs at their backs. It means Mathilde and Luc are missing.

All the rest of that day and the next, Céleste and Henri tried to help me fit together fragments of news into some sort of order. One paper said ten thousand people taken, another said twelve thousand, yet another said six thousand internees were packed into a detainment centre at Drancy, while seven thousand, including four thousand children, were sent to Vélodrome d'hiver, a glass-roofed sports arena in the 15th arrondissement with big grandstands where bicycle races are held in winter. The Germans closed down the *Métro*, sealed off five arrondissements, and then the French police moved in, drawing the noose ever tighter.

Bernard Levy was right. The very first step the Nazis took against the Jews in Paris made the last step easy: the Jewish register told them where to come pounding in the dawn, whom to look for and who might be missing. And if they have taken the ill, the elderly and the infants, it can't be to put them to work at hard labour. This is for something else.

During the day, Sophie is quiet and unnaturally still. She clings to me, follows me from room to room as if I too might vanish. At night, I rock her in my arms while she cries for her Maman, her Papa and Mathilde.

I never believed anything could hurt this much.

I must try to take her into the countryside by myself, but we must wait. Henri says the Germans are searching all the trains now, as some Jews were warned of the roundup by sympathetic *gendarmes* and are trying to flee the city. But where can they go? Pétain's Unoccupied Zone is patrolled by paramilitary bands of thugs who are viciously anti-Semitic. There is little hope of sanctuary there. Rumours are spreading that over a hundred people have committed suicide.

I took the train to Drancy today to stand dumbstruck with a group of others on the bridge over the railroad yards.

Drancy is an abomination, an unfinished housing project

surrounded by barbed wire and watchtowers. It stinks from a block away, the stink of raw sewage, sweat, misery and death. Even the weather has been cruel, incredibly hot all week. People have been stuffed inside for five days with no food and little water. Any strength they may have had left has slowly been drained from them. An old woman beside me leaned over the bridge and began to cry. She told me she's been here every day and has counted 130 bodies being carried out, including two pregnant women who died in premature labour.

I could feel my stomach twist into knots as the Nazis with their French lackeys began the process of boarding people onto the trains. First, the internees milled around, dazed by the glare of the sun. Hands reached for other hands, several couples embraced. Their clothes were wrinkled and stained with perspiration and worse. Their faces were sombre or bewildered or blank. I scanned the crowd as the *gendarmes* began pushing and shoving people into lines. People screamed and shouted out names. German guards surged forward with guns and snarling dogs. Some of the older men and women collapsed and were hauled roughly to their feet. Four or five men and two women broke from the lines, but soon crumpled under the blows of rifle butts.

Several times, my vision blurred and my legs turned to water, but I forced myself to watch, praying that I might see Luc or Mathilde, and praying that I would not. Praying that their flimsy pieces of paper that identified them as non-Jews had saved them.

Then I saw her, thin as a seedling hatched in the dark. She looked up and our eyes met. *Yes*, I nodded, *Sophie is safe*. I made an L-shape with my hand, a silent question. She shook her head sadly from side to side.

A guard pushed her from behind and she staggered forward. A dozen anonymous hands from inside the train reached out to break her fall and pull her into the railway car.

Mathilde was gone, swallowed into the crush of bodies.

I searched the faces disappearing into the train, a scream strangled in my throat.

The deep, rumbling sound of the boxcar doors closing ripped through my consciousness. A part of my life closed with them.

Once you've been to Drancy, once you've heard people cry out for help and go unanswered, nothing is ever the same.

Now I write hurriedly, trying to crush everything I'm feeling into a few last sentences. Henri is worried. He fears that Max has been arrested. We were careless when we met him, using our own names, innocent about what was coming. Henri wants to leave tomorrow for Burgundy and I will go with him with Sophie. She doesn't speak anymore. Her voice has been stolen away as surely as her sister and parents have been. The *gardien* knows she's here and doesn't like it. Yesterday, he insinuated to Céleste that he wants money in exchange for his silence.

Luc has vanished. I do not know what Mathilde was trying to tell me. Perhaps she didn't know what happened to him. Perhaps she meant he wasn't taken. Perhaps she meant he'd been arrested. Perhaps worse. All I know is that if he were free, he would come to me.

The telephone is ringing.

I do not think I can write anymore. I have lost my country, my name and now my voice.

Only one ring. *Why? A signal?*

SUMMER

1942

G

᷂

August 15, 1942

She knelt alone before the altar, her eyes fixed on the wave of white before her — white gardenias, white daisies, white phlox — like seafoam breaking over the carved wooden pews and spilling across the stone floor of the nave.

The flowers were for her husband, Jean Aubin, his hands tied behind his back, waiting outside in the market square to be shot.

Gabrielle felt she could not pray any longer, but she stayed on her knees, unable even to lift her head. She had been baptized in the church of St-Léger, and walked up the aisle in a white dress with a blue satin sash when she was confirmed. That day, she and Jean had stolen away from the village *fête* and he had kissed her for the first time in the narrow lane behind the *boulangerie*. Afterwards, they had eaten cake with pink icing from Madame Pascal's pastry shop, and Gabrielle had given him the ribbon from her black hair.

She leaned forward and placed her hands flat against the stone floor as if to pull strength from its polished surface. She had stood just here as a young bride at nineteen, Jean strong and proud at her side, their lives full and without horizons.

But the war had come to St-Léger. At first, the fall of France was too large a thing to believe, but the reality soon rumbled in on German trucks and marched in jackboots through the town. Who would care about tiny St-Léger? It was no more than a dot on the map of France, a few hundred inhabitants, a stone church on a slight hill at the top of a dusty square. On either side, there was a line of modest shops — a *boulangerie*, a *charcuterie*, a small grocery, a *tabac*, a bar with a couple of outside tables. The peeling colours were different shades of faded pink and yellow ochre. Most of the buildings were of weathered stone or stucco, with brown wooden shutters.

But still the Germans came and the St-Léger of Gabrielle's childhood became a foreign country. Swastikas hung from the flagpoles and the offices of the *mairie* where Jean was a clerk. German orders and German laws were plastered to the sides of buildings and the fronts of shop windows on brown broadsheets with double columns of red printing. Most began with the word *verboten:* forbidden to keep firearms, forbidden to listen to foreign radio stations, forbidden to walk after curfew, forbidden to aid or abet the enemy. Orders upon orders, some ending with the stark warning, "On pain of death."

Food became scarce as the Germans stripped the land of live-stock and produce. Everything was rationed — butter, eggs, meat, clothing, soap, fuel. Gabrielle spent long hours in queues for bread or a tiny wedge of cheese. During the icy winters of 1940 and 1941, people had struggled to feed their families, and scurried to meet curfews with newspapers under their clothes to insulate them from the bitter winds. All around them, propaganda posters spread lies of a peaceful Occupation: one image was of a German feeding bread and jam to a group of rosy-cheeked boys and girls. "Trust the German Soldier," it exhorted. But every day, the real children of St-Léger grew hungrier and more ragged.

From the beginning, Gabrielle was split into two selves, living two lives. In town, where the shadow of a German soldier falling across a café table could strike fear into the stoutest heart, she often felt remote from herself, a cardboard cut-out moving stiffly across a frozen tableau. Long after the handful of Germans billeted in St-Léger knew the villagers by sight, she was sometimes ordered to show her identification papers.

One of these soldiers was Hans Meyer. He was shorter than the others, with thinning hair and small eyes lost in a pudgy face. He enjoyed inflicting the needless humiliation, grasping her papers in his fat fingers and eyeing her up and down. At these moments, Gabrielle felt a rending of time and space, as if she were looking down at herself from a great distance. She knew it was important to question nothing, to betray nothing. But Meyer always laughed at the anger she could not keep from darkening her green eyes.

Away from the town square, in her cottage just a kilometre away from St-Léger, she would slip back into her own body. The stiffness would melt away and, when she was alone with Jean, she would be liquid in his arms. Their bed was inviolate. There, in a tangle of sheets, supple arms and legs, the arch of her back, the curve of his spine, the taste and smell of his skin, she could be the Gabrielle she remembered.

Sometimes they would wander into the great forests of the Morvan that loomed at the edge of the fields skirting their cottage. There they could almost pretend to be free. The Morvan was remote; in places, almost impenetrable. They knew its thin green light filtering through the heavy boughs of pines and the canopy of ancient oaks and beeches. They knew its rushing streams, sheer drops and fissured rocks. They knew its paths, sometimes only thin lines traced among crowded trees. They knew its caves and clefts, its mushroom smell of moss in the summer and its bursts of yellow marsh flowers in the spring. They also knew, but never spoke, of the activities of the Resistance hidden in the darkest part of the woods.

The loss of freedom rankled, but almost worse was the loss of trust. Gabrielle could no longer predict how anyone she knew might behave. Ordinary people, people she loved and people she hadn't even noticed or liked, were transformed by the Occupation. The town doctor, once so meek, became a pillar of strength, badgering the German Kommandantur in Avallon for more medicine and more food for the old and the ill. Joseph Thibault, the shy *garagiste* forced to service the Germans' trucks and the sleek black Citroëns of the Gestapo, did his job with a kind of grim dignity that even the *boches* grudgingly acknowledged. Kind Madame Pascal of the cakes of Gabrielle's hungry dreams became so cross that her gruffness toward Hans Meyer bordered on the dangerous. An old school friend, Marie-Claire, was often seen walking with a handsome German named Klaus: the older women on market days whispered that she'd become an *horizontale*, the shame of the village, sleeping with the enemy.

And lately, Jean had changed too. Even Jean. A son of the village, amiable and gregarious, he had become increasingly reserved. His laughter dwindled and his eyes became grave. Each day when he walked home from the *mairie*, where he supervised the distribution of ration cards under the watchful eyes of the Germans, his steps seemed to grow slower. Gabrielle knew why he worried, and did not press him for explanations. He took risks, she knew, slipping extra ration cards to women in the village with young children to feed, or to women left alone, their husbands prisoners of war or deported to Germany to work in the factories there. Yet, it seemed so small an infraction, such an ordinary act of kindness, Gabrielle hadn't the heart to caution him. As long as he stayed away from the *résistants*, as long as he didn't become reckless.

Then one night, as she spoke of the scurrilous gossip about Marie-Claire and her trysts with the German named Klaus, Jean had become angry.

"How can you judge her, Gabrielle, you of all people? Can't you see what's happening? She's poor. She's hungry. Worse than that, she's afraid. The good people of St-Léger have lost their spirit, their *esprit d'opposition*. Every day they become smaller, breathing in fear like poison. Letters come to the *mairie*, anonymous letters from neighbours accusing neighbours. *Where does Madame Pascal get her sugar? I saw Guillaume Sorel out past curfew. The Carons have a radio. There were lights in the forest two nights ago.* It makes me sick."

Gabrielle was ashamed. The next day, she rode her bicycle to Marie-Claire's house and gave her a bar of perfumed soap, not the revolting black stuff made from ashes. She hoped to please her husband, but the alarm she was beginning to feel about his mood did not abate.

She began to watch him more carefully. On one of the first warm days of March, when they were drinking rough red wine outside the Café du Sport with a group of friends, she saw him slip something into the pocket of Joseph Thibault. A ration card? A note? It was clumsily done. She'd looked around quickly and caught the eye of Hans Meyer, sitting just inside the café by the window. He'd grinned, a sly grin, thick fingers around the stem of a wine glass, lifting it in a delicate arc. Her heart stuttered. She was sure he'd witnessed everything. For the first time, she knew for certain that Jean kept secrets, dangerous ones.

One night two months later, after curfew, she woke with a start and a feeling of dread, sensing coldness on Jean's side of the bed. She shivered in the darkness, afraid to move, afraid to light the oil lamp on their night table. In the stillness as intense as prayer, every sound was magnified. The soft rustling of the countryside became ominous, the barking of a fox or the shriek of a bird like needles pricking her skin.

After what seemed hours, she heard his footsteps. She heard the door open. She saw a thicker blackness as he stood watching her in the doorway of their bedroom. She rose and opened her arms to him, her naked body a thin, pale column in the shadows. His hair was wet, and his face, burrowing into her neck, was clammy with sweat. His hands trembled across her breasts. Hungry for him, afraid for him, she dragged at his rough clothes and then wrapped her arms around him. Whatever he'd done, she didn't care. He was safe. He must be safe. She traced the curve of his lips with her fingertips, then his chin, the bridge of his nose, his cheekbones, his forehead. She kissed his eyes. With her touch, she memorized him — a lover's Braille.

He took her small hand and tucked it into his own.

"Gabrielle," he whispered. "*Je t'aime*, Gaby. Whatever happens, believe this. I buried him, but I did not kill him. I would never have put you at risk. I washed in the stream as best I could. But there wasn't much time. The grave is shallow. Sooner or later they'll find him."

Gabrielle shuddered, but she did not cry nor question him. She trusted him as she had trusted no one else in her life. Eventually, they slept.

In the morning, when Jean left for work, she rose stiffly. She stripped the bed, the sheets dirtied with mud and bits of pine needles, and, across one edge, a rusty streak of blood. She soaked the sheets in cold water and scrubbed Jean's discarded clothes. With her kitchen shears, she cut off the end of one stained jacket sleeve and burned it in the fire. Carefully, she sewed on a new patch of material that almost matched. Who would notice? Everyone's clothes were worn and patched these days. There would be no easy trail to lead the Germans to Jean. She took up her market basket and bicycled into St-Léger, as she always did, to line up for food.

The transformation of the town hit her like a body blow. She could smell the fear. The handful of German soldiers had swelled to more than two dozen. Outside the *mairie* where the Germans had set up their civil headquarters when they occupied the region, she saw the black Citroën of the Kommandantur. She saw the malevolent black uniforms of the Gestapo, two rigid men, standing guard like tightly reined dogs. No one spoke. No one looked at anyone else for very long.

She shuffled forward slowly along the line in front of the bakery, finally reaching her turn.

"You're late today," grumbled old Madame Pascal. "I've nothing left but stale bits and pieces of bread from yesterday."

"It doesn't matter, Madame. Whatever you have is fine. What's going on?"

"Hans Meyer is missing. The fat fool. I told them, he's probably fallen down dead drunk, pissing behind somebody's barn. Always stealing away at night to one of the farms, hoping to grab a chicken. Worse than a fox, that one."

"Shush — you mustn't say things like that. The Gestapo are here. I saw them outside the *mairie*. Please be careful, Madame."

Hans Meyer. Dead. Buried by her own husband somewhere in the Morvan.

When Gabrielle reached for the bread, her hand was shaking.

Madame Pascal looked up, surprised. "Don't worry, *ma petite*. They'll soon be gone. They'll find him, you'll see."

Gabrielle did not want to believe it, but the simple words of her old friend cut her with a terrible sense of inevitability.

Six days passed, as if in slow motion. Six days of roundups and questioning. Six days of anguish while the villagers quaked in fear.

But the animals in the Morvan were hungry, too, and the grave was shallow.

The notice went up only hours after the body was retrieved. Hans Meyer had been stabbed to death. If no one came forward, reprisals would be swift and unsparing, as they had been elsewhere: five men shot for every German killed.

The words reverberated in Gabrielle's head like the tolling of a funeral bell. With an aching heart, she'd watched Jean's struggle.

She sensed at once that he knew the identity of the killer. Perhaps the death was an accident, or self-defence, or an act of resistance, but it didn't matter. If he spoke out, that person would die. If he did not speak out, five people would die. It was not a choice. If the Germans could not find the real killer, or if he did not confess, the burden Jean carried would eat him alive.

In the end, the decision was made for him. Without warning, the Germans had come at dawn, pounding with fists and jackboots on the cottage door. Jean had grabbed both of her hands and pulled them to his chest.

"Say nothing, Gaby. Be safe," he'd whispered. Quickly, he'd pulled on a pair of trousers and opened the door.

The first soldiers burst in, propelling him to the floor, smashing the side of his head with the butt of a rifle. Gabrielle screamed and felt the iron clamp of hands on her arms as one of the soldiers flung her aside. On hands and knees, she crawled after them to the gaping doorway, and watched them drag Jean away, his bare feet trailing limply across the ground.

Her mind was numb. Her body felt hollow, as if her heart had been scraped away. She could not move.

The old priest, Père Albert from the church of St-Léger, found her still lying in the doorway an hour later. He had buried her father when she was fourteen; he had buried her mother seven years later when influenza had struck the village. He had confirmed her on that day of the first kiss, and three short years ago, only a heartbeat ago, he had blessed her and Jean on their marriage day.

"Come, come Gabrielle. You must get dressed. I will ask the Kommandantur if you might see him."

"Where have they taken him?"

"Only to the *gendarmerie*, not to Château-Chinon."

Gabrielle dared to feel hope. Château-Chinon was the headquarters of the Gestapo for the Morvan region. If they hadn't taken Jean there, perhaps they would soon let him go.

And so all of that day, and all of the next, wearing a pale yellow cotton dress with her hair falling like a black river to her waist, she had stood waiting outside the *gendarmerie*.

At first, the villagers were afraid to approach her. Some were glad that Jean was in custody, hoping that the Germans would be satisfied and that there would be no further reprisals, and some were ashamed of their hope. Others were alarmed for her safety, and urged her to go home. Still others — Marie-Claire, who brought her a shawl when it began to rain, and Madame Pascal, who brought her bread — were moved by her stubbornness.

On the third day, Étienne Fougères, one of two *gendarmes* stationed in the area, told her that the Kommandantur wished to speak to her. She nodded mutely and followed him across the square to the *mairie*, where the Germans had commandeered the offices of the mayor.

As she entered the swastika-draped room, the Kommandantur rose from behind the desk and gestured her to a chair. Gabrielle had never seen him before and she studied him carefully. She supposed he was too important to waste his time in St-Léger. He was perhaps thirty-five — young for his position, she thought — tall and slim, with close-cropped blond hair and an angular face. Yet there was something in his demeanour that surprised her. Had it not been for the uniform and the stiff posture, she would have called it gentleness.

"I am Gerhardt Dietsz, Madame Aubin. I understand you wish to see your husband." His French was correct, but his intonation carried the dregs of the harsher German language.

"He's innocent."

"It is natural that you should think so. But we have proof."

"Torturing a man to confess is not proof. He didn't kill Hans Meyer."

"Madame Aubin, I did not torture your husband. I am a Wehrmacht soldier headquartered in Avallon, not Gestapo. It is my sad duty to inform you that your husband will be shot tomorrow at five o'clock in the morning. I am sorry for you."

Gabrielle's stomach clenched. She closed her eyes, long dark lashes lying like shadows on her cheeks. When she opened her eyes, they were filled not with fear, but with accusation.

"You may see him," Dietsz said softly. "But only for a half-hour, no longer."

"You must stop this. Can you do nothing for him?" Gabrielle's voice was urgent, barely audible.

"I cannot. Even to allow you to see him, Madame — you must

understand. It is against all protocol. It is all I can do."

Gabrielle rose stiffly from her chair and walked to the doorway. She looked back at Dietsz once, and her voice was clear, edged with contempt.

"In that case, Herr Kommandantur, you are no better than the Gestapo."

Dietsz flushed and opened his mouth as if to object, but then closed it firmly and turned away.

Étienne Fougères was waiting for her outside. He took her arm and they walked across the suddenly deserted square. As they neared the *gendarmerie*, Père Albert materialized as if from nowhere and stood in their path.

"A moment, please, Étienne," he said. He took Gabrielle aside. "Be prepared, *ma petite*. He has been beaten. You must be strong, *hein?* Say nothing that you wouldn't wish to be overheard. I'll wait here, and take you home."

But the warning to be guarded in her words was unnecessary. There was so much to say, a whole lifetime crowded into a half-hour, that she and Jean had said nothing, choosing instead the syllables of touch. They sat facing each other, their fingers entwined. Only their eyes were eloquent. Gabrielle looked beyond the broken nose and the swollen lips, to the face she remembered and loved.

When she was ordered to leave, Jean whispered to her. "It's better this way, Gaby. One man for five. The Kommandantur has promised. In the morning, go to our church. I will think of you there."

Père Albert had sat with her at the kitchen table in her cottage through the long bitter night. They barely spoke, listening instead to the rainy wind. Like a child, Gabrielle had hoped that the swirling clouds would block out the light and dawn would never come. The ticking of the clock was remorseless.

Finally, under a still-dark sky, the priest had accompanied her to the church, and then left her to cross the square to Jean. She'd swung back the heavy wooden doors, smelled the flowers, their petals still wet with rain. It was all Jean's friends could do for him.

Now, unbidden, a pale wash of light began to seep through the stained glass windows. Gabrielle's hands had been clenched for so long she could barely open them.

She looked toward the alcove, where a painted plaster statue of the Virgin stood upon an altar. A metal crown of stars formed a halo around the figure's head, and a half-dozen flickering candles illuminated her face from below. Gabrielle realized she had never properly looked at her before, at the filigree of cracks across her face, the coldness of her eyes, or the rigidity of her arms, raised in endless supplication.

The explosion of the guns ripped through the dawn, through the thick stone walls of the church, through her heart.

Her mouth opened as if to scream her grief, but her vocal cords were tensed thin as taut wire, and she could make no sound at all.

Gabrielle sat alone in her stone cottage, chilled from the rain and numb with loss. There would be no funeral. The Germans would not allow it. There would be no slow cortège through the village, no friends with bowed heads pacing solemnly behind a wagon pulled by black horses wearing black plumes. There would be no graveside mourning, no ceremony that the villagers might use to turn Jean into a martyr. Would there even be a coffin, or would the *boches* simply dig a hole and roll the body into the dirt? Gabrielle swallowed a wave of nausea. No, she prayed, not that.

The tea that Père Albert had made for her from hot water and mint leaves had grown cold. She hadn't noticed when he'd slipped away, nor asked when he might return. She was unable to think, unable to move.

She stared at her familiar surroundings as if she'd never seen them before. One large open room running the length of the cottage, a plain staircase leading to two small bedrooms above. Jean used to complain of the lack of space that now seemed to yawn before her. The heavy pine table where she sat was heaped with onions and tomatoes. A hutch filled with blue pottery bowls and plates stood beside the washing-up tub. At the opposite end of the cottage was an old stone fireplace grown cold, two stuffed chairs and a blanket chest. The pride of the room had been their radio, but that had long been confiscated.

It wasn't much, but she had loved the cottage, loved sharing it with Jean. Mindlessly, she began tracing out the pattern of the oilcloth on the table with her fingers. Over and over, she followed the swirls and curving lines of the pattern, not thinking, keeping her mind empty. She felt she could do this forever and never have to look up. Loneliness was waiting for her there, like an animal in its lair.

She became aware of a soft knocking at the door and wondered how long it had gone on, but still she didn't move. As if from a distance, she heard the door open, heard a voice at the edge of her consiousness. Joseph Thibault leaned toward her, touched her shoulder.

"Come, Gabrielle. Come and see this." He helped her up and led her to the small garden that fronted her cottage.

There, in a heap beside the path, was a basket of eggs, a whole roasted hen wrapped in a white cloth, a jar of wild raspberry jam, a small sack of potatoes, a casserole of rabbit. She knew what it meant. The villagers would not be cheated of their sense of ceremony, of rites of passage as deep as memory itself. The food, so hard-won in these times of scarcity, so carefully prepared, was an act of respect, but also of defiance. The war, Gabrielle realized, was being fought in kitchens all over France. She felt something hard inside her begin to melt, releasing her tears.

"Here. I'll help you," Joseph said gruffly. He carried in the food, looking away from her face.

Gabrielle shook herself as if waking from a disturbed sleep. The rain had stopped. The daylight was fading. Joseph would not be able to stay long before curfew began, and she had much to ask him.

Reaching for a towel, she washed her face in the kitchen basin and combed her fingers through her hair. She found a bottle of table wine in the cupboard and brought two glasses with it, pulling out a chair for Joseph.

"Tell me," she said, pouring the wine. "I need to know what happened. I need to know where they took him."

Joseph squirmed in his chair. "I think perhaps the priest …"

"No. Not Père Albert. He'll try to spare me. He'll not tell me everything. Do you think there could be anything worse than what I'm imagining?"

Joseph shrugged and took a long swallow of the wine.

"They wouldn't allow anyone to attend, except the priest. But people watched from windows around the square. We — the doctor and I, a handful of others — were with Madame Pascal. She cursed the soldiers like a sailor. I wouldn't be surprised if she spits in the bread dough she bakes for them."

Gabrielle smiled. Encouraged, Joseph reached for her hand.

"Are you sure you want to know this?"

"Go on."

He leaned forward and tipped some more wine from the bottle into her glass before he continued. "They led him out from the *gendarmerie*. The rain was pissing down. Old Albert walked alongside him, his cassock trailing in the mud. Jean's hands were tied behind his back, but he looked over at the windows and nodded as if he knew we were there watching. He didn't look down, not once. The Kommandantur was there too, but he didn't give the order to the firing squad. It was someone else, a man in a suit. Gestapo, I think, from Château-Chinon. They didn't use any of the *boches* stationed in the village, as if that would make any difference to us.

"Then they offered him a blindfold, but he shook it off and looked toward the church. He was thinking of you at the end, Gabrielle. Only of you."

Gabrielle's body slumped forward, but she lifted her head for Joseph to continue.

"When ... when it was over, four soldiers came forward to take the — to take Jean away, but the Kommandantur waved them off. He was arguing with the Gestapo guy, and he called out for Père Albert. Finally the soldiers left. After talking to the priest, the Kommandantur left too. So we got our chance. Père Albert told us to move quickly, before the Germans changed their minds; then he went ahead to find you and get you home. We carried Jean into the church after you'd left. Madame Pascal washed him up a bit, while the rest of us headed for the Sorel farm — Guillaume said there was enough wood in his barn to make a coffin. It wasn't much. We had so little time."

"No, Joseph, I'm thankful. Relieved. I couldn't bear the thought that they — you must know what I feared."

"We couldn't take him to the village cemetery. Père Albert said no procession of any kind and we would've had to carry the coffin through the streets to the edge of town. So we buried him right there in the churchyard among all the ancient gravestones. It's a narrow space, but it was done good and proper. The priest said a short prayer. There's no marker, I'm afraid."

"It's all right. I'll know. They can't stop me from visiting an unmarked grave. Bless you all."

Joseph pushed back his chair, the legs scraping across the floor. "Well," he began hesitantly, not sure where the sentence would take him and feeling uncomfortable with the emotion in the room. "If there's anything more I can do ..."

Gabrielle caught his arm as he rose. "Tell me what Jean was doing in the forest the night Hans Meyer died."

His eyes widened involuntarily. "I don't know."

"Yes, you do. How long have we known each other? You can lie to the Germans, but not to me. I saw Jean pass a message to you once. Meyer saw too. Is that why he was killed? Was it the Resistance?"

Joseph sat down abruptly, as if he'd been hit by a stone. Sprawled on the kitchen chair, he seemed even taller than his six-foot frame, and he flexed his workman's hands awkwardly as if not sure what to do with them.

Gabrielle might have felt sorry for him if she hadn't needed to know the answer to her question so badly. She let the silence in the room thicken until it was almost unbearable.

Finally, his voice. "I — we — didn't know that Meyer had seen anything. It wasn't us. Even if we'd been suspicious, we wouldn't have been foolish enough to kill him. We'd have shut down, disappeared into the Morvan instead. Sometimes Jean carried messages for me, from one group of *résistants* to another, that's all. He didn't know anything, didn't want to know. He just left the messages in a certain place, didn't wait to see who might collect them. If Meyer caught him, he must have panicked and killed him to get away, hidden the body in the hope that it wouldn't be found."

"Jean did not kill him."

"What?"

"Jean buried the body, that's all."

"But then who? Why would Jean?..."

There was no need to finish his thought. The answer was plain enough. Jean died to end the threat of reprisals, died to protect someone or something.

Gabrielle sighed as if the words had been spoken aloud. "So, you see, Joseph. Even if Jean was not deeply involved, a messenger boy as you say, he must have thought Meyer was killed by the Resistance. You don't know who he might have seen in the forest? What about these other *résistants?* Might one of them have done the killing?"

Joseph shrugged. He was a pretty good liar, not at all proud of it. But he was caught unprepared. And this was Gaby asking, not some stranger, not an enemy. He owed her something.

"Gabrielle," he began gently. "Your questions, you must see, are dangerous. I can give you the broad picture, yes? But nothing more. There are half a dozen Resistance groups spread across the Morvan based in a string of villages and towns. Half the time, the left hand doesn't know what the right hand is doing. Some are Communists, some are Gaullists, some don't care about politics but are just trying to hide from the Germans. I don't know many of these men. Like Jean, I don't want to know. If we're caught and tortured, better not to know names.

"Here, in St-Léger, we are a small part of an escape line. I don't know where it begins or ends. If Meyer stumbled onto something that may have compromised another cell, then perhaps, yes, he would have been killed by the Resistance. But I'd not be told. The Resistance is not a single entity, not united, not yet. I can't help you more than that."

"I see," Gabrielle whispered.

But the truth was she did not see. She didn't believe that Jean would have died for a stranger, would have left her to cope alone for an abstract ideal. He was a brave man, but not stupid, not rash. She needed to believe that he died for a reason that made sense to him, if not to her. An escape line? Yes, that would be just the sort of thing Jean would be sympathetic to, not sabotage or armed rebellion. And she was certain now that he'd looked upon the face of the killer and recognized it.

She could accept that, but for one chilling fact. How, out of all the villagers who had been hauled into the *mairie* and questioned, had the soldiers known to accuse Jean?

She played that night over in her mind again — Jean, wet and shivering, crawling into bed with her; the streak of blood on the sheets in the morning. But she'd bleached out all the signs, mended his jacket sleeve. It had been so dark and he knew the forest so well, no one could have followed him. Could a second person have witnessed the killing? No, that was stretching credulity. Could someone have denounced him? Pulled a name from thin air just to stop a beating? No, she couldn't believe that and continue to live in St-Léger.

That meant that the person who stabbed Meyer recognized Jean too. That meant that Jean had been betrayed.

She thought about how ugly the word sounded.

Le traître. Treacherous, cowardly.

And she knew she could not ignore it. She would have to know who did this thing, even if she didn't know yet what she would do with the knowledge.

A glimmer of a path opened up before her, and she immediately took her first step upon it.

"Joseph," she said. "I want to take Jean's place. I want to join the line."

He stared at her, made an explosive sound with his lips.

"*C'est impossible.* This is no place for a young woman."

"No, but it might be just the place for a widow." She saw him wince and was sorry for her anger.

Her voice softer now, she took his hand. "I know you want to protect me, for Jean's sake. You're a good friend. But I can be useful. If the Germans are human at all, they'll look away from me, ashamed of what they've done."

"Or they'll look more closely, suspecting you know Jean's secrets."

"Perhaps. Don't say yes or no right now. Go home and think about it. I need this, Joseph. I need some purpose."

She smiled, kissed him on the forehead, walked him to the door.

Child's play, she thought, watching his broad back disappear into the twilight. She felt not the slightest pang of guilt for her manipulation of him. If this is what it took to be a *résistante,* perhaps she was more skilled than she knew.

August 17

Two days later, and still she had not heard from Joseph. She supposed he must be delaying the inevitable, reluctant to involve her but knowing he had little choice. The thought that she might be useful, might at the same time do something to avenge Jean's death, had gotten her through the first terrible hours of her grief. The echo of her footsteps on the stone floor of the cottage only served to remind her of its unnatural quiet, so she'd stopped pacing, slumped into a chair, eaten a little, slept less. *Jean, Jean.* She'd thought of the colour of his eyes, the gracefulness of his hands, the way the small of his back curved, the contours of his face. Would there be a time when she could not remember every detail and line of that face?

Once she'd had an urge to go into the forest, lay her face against the smooth bark of a tree, put her hands against something living, but when she opened the door, she saw that someone, probably Madame Pascal, had left a fresh baguette on the step, and the simple gesture reminded her of the enormity of what had happened. She closed the door, not yet ready to leave the cocoon of her sadness.

She'd busied her hands with small tasks, washing dishes, braiding her hair, fastening the line of tiny buttons on the black dress she'd first worn on her mother's death. She'd smoothed her palms over the sheets of the bed, the marriage bed as the old women in the village still called it. She would not sleep there again. She'd moved her brush and comb, her oval mirror, her bits and pieces of clothing into the second bedroom. The shift in space was disorienting, and for that reason, felt right. She'd fingered his clothing, wrapped her body in one of his sweaters, letting his smell envelop her. She'd picked up her wedding photo, stared at the two open, smiling faces in a kind of wonder. How long had she held it to her breast — a minute, an hour? At last, she'd given in, collapsed onto the narrow bed, and slept a deep dreamless sleep.

She was in the kitchen making ersatz coffee when she heard the two sharp raps on the door. Joseph at last, she supposed, or Père Albert. She suddenly felt a sense of welcome, of wanting to see people again.

But when she opened the door, the expectation on her face froze, and the words of welcome died on her lips. Backlit by the sun, the face of the Kommandantur was shaded. Just over his shoulder, she could see a second figure, the tall blond soldier — Marie-Claire's soldier, Klaus something, she remembered. She looked for a car or even a motorcycle with a sidecar attached, but there was nothing. They must have walked from the village, not wishing to draw attention to themselves. Why?

"*Bonjour*, Madame Aubin. I am most sorry to disturb you."

She didn't speak, merely held his gaze. She watched his eyes slide away from hers, take in the black dress, the sleeves of the too-large black cardigan that trailed beyond her fingertips, the single plait of hair. For the second time in only a few days, Gerhardt Dietsz averted his eyes momentarily, unable to bear the accusation in the green eyes, so vivid against the pale skin and the black clothes.

He stiffened, she thought she could actually see his backbone straighten, and when he spoke again, the voice was commanding.

"We will enter, now. Information has come to us that makes it necessary to search here."

"You must know your soldiers already searched here the night my husband was taken."

"We must search again."

He brushed her aside, waving Klaus forward.

Gabrielle bit down on her anger, tried to keep her face still. The two men seemed grotesquely large under the low ceiling. Dietsz glanced briefly around the room, said something in German to Klaus. While the soldier climbed the stairs, Dietsz surveyed the kitchen. The uniform fit his whip-like body perfectly. His hair looked like it had been parted on the side when he was seven and hadn't been out of place since. Perversely, she felt like laughing aloud at how ridiculous he seemed, at how ridiculous it all seemed. There was nothing more they could do to her, and the realization filled her with a sense of power.

"What are you looking for? Perhaps I can help, *non?* Here is some of the food my friends brought me after Jean was executed. Over there is the fireplace where we would sit together on winter evenings and read to each other. Be sure to look there — we may have stuffed a radio or some weapons up the chimney. Then over here ..."

"You will stop this, Madame Aubin. I am not without feeling. I understand that you are angry. If you should speak this way to the Gestapo, I cannot protect you."

A series of crashes from upstairs saved her from replying. Dietsz shouted out in German again and the crashing stopped. She retreated to the end of the room, sat down stiffly in one of the armchairs and folded her hands in her lap. Carefully, slowly, he searched the kitchen, pulling out drawers, opening cupboards. He studied the grout between stones in the flooring, looking for any sign that a stone might have been removed and resealed. He did, indeed, check the chimney, move the curtains aside, even tap along the curtain rods listening for a change in sound. While she watched, he opened and prodded and scrutinized everything she owned.

What is he looking for? she wondered. Some weapon, some evidence of Resistance activity? She didn't worry, for she knew there would be nothing. She considered how much a violation the search would have seemed if Jean were still alive, but it didn't matter now. These objects in the room, these things, meant little to her now.

At last he seemed to be satisfied, and called for Klaus. She rose from her chair, glanced up and caught him staring at her. She opened her arms.

"You wish to search me?"

This time, he did not look away, but shook his head.

"Kommandantur —"

"My name is Gerhardt Dietsz."

"Very well, Herr Dietsz. I wish to thank you for allowing the villagers to bury my husband."

The blue eyes seemed to soften, but Klaus entered the room, breaking the moment. Dietsz nodded briskly and she followed both men to the doorway.

At the gate, Dietsz looked back at her standing there.

"But I will never forgive you," she said coldly, just loud enough for him to hear. She felt dangerous, wild with grief and anger.

August 30

Gabrielle sat at the kitchen table counting her money. Life came down to one hundred and twelve francs. She needed to find a job. In the Unoccupied Zone, she knew, Pétain had restricted married women from working and many of his measures had been adopted north of the demarcation line. But she supposed exceptions would be made for widows.

She rode her bicycle into the village. People were staring but she kept her head up and slipped into Madame Pascal's shop. The old woman was like the bread she sold, tall and thin as a baguette, with a hard crust but a soft centre. She nodded at Gabrielle, twisted a loose strand of iron-grey hair back into her bun. There were few customers, and she dealt with them brusquely, taking their ration tickets and their coins and shooing them away. They were happy enough to go. Gabrielle's presence in the room weighed on them. Some took her hand on their way out, shook their heads sadly; others just shuffled by awkwardly, unable or unwilling to meet her eyes.

When they were alone, Madame Pascal closed the shop and embraced her.

"*Bienvenue, ma chérie.* You've become a *spectacle, non?* The memory of the execution is still raw among us. As quickly as the Gestapo disappeared, they can reappear. That's what they're thinking when they look at you. They worry they'll not be satisfied with Jean's blood, that there may be further reprisals. But let me look at you. Too pale. Come. We'll drink some of that vile roasted barley corn that passes for coffee now. I've given up on chicory infusions, too bitter."

She ushered Gabrielle into the backroom, furnished sparsely with a dilapidated couch, its springs sagging, a small scarred table and a few pots of straggling gardenias. But the leather top desk where Madame Pascal did her accounts was exquisite, the papers impeccably ordered. Gabrielle smiled to herself. The seventy-year-old woman had an uncanny business sense and a reputation for leaps of intuition. She'd always known what the naughtiest children were up to, and could wring the truth from anyone. It was her trademark.

Once they were settled with their hot brew between them, Gabrielle leaned forward to speak.

"Not yet," Madame Pascal interrupted. "Take a sip."

The liquid was laced with brandy, so strong Gabrielle began to cough.

Madame Pascal grinned. "A good nip will clear out the fog. Your eyes are looking dull, *ma petite*. Mustn't let your sadness blunt you. Better to let the pain sharpen you, make you more conscious of life. Do you know who killed Meyer?"

"Not Jean."

"Of course not Jean. Never crossed my mind. Now, why have you come? I expect Joseph sent you."

"Joseph? No. I've been waiting and waiting to hear from him, but he's not come. I was hoping — you see there's not much money. I need to work. If not here, maybe you could advise me where I might ask?"

"It's all been arranged. Ah, Joseph. Just like a man, hoping you'll forget all this Resistance business if he drags his heels long enough. But I don't mind telling you, we need all the help we can get. Some people have dropped out since that idiot Meyer got himself killed. They're sympathetic, but you know how it is."

Gabrielle's eyes widened. Madame Pascal was talking about the Resistance as if she were discussing the weather or the price of flour. She'd expected innuendo and stealth, not a casual conversation over spiked ersatz coffee.

"I'll need you here every morning by seven. Can you manage that? If you serve the customers, that'll leave me free to make deliveries to the outlying farms. I've an old white van that Joseph is adapting with a twenty gallon steel cylinder for burning wood — a *gazo* he calls it. It's what we French have to make do with since the *boches* are so stingy with petrol."

"Is that all?" Gabrielle could not hide the disappointment in her voice.

Madame Pascal narrowed her eyes and her voice dropped an octave.

"Be patient, Gabrielle. Establish a routine, every day do the same chores, follow the same route, never vary. Soon the *boches* will grow bored with you and stop watching. After that we'll see."

"Are they watching me?"

"They searched your house again, didn't they?"

"How did you know that?"

"Marie-Claire."

"Is she ..."

"No. Poor little fool. She's not a *résistante*. It's much worse. I think she's fallen in love. And you mustn't ask for names, not ever. Now go, and I'll see you tomorrow."

Gabrielle pushed her bicycle across the main square of St-Léger toward the church. She passed the Café du Sport and saw Marie-Claire sitting with Klaus, but didn't stop. Propping up the bicycle against the church doors, she took a deep breath and peered around the walled grounds to the north side, crowded with ancient tombstones. This was her first visit to the grave, but to establish a routine, she vowed she would come here every day.

Many of the inscriptions had long since been sponged away by wind and sun and snow, the stones leaning drunkenly and encrusted with lichen and climbing vines. She stumbled among the grey stones and the clumps of sharp green grass until she saw the narrow mound of raw earth. Her throat tightened, but she would not show her pain, not here. Instead, she began gathering small stones, arranging them in the shape of a flat cross on top of the bare grave. She did not notice Marie-Claire until she heard her voice.

"Gabrielle. I'm so sorry. I wanted to bring flowers, but Klaus said I'd better not. Jean was kind to me, to my parents."

Gabrielle stood, brushed the dirt from her hands, kissed Marie-Claire once on each cheek. "Thank you. Come and see me anytime, you're always welcome. But I must go now."

She turned to leave, and Marie-Claire reached out, grasped her hand. She looked around, almost furtively, though they were completely alone.

"Wait. There's something I need to tell you," she whispered. "There was something funny about Hans Meyer. The soldiers have been talking among themselves. Klaus says he was a *voleur*, a thief. He used to be stationed in Paris, you know, but they had to shift him because of his looting, stick him down here instead. The rumour is he was about to be shipped to the Eastern Front, to

Russia. It's terrible there, really terrible."

Gabrielle sighed, tried to pull her hand away.

"No, wait. I know you don't care about what kind of person Hans was, but Klaus said he wasn't the only one with a shady past. Meyer was blackmailing someone. He bragged about how rich he'd be when the war was over. He wasn't even worried about Russia, said he could buy his way out. He'd already been to see Dietsz. That's why your place was searched. Dietsz was looking for something that Hans had stolen, maybe something he'd hidden in the forest that Jean may have stumbled across."

"Dietsz told Klaus this?"

"Not in so many words. But Klaus is intelligent. They searched the house where he and Hans were billeted too. Why else would they do that? Besides, they'd already found some things that Jean had taken, hidden in his desk at the *mairie*."

Gabrielle's head snapped up. "What?"

"Oh, yes, but don't worry, I've told no one. They found a ring that Hans wore and a cigarette lighter, I think. That's why Dietsz agreed not to pursue the reprisals. He figured Hans had been killed for money, nothing to do with the *résistants*. So, be careful, Gabrielle. If you know where Hans hid his stash, just give it to them. I couldn't bear it if they —"

"Don't be ridiculous, Marie-Claire. Think about what you're saying, you *knew* Jean. He'd never steal. And he didn't kill Meyer either."

Marie-Claire shook her head as if she hadn't heard or couldn't believe what Gabrielle had said. "I know you loved him," she whispered. "But these are hard times. People change, do desperate things."

"Is that what you're doing, Marie-Claire? With Klaus?"

Marie-Claire pulled away, took a step back, her pale blue eyes filled with hurt. "How can you say that? I thought you understood. Klaus isn't like the rest."

"No, of course not, *mon amie*," Gabrielle took her hand. She studied her friend, her slight body, her thick dark blonde hair, her soft mouth, so vulnerable. "I'm just saying you should be careful, too."

"Oh, I already know what the village thinks of me. The German whore, they call me, even the *collabos* who take the Germans' money and meet with them in private. I know who they are. At least I don't hide, don't try to pretend I'm something different. I'm not ashamed of Klaus."

Gabrielle tried to make her voice sound casual. "These people who pretend to be other than they are, did any of them meet privately with Hans Meyer?"

"I don't know. Why?"

"Because I mean to find out who killed him. Listen, Jean died because he tried to protect someone, tried to protect the village. And now you tell me the Germans think the killer was a common thief. I can't live with that, Marie-Claire, I won't. Will you help?"

Marie-Claire shook her head, her eyes wide with alarm. "No, Gaby. No. If Jean was innocent as you say, then the killer is still out there. You could be next."

"All the more reason to find him. Please help."

She hung her head for a moment, then shrugged one shoulder. "I'll try."

September 7

Every day of the next week, in the late afternoons when the bakery closed, Gabrielle walked across the fields and into the forest to search for whatever it was Hans Meyer might have hidden. She knew her search was probably futile, but she clung to the idea that if she could find what the Germans were still looking for, she might also find a clue to whomever killed Meyer and betrayed Jean. The ring in Jean's desk had been deliberately planted there, like a finger pointing Dietsz in the wrong direction. She felt almost grateful that Jean had died without knowing about this last act of cowardice.

She remembered how greedy Meyer was, how stupid. He would pick somewhere obvious, she thought, the hollow of a tree or maybe the entrance to one of the caves. The trouble was there were so many trees, so many fissures in the rocks. But she knew the forest better than Meyer ever could, better than Dietsz could, and she thought she deserved some luck.

At first she explored only the fringes of the Morvan where the trees were widely spaced. Then she remembered that Jean had washed after burying the body, so she walked further into the woods along the beds of several streams, paying close attention to the slanting willows and slabs of rock that lined the banks. Sounds were muffled here, soaked up by moss, pine needles and the green canopy overhead. She listened for any sign that she was being followed but could detect nothing.

As each day passed, yielding nothing, she became more dispirited, losing faith in her intuition, almost giving in to the inner voice that nagged her about the pointlessness of her task. Still, she remembered what Madame Pascal had said about setting a routine, every day the same — work in the shop, visit the grave, come home, change into a hemmed pair of Jean's trousers and an old sweater, wander into the woods. It was something to do, and she had to *do* something, even though she was aware she was beginning to lose focus, that her motives for coming here were mixed. Yet being alone in the cottage at night was a struggle, and at least the Morvan was as huge as her loneliness.

At the edge of a stream, she happened upon a trail of recent footprints and decided to follow them. They led her deep into the woods where the trees were crowded, their leaves darker, their boughs twisting and snagging the wool of her sweater. She cursed aloud, startling a flock of crows that flew up out of the branches in an explosion of black flapping wings. As her eyes followed them to the sky, she saw that she had lost track of time. The light was fading, too quickly for her to reach home before curfew.

She stood very still, wondering what to do, listening to the night settling over the forest. A sudden movement caught her eye and she turned her head. A single fir branch was swaying back into position, as if it had been pushed forward, then released quickly.

Her mouth went dry and she felt her heart thud.

She was not alone. Someone else was in the forest. Meyer's killer? A German soldier?

She moved forward silently. Her instinct was to climb to higher ground, to one of the rocky plateaus where the trees thinned and where there were swathes of grass forming a rough sort of meadow. Whoever might be following her would find little cover there.

Slowly, carefully, she pressed through the undergrowth to the face of the rock cliff. She would have to climb up about twelve metres. She pressed her fingers into the cindery soil, feeling for the fissures that would give her a grip. Closing her eyes, she let her sense of touch, her memory of past climbs, guide her. Hand over hand, her body flattened against the rock, finding whatever leverage she could, she inched her way up until finally her fingers found a tuft of thick grass and she knew she had reached the meadow.

On level ground again, she stretched, brushing the dirt from her clothing, breathing in the night air. Above her, she saw a narrow crescent moon, a vastness of stars. Then, at the opposite end of the clearing, she saw a flash of light — not moon, not stars.

She dropped to her stomach, elbowed forward to the rim of a small hollow in the field and rolled into it, straining against the silence.

Then, in the distance, there came a hoarse sound like intermittent breathing, gradually deepening into a low hum. Gabrielle lay on her back, her eyes opened wide, her stomach clenched. The noise grew louder, becoming a pulsing growl, continuous now. She heard men shouting. Flipping over, staying low, she raised her head cautiously to see a line of shadows strung across the clearing. Torches blazed once, then blazed again. She took a quick look up just in time to see the plane pass directly above her, the engines thunderous, the ground trembling beneath her. The belly of the plane was a black square against the white moonlit clouds, growing swiftly in size as it began to descend.

Just as she thought it must crash, it began to rise, banking slowly to its right. The sound of the engines was almost lost in the long heavy turn, only to increase again as the plane made its second approach. She saw the torches again, this time in a steady line marking the length of the meadow. The plane dropped closer above the lit field. Its belly broke open, and heavy white blossoms filled the sky behind it. She counted the strange flowers, three of them, with stems of metal — parachutes dangling long cylinders spinning in narrow arcs to the ground.

As the propellers echoed in the distance, men swarmed across the field, collapsing the parachutes and wrenching free their metal cargo. Mesmerized by the scene playing out before her, Gabrielle rose to her knees. She peered through the darkness and saw two men dragging the cylinder that had landed closest to her across the ground to the far end of the meadow.

Suddenly, light from a torch blinded her. Her instinct was to dart away like a fish from a baited hook, but she knew it was too late. Behind the torch, a tall shadow loomed above her.

"Who are you?" French, not German. Her rigid body relaxed. His voice was harsh. "What are you doing here?"

Gabrielle didn't know which question to answer first, so she said nothing. The light burned her eyes and she turned her head away from its glare. A hand reached out, grasped her arm, tugged her forward.

"C'mon, follow me. You've seen too much already. Quickly now."

She stumbled along behind him, trying to keep up with the long strides. They passed other groups of men dragging the cylinders, making for the blackness of the forest at the end of the meadow. As they ducked under the first low branches of trees, she heard the snuffling of a horse, the sharp sound of a hoof striking against a stone. She glimpsed the outline of a wagon waiting for its cargo at the edge of one of the old logging roads that criss-crossed the Morvan.

The man reached for a shovel from the wagon, tossed it to her. She saw his face as he leaned toward her — deep-set eyes, high cheekbones, a square jaw.

"Dig," he said. "Over there, under the trees. Keep away from the road." He paused, seeing the alarm in her eyes. "For the parachutes. We bury them."

Gabrielle didn't think of disobeying. She moved quickly, understanding at once that they were all in danger, that German patrols might have seen or heard the plane and may even now be combing the woods. She found a spot at the foot of a towering pine, leaned all her weight on the handle of the shovel, felt the earth turn. She dug steadily for what seemed a long time — five minutes, ten? She wasn't sure how deep the hole should be or how wide. Sweat trickled down the channel between her breasts. From somewhere behind her, the man appeared again, this time with a comrade carrying the pillows of silk in his arms.

"That's fine, that's enough," he said, taking the shovel from her hands.

She watched as they packed the parachutes into the hole, shovelling the loose dirt over them. The second man gathered up pine needles and leaves to disguise the freshly turned earth. He straightened up when he finished his task, looked into her face, gasped.

"Gaby! *Mon Dieu!*"

"Joseph! Tell him who I am! I didn't know. I came for a walk, lost track of the time."

"You know each other?" the tall man asked.

"She's all right. She's —"

"I don't want to know." He cocked his head, listening for the sounds of a German patrol. "Let's get out of here."

They ran for the wagon where the other men had hidden the canisters beneath a load of logs before melting into the woods. The tall man swung up onto the wagon and, without a backward glance, urged the horse forward with a flick of the reins. Joseph grabbed her hand, pulling her into the forest and away from the logging road.

She kept her head down, watching her feet fly over the hint of a trail, listening to the pounding of her heart and, in the distance, the sharp yelps of barking dogs.

September 8

After what seemed to Gabrielle an endless night, the morning sky was a wash of pink, turning the landscape beneath it into a muted watercolour. She hadn't slept. Her muscles ached as she cycled into town to open the shop, but it was a satisfying ache. At last, she had been part of something important, a small strike against the Germans, something better than doling out bread and collecting ration tickets so that Madame Pascal could be freed to do whatever she did when she visited the outlying farms.

Her mind was filled with ideas and questions. She remembered her moment of panic when she thought she was being stalked, but it must have been someone on the way to join the *résistants* in the meadow. So much for Joseph's activities being confined to an escape line. It wasn't people in those canisters. Standing on end, each one was taller than her, and they were heavy enough to require two men to drag them. What was in them? Guns? Ammunition? Supplies? She hadn't gotten close enough to see the others, only Joseph and the tall man. Who were these men? Did they come into the shop for bread? Did she know them, and not know them at the same time? She thought she understood why the man who had discovered her had put her to work with the shovel. It made her part of what was happening, it made her complicit just in case she wasn't the sort to be trusted. From his manner and his voice, she was sure he was the leader. He'd taken the greatest risk by staying with the cumbersome wagon and its incriminating load.

Even before she pushed open the shop door, she was enveloped by the yeasty smell of baking bread. Madame Pascal looked out from the kitchen, waved her forward. Gabrielle took an armful of still-warm baguettes and began arranging them on the shelves.

"Sleepless night?"

Gabrielle looked up, saw Madame Pascal watching her.

"Ah, well. You know how it is. The nights seem longer without Jean."

Madame Pascal made a sputtering sound, almost a snort. "But not, I think, last night. Still, it's a good enough answer for most."

How did she know? Gabrielle raised an eyebrow.

"Your colour is up. There's a certain spring to your step. Don't be seduced by the adventure, *ma chérie*. Remember, always remember, that it's your life, maybe worse, if the *boches* catch you. You must be vigilant, take for granted that you're under suspicion. We must all live deep down inside ourselves now, remain calm on the outside. Can you do that?"

"I think so."

"I hope so. The *gendarmes* tell me the Kommandantur is coming here today. He likes my bread. Or maybe he's intrigued by the enchanting Gabrielle who serves it. Or maybe he's read the reports of a suspected drop last night, and is coming to sniff the air, in the manner of a dog meeting another dog. Be careful. Here's a baguette for Guillaume Sorel. Keep it under the counter. If it's safe, give it to him. If not, pass him one of the others and say 'This is all I have today.' Can you manage?"

"I can."

But it was easier to say than to do. Gabrielle was jittery, her eyes darting to the window again and again, waiting for Dietsz, waiting for Guillaume, old man Sorel's son, the slowest boy in school. Should she thank him for helping to bury Jean, or stick to the script? Was Guillaume one of the men in the field last night? She began to understand the gravity of secrets. She began to understand that, though she did not fear for herself, she was frightened for others whose identities she could now name.

She worked her way through the morning queue, then closed for lunch. Sitting in the little backroom with vegetable broth and a piece of cheese, she wondered what sort of message could have been baked into the bread, then realized that she, like the tall man, didn't want to know some things, didn't need to know. None of these people would have betrayed Jean. *Would they?*

The afternoon brought the farmers' wives into town. They would have finished their chores by now, weeded their vegetable gardens, more important than ever now as their main source of food, tended what few animals the Germans had thought were too old or broken down to steal. She looked down toward the end of the queue, saw Madame Sorel, Guillaume's mother, and behind her Marie-Claire, looking dreadful with red-rimmed eyes.

"Madame Sorel. How lovely to see you. How's your family?"

"No better than they should be. That fool of a son of mine sprained his ankle last night. I've all his chores to do now besides my own."

"I'm sorry."

"You shouldn't be. Serves him right. He says he went hunting, but I know he was probably drinking at the Café du Sport with the other village idiots. I mean, who would go hunting in the forest in the dark?"

Mon Dieu, Gabrielle thought, *suppose Dietsz had strolled in and overheard this?* She had to get the woman to be quiet. She looked over Madame Sorel's head, pretended to see Marie-Claire for the first time.

"Marie-Claire, why, whatever's happened? Are your parents unwell? Come, I'll fix you something to drink." Gabrielle came out from behind the counter, took Marie-Claire by the shoulders and ushered her toward the backroom. "*Excusez-moi*, Madame Sorel. I'll be right back."

It worked. Madame Sorel's mouth clamped shut with disapproval and she turned her back on Gabrielle, leaving the shop in a huff.

Gabrielle turned her attention to her friend, who really did look unwell, her face strained and pale. She slipped into the kitchen, found Madame Pascal's brandy.

"Here, drink some." Gabrielle waited until Marie-Claire had swallowed some of the liquid. "Tell me what's wrong."

Marie-Claire looked up from the glass, her eyes brimming with tears.

"It's Klaus. They've shipped him to the Eastern Front."

Yes, well, there's a war on, Gabrielle thought, but she didn't say it. Though she cared little for Klaus, her heart twisted at the sight of Marie-Claire, stricken by the news, bent over from the waist now, her thin shoulders heaving with her sobs. Gabrielle leaned forward, held her friend's face in her hands, smoothed back her hair.

"Shush, now. Perhaps he'll come back."

"N-no. I know in my heart I'll never see him again. This is Dietsz's doing. Don't you see? He's gotten rid of him because he roomed with Hans, because he knew about his past. Oh, Gabrielle, I'm so frightened. What will happen to me now?"

"Why should you be frightened? The villagers will soon forget."

"You think I care about their gossip? It's Dietsz I don't trust. He could do anything, call me in for questioning, deport me, anything. Klaus told me things. I know who Hans was —"

Marie-Claire froze as the bell on the door of the shop jingled.

Gabrielle raised a finger to her lips, and slipped out of the room, closing the door behind her.

Dietsz. As if summoned by the sound of his name, he leaned casually against the counter, straightening up when he saw her.

"Madame Aubin, you are working here now?"

As if you didn't know. "May I help you with something?"

"Six baguettes, please. The bread is better here than in Avallon. But perhaps I am disturbing you?" He cocked his head toward the backroom.

"No, not at all." Gabrielle turned her back. She saw there were only four baguettes left. She gathered them up, trying to keep her hands busy, trying to keep them from shaking. Had he seen the baguette set aside for Guillaume when he was leaning over the counter?

"And where is Madame Pascal today? I miss her rough tongue."

Gabrielle paused. Did he know about the white van and the deliveries? She wasn't sure how much to say.

"She often rests in the afternoon, or visits friends. It's hard for her at her age, being on her feet all day."

The blue eyes narrowed. He had detected her hesitation, she was sure.

"I'm afraid I've only four left," she said. "It's late in the day. Please, take them."

"No. I insist on paying."

He held out the money, German coins, not French. She reached for them. Ever so lightly, his fingers grazed the back of her hand.

"You're sure there's no more? Perhaps in the kitchen?"

"There's nothing. You should come earlier in the day, but I expect it's a long drive from Avallon just for bread."

"Oh, no. Not so long, not so long at all. Good day, Madame Aubin."

At the door, he paused, looked back. "Please, you will give my best to the young lady. I am sorry she's upset."

Gabrielle's palms were sweating. She wiped them on her apron, walked to the shop windows, watched his back disappear down the street.

The door to the backroom opened behind her.

"You see, he's following me. I heard everything. Tell me again how I shouldn't be frightened." Hard-faced, Marie-Claire brushed past her and reached for the door.

"Marie-Claire, please." Gabrielle touched her friend's arm, but she stepped away and was gone.

An hour or so later, Madame Pascal returned and found Gabrielle waiting for her. In a rush, Gabrielle told her everything about Guillaume's ankle, Dietsz and Marie-Claire, but nothing about Meyer, no word that her friend might know whom he had been blackmailing. That was for her, for Jean, nothing to do with any of the others.

Madame Pascal reached for the brandy. "It's clear Dietsz is up to something. What puzzles me is that he's not even trying to hide it. Buying bread from an old woman's shop miles away from Avallon? He knows how flimsy that is."

"So you think Marie-Claire really may be in danger?"

"Oh, yes. But not from him."

"Then who?..."

"Ah, Gabrielle, you are still a child, a good Catholic girl whose husband was loved. You don't hear the ugly things they say, but around me they aren't so careful, *hein?* Spreading her legs for a German sausage — that's the way they talk about Marie-Claire. They feel shamed. The Germans have made them impotent, and one of their own daughters has welcomed a *boche* into her bed. They're angry, and she's lost her protector now."

"You don't think they'll hurt her, do you?"

Madame Pascal shrugged. "She bears watching. But I'm more worried about Dietsz. And with no Guillaume ... well, the message was vital. I'll have to deliver it myself."

"No, you mustn't. Dietsz didn't believe me today, I'm sure of it. He's watching the shop, not me. I'll deliver the message."

Madame Pascal looked at her for a long time, saying nothing. Then finally, "Last night was an accident, Gabrielle. You shouldn't have been involved. I could even explain away the message in the bread if I needed to, should it be discovered. But this is something different, a deliberate act. You'd be meeting another agent from another town, learning about our drop site. You understand what will happen to you as a courier if you're caught? You'll have no weapon to defend yourself with. I believe Dietsz has a certain sympathy for you. Perhaps he even suspects that Jean was innocent, and so his conscience is pricked. But if he catches you at this, neither your beauty nor your vulnerability will be a shred of use to you. In fact, rather the opposite. Dietsz will crush you as easily as he smiles at you."

"I know the risks."

"*Non, ma petite*, you only think you know them. And then, only in your head, not in your heart."

"These last weeks, my heart has grown old. Please, Madame, let me be of use."

"Grief is not reason enough, Gabrielle. If you don't care what happens to you, you'll be careless. You can only succeed if you want desperately to live."

Madame Pascal took hold of Gabrielle's hands. "If I allow you to do this thing, I'm placing my life in your hands, and the lives of others. Some you know, some you'll never know. They may be villagers you've known all your life, pilots whose aircraft have crashed over enemy territory, children whose only crime is to have been born Jewish. We want to live. Do you?"

Gabrielle squeezed the old woman's hands in her own. "I do."

"I hope so, for all our sakes. I'll get the message from the baguette. Take it into the Morvan, to the old logging camp. You know it? Very well. You must get there and back before curfew. No more skulking in the forest after dark. Your code name is Amélie. The man you'll meet is Yves. He'll ask who you are. Say 'I am a farmer's daughter.' He'll tell you he is a tailor's son. But we're late, he may not have waited. If there's no one there, put the message in the hollow of the oak to the left of the camp and leave immediately. If he's there, and doesn't say the right words, run from him as fast as you can, and get rid of the message. If you're caught, you have forty-eight hours."

"Forty-eight hours?"

"It will seem a lifetime. Forty-eight hours to endure whatever is done to you before you talk. It will give the rest of us time to disappear as best we can."

The old woman crossed to the counter and dug a small fold of paper from the baguette. She held it up. "Are you sure, Gaby?"

Gabrielle nodded. The message seemed to burn in her fingers as she slipped it into her shoe. She turned to leave, already thinking of the old shed at the logging camp, seeing the oak, the hollow where she and Jean used to leave love notes for each other when they were teenagers, knowing he must have chosen the site of the drop, and that she was following in his footsteps. She should have guessed much earlier. Was this the place where Meyer was stabbed?

She opened the door, and just as quickly Madame Pascal slammed it shut.

"What a blunderer you are. Look at yourself. Your cheeks are blazing, you're about to rush into the street. And would you have remembered to visit Jean's grave, to keep to your routine? Patience is as important as courage, my girl, maybe more so. Have the good sense to see you're not followed, at least. Learn to look without others knowing that you're looking. Act normally."

Gabrielle hung her head. "Of course, you're right. I'm sorry. But what's normal these days?"

"Danger, and you'd best not forget. Godspeed."

Slowly, Gabrielle approached the church at the top of the square, leaned her bicycle against the church doors, walked to the grave. *I can do this*, she promised, *I can learn to see myself as others see me, learn to suppress all outward signs of emotion.* She knelt down, touched the flat cross, hot from baking in the afternoon sun. One of the stones was slightly out of place. She nudged it aside, saw the small square of paper underneath. Quickly, she slipped it into her pocket.

When she reached home and opened the note, she cried aloud at the message: *You were lucky last night. Give me back what's mine if you want to survive your husband.* The printing was childish and uneven, as crude as the threat. She crumpled the note in her fist and lit a match to it.

An hour later, dressed again in Jean's clothes, she stepped out of the shade of the forest into the clearing of grass that marked the approach to the logging shed. The makeshift roof of branches strapped together with weathered twine seemed to sag, the old door leaned crazily. She moved without being conscious of moving, pushed against the door that swung open easily, stepped into the windowless gloom. No one.

She turned to leave, saw a man's shape backlit in the doorway. She could not make out his features, saw only that his hair was dark, his body lean.

"Who are you?" he asked.

"I am Amélie. A farmer's daughter. Who are you?"

"Yves, a tailor's son."

Gabrielle nodded, bent down to remove her shoe. She heard his soft laughter.

"You're new. It's the first place they'd look. Also, not very bright, if you don't mind my saying. If you wanted to get rid of the message in a hurry, would you have time to take off your shoe?"

"Where, then?"

"Use your imagination," he grinned, holding out his hand. She caught the glint of dark eyes in a handsome face, very young, maybe mid-twenties. "Thanks, Amélie. I'll wait 'til I see you safely gone."

She didn't want to go. The meeting felt like an anti-climax. She wanted to study him, hear the voice again. The French wasn't quite right, she couldn't place the accent. Then she heard Madame Pascal's voice inside her head. *Patience.* She gave him her best smile, turned away and disappeared into the woods.

September 10

Gabrielle was beginning to learn that, with an act of will, she could appear deceptively calm, even while her mind was a maelstrom of questions about Meyer's killer and the message he'd left. She must speak to Marie-Claire, let it be known that she didn't have Meyer's stash. She wondered too about the tailor's son, unanswered questions about who he was, where he came from, whether he'd ever known Jean. She was learning to be still, to create a quiet pool inside herself from where she could watch others more intently. Perhaps, little by little, day after day, she was learning to perceive herself as an independent woman, not as daughter, not as wife, though Jean's voice was always with her, like a gentle friend inside her head.

She discovered that danger could sharpen the senses more keenly than curiosity. She found herself studying the expressions of the people who came into the shop, people she'd often taken for granted, surprised that she could often discern when they were being evasive or guarded. Étienne Fougères, for example, the *gendarme* who had first escorted her to the Kommandantur's office. *Gendarmes* were never locals, but assigned to districts by the central authority as a way of ensuring objectivity. Yet Étienne, thin and boyish, with a lean, serious face, seemed fond of the villagers. When Gabrielle caught his eye, he would smile shyly, but when he thought she was not looking, he studied her, often frowning, his brow furrowed, as if she were a mystery he could not solve.

Gabrielle would often watch Madame Pascal and Joseph with their heads together beside the white van, and guess that there would be deliveries on certain days to outlying farms that had nothing to do with bread. She wondered if the message she had delivered meant a whisper of hope for some unknown person in the escape line.

But it took none of her burgeoning talent to read what was happening between Marie-Claire and the villagers. Their mutual antagonism was plain for even the most dim-witted to see. That Marie-Claire made no secret of her distress over the loss of her German soldier was salt in the wound as far as most onlookers were concerned. More and more frequently and more markedly, people had begun to shun her, turn their heads away if she spoke, step aside if she were in their path.

Gabrielle watched the growing isolation with alarm. She knew what it was like to have your future snatched away, and whatever Marie-Claire had done, she felt a tenderness for her.

She came into the shop one morning and Gabrielle made a fuss over her, tried to slip her more bread than the ration ticket allowed, while others looked on askance.

"Come for supper," she urged. "Come tonight. We'll talk."

But Marie-Claire only shrugged and scurried away.

"Careful," Madame Pascal cautioned. "The villagers have enough resentment for two."

"It's what Jean would want. I don't believe people would so easily forget his kindness."

"Memory's the first to go when people feel offended."

Gabrielle felt frustrated, partly because she cared, partly because she was burning to find out everything she could about Hans Meyer. Who, among these people she'd thought she'd known so well, might he have been blackmailing? Who would be callous enough to leave a threatening note at Jean's grave?

As the day wore on, Gabrielle felt her spirits lag, dragged down by petty resentments and gossip. By the time she reached the graveside, her legs felt leaden. She sat on the ground, one hand on the makeshift cross, and tried to remember what joy tasted like.

Joseph's hand on her shoulder interrupted her gloom.

"Gaby? Are you all right? I need you to come, quickly."

She stood up, brushing the loose dust from her skirt. "What's happened?"

"Not here. C'mon. I've borrowed a motorcycle from the garage. Leave your bike."

She climbed on behind him, wrapped her arms around his thick waist, felt the wind scrub her clean as they bounced along the dirt road to her home.

Once inside, Joseph spoke quickly, his voice urgent.

"Jean's clothes — do you still have them?"

She nodded.

"We've got to hide someone. We need French clothes — pants, a shirt, maybe a jacket, shoes if you have them. Hurry, I can't be away from the garage much longer."

She obeyed instinctively. On the rail inside the wardrobe in the bedroom she had shared with Jean, his clothes hung like discarded selves. She didn't pause to think. She gathered what was needed into a bundle, held it out to Joseph.

"No. I can't go." He took the clothes, began wrapping them in newspaper. "You must take them to Dun-les-Places, to the church."

"But how? It's — what, fifteen kilometres away?"

"Only ten if you go through the forest. Someone's waiting for you now, with a horse, just across the field under the trees. You should be able to make it to the town in an hour or so. Do you know the way?"

"Yes, I think so. Who's waiting?"

"Gabrielle, just go. If you suspect you're being followed, turn back. If you get to the church, go into the confessional. Leave the clothes there."

The door closed behind him. She stood still for a moment, clutching the package of Jean's clothes to her breast, felt a flash of sorrow, a tightness in her chest. Then she turned, resolute, and changed into her forest clothes, shut the door behind her. She crossed the field, pacing herself, reminding herself not to run, not to hurry. At the fringe of the woods, she stopped to listen. There, to the left, she could hear the snuffling of an animal. She stepped under the branches of the trees into the dappled light.

He held the reins out to her, with the same wry smile as before.

"We meet again. Can you ride?"

She smiled back. "I really am a farmer's daughter." She took the reins, swung up easily onto the black mare's back and looked down into the face of Yves.

He reached up, touched her hand. His dark eyes met hers. "I'm sorry about your husband."

"You know who I am?"

He nodded in the direction of the field she'd just crossed. "We make it our business to know the safe people. Don't worry. You'll always be Amélie with me."

He swatted the mare's rump and she was off, urging the horse across the first stream, threading through a stand of beeches, stretching low across its neck as she found the logging trail and risked a gallop. Twice, she had to double back, had to scour her memory for the route, but eventually she came to the edge of Dun-les-Places, no more than a dozen houses and a few shops that serviced the neighbouring farms. She dismounted, patting the mare's nose, tethering the reins to a tree, and approached the church from behind, its pale yellow stone now golden in the sunset.

She stopped for a moment, felt the softness of the summer air on her skin, damp from the riding. She knelt by a small pooled fountain to the left of the church, dipped her hand into the water and washed her face. The village was serene, sleepy in the twilight. *Entre chien et loup*, she thought — the twilight time between the dog and the wolf, between the tame and the wild. On this mission, she knew, she was on the side of the wild. She picked up the bundle of clothes, circled to the front of the church and pushed open its heavy wooden door.

The quietness of the village was intensified inside, the air cool and dark, scented with a scattering of lit candles. She halted abruptly, saw two figures kneeling with bent heads in the front pews before the altar. The confessional was close to her at the back of the church, a wash of light coming from one side of the carved wood double doors. One side was occupied, the other empty. She had not been told that anyone would be there. She hesitated. But what if one of the supplicants at the front should turn and see her? She had no choice. She slipped into the confessional, held her breath.

She heard the panel between priest and sinner slide open, a ray of light falling through the grille across her profile.

"Do not be afraid, my child."

"Père Albert?"

"Of course. You have something for me?"

"Yes."

"Then leave it now. But first, have you no sins to confess?"

Gabrielle felt a sudden desire to laugh, to hug her old friend. She placed a hand against the grille, felt his hand meet hers there.

"I fear I'll be out past curfew, Father."

"That is not a sin. Unless you should be caught. Go now."

Buoyed, she stepped out of the confessional as quietly as she could, reached the church doors and looked back once. The smile died on her lips. One of the praying figures was standing now, watching her. A man, tall, and in the dim light, almost gothic-looking in the monk's robes. Sensing her fear, he reached up, slipped the hood away from his head. She blinked, looked again. It was the man from the parachute drop, she was certain. His features were obscured, but there was something in the bearing, some grace she felt she recognized. Drawn to him, she took a step forward, but he held up a hand, shook his head slightly. Oddly deflated now, she made her way back to the edge of the forest, and led the black horse into the cover of the trees.

The journey back was more arduous than she had expected. Darkness meant she had to dismount several times and lead the horse through the maze of trails, taking whatever measures she could to dull the sound of their passage. When she reached the place where she had met Yves, there was no one waiting. In the end, she decided to leave the animal where she had found it, and make her way across the field on foot. Conscious of the time, she kept close to the hedgerows, avoiding the exposure of the open field.

She stepped inside the cottage, leaning her back against the door for a moment, feeling the tension drain from her body. Then instantly she straightened up, an intuitive part of her aware that something was wrong in the tidy space she'd left only a few hours before. There was nothing obvious, no gaping drawers, no obvious disorder, but she was sure someone had been here. There were small signs of searching — a kitchen towel left askew, a cupboard door not quite shut. She lifted her eyes to the staircase, felt her unease flare, the corrosive taste of fear in her mouth. Was she alone?

She forced herself to move across the floor, mount the stairs. Close to the top, her hand slid into something sticky on the railing. She jerked it away and looked down at her palm and fingers. Blood. There was a smear of it on the railing.

Slowly she backed down the stairs. She listened intently, but could hear nothing from the rooms above. She scanned the floor and the lower stairs, but saw nothing. There was only the small dark stain of blood on the railing. Slumped in a chair, she wiped at her hand with her handkerchief and thought about what she must do. She must will herself to search the bedrooms.

Very, very slowly, she began to climb again and this time reached the landing. She switched on the lights, edged open the door of her room and saw her work clothes scattered on the bed where she had left them. She looked into the second room. The closet door was still agape from when she had rifled the closet for Jean's clothes. She peered inside.

There was no one. She was alone. Puzzlement edged away her fear. What had happened here? She hadn't locked the door when she'd left on her mission. Before the Germans came, no one had locked their doors in St-Léger. Once Jean had been taken, she'd realized how futile locks were and so had reverted to her old habits. But who would have come?

Instantly, she thought of Marie-Claire, of the dinner invitation that she had shrugged off. Had she changed her mind, only to find an empty cottage? Or worse, a cottage that someone else was searching? Was Meyer's murderer still looking for his missing stash? She looked down at her hand again, at the traces of blood, and was filled with a sense of urgency. In three steps she was back out in the night, heading for the shop and Madame Pascal's telephone. She had to know if Marie-Claire was safe.

Outside, the moon turned the road before her into a silver trail. Missing her bicycle, she walked quickly, feverishly rehearsing the words she would use should she be spotted by a German patrol. *An emergency. I need to find a telephone. I'm worried about ...* then her words crashed into each other inside her head and her body jerked to a halt. She'd caught sight of something pale in her peripheral vision, there, to the left of the road. A small white hand lying in the verge of tangled grass.

She swallowed, her pulse racing. She steeled herself to step over the shallow ditch onto the verge and lift up the thicker undergrowth, uncovering first the arm, then the body. A sob bolted through her chest. Marie-Claire was lying on her back, one arm flung outwards, her head turned sideways, the thick blonde hair obscuring her face. With a low moan, Gabrielle knelt beside her, searched with her fingertips for Marie-Claire's lips, already knowing she would feel no breath there.

She forced herself to look at the body, stared at the stained punctures in the clothing. Marie-Claire had been stabbed several times. Gabrielle shook with revulsion, realizing she was kneeling in blood. She tried to stand and slipped forward.

Something was twisted around Marie-Claire's neck. Gabrielle leaned closer to look, and recoiled.

It was a miniature coffin six inches long with a raised cross carved into its upper end, and a thin piece of leather looped through its tapered bottom. In a rush of anger, she untwisted the leather and yanked the malignant coffin from her friend's neck. Her skin crawled as she grasped the foul object in her fist. Fighting the urge to throw it from her, throw it away as far as she could, she swallowed her nausea and stuffed the coffin into her pocket to show to Madame Pascal when she reached the *boulangerie*.

She sensed a presence, a movement behind her. She swung around, her heart racing. Still in her crouching position, she saw the boots first, black leather to the knee. An enigmatic face bent toward her.

"What are you doing, Madame Aubin?" whispered Dietsz.

*

J

July 30, 1942

Juliette snatched up the phone the moment it rang again.

"Get out. Hurry."

The line went dead in her hand. She'd barely had time to register the sound of Henri's voice.

For a moment, she felt a dreadful lethargy, an urge to sink to the floor and wait for whatever would happen to her when she was found.

But Sophie. She ran to the bedroom where the little girl was napping; it was all she could do to stop herself from scooping her into her arms, hugging her. She knelt beside the bed and whispered urgently into her ear.

"Wake up now. Wake up. We're going to see Céleste. You'd like that, wouldn't you? Here, put on your shoes. You can take your doll."

Sophie sat up, dazed, as Juliette struggled with her laces and shoved her feet into the shoes. Juliette tried to smile, failed, watched Sophie's eyes grow wide with fear. There was no time to comfort her. She grabbed her hand, reached for the suitcase already packed for the flight to Burgundy.

Picking up her journal from the desk on the way through the living room, she slowly opened the door of the flat. The hallway was quiet. Quickly, she reached up, slipped the small book into its hiding place, then pushed Sophie gently toward the stairs, one finger raised to her lips, the other hand grasping the suitcase.

The stairs had never before seemed so threatening, plummeting down to the front foyer — so open, so unprotected. She urged

Sophie forward. There was no time to think, to imagine what might be waiting on the other side of the door to the street. There was just the urgency to move, one step, then another. The child was slow, each step had to be maneuvered. Juliette lifted her up, hefted her weight onto one arm, bumped the suitcase down the stairs.

At the bottom, she set Sophie down, took a deep breath, wrenched open the door. Which way? It didn't matter. They turned down the street, in the direction of the market and Luxembourg Gardens beyond. The open air was like a tonic. She squeezed Sophie's hand, smoothed the black corkscrew curls away from her cheek.

"Better now?"

Sophie nodded, her face solemn as ever.

At the end of their street, about to turn into rue de Seine, she heard the engine, tuned to a perfect hum. She forced herself to look back casually as she slipped around the corner, Sophie's hand tightly in hers. A black Citroën, a Gestapo car, had pulled to the curb in front of the apartment. The driver got out and held the back door open. A tall man with a hawk nose walked toward the building, took something from the inside pocket of his suit and seemed to study it. An address? A document of some kind with her name on it, or Sophie's name? Or Céleste's? She saw the *gardien* scurry into the street, only too glad to welcome authority. She watched him stretch up his neck, as if trying to grow taller, gesticulate toward the front door.

So that was that. She turned her back, kept walking. The little worm had turned them in, probably. But then how had Henri known? Had he warned Céleste? She'd left the flat in the late morning, but the restaurant where she worked didn't open until eight in the evening. In the meantime, she could be anywhere.

"Are you thirsty, Sophie?"

A nod in reply.

Juliette found a café and a table at the back away from onlookers. She checked the clock — it was just after five. What were they to do for three hours?

A waiter sauntered over, bored. Juliette pushed the suitcase out of sight under the table and ordered coffee, and a glass of water for Sophie, who drank it quickly when it came, staring at her over the rim of her glass.

Juliette stared back. There was a sadness in the black eyes, a distance plain for anyone to see. She needed to pull her back into the present. She needed her to be alert, if she were to have any hope of protecting her.

"You and I are alike, Sophie."

The black eyes blinked. She turned her face away, began looking around the café as if she didn't want to hear what Juliette had to say, didn't even know her.

Juliette took a deep breath. She was sorry, but it had to be done.

"My family is far away. I don't know if I'll ever see them again. I hope to, someday."

Sophie turned her head toward Juliette, and hugged her doll.

"I wasn't born here, in France. I grew up in another country, Canada, across the ocean. But I was here when the war came — did your maman explain about the war? — and I chose to stay. Now my country is fighting the war too, so I need to pretend to be someone else. I promised your sister, and your maman and papa, that I'd take you to a safe place where people will look after you, but if the Germans catch me, they'll separate us. We can't go back to the flat anymore. We have to find Céleste, and then try to leave Paris. We have friends to help us, but I need your help, too."

Nothing. Sophie merely looked away again and began rocking her doll.

A part of her wanted to shock Sophie out of her walled-up silence. *Look, kid. They're gone. I'm it.* How truthful should she be, how brutal? How do you explain the evil adults are capable of to a seven-year-old child? She would have to be more resourceful than ever before to drag them both from the quicksand the world had become.

She felt the crawl of time. She beckoned to the waiter, ordered red wine. The coffee, a pale brown, sludgy liquid, was cold now, a thin scum forming on its surface.

"I don't blame you," the waiter said, taking the coffee away. "It's practically undrinkable these days."

Juliette glanced up, took in the sloping shoulders, the shrunken face, the weary smile. A few minutes later, he returned with the wine, leaned in toward her.

"She's Jewish, isn't she?"

"What?"

"The little girl. She doesn't look like you."

Juliette stiffened and reached for her purse.

"No, no. I don't care, but in an hour, this place'll be crawling with *boches*."

Juliette nodded, her anger dissolving. But where could she go? She looked up at the waiter, a question in her eyes.

"Follow me. Bring the suitcase."

He led them to the far side of the bar, through a swinging door to a kitchen where an old woman, completely oblivious to them, was reading a newspaper, and on into a small sitting room.

"You can rest here for a while. If you take my advice, you'll dump the suitcase. It's a red flag. They're looking for any Jews that escaped the net." He jerked his head toward Sophie. "They took her family, *hein?*"

Juliette winced. Despite Sophie's apparent fascination with her doll, Juliette knew she was following every word.

Without waiting for her reply, the waiter left. Juliette looked around the room with its shabby furniture, saw a telephone. Quickly, she dialled Henri's number.

"Oui? Bonsoir?"

Gently, she replaced the receiver.

It wasn't Henri's voice.

She felt the panic rise in her stomach. She'd only been on her own for an hour or so. Had she already led them into a trap? She reached for Sophie's hand, picked up the suitcase and turned to see the waiter watching her from the doorway.

"That's good. Can't trust anyone these days," he sighed. "But I'm not the enemy. Take these." He handed her two pale blue kerchiefs and a large straw shopping bag. "Cover her hair, at least. And put the things from your suitcase in here. Most women on the streets will be carrying a shopping bag, so you won't draw attention to yourselves. You can stay until we get busy out front. Then you'd better leave. Through that curtain, down the stairs and through the back door. It opens onto an alley. *Bonne chance.*"

Juliette and Sophie stood on the sidewalk outside Celeste's bistro, Le Petit Zinc on rue de Buci. The warm summer evening had lured people out-of-doors and the street was busy, almost gay. Juliette stepped toward the large front windows and peered inside. Through the distorting panes of glass, she saw the slim figure of a waiter leaning against the bar, but no customers and no Céleste. Quickly, she rapped on the window, and waved.

The waiter sprang forward, opening the door. "*Vite, vite.* Céleste is in the backroom, waiting for you."

In a moment, Céleste was kissing her cheeks, sweeping Sophie into her arms.

"We've been so worried," she said. "Come, you've just time to eat before we leave."

Juliette felt her body relax, realized how tense she'd been. She and Sophie sat at a little table in the corner of the kitchen and the cook brought bowls of hot soup with chunks of meat and vegetables in it, and thick slices of bread and cheese. When they had eaten a little, Céleste pulled Juliette aside.

"Does she know what's happening?" she asked, nodding at Sophie.

"I think so, but she still hasn't spoken. Henri? I tried to call him, but someone else answered. What happened? Was it that little runt of a *gardien* who turned us in?"

Céleste shrugged. "Maybe. But that wouldn't explain why they were on to Henri. I was on my way to his apartment when I saw the Gestapo pull up. They didn't find him. I knew he would leave a message for me here."

"Are we leaving Paris tonight?"

"Not yet." She looked over Juliette's shoulder to where the cook was trying to catch her eye. She nodded. "Let's go. I'll get Sophie."

They went through the back door of the bistro. A small delivery van was waiting for them a little way up the alley. There was a shutter in the back instead of doors and the name of a bakery painted on the side. Céleste rolled the shutter up and hefted Sophie inside, then vaulted up and turned to hold out a hand for Juliette. She scrambled in and immediately the truck began to move, bouncing on its springs. Caught off guard, she stumbled to the side and almost lost her balance.

Then she heard a wonderful sound. Sophie, laughing.

She deliberately exaggerated her stagger, twirled around several times as Céleste joined in the laughter, and finally dropped to the floor of the van. The driver rapped sharply on the dividing panel.

"Settle down back there," he ordered.

Juliette gave a mock salute and winked at Sophie. "Where are we going?" she asked Céleste.

"Close to your old haunt in the Montmartre. A place Henri knows in Pigalle."

When the truck finally stopped bouncing, Juliette lifted the shutter and looked out. Place Pigalle was transformed by the blackout. Once gaudy in neon flashing light, it looked like a peacock stripped of its bright plumage. Even the red windmill of the Moulin Rouge was just a silent shadow on the skyline. The driver hurried them along a shabby alley and through a doorway of stringed beads, and then he was gone.

Behind a thick blackout curtain, a narrow corridor led them past several small windowless bedrooms to a sitting room that also served as kitchen and office. The tiny bathroom beside it smelled of musty pipes and drains that must have dated from the turn of the century. The entire apartment seemed sunk in perpetual gloom, like a block of darkness propped up between peeling walls. Sophie pressed against Juliette's legs, trying to hide behind her skirt.

They heard the strike of a match, and watched as a tall woman leaned toward an oil lamp. In the pool of yellow light, her lips shone with dark lipstick and the blue smoke of her cigarette swirled around her face. She looked exotic, with cat's eyes and high cheekbones, a feathery shawl wrapped around her shoulders.

"Don't worry," she said, her voice low and husky. "As long as you don't go through the far door, the customers won't bother you. Wait here. Henri will be along shortly. You can use the first bedroom on the right."

She turned to leave, moving elegantly toward the forbidden door, the rustling of her silk skirt like soft music in the shadowy light. Then, looking back, she smiled and the illusion of mystery dissolved. She had a small gap between her front teeth, making her seem little more than a child in grown-up clothes.

"I'm Monique," she shrugged. "For the duration."

She opened the door — a glimpse of brilliant light, a snatch of sound, tinkling glasses, male voices — then closed it firmly behind her.

Juliette and Céleste looked at each other, amazed that Henri had chosen to hide them in a brothel, but they said nothing, and together helped Sophie get ready for bed. The child's eyes, filled with questions, never left Juliette's face.

"It's all right, *ma petite*. I'll be here when you wake, I promise." One lullaby later, Sophie was fast asleep.

"Well, well," Céleste mused. "Henri has hidden depths."

"I'm beginning to believe there's quite a lot about Henri that's hidden. How old do you think Monique is?"

"Wise beyond her years. Have you heard anything at all about Luc?"

"Nothing."

"Perhaps Henri will find him. He's been looking."

"Perhaps," Juliette whispered, but she felt starved of hope. If he were anywhere alive in that vast city of soldiers, strangers and lovers, he would have reached her somehow.

The two sat quietly together in the pale glow of the oil lamp, each of them preoccupied with disconnected images of the men who were not in the room.

"You know, I think women have a gift for this," Juliette murmured.

"Hiding?"

"No. Waiting."

An hour or so later, Henri finally arrived, the banker's suit as pristine as ever. Behind the blackout curtain, there was a grille door which he closed and locked. "Sorry I'm late. And I haven't much time. Where's Sophie?"

"Asleep." Juliette explained how she had left the apartment. "Do you know who turned us in?"

"We're not sure. We think Max."

"Max? I don't believe it. They've arrested him?"

"I've only just heard. They've killed him, I'm afraid. The body was disfigured. He may have talked first."

Juliette felt an icy breath enter her body. Poor Max. He'd always known his time was limited. She hated to think what he must have suffered. "And Luc?"

"We haven't found him. But that's a good sign. One of the clerks working with the Germans says they've got lists of names of the people they're deporting. So far, there's no record of him. He may have escaped the net."

Escaped where, Juliette thought, *hiding where?* As much as she wanted to believe otherwise, she sensed Luc was slipping further away from her, like a drowning man sinking below the dark surface of the Seine. She shook the image from her head. "When do we leave Paris?"

"Not yet. You'll need new papers now, both you and Sophie. Give me the old ones."

Juliette left the room to get them, found Henri and Céleste whispering together when she returned. She handed Henri the identity documents and raised an eyebrow.

"What's going on? We're all leaving together, aren't we?" But she'd known the answer as soon as she'd looked at their faces.

August 6

Juliette walked along the avenue Foch with downcast eyes. In a week, she had been transformed again. She was now Renée Lachaisse. Her husband was a prisoner of war, and she had taken up private tutoring to make ends meet. If all went well, she would be taking her young cousin, Sophie, into the countryside near Beaune to live with their common grandparents. Henri had managed to find her and Sophie appropriate travelling clothes and a new suitcase. Juliette's identity papers listed her place of birth as Paris, and included a physical description, a photo of a plain brown-haired woman in glasses, and a thumbprint. The bland blonde hair of Renée Benoit from Switzerland had been dyed in Monique's sink in Place Pigalle.

Turning away from the avenue Foch, she looked back once, sadly, at the building that in pre-war days had been the Canadian Embassy. It now housed the *Sicherheitsdienst*, the SD, secret police of the SS, more feared than the Gestapo itself. The sinister takeover seemed a particular insult to her country, and she allowed herself a moment of yearning for just one lungful of Chapleau's clean air to wipe away the stain of the SD. But only a moment, for she had directions from Henri to follow.

She found the small café and walked easily past a group of lunching soldiers. They barely glanced at her, a woman in a loose, unstylish dress, ankle socks in sturdy walking shoes, and not a speck of makeup. Juliette smiled to herself. As plain as pikestaff, her mother would have said. She knew her papers were the best Henri could get, the names taken from pre-war issues of the *Journal officiel*. If the police should be suspicious and call a district official to check on her identity, the records would confirm it.

Inside, she nodded to the man behind the bar, who jerked his head in the direction of the phone. She entered the narrow corridor, quickly dialled the number she had memorized of a library near the Sorbonne.

"*Oui?*"

"I wonder if you can help me. I'm looking for a book on the wines of France. The Burgundy region."

"I'm sorry. The last one was checked out yesterday at two o'clock. You might try another branch, just off the Jardin des Tuileries. Might I help you with something else?"

"No. Nothing, thank you."

"*Au revoir.*"

Juliette sat on a bench under a spreading plane tree in the Jardin des Tuileries, watching a group of children playing in the summer dust, their bodies flashing in and out of the sunlight filtering through the branches overhead. She thought how utterly ordinary the scene was, how beautiful, even. But that was the danger, of course — a deceptive illusion that might lull you into believing that the reality underneath had not turned ugly.

In her peripheral vision, she saw an elderly veteran in a beret pause slightly on one of the paths leading to her bench. He carried a shopping basket in one hand. As he drew closer, she saw that one arm was missing, the useless left sleeve of his jacket folded over and pinned just below the shoulder.

Sighing, he took a seat on the bench, placing the basket of bread and vegetables between them, staring straight ahead.

"You're looking for the book on Burgundy wine?"

"Yes." She could see how bony his single hand was, covered in brown splotches betraying his age.

"The name of your contact there is Louis. There's a false bottom in the basket. You'll find a map of Beaune there, with the meeting place marked. How is Monique?"

"She's a marvel." Juliette hesitated slightly. "She's very young …"

"To be a prostitute? Young, but very experienced. In the important matters, much older than her years. You needn't feel sorry for her. She doesn't forget who she really is underneath the paint. That's good advice, *hein?* Don't forget who you really are, young lady, behind those glasses."

"I'll try."

"We all try. This country has gone to the dogs. Best be off now. Give my best to Monique."

"Who should I say was asking?"

"Her father."

Juliette picked up the shopping basket and strode away, humbled by the thought that there were people willing to sacrifice far more than she.

Back in the Pigalle late that evening, Juliette and Céleste stared out at the street from the mouth of the alley.

"So," Céleste said, turning back to her in the shadows. "You leave tomorrow. I'll miss you."

Juliette turned her head away. She felt bereft. "It's not what we planned, is it? To be parted. When I chose to stay in Paris, I thought I would always be surrounded by my friends. But now Pierre is dead, and Max. Will we ever —"

"Don't say it. If all goes well, you'll be back in a month or so."

"Of course. Has Henri found new work for you?"

"I'm to be a secretary, working in the Crillon. I'm Yvonne now."

Juliette felt a flicker of worry for her friend. The Crillon was one of the five great hotels of Paris, all of which had been taken over by the Germans as offices and residences. Céleste would be working under their noses.

"I can see you frowning." Céleste reached out a hand and smoothed Juliette's forehead. "You have the hardest task."

"No. It's simple really. I'll take the train to Beaune and meet my contact. There's an orphanage nearby where the children arrive in twos and threes. From there, the *passeurs* take them into the Unoccupied Zone and eventually into Switzerland. The irony is I might have been able to help them if my passport were still Swiss."

"Do you think Sophie will ever be reunited with her family?"

Juliette closed her eyes and the filth and smell and blood of Drancy came flooding back. She lowered her head, but didn't speak.

Céleste leaned forward and kissed both of her cheeks. "I must go now. Henri's waiting. *Bonne chance.* Give Sophie a kiss from me."

"I will. Just remember that Yvonne is a meek little secretary, not so spirited as Céleste."

Her friend laughed. At the mouth of the alley, she turned back, the classic face serious, her voice a whisper.

"Juliette?"

"Yes."

"Take great care."

"And you, *mon amie.*"

Juliette lingered in the alley, listening to the tapping of Céleste's heels on the pavement until they were swallowed up in the Place Pigalle.

She leaned against the wall a moment, running through her instructions in her head. Women with children were safer than others, she knew. The Germans rarely bothered them. She knew where she must go, she knew how to make her contact and the number she could call if anything went amiss. It would be all right.

She slipped through the blackout curtain, and locked the grille behind her. As she walked down the dingy hall, she heard the lapping of water and tapped on the bathroom door.

"Monique? Are you all right?"

"*Entre.*"

She opened the door and immediately wished she hadn't. Stripped of the glamorous clothes, Monique sat in the bathtub with her knees drawn up, arms around her colt-like body. She'd scrubbed her skin until it was almost raw.

"Oh, Monique."

"*Rien,*" she shrugged. "It's what I do to take away the stink of them. Go now. Go away."

Juliette stumbled down the hall, undressed, crept under the covers next to Sophie. Compared to Monique, she was being asked to do so little. The child turned in her sleep and cuddled into her shoulder. Juliette put her arm around her, finding comfort in the damp little-girl smell of her.

August 7

The train was mobbed with people carrying baskets, sacks and bags of all sizes, hoping to fill them with food from the countryside. Juliette was scrunched up on a wooden bench beside a window with Sophie on her lap, Sophie's mass of black curls tamed into a ponytail. They wore the blue kerchiefs given to them by the old waiter in Paris. Their carriage was stifling, the air heavy with garlic and sweat. Juliette pulled off her kerchief and used it to wipe the perspiration from Sophie's brow, then tugged at the window which seemed to be stuck. She looked around, saw several people watching her, but no one offered to help.

"First trip?" A middle-aged woman was sitting across from them, a sulky looking teenaged boy in tow.

Juliette nodded.

The woman looked at the suitcase Juliette was trying to balance between her knees. "You're not after food, then?"

"No. We're going to move in with my grandparents, near Beaune."

"Lucky. They say folks have it easy in the country, not like in Paris. Those windows won't budge, by the way. But it'll get better the farther we travel from the city. People will get off along the way. Not many will go as far as Beaune."

Juliette wasn't sure she should feel relief. The cramped carriage was uncomfortable, but there was anonymity in the crowd. The woman seemed to have lost interest in her, so she turned her head toward the window and watched the factories and the suburbs crawl by. When they reached the fields, the train seemed to gain speed, rocking from side to side. Twenty minutes later, they reached the first stop, and the crowd seemed to shift and then reform itself into a slightly smaller mass. Juliette could see soldiers patrolling the platform, checking papers, looking through bags. She waited to see if they would board the train, felt her shoulders ease once she was sure they wouldn't.

As the train started up again, she caught the woman studying her. Juliette held her gaze, kept her face still.

"They don't usually board when it's this crowded. It's too hot for them in their uniforms. Unless they're looking for someone?..." There was no mistake that the last comment had the slight inflection of a question.

Juliette shrugged, grateful to Luc for the lessons in Gallic body language, and did her best to look bored. She rummaged in her purse, found a withered apple and gave it to Sophie.

"She's very quiet, your daughter."

"My cousin. Yes, she's a good girl."

As if on cue, Sophie took a bite of the apple, gave Juliette a huge grin.

You little actress, Juliette thought, grinning back. Her spirits instantly lifted. Was Sophie beginning to venture out from her inner, protective world? Clearly, she was paying attention. Juliette gave her a little hug, and ignored the woman, effectively shutting down further conversation.

The journey continued in its stop-and-go fashion. Juliette remained glued to the windowpane, gazing at the landscape. When the woman reached her destination, she and her son shuffled off. Juliette said goodbye, but she didn't reply, probably feeling snubbed. The crowd had thinned, and over the miles, its character had changed. There were fewer sacks and more suitcases, people on the move like her, and salespeople, she supposed, with display cases and newspapers. She shifted Sophie from her lap onto the seat beside her. Only two stops to go.

The *gendarmes*, with an armed guard of two German soldiers, boarded the train at Avallon. They went politely up and down the aisles, asking for papers. Juliette waited her turn, controlling her breathing, feeling the air flow in and out of her lungs.

A gloved hand extended toward her. She put the identification papers and her travel permit on the glove, not sure if she should look up or straight ahead.

She felt Sophie tugging at her arm.

"I have to go to the bathroom."

Juliette was startled, her expression registering both the shock and the joy of hearing that crystal clear voice.

The *gendarme* and one of the Germans started to laugh. Her papers were thrust back at her, barely glanced at.

"Better hurry," the *gendarme* grinned.

She led Sophie down the aisle and into the tiny cubicle, closing the door and covering her face in kisses.

When they returned to their seats a few minutes later, the *gendarmes* and the soldiers were gone.

Sophie and Juliette held hands and watched through the windows as Avallon shrank into the distance. Soon, the train tracks were flanked on either side with endless rows of vines, thickly woven over low hills, touching the resplendent skies of Burgundy.

By four in the afternoon, Juliette and Sophie were sitting in the courtyard of the Hôtel-Dieu in Beaune on a bench at one corner of its cobbled square. The glazed roof of the building, ornately patterned with red, green and black tiles, descended steeply over rows of dormer windows and a timbered first-floor gallery resting on slender pillars. Against the background of a deep blue sky, the roof was dazzling, its rich tones burnished gold by the sun.

"Is it really a hotel?" Sophie asked.

"Sort of — a hotel for the poor. The name means "charity hospital," but it's a general hospital now. Don't worry, we won't be here very long. We're just here to meet someone."

"Henri?"

"One of his friends. A man named Louis."

Tourists, some French, some German, wandered in and out of

the courtyard, admiring the view. Juliette scanned the faces. Louis was late. Almost a half-hour late, but she didn't want to alarm Sophie until she had figured out what to do. She knew it would be dangerous to linger in the courtyard much longer. She thought fondly of old Lucette, the woman who had been so kind to the four Paris friends when they had visited the Dumais winery. She had an emergency number to call. Maybe Lucette, if they were lucky, would answer.

By a quarter to five, Juliette's palms were sweaty. "Are you hungry, Sophie?" She managed to keep her voice even.

"Louis isn't coming?"

"He seems to be late. Let's find a restaurant, and I'll call him."

They rose to leave, Sophie clutching her bedraggled doll tightly to her chest. Looking down at her slim figure and the dark aureole of curls that had escaped from the blue kerchief, Juliette felt a wave of love for the child, so acute as to be almost physically painful. When the moment came, would she be able to turn her over to strangers and send her into the unknown without a single friend?

She felt a hand on her shoulder from behind and gasped involuntarily, whirling around.

"I'm sorry to startle you. Are you Renée?"

A tall angular figure stood before her, her eyes, under beautifully arched brows, the same colour as her black habit.

"I'm Soeur Hélène. Louis has been delayed. Please, follow me."

Juliette reached for Sophie's hand, and nodded. After the brightness of the courtyard with its glittering colour, the foyer seemed shadowy and cool. Without a word, they followed the nun through a cavernous corridor flanked by doorless frames through which Juliette could see neat rows of white hospital beds, some covered with mosquito nets that shifted in the air like trapped clouds. She could hear groans and see glimpses of human shapes through the netting. Juliette felt the little hand she was holding tighten, and the little steps drag.

Juliette picked up Sophie and hurried forward. Ahead of them, Soeur Hélène was turning a corner at the end of the corridor, the long skirt of her habit dragging behind her like the train of a bridal gown. They followed her down a brightly lit flight of stone steps to the building's basement.

Soeur Hélène opened a wooden door onto a huge kitchen area, all white stone and marble, with vaulted ceilings and open archways. It was a warm, welcoming space with fires lit in several fireplaces and a long table stretched across its centre. She led them to stools at one end of the table where several nuns were busy arranging food on trays.

"We do all the cooking here for the patients upstairs. Please, you must be hungry after your journey."

The Soeur was a formidable figure, her voice soft and low, but commanding nonetheless. Juliette was surprised to see that she was young, perhaps only a few years older than herself. Setting aside the questions she wanted to ask, she smiled her thanks and accepted the bowl of thick potato soup. For dessert, Soeur Hélène brought her a glass of fortified wine, and for Sophie, bread with real jam. Soothed by the food and the warmth, it wasn't long before Sophie's head was nodding like a heavy flower.

"You can put her to bed now, if you like. She can bathe in the morning."

"You've been very kind, Soeur, but is there someplace other than the wards? They frighten her."

"Come. I've a room where both of you can stay."

Juliette carried Sophie, who curled into her shoulder. After climbing the stairs to the second floor, they passed several closed doors on their way down the upper corridor.

"There are some patients on this floor, several children too, but it's quieter here. Some of the rooms are used by the Sisters. You may use my room, but I'm afraid there's only one bed. Take a few minutes to settle her. Then we must talk. You'll find me with the patients down the hall."

It was a bare room, more typical of a convent than a hospital, with a narrow bed, a washstand and basin, a crucifix on the wall. Juliette helped Sophie out of her clothes, unloosed the ponytail and finger-combed her long hair as best she could.

Sophie was fast asleep by the time Juliette re-entered the hallway. She found Soeur Hélène in a small ward with several children, and wondered if these children too had been suddenly orphaned by the state.

The Soeur led her to a small office and lit several oil lamps.

"We try to preserve electricity whenever we can. It's at best unreliable these days."

Juliette thought again how attractive she was, the soft light sculpting her face, highlighting her cheekbones and the graceful brow. Suddenly, she realized that the Soeur was studying her just as intently.

"The other children ... are they also making the journey?" she asked, to fill the awkward silence.

"No. They're patients rather than packages."

"Packages?" Juliette's voice betrayed her distaste for the word.

"It's what we call the children passing through. We mean no disrespect. It's just a way of saying that we hope they reach their destinations, and a way of protecting ourselves from becoming too attached to them, too attached to let go when the time comes."

Juliette looked away, choosing not to acknowledge the implicit warning.

Soeur Hélène leaned toward her. "Look, I'll not mince words. It's a bad sign that Louis didn't come. If he were merely being followed, he would have gotten a message to us somehow. But we've heard nothing."

"I've a number to call in emergencies."

"Good. Then you may rest here for a few days until we discover what's happened to Louis. A woman travelling with a package is safer than a man. Louis will need you to stay with her until he makes contact with the *passeur*. After that, you must let her go."

"I understand."

"I needn't tell you that the easy part of the journey is over. Sleep well, Renée. You'll need your rest."

But later, her face resting against Sophie's head on the pillow, Juliette couldn't sleep. The world outside the Hôtel-Dieu seemed huge and predatory. As the hours passed, she was lulled by the sounds on the ward, footsteps echoing down a hallway, the rustling of habits, someone coughing. She wished she could curl up in this sanctuary, remain safe and hidden with Sophie until the world regained its sanity. She drifted into memory, saw the apple orchard behind her house in Chapleau where she would often hide as a child when she was in trouble. There was one tree she could easily climb, where she'd sit on a limb, screened by a blanket of leaves, her worries receding as she looked down upon the ground she'd left behind.

A rhythmic pounding bled into her dream. Then shouting. She leapt to her feet just as the door to the room opened.

Soeur Hélène pushed a habit into her hands. "Get into this. Quickly."

Her hands were clumsy in the darkness. The cloth slipped through her fingers, landed at her feet like a black puddle.

"Hurry. Here, raise your arms."

She felt the material slide across her body, heavy and surprisingly soft. Then the Sister was smoothing back her hair, pinning on a white headpiece, not the full wimple of a nun, but a broad band with a drape of white cloth that reached her shoulders. The cross on a leather thong weighed heavily against her breast.

"Sophie?" she asked. The little girl was still asleep.

"Leave her. Follow me and say nothing. Keep your head down."

Juliette pushed her feet into black slippers and raced after Soeur Hélène. On the first floor, the pounding was louder.

They paused for an instant at the heavy door. The Soeur took a deep breath, and called out, "Who's there?"

"Open up. Immediately."

Juliette thought she could hear the man swearing in German while the Soeur patiently worked her way through an intricate system of locks. Finally the door yielded several inches, revealing a vulturine face, flushed with anger. The Soeur moved deftly aside as the man gave a push. He was large, broad-shouldered and heavy, wearing the uniform of an officer. Behind him a group of helmeted soldiers stood like spectral figures under the charcoal arch of the entrance.

"We have orders to search this hospital." With an arrogant wave of the hand, he signalled to the soldiers, half a dozen of them, who swept past, boots thudding as they started down the hallway and dispersed into the wards.

"Now. If you would be so kind, I would like a tour." His lips curled back into the caricature of a smile.

Soeur Hélène inclined her head. "*Soit.* Follow me."

She glided down the hall, Juliette following mutely, the man towering and impatient beside them. Many of the patients were by now awake, groaning, calling out into the darkness in bewildered voices. Soeur Hélène lit a lamp and moved unhurriedly among them, offering comfort. The shadowy light obscured the details of their features so they seemed to Juliette like a collection of wax figures, some prostrate, others sitting up with glassy eyes staring in alarm. Several times, Juliette was instructed to adjust their bedding or pour glasses of water.

"Enough of this," the officer complained. "My men can check the wards. Where are your offices and private rooms?"

Without a word, Soeur Hélène led him to the stairs. As they all began to climb to the second floor, Juliette's fear for Sophie mounted. Soeur Hélène's pace did not alter as she began to pass the series of closed doors leading to the open wards.

The officer halted. "Just a moment. You will open these doors, please."

For the first time, the Soeur showed reluctance. She lowered her voice to a whisper.

"These doors are not locked. The rooms are the private quarters of the Sisters on duty. In respect for our vows, I ask that you not disturb them. The Sisters will be in their night clothing, without the protection of their habits."

"Open the doors."

"Very well. As you insist." A sharpness had crept into her voice, not of anger, but of weariness for a man who would commit a sacrilegious act.

One by one, she slowly opened the doors, holding the lamp high so that the light fell softly across the beds of the sleeping nuns, the officer peering over her shoulder. Juliette's mouth was dry. She was having difficulty swallowing. She knew that Soeur Hélène had hoped to shame him, but the officer seemed unperturbed.

They came to the fifth door. Juliette's hands inside the sleeves of her habit were shaking now.

Soeur Hélène held up the lamp. In the spill of light, a woman knelt in prayer, her bare arms and feet exposed, her hair shorn. Slowly, she turned her head. Her eyes were open and white, like broken eggshells. In her blindness, she cried out and scrabbled to cover herself with the bed linen.

"Who's there?" Her voice was a wail, filled with shame and panic.

"Forgive me, Mother. It is Soeur Hélène." A long pause, and then in a deliberate, clearly enunciated voice. "With an officer of the Germany army."

A thin gasp came from the room, followed by an old woman's sob. The officer stepped back as if slapped. Juliette felt a flare of hope, as Soeur Hélène closed the door and began to move away down the hall.

"And here," he ordered, stopping at the sixth door.

Soeur Hélène turned to Juliette without a murmur. Their eyes met but Juliette could read nothing from her expression. "Step away from the door, my child."

Juliette obeyed automatically, watching as the Sister drew two squares of white linen from the pocket of her skirts. She held one toward the officer, and placed the other over her nose and mouth.

"What's this?"

"I advise you to protect yourself. The child in this room is highly contagious."

"A child?"

"There are half a dozen children here. This one has been quarantined. Please, take the handkerchief."

"What's he have?"

"He is a she, with a severe case of German measles. She will probably survive, but adults who catch this disease suffer greatly with fever, sometimes resulting in disorders of the brain."

Backed against the far wall of the corridor, Juliette squeezed her eyes shut and heard the door of Sophie's room open and close, quickly. She felt a wildly inappropriate urge to laugh.

When the soldiers were finally gone, Soeur Hélène shook her head sadly.

"I fear the worst for Louis. These men will be back in the morning to check papers. I'm sorry, but you cannot stay. Be ready in an hour. I'll lead you through the underground tunnels to the convent, and from there you can slip away unnoticed. How well do you know the area?"

"Not at all. I visited here once, long ago."

"Then I'll find a map of the Côte d'Or for you. If you can't make your contact, the orphanage is near the border crossing in Chalon-sur-Saône. Follow the river Saône. I'll bring food."

At mid-morning, Juliette found a post office and a telephone. Through a square of dusty window, she could see Sophie waiting for her with their suitcase, and a bicycle that Soeur Hélène had found for them. She dialled the number she'd memorized.

"*Bonjour.*"

"I wonder if you can help me. I'm looking for a travel book on Paris."

"Yes. I'm sure we have something. If you could come by around two o'clock? Is there something else I can help you with?"

"No, thank you."

Silence. Then the voice dropped, became urgent, almost coaxing.

"We'll see you at two o'clock then?"

"Yes. Goodbye."

Juliette replaced the receiver gently, and bit her fists so as not to scream. The escape line had been infiltrated. They were probably already watching the public phones. At any rate, they would trace the call. She had to move quickly, if she and Sophie were to survive.

Though she longed to find the Château Dumais, instinct warned her that she could not go there without putting others in danger. As if it had a voice of its own, her body was telling her to move. She went outside, lifted Sophie onto the seat of the bicycle and began to pedal.

August 15

The next eight days passed in a blur of exhaustion and nerves stretched taut. They kept to the rutted and gravelled side roads, skirting the villages except when they needed food, and trying to follow the river as best they could. Several times, they got lost, adding needless miles to their journey. In late summer, the nights were still gentle, and they slept among the vines which stretched around them for miles. Twice, they risked a shabby hotel with their dwindling funds, where they could wash the grime and the fear from their skin and pretend to be normal for a few hours.

Sophie had grown quiet again, her white face pinched and serious. She asked no questions, merely succumbed passively to whatever Juliette said, trudged along in whichever direction she pulled her.

Only at night, when they huddled together, did she seem a child again.

"Tell me stories," she'd ask. "Tell me about the place where you grew up."

So Juliette unwrapped her memories for her, telling of apple trees, and red-winged blackbirds flying above summer corn, and lakes that glittered green in the sunshine and turned to sheets of white when the deep frosts came. She told her about rabbits she'd had as pets, and about the deer that would watch you from their hiding places in the forest. When her memory faltered, she made up a story of a snow queen in rich furs riding on a sleigh pulled by silver timber wolves.

Only then would Sophie smile and grow heavy in her arms, finally disappearing into the kind of deep sleep Juliette could only imagine, leaving her to think of Céleste and Henri and Luc, already disappearing from her life, growing translucent like figures wavering on a distant horizon.

In the morning, they would get up and do it all again, moving closer to Chalon-sur-Saône and the orphanage that Juliette was no longer sure would be safe.

When they reached the outskirts of the city, it was almost noon and a fresh breeze gave the sky an intense blue. But at eye level, the edges of Chalon-sur-Saône were not pretty. They pushed the bicycle past several factories with weedy lawns and reached a series of narrow streets, grimy with smoke and smelling of open drains. They saw no soldiers, but several workmen queuing up outside the lunchtime cafés watched them with curiosity. Juliette pushed on, her legs like lead after the days of travel, eager to reach the centre of the town, where they would be less conspicuous. Eventually they came to a stone bridge stretching across the Saône to the old town on the far side. They had only to cross it. They had only to pass through the checkpoint at the far end of the bridge.

Juliette took Sophie's hand, and began the crossing, her steps determined and steady.

"Papers, please," the *gendarme* asked.

Juliette saw that there were several *gendarmes*, but no Germans. She leaned her bicycle against the railing of the bridge and handed him the papers from her purse. While he studied them, she lifted Sophie into her arms.

"Look," she exclaimed. "There's a barge on the river." With Sophie occupied, she turned back to face the *gendarme*.

He was watching her, with narrowed eyes in a pink face with a pencil moustache.

"Renée Lachaisse. It says here you're from Paris."

"Yes, that's right."

"What are you doing here?"

"Just visiting friends. It's good for the child, to be out of Paris for awhile."

"Address?"

"Pardon?"

"What is the address of your friends?"

"Oh, the rue Foch." She spoke quickly. *Surely there was a rue Foch in every town in France.*

The *gendarme* looked at her photograph, then looked again at her face. He seemed puzzled, uncertain.

"Where are your glasses, mam'zelle?"

Juliette felt a spike of fear. She'd stupidly forgotten them, hadn't worn them for days. She put Sophie down, opened her purse, made a show of digging around. Her fingers closed around them like a vise, and with a surge of strength she felt them snap. Slowly she withdrew her hand, and held out the pieces to the *gendarme*.

"I've broken them," she shrugged. "I can see distances, but I'm afraid you're a bit blurry."

The *gendarme* watched her eyes. She could tell he was trying to decide if she were lying.

"Open the suitcase, please."

She reached over. The suitcase was lying in the *panier* of the bicycle. She swung it to the ground, snapped open the locks. Sophie's rag doll lay on the top of a pile of wrinkled, soiled clothes. The *gendarme* seemed reluctant to touch them.

He looked at his watch. "End of shift," he said. "You can go."

When they reached the centre of town, the streets broadened. St-Gabriel's Orphanage, its red-brick facade dotted with dagger-shaped windows, stood in the middle of a grove of plane trees at the top of a narrow, winding street that led up from the town's main boulevard. The whole building was crowned by arches and towers, as imposing as a Gothic cathedral. Juliette and Sophie entered the leafy garden. Here and there cobbled paths meandered among the trees, past a fountain adorned with a mould-covered angel. Although the place was daunting, it had an air of tranquility, as if it had turned its back on the worldly concerns of the bustling town below and hidden in another century.

Juliette urged Sophie forward. As they neared the front door, she saw an elderly priest there, watching them. His hair was silver, his slight frame leaning on a wooden staff. He smiled, and Juliette was instantly reassured by his look of an emaciated cherub.

"We've come from Beaune," she began. "From the Hôtel-Dieu." She had no code words for the meeting, and hoped her appearance would be enough for him to understand their plight.

"You've come alone?"

"Yes. Louis was unable to make the trip."

The priest inclined his head to the side, and waved them up the stone steps, opening the door for them.

Inside, the air was cool and had the sweet, musky smell of incense. Following the priest, they crossed a huge open room with several staircases leading to a three-sided upper mezzanine. Crossing the echoing space, they reached an inner door which opened onto a large treed courtyard.

"Rest here," the priest said, leading them to a bench in the sun and then leaving them.

Juliette sank onto the bench and clasped both of Sophie's hands. "We've made it. Someone will help us now. You've been so brave. I'm proud of you."

With relief came a wave of exhaustion, not only from the

journey, but from the constant need to be vigilant. Above anything else, Juliette wanted to sleep. Sophie stretched out on the bench, her head in Juliette's lap. The minutes passed. A light breeze blew strands of hair across her face, and the sun melted the tension in her shoulders. Her head nodded forward.

"Juliette?"

The voice seemed to come from a distance, almost from another time. *Jules*, she remembered, *he used to call me Jules*. And for a moment, she saw Luc's face, felt a spurt of joy, then a wash of sorrow, like high tide on a stony shore. She started awake.

"Juliette?"

She looked up, disoriented, then astonished. "Bernard — is it really you?" She took in the monk's robes, the handsome face, the dark hair greying at the sides.

"Frère Jean-Claude, remember? And who is this?" he asked, grinning at Sophie.

She was pressed against Juliette's side, as if she could make herself invisible.

"It's all right, *ma chérie*. This is an old friend." She made her voice sound light, but her heart ached at seeing how Sophie had learned fear.

Bernard knelt down to the child's level. "Pleased to meet you, Sophie. Are you hungry? Yes? Then both of you, come with me."

He led them back into the building and up a staircase to a large, open room furnished like a nursery. Several children glanced up from a corner where they were playing with an assortment of toys. A small wooden table was laid with two places, a tray of chicken legs, olives and bread in the centre. While they ate, Bernard took a book from a shelf and began reading it aloud to the other children, two boys and a small girl. Sophie's eyes followed him, though she looked away quickly whenever he raised his head toward her.

"Do you want to join them?" Juliette asked.

Sophie hesitated. Her face and hands were grubby, her hair damp with sweat. The blue kerchief had long ago slipped down and now encircled her neck. Juliette thought how pretty she was, how much like her sister Mathilde, how vulnerable.

"I'll be here. I promise, Sophie." So many times she'd spoken these same words to calm the child's fears. Was the moment approaching when the words would be a lie, when she would have to give Sophie to strangers?

Slowly, the little girl slid off her chair, shyly moving ever closer to the other children. One of the boys edged over, made a place for her beside him. By the time Bernard finished the story and extricated himself from the group, the four small heads were leaning together in the special conspiracy that adults couldn't join, but only remember.

"She'll be fine, Juliette. Children mend, especially among other children."

Juliette sighed. "I hope you're right. She's lost so much."

"She's alive."

Juliette nodded and followed Bernard back to the courtyard. Somewhere from inside the building, a child laughed.

"Do you know what happened to Louis?" Juliette asked.

"Arrested, I'm afraid."

"I thought so. The phone call went wrong. Soeur Hélène?" She turned to search his face when he didn't reply, saw the pain there.

"Oh, no, Bernard," she gasped.

"She's not been captured, but the Germans are looking for her and for a young novice, accompanied by a black-haired female child, possibly ill."

"So we have little time. We must get Sophie out."

"The line is broken. I've come to take you back, not to Beaune, but to the Morvan, to the *abbaye* where we can hide until a new route is pieced together."

Juliette shook her head determinedly. "No! We can't go back. We've come so far and we're so close to the border now. I can't explain it, but I know our only chance is to keep going forward. I'll take her."

Bernard shook his head. "You don't understand. The escape line has been compromised. We can't go through Switzerland as we usually do. We're trying to make contact with lines in the South. There is one we know of, called Alliance, run by someone known only as Hedgehog. The Germans call the line Noah's Ark because its operatives take the names of animals. As far as we know, Alliance deals mainly in information, feeding it back to Britain. But we have information to trade. Maybe, just maybe, they could get Sophie through the Pyrenees and then to England. But the journey would be hazardous at best, and we have few contacts."

"But you have some? And there would be a place for Sophie in Britain?"

"In Scotland, yes. I know a family who would take her."

"Then let me make contact with Alliance. Let me set up the line."

"Do you know what the South has become? They're no kinder to Jews there. They round them up willingly for the Germans. It is safe for no one. Minister Laval, fool that he is, has offered to trade young Frenchmen for prisoners of war. Three skilled workers for every POW. Armed thugs now hunt their own countrymen like the scavengers they are. I could not, in good conscience, send you there alone."

"Can you guarantee that Sophie will be safer in the Morvan?"

"There are no guarantees."

"Exactly."

The two friends fell silent, sitting shoulder to shoulder in the sunshine. Language was a clumsy tool for all that needed to be said between them.

Bernard rubbed his face in his hands. "How is Céleste?"

"Well. Henri has moved her from the restaurant. She'll have a new identity by now as a secretary working for the Germans."

"And Luc?"

"Nothing. Henri has tried, but ..." She spread her hands open to indicate that on this point she'd never be certain, never be able to admit his probable death.

"I'm sorry."

"When do we leave?"

"Tomorrow night. But I can't journey with you. You understand?"

"Yes."

August 16

Two-twenty in the morning: a breeze sighing across the fields, the ribbon of the Canal du Centre silver in the moonlight. Juliette lay on her stomach at the top of a low hill, wrapped up in a thick sweater, with Sophie and a small valise by her side. At the foot of the hill, a narrow road of packed dirt skirted the canal. This close to the Unoccupied Zone, it was subject to frequent patrols. Beyond the road, a symmetrical row of plane trees, their trunks gleaming soft white in late summer, lined the grassy banks of the canal. In the stillness, Juliette could hear water lapping, and could just make out the large floating shadow that was the barge.

Bernard shifted his position, raised his hand in caution. From a distance, Juliette heard the sound of a truck engine, heard it draw closer, very loud now. Then stop. She pressed her face into the grass, wet with dew, one arm around Sophie's shoulders. She listened as the border guards — two, perhaps three? — piled out of the truck and called out to the bargeman. She picked out the voices, a mix of rough German syllables and slurred French. When she heard the boots, heavy on the wooden planks of the boat, she risked a glance. The moonlight made a pale glow on the helmets of the border guards and on the butts of the rifles slung over their shoulders. She caught a flash of reflected light as a bottle was raised. They were sharing a drink now, and the tips of their cigarettes glowed in the darkness.

Beside her, Sophie wriggled in impatience.

"Not long now," Juliette whispered.

The sentries shared a final laugh and jumped off the barge, flashing an electric torch along the line of trees in a desultory fashion as they headed back to their vehicle. The truck moved off.

At a nod from Bernard, the three of them rose to a crouch and ran, staying low to the ground, slipping down the bank, two huge hands swinging out over the side of the barge to catch Sophie and swing her aboard.

They climbed down into a small cabin behind the pilothouse. There were two benches made up as makeshift beds.

"You can sleep here," the captain said. He'd seen better days; his nose and cheeks were covered in the pencil-thin red lines of broken veins. His mouth was glued to a half-smoked cigarette that seemed to grow out of a thick moustache.

Bernard touched her shoulder. "Here is the information," he said, handing her a pack of cigarettes, *tabac national*. Whatever you do, don't smoke them unless you're caught. Then light up as soon as you can. Understand?"

Juliette nodded.

"The barge will take you close to the town of Vichy. Wait for a man named the Fox. He has your description and he'll be looking for you. They wouldn't give a specific place. They've no reason to trust us. That's all I could find out. *Bonne chance.*"

She stepped into his arms, tried to memorize the brief moment of safety she felt with her head against his chest. Then she let go and followed him back up the stairs to the deck. She stood there, watching him walk away down the perilous road until his silhouette blended with the darkness.

Sophie was waiting for her in the cabin. They squeezed together on one of the benches, pulling a blanket over themselves, leaving the other empty for the captain who strode the deck above them. They listened to the rhythm of his strides, felt the boat rock gently as he moved from side to side.

Sleepily, Sophie murmured, "Tell me a story."

"Once, in a country far away, there was a beautiful snow queen, with hair as black as jet and eyes like stars ..."

The throbbing of the engine in the morning woke them. It seemed to make the wood shiver. Juliette could feel the water sliding by. The captain ducked below, brought them bowls of lentils with mustard.

"It's better if you stay below where no one can see you," he said. "We'll be over the border by the time you finish your breakfast."

And so the morning passed, and the days after it. Juliette found a greasy pack of cards and taught Sophie every game she could remember. The child was smart, sometimes winning even when Juliette wasn't trying to let her. There were no windows so they made up landscapes, and the snow queen sped over the frozen tundra in her golden sleigh pulled by wolves. They slept a lot, their bodies recovering from what they'd left behind, preparing for what lay ahead. Sometimes at night, under cover of dark when the barge was moored, they would climb onto the deck and breathe in lungfuls of fresh air, scented with grass and leaves and green water. Other times, when Sophie was sleeping, Juliette would stand on the deck alone and watch the mist rise from the water. It made everything seem unreal, wrapping the trees along the canal in a moist, grey twilight.

Once, she asked the taciturn captain if he knew the Fox.

"I know nothing," came his reply from the darkness. "I don't know you. You don't know me."

Juliette didn't blame him. She was an albatross around his neck. She could ask for nothing more than their passage and the food he magicked for them at the stops along their way.

August 23

Vichy, the elegant spa town of *Belle Époque* architecture, stank of fear. Juliette sat in the shaded park staring at the Opera House. Its curved rotunda was balanced by two long wings, its front graced with a glass Art Nouveau portico and its top by a dome that glittered white in the sun. The building had been taken over by the Pétain administration, and inside one of the rooms on the first floor, members of the government fleeing from Paris had self-righteously claimed to embody the spirit of a reborn France. The park itself was beautiful, an ornate bandstand and a carousel tucked amid huge plane trees. A circular building with tall windows housed one of the town's oldest mineral springs, and boardwalks topped with delicate white roofs ran along each side of the park.

It was all a sham. Draped in tricolours, Vichy was like a folk village in a pop-up book. Among its opulent facades, Juliette had seen posters already beginning to fade. "La France Éternelle" displayed an idealized French village, with neatly mown fields and a church, and not a German soldier in sight; "1941: L'Année du Nettoyage," the year of the birth of the puppet government, showed a blonde, barefooted woman, Pétain's version of patriotic femininity. It made Juliette's skin crawl.

And everywhere, the Milice strolled the streets, uniformly attired in breeches and boots, khaki shirts with black ties, black berets, pistols in holsters on their belts. Their presence betrayed the true Vichy, the shame of collaborationist France.

Away from its administrative centre, the town seemed less oppressive. Not knowing how long it would take the Fox to find them, Juliette had rented a room along a narrow lane of narrow houses, with a landlord whose husband was a prisoner of war and who was poor enough not to ask questions. During the day, she seemed happy enough to let Sophie play with her own young daughters, while Juliette pretended to look for work, in reality wandering the town, waiting for the Fox to approach her. Bernard had managed to get her a German *Ausweis*, stamped in Lyon to explain her presence in the Free Zone. He had given her money too, but she could not get a ration card without registering with the local authorities, and black-market food was expensive.

Every day she said goodbye to Sophie, who watched anxiously until she had turned the corner at the end of the street. Every day she promised to come back for her, each time conscious that there were no guarantees.

After four days, the task of finding the Fox seemed hopeless and her only plan was to keep moving further south. Perhaps they could take a train as far as Toulouse if they could afford the passage. She took a different route, away from the park's trumped-up beauty, toward the railway station. She felt exposed and vulnerable on the hot streets. She missed the cool nights on the canal and the mist that had seemed to blanket her from curious eyes.

The station was busy, people from a train that had just pulled in milling around on the platform, beginning to form a queue for the checkpoint. She bypassed them and entered the empty stationhouse, approached the ticket window and the man behind it.

"How much for passage for two to Toulouse? I'll be travelling with a seven-year-old."

Shouting from the platform. Juliette whirled around, saw a man streak by the windows. Several Milice were pounding after him. When people saw the drawn pistols, some screamed and ran. Others dropped to the ground. The man leapt over them, head down, running with long, loping strides. He skidded at the edge of the platform, jumped toward the open tracks. The bullets ripped into his torso in mid-air.

Juliette stared. Her lungs felt compressed, as if she were trying to breathe underwater. She had to get out of the stationhouse or she would suffocate. Her stomach heaved.

She looked back at the ticket man and stared in astonishment. His dark eyes were flat and cold as stones. Outside a man lay crumpled on the tracks and the platform heaved with panic, while he stood like a statue as if nothing had happened.

He moved then, more quickly than she could have predicted. The door to his booth opened, his hand snaked out, grabbed her arm and pulled her inside the cubicle.

"*Taisez-vous!* Hide here," he hissed, giving her a quick shove.

She crouched down in the corner under the ticket counter, head pressed against her knees, arms wrapped around her legs, listening to the melee outside. *This is it*, she thought, *this must be him*. The Fox. After a while, the panic began to ebb. People started to drift inside, inquiring after schedules, buying tickets. His voice was dry and even. The next train came and left, the passengers kept coming in a steady flow. She studied his worn shoes and the crease in his trousers. She couldn't see his face. He paid no more attention to her than if she were a piece of furniture. She stayed that way as the day wore on, her muscles cramped, until she thought she would scream.

Finally, she heard him close the ticket window. He knelt down and helped her up. "I'm the Fox. We've been watching for you. We knew you'd come to the train station eventually."

Her legs were numb and she staggered against him. Her cheek grazed his face, smooth and shaven, smelling of soap. He was younger than she had realized, the eyes softer this time above a generous mouth.

"Rub your legs," he said, in the distinctive dry voice she thought she would recognize anywhere from now on. "I'll just check the platform. Be ready in five minutes."

Darkness had settled on Vichy by the time they crept away from the railway station. Even in Pétain's fantasy of France there was a curfew. They darted from corner to corner, the Fox leading the way. They crossed a small park and climbed up the steps of a shabby building, its pink neon sign flashing "Hôtel de Londres." The Fox tattooed a complicated knock on the glass door, a sleepy night clerk materializing from the shadowy interior to open it.

"Through here," the clerk hissed.

They followed him through the tiny lobby and down a corridor of stained carpet to a side door opening onto an alley. Beyond it was a wide boulevard, a strip of parkland and the curve of a river.

The Fox nudged her. "You see the van parked at the edge of the grass?"

"Yes."

"You'll be getting into it. Walk over as quickly as you can, but don't run."

Juliette started to say goodbye.

"Go," he interrupted. "Right now."

The van was marked as a maintenance vehicle. As she approached, the driver, tall and pale with a Slavic face and a worker's cap, leaned out from his window. "In the back."

She did what she was told. There was no time for why or where. Wooden racks were bolted to the walls of the van, holding a variety of pipe wrenches and shovels. The truck smelled of lubricating grease and burnt cinders. She sat down on the metal floor, holding onto one of the racks as the truck pulled smoothly away. There were no windows, and it seemed to her that they drove in circles for a long time.

By the time the van pulled to a stop, the sky was an inky black.

"In there," the driver said, helping her to the sidewalk. "Number forty-one."

She had no idea where she was, but that, of course, was the intent.

She walked to the flat, climbed up a flight of rough concrete stairs, and knocked on the dull brown door. A small brass eyehole stared blankly. Juliette heard a rustling from the other side of the door, heard an unseen cover scrape off the eyehole. She swallowed hard in the long interval that followed. The door opened slowly.

In the gloom stood a slight small-boned woman of middle-age, her fair hair pulled back from a high forehead above an aquiline nose. She was handsome rather than pretty, her face a curious mix of strength and delicacy.

"You are Renée, yes? Come in."

The room was cluttered with small bits of furniture and stacks of papers, more like an office than a living space. But Juliette wasn't really paying attention. Her gaze was fixed on the woman, on the ungainly hitch in her step as she limped across the room.

The woman turned, caught Juliette staring.

"It's my hip," she smiled. "A congenital condition. I find it's quite useful as the Germans equate it with a crippled mind. I'm Hedgehog. You've brought information?"

Juliette was stunned. She fumbled in her purse for the pack of cigarettes entrusted to her by Bernard, glad to have a task that would mask her surprise.

Hedgehog took the cigarettes from her and nodded toward a chair.

Juliette sank into it, waited while the woman carefully split open the paper and brushed away the tobacco. She held the thin wisps of almost translucent paper up to a table lamp, reading the minute lines of writing.

"Good," she said. "We can use this. Now, tell me what you need. There's a child?"

"Yes. Her name is Sophie. Her family's been taken and we need to get her out of France, to Britain if possible. I have the name and address of a family in Scotland who will look after her."

It was the first time Juliette had spoken. Hedgehog studied her, obviously trying to place the slight accent.

"You are from the north of France?"

"No. I'm Canadian. It's a long story."

"And will you be going with the child, or staying?"

Juliette opened her mouth, and closed it again. The question jarred her. Two futures flashed before her. One was a dream. She could flee with Sophie, never have to turn her over to strangers, never again have to feel terror sinking into her like a claw. Sophie was spun from light. She could follow her into the light.

But could she? The other future stared at her unblinkingly, like a predatory creature. She closed her eyes, tried to call up that long-ago girl from Chapleau. But she was gone. Instead she saw a young boy distributing butterflies, an old waiter handing her a blue kerchief, Monique crouched in the bath, Soeur Hélène's face. She saw an unknown man beaten to death on a street, and a line of children, so many children, being boarded onto a train.

Finally, she spoke. "I'll be staying."

"Why?"

"It's not a question of being French, or not being French. It's a question of being human."

The two women sat very still, strangers and yet together, bonded by the moment. Juliette felt something subtle shift inside her, like a shaft of cold air clearing her head and intensifying her senses.

Hedgehog broke the silence, her voice gentle and low. "You are a brave woman, I think. I'll do what I can to help. You must make your way to Toulouse. The Fox will see to the tickets. Go to the Basilique in the old town. Someone will watch for you. He's known as the Wolf."

August 25

The city of Toulouse sprawled across the southwestern landscape of France, but at its heart was the lovely old *ville rose*, named for the pink-brick streets making up the old town, hardly larger than a village. It was dominated by the Basilique St-Sernin, a huge Romanesque church, one of the stops on the pilgrims' route to Santiago de Compostela in northwest Spain. For thousands of years, pilgrims had rested and worshipped here before crossing the Pyrenees at the passes of Roncesvalles or Somport.

Juliette and Sophie, two pilgrims of a different sort, entered through the elaborately carved south portal and strolled down the nave, past glowing frescoes and tapestries, painted capitals and carved choir stalls. Heads bowed under their blue kerchiefs, they felt subdued by the grandeur of the church. They took seats, their case tucked between them, in a pew near one of the chapels radiating from the centre, and waited.

It seemed to Juliette that her days and nights had fallen into an inexorable rhythm, one she could not control: idle times of wondering and waiting, followed by tightrope dashes to the next place, the next contact, the next swelling of hope. Only a dark thread of fear held the waiting and the running together.

Beside her, Sophie pointed up to one of the capitals. "Look," she whispered. "There are seashells. Maman and Papa took me to the ocean once."

Juliette looked and saw that Sophie was right. A motif of scalloped seashells was carved into marble and wood, even painted into the frescoes.

"They're everywhere. It must be a symbol of some kind, but I don't know what it means."

"It's the sign of the pilgrims," said a voice behind them.

Juliette turned. It was a young man, younger than she, dressed like a schoolmaster in a blue-and-white striped shirt, a dark blue tie and a black waistcoat. His eyes were a vivid blue in a face with more angles than curves, his hair a gypsy black.

He smiled, a smile as open and innocent as Sophie's, and just as unexpected. "You are Renée, yes? I am the Wolf." He turned his attention to Sophie. "The seashells tell the story of St. James, the disciple who brought Christianity to Spain. He was murdered by Herod. When his followers brought his body to Galicia, they saw a vision of a man covered in scallop shells rise out of the waves on horseback. If ever you're lost, remember that the pilgrims believe you can follow the sign of the shell on the wayside shrines and chapels all the way from here to Spain. But for now, follow me."

After the cool air of the church, the mid-afternoon heat of the Place St-Sernin was smothering. The huddle of buildings around the square shimmered in white light, blinding Juliette, and for a moment bleaching the Wolf of his features. He led them to a pair of bicycles outside a small café.

"How far?" Juliette asked.

"About ten kilometres. I can take you most of the way." He picked up their battered suitcase and strapped it into the basket between the handlebars of his bicycle. Then he turned to Sophie. "Would you like to ride with me?"

Juliette looked down at the trusting face, the black eyes watching her under the corkscrew curls. A package, Soeur Hélène had called her, and the description seemed more apt than ever. "It's okay," she nodded. "I'll be right behind you."

They pedalled away from the old town, through a maze of streets leading out from the sprawl of the modern city. Faded blue and magenta shutters were closed tight against the heat, and it seemed as if all of Toulouse was dozing in the sun.

But not quite.

Close to the edge of the city, a hundred yards ahead of them, three men stepped out of the shade of a tree-lined avenue. They were wearing armbands.

The Wolf slowed, but did not stop. "Keep going," he ordered. "Follow my lead. When I lift my hand, go as fast as you can." Still pedalling, he shouted back to Sophie. "Hold onto my belt. Both hands. Hold on tight."

"Who are they?" Juliette asked.

"One of Pétain's militia units — *La Jeunesse du Maréchal, La Jeunesse patriote*, they have all sorts of names."

As they drew closer, one of the men, as fair-haired as any German, stepped into the street, holding up his hand.

"Stop," he ordered. "Where are you going?"

The Wolf lifted his hand as if to wave, then stamped down hard on the pedals, Juliette close behind him. The blond man leapt from their path, cursing, shaking his fist.

Juliette crouched low over the bike, her legs and heart pumping. Angry voices swelled behind her. The paved street beneath her streaked by. She felt the resistance of an incline, pumped until her legs burned and her lungs gasped for air. Then she was shooting down the other side of a hill, Sophie's curls flying just ahead of her, the voices fading, the sudden green and corn-coloured countryside blurring in her vision.

The Wolf slowed slightly but kept a steady pace until Toulouse was several kilometres behind them. Finally, to her relief, he pulled to the side of the road. She dismounted and fell to the verge beside him.

"They won't follow now," he panted. "But they'll report us. I must leave you here. This road will take you to the Villa Lamy in a small vineyard. The gates will be open. Sylvie Lamy is expecting you. She'll make arrangements for you to cross into Spain."

Juliette drew Sophie to her, pointing across the road. "See the wild flowers over there? Will you pick some for me?" She waited until the child was out of hearing.

"Why didn't you stop back there? Sophie and I have papers that have passed inspection before. Why risk a report? Now they'll be looking for us."

The Wolf opened his waistcoat, slid his hand into an inside pocket and drew out a small blunt-nosed pistol. "Do you know how to use this?"

"Of course. I grew up in — I mean, my father taught me."

"Take it."

"No."

He raised his eyebrows in surprise. "The Pyrenees are patrolled. Sometimes we hear rumours that the guides are unreliable. Are you sure?"

Juliette pushed his hand away. "If we run into trouble, it'll only be made worse by having that."

"Ah, I see. You're afraid to use it."

"No. I'm afraid I might use it." She read his face, saw that he didn't understand. "Look, do you know the old saying that a person grows to resemble his dog? Well, where I come from, the saying is that a person grows to resemble his dog and his enemies."

"It's a fine principle," he shrugged, "but hardly practical. War changes everything."

"Even so. It's all I have left."

The Wolf shook his head. "Grow up. It's not about you. It's about her, isn't it?" He nodded toward Sophie. "Or did we get that wrong?"

Juliette felt as if she'd been slapped. Was she wrong, she wondered? Was she being selfish?

She listened to his voice, gentler now. "You want too much. You think you can survive unscathed? You can't. There's a chapel a mile or two from the villa, marked with the scallop shell. I'll leave the gun behind the statue of St. James. Think about it."

She broke the silence. "Can I ask a question?"

He nodded.

"You gave me her name — Sylvie Lamy. Doesn't she have a code name?"

"No. She's not part of the Alliance. But she's helped people in the past. You can trust her. I'm going now."

Juliette reached out, touched his shoulder. "Thank you."

"There's nothing to thank me for."

"Not even for the lesson? How old are you, anyway?"

"Sixty-five."

She laughed out loud.

"Goodbye, Sophie," he called with a wave, and pedalled away.

The pink, vine-covered villa with its slanting roof of red tiles was not large, not at all like the Château Dumais in Burgundy. But its windows and archways gave it a sense of airiness and grace, and the courtyard smelled wonderfully of lavender and thyme. They pushed the bicycle to an open arch that framed a path leading to rows of vines heavy with clusters of ripening grapes. Juliette looked toward the window, and through the reflected light of the late afternoon sun, saw a watery shadow move across the other side of the glass.

A door opened onto a terrace and a tall, slim woman, shoulders braced and head held high, waved them forward. She carried herself like an *haute couture* model in the days before the war, with a once common air of self-confidence all but snuffed out now by the Occupation in the North. Her shoulder-length dark red hair was fashioned in a stylish roll that curved back from a high forehead, blue veins at the temples. Her eyes were green, her smile bright red. She seemed somehow older than she looked, possibly in her mid-forties.

"I am Madame Lamy. Come in, come in." Her accent was polished, her voice slightly husky.

She shooed them forward through an elegantly furnished foyer of gleaming wood, and down a hallway into a pristine kitchen. The room was commanded by a grey-haired woman whose body resembled a large square block.

"This is Laurette."

Juliette thought it a frivolous name for such a formidable figure. The woman barely glanced in their direction. Juliette had a sudden vision of the large hands wringing the neck of a chicken, and then wished she hadn't.

"Renée and Sophie will be staying with us for a short time. I expect they're hungry."

"That dog's got out again."

Sylvie looked cross. "Well I haven't time to look for it now. There are guests coming from Toulouse." She gave a quick nod to Juliette. "Laurette will show you around." And with that, she swept from the room.

Laurette scowled after her, her hands on her hips.

Sophie clung to Juliette's side, a fistful of wilting flowers still clutched in her hand.

"What's this?" Laurette asked.

"Sophie picked them from the fields."

"Well, you'd better not pick any from the gardens. She'll have your head. Bring your case."

They left through the kitchen door, which opened onto an herb garden encircled by a low wall. Beyond it were a number of outbuildings.

"We're not staying in the house?" Juliette asked.

Laurette made a snorting noise, not quite a laugh, but didn't answer. She led them through a gap in the wall. They passed a tool shed, a large stone building of the type that held equipment for making wine, an open stable that now housed machinery. To the left was a small cottage.

The door creaked when Laurette opened it. There were four beds along the walls, a small table with a basin for washing up at a pump, an oil lamp. Nothing else.

"The workers sleep here when it's time to harvest the grapes. I'll be back. She won't like you walking around the property."

The door scraped shut.

Two of the beds were made up with sheets and blankets; the other two were bare, the thin mattresses rolled up. Juliette walked to the window and tried to open it, but it wouldn't budge.

"Let's get some air in here, okay Sophie?"

She pushed against the door, and it groaned open. A small dog with silky black fur and a white patch over one black eye studied them from the threshold, a low growl vibrating from its throat.

"Hello you." Juliette stood very still, Sophie pressed to her side. Tentatively, she stretched out her hand.

The dog leaned forward, sniffed it. The growl stopped.

"Would you like to pet him, Sophie? Gently."

The small fingers reached forward, just tickled the fur. The dog's tail began to wag. Another pat, more confident this time, was greeted by a pink tongue licking Sophie's face. In a moment, they were rolling together on the floor, the child laughing, the dog's tail thumping.

A shadow loomed in the doorway. Laurette was back, carrying a basket of food, some towels, a bar of black soap.

"Figured that dog would find you. His name's Jacques. I let him out of the house whenever I can." She jerked her head in the direction of the villa. "She wants to see you. Just you. Leave the child to play. I'll keep an eye out."

Juliette found Sylvie Lamy in the drawing room, light glittering from the glass surfaces of mirrors and the teardrops of a large chandelier.

"Come in, dear. You can call me Sylvie." She patted a velvet chair.

"It's a beautiful room."

"Oh, not like it used to be. I've had to sell some of the furniture. Hard times, you understand."

Juliette didn't think the villa showed much sign of deprivation, but she smiled anyway.

"I'm sorry I can't have you in the house. I often have visitors, and the sleeping quarters for the grape pickers is safer. Should anyone notice, I can explain your presence by saying that you're here to help out Laurette. You wouldn't mind, would you? Helping out I mean."

"I'd be glad to do whatever you need. But we won't be here for long, will we?"

"Oh, no. Not too long. But these things take time. We must be cautious, yes? I must choose the guide carefully. One sometimes hears dreadful stories."

"What stories?"

"Well, some of the guides demand a great deal of money for the passage. Some people say they take money from both sides. We pay at this end, and then they turn their charges over to the patrols and collect from them, too."

"But I don't have any money, only a few francs."

"Don't worry, dear. That's what I'm here for. But, you understand, it may take awhile. Didn't your contact explain any of this? These young boys, they're only in it for the adventure. They don't understand the larger picture, the sacrifices that need to be made. If I could speak to him directly, we could avoid this confusion. What was his name again?"

Juliette lowered her head. She thought about the gun the Wolf had offered her. Whatever his motivation, it wasn't adventure.

She looked up, caught Sylvie studying her.

"His name, dear?"

"I don't know. He didn't say. He calls himself the Wolf."

"The Wolf? How ridiculous. Oh well. I think we should change your hair. Laurette could cut it, maybe make it darker. Somewhere, there must be an old uniform that would fit. Yes, a maid would be a good disguise for you. The child should stay in the background as much as possible."

"Her name's Sophie."

The red lips parted in a smile.

"Such a pretty little girl. I know you'll do your best for her. Now, I expect you're tired. We'll talk again, tomorrow."

Juliette walked back to the cottage, replaying the conversation in her mind. *How long?* she wondered. She'd come to dread the idle times. Twice now, she'd been warned about the guides. But Hedgehog had sent her here. It must be safe.

That night, she lay awake for a long time, voices and laughter from the villa seeping through the darkness over the stone wall that hid the cottage from view. She listened to Sophie's even breathing and the snores of Jacques, who was curled up on the child's bed. When she finally fell asleep, something startled her awake. But by the time she opened her eyes, whatever had disturbed her had vanished.

AUTUMN
1942

G

~

September 10, 1942, midnight

Gabrielle stared, paralyzed, from beside the body of Marie-Claire, afraid to move, afraid to speak. Above her, clouds drifted across the night sky swallowing up the moon, momentarily blacking out the face that leaned toward her.

His voice penetrated the darkness. "Move away."

She stood, took several shaky steps backward. At first, she could see nothing, then the clouds shifted and the moon reappeared. Dietsz took her place beside the body, removing his gloves and touching his hand to Marie-Claire's neck, searching for a pulse. Gently, he brushed her hair from her face. Her eyes were open, frozen, her features already turned to pale marble. He studied the horrifying expression for a few seconds, then drew his hand over her forehead and eyelids, closing her eyes.

Gabrielle turned away. The moonlit scene was like a strange nightmare and yet, at the same time, an excruciating reality.

"What happened?"

Her temper flared. She whirled around, confronting him. "She was terrified of you. She tried to tell me she was in danger. You bastard!"

Dietsz looked shocked. He reached out, grabbed her hands. He looked down at them and then turned the right one toward her.

"And yet, it is you, Madame Aubin, whose palm is streaked with blood."

Blood from the stair railing. Gabrielle stared at it. "I didn't ..." she stammered. "I saw the blood and came to look for her."

"Where did you see the blood?" he demanded, still grasping her hands.

Gabrielle's eyes widened and she searched his face. He seemed genuinely puzzled. He had no need to pretend innocence to her. He could shoot her just as easily as listen to her. The grotesque coffin weighed heavily in the pocket of her cardigan. She could think of no reason why Dietsz would have put it on the body. But if not him, then who had killed Marie-Claire? She was the ideal suspect, caught here literally red-handed.

She closed her eyes, realizing how precarious her situation was. How could she explain, keep her identity as Amélie from him?

He shook her, and her mind went blank. "Talk to me. Right now I am all that is standing between you and the Gestapo. I must report this. It is my duty. She has already been dead for several hours."

"I didn't kill her. She was my friend, a better friend to me than I was to her. I came looking for her and — and I found something on the body. It's in my pocket."

"Turn around. You will clasp your hands behind your head."

He let go of her and she did as he asked. She felt his hands slide from her armpits to her hips, suddenly stopping when he felt the object in her pocket. He removed it and she heard the sharp intake of his breath from behind her.

"You may put down your hands. We will go to your cottage now, and you will tell me everything."

They did not speak again until the cottage door closed behind them.

Dietsz surveyed the neat room, the cold stove with no signs of a prepared evening meal. "Show me where you found the blood."

She pointed wordlessly to the railing and slumped into a chair, her legs trembling, her mind numb as she listened to his boots mounting the stairs and thudding from room to room. When he returned, he sat across from her, his back rigid.

"The cottage is as you found it? No sign of a struggle?"

She nodded.

"Why was Mademoiselle here?"

"I was worried about her. I'd invited her to supper, but she hadn't said she would come. I — I went walking in the forest as I often do. When I returned I found the blood and went looking for her."

"How long was the cottage empty?"

"Several hours."

He sighed in exasperation. "Madame Aubin, you are in serious trouble. A woman is dead. You have been found beside her body, after curfew, with an object you either removed or were about to place on the body. She was in your cottage, from which you have an unexplained absence." He held up a hand to stifle her protest. "You have no reason to trust me, nor I you. But unless you give me a fuller account of the evening, I cannot help you. Now, begin again. What did you do after leaving the shop?"

I became Amélie, she wanted to say, but could not. She would tell him almost the truth, but not that. She thought of Jean, understood more profoundly the choices he had been forced to make. Whatever happened to her, she would protect the people who knew her as Amélie.

"I visited my husband's grave. Joseph Thibault found me there and offered to drive me home. I changed and went to the Morvan. I walk there often, revisiting the places I shared with Jean, and I lost track of the time. That's all. When I got back, maybe ten-thirty, maybe eleven, I felt someone had been here. I was frightened. I searched and found the blood, remembered Marie-Claire, and hurried out to telephone her from the shop. On the way, I saw her. That coffin, that thing — it was like a desecration. I yanked it from her throat. And then you found us." She paused, raised her chin. "And why were you there? She told me she was frightened of you, because Klaus had told her about Hans Meyer."

His eyes widened. "What about Meyer?"

"He was a thief and a blackmailer. He had something hidden, perhaps something very valuable. Klaus thought that was why you'd searched here. Marie-Claire thought you sent him to the Russian front because of what he knew about Meyer, and that you would also get rid of her somehow."

"Why would she tell you this?"

"Because she was trying to help me find who killed Meyer. The things that were found in Jean's desk — the ring, the cigarette lighter — were planted there. I've told you before. Jean didn't kill him. He only found the body, and buried it to try to protect the village. She said Meyer sometimes met secretly with people. I think she was about to tell me who he'd been blackmailing."

If her confession surprised him, he hid it well. He regarded her calmly, watched as she nervously tucked a wayward strand of hair back into her braid. He seemed to be thinking, reaching some sort of decision. She saw his body relax slightly.

"Very well," he said. "I, too, have come to believe that Monsieur Aubin was innocent, but I did not learn these stories about Meyer until it was too late. Meyer did come to me, said he would make me a rich man if I kept him from the Front. But I did not believe him. Many men are desperate to avoid that fate. So I must bear some responsibility for your husband's death."

Gabrielle turned her face away so he would not see her tears. She felt relief that he believed in Jean's innocence. Knowing what his admission must have cost him, she wanted to trust him. But she was wary still. He was the Kommandantur. He was the clever enemy. And how had he happened upon her beside the body?

"Do you not know what this is?"

She brushed her tears away, looked again at the ugly little carving that Dietsz had placed on the table. She shook her head.

"I have seen one before in Avallon. It is a sign, a brand of sorts. The brand of the collaborator. Members of the Resistance leave it as a warning to others who may give us information. So perhaps you will understand now that some members of the Resistance are not the unsullied heroes you wish them to be. The villagers are angry, are they not, that your friend fell in love with a German soldier? Perhaps this is their punishment."

Gabrielle felt a new ripple of repulsion as she stared at the coffin. Marie-Claire's murder as an act of blind revenge was bad enough, but the carving spoke a different language, one of cold calculation and malice. Perhaps she was naive, but she could not believe the anger against Marie-Claire ran so deep nor was so cruel.

"I ask you again, Madame Aubin. What were you doing in the forest? Why do you go there night after night? Why did Joseph Thibault offer you a ride, tonight of all nights? Were you perhaps performing an errand for him? Is this not the true reason why you failed to keep an arrangement with your friend?"

"No. As I told you, she never said she'd come. That day you came into the shop to buy bread, she was about to tell me who

Meyer was meeting, but you frightened her. Do you think I would have missed a chance for her to tell me?"

"And Joseph Thibault?"

"An old friend. I've known him since I was a child. He saw I was tired and offered me a ride."

"And, yet, not too tired to wander in the forest for over three hours."

"Perhaps you can't understand the grief a woman has for the man she loved."

"Perhaps so. It must be a grief too sacred to pander as an alibi."

Gabrielle's cheeks flushed with shame, as good as an admission of guilt. She dropped her head, hid her face from him, but it was too late. He'd caught her.

"I see," he said, his voice low and gentle. "I owe you one chance, Madame Aubin, but only one. If you are mixed up in Resistance activities, you must stop at once. You must see now how treacherous these people can be."

He stood up, pocketed the carving, walked toward the door. Gabrielle spoke to his retreating back.

"I won't make the same mistake twice, Kommandantur. But neither should you."

He froze, then turned back to her, looking down into her face, studying her — the black glossy hair, the deep eyes, translucent green, the green of the sea. Her fear was gone. She did not break his gaze.

"What do you mean?" he asked.

"Marie-Claire was stabbed, just like Meyer. You thought once that his murder was an act of resistance, but now you're not sure. Someone may have killed him for his secret money, money no one has found. Greed may have been the motive, nothing to do with the war. Marie-Claire may have been killed for what she knew, not for whom she slept with."

Gabrielle was not sure what reaction she was expecting, but it was not the one she got.

Dietsz smiled. "I agree. You are an intelligent woman. Have you also realized what it means if your theory is correct? No? You have been seen often with Marie-Claire, and she has been known to spread a story or two. Your own husband, you tell me tonight, found Meyer's body. Might he have also looked upon the face of his killer and spoken that name to his wife? You are in danger, Madame. The slim possibility that this danger may be from a German is why I have been watching you. It is why Klaus was removed. It is why I saw you leave the cottage at midnight, find the body and hide something in your pocket.

"I will go now to report the murder of your friend. I will give the Gestapo in Château-Chinon the coffin, and tell them I found it on the body. They will be alerted to the possibility of Resistance activity, but beyond that, they do not care if the French kill the French. I will not tell them Marie-Claire was in your cottage, because I do not believe you killed her and because you have suffered enough at my hands. They will turn the investigation over to the *gendarmes*, and turn their eyes to the Resistance. I warn you again. Be very careful. I believe I have done what I can to settle the debt I owe you. Good night, Madame Aubin."

The door closed behind him. Gabrielle sat rooted at the table, listening to the whisper of wind in the trees, and the whisper of Dietsz's warning in her head.

September 11

Madame Pascal met her at the door of the shop and kissed her on both cheeks. "*Ma petite*, I've been so worried. Dietsz is here, at the *mairie*, and at dawn a Gestapo car arrived."

"It's Marie-Claire. She's been murdered."

"*Mon Dieu!*"

"I'd invited her for supper. When I returned, when Amélie returned from the forest, I found blood on the stairs in my cottage and I went to look for Marie-Claire. Dietsz has been watching me. We happened upon the body at the same time." Gabrielle stopped, biting her lip. She didn't want to reveal the connection to Meyer, her private mission to find his killer. Yet she had to warn her friends that the Gestapo would have a renewed interest in the Resistance. "Madame, please don't go out in the van today. They'll be watching everyone. Dietsz saw ... there was a small coffin around her neck."

Madame Pascal suddenly looked her age, her face drained of colour.

"I need a drink," she murmured.

Gabrielle followed her to the backroom, waited while she poured herself a small brandy, braced herself for the questions she knew would follow. The old woman closed her eyes for a moment, thinking, then she leaned forward.

"Poor Marie-Claire. She was foolish, but an innocent. I fear I have failed her. Killed because she was an *horizontale?* Perhaps. But not by the Resistance." Then her eyes narrowed. "Why did Dietsz not arrest you?"

"He knew I didn't kill her. He saw me leave my cottage and stumble upon the body. Of course he asked me why I'd gone into the forest. I think I've convinced him that I was mourning for Jean. But his suspicions are aroused. We mustn't take any chances."

"*Mais, non.* Now we must take the greatest risk. There are people already in hiding. If they stay too long in one place, they'll be found. I can warn the St-Léger line by telephone, but we must also warn the others, and we'll need their help now to move people away from the outlying farms and into the forest."

"The others?"

"Think, Gabrielle. You witnessed one of the air drops. There are armed men in the forest, the *maquis.* They're a small band, but growing. They're men from villages all over the Morvan. Our only contact with them is Yves. He's their radio operator, their link to the Allies who supply them with guns. They'll help us now, as we've sometimes helped them. I must get a message to Yves."

"Amélie will do it."

"*Incroyable.* You've just told me Dietsz is watching you."

"He isn't watching me now. Besides, we have no choice. No one else knows about Marie-Claire yet. It may be the last time I can help as Amélie. Please. I have my bicycle. You phone the others and I'll go to warn Yves."

Madame Pascal hesitated, then nodded. "You may be right. This must be done quickly. You know where to leave the message. A single word. *Gestapo.* It's all you need. Hurry. But first, where did you find the body?"

"In the underbrush beside the road. Not far from the cottage."

"Then the Gestapo will surely question you. God help us if they don't find you at home. I'll do my best to stall them, should they look for you here first. Now go."

The sun had not yet burned off the dawn's mist by the time Gabrielle reached the logging camp. Wreathed in strands of ground fog, the lean-to cabin seemed more insubstantial than ever. She paused, cocked her head, heard only birdsong. Cautiously, she stepped into the clearing and then ran to the oak tree. On her toes, stretching up to leave the message in the hollow, she heard a twig snap. She froze.

"Amélie?"

She turned, saw Yves and collapsed in relief in his arms. Then she pushed him away and held out the message.

His arms released her reluctantly. He took the note, glanced at it quickly, then stared at her. She'd taken no time to change, still wore the black dress she'd put on for the shop. Her shoes were wet.

"What's happened?"

"There's no time. I must get back." She was already turning away.

He followed her. "I'll go with you."

"No. Warn the others. We need their help."

"Will you be all right?" His dark eyes were filled with concern for her.

"I can handle them. Just go."

He nodded and she ran away from him, back the way she had come, slipping in her wet shoes, catching her legs on low-lying branches, until she reached the field behind her cottage. She had to make an effort then to walk normally, to walk across the open space with the anonymous grey calm of people who have no secrets to hide.

She was in time. Unless the Gestapo had already come and gone, she had beaten them home. She went upstairs and changed into a fresh dress, combed her hair, wild from running, and pulled woollen stockings over the scratches on her legs. Madame Pascal had told her once that the members of the SS had taken a personal blood oath to Hitler. Perhaps this was one reason why they so frightened her, these men in black, with silver lightning bolts on their collars and skull bones carved into their rings. They stalked like vampires, creatures of the night, choosing dawn to sweep in for arrests, when people were asleep and disoriented. Five o'clock in the morning was the hour of the Gestapo, the hour of death. But another day of summer sun shone brightly now. Her anger over what they had done to Jean was her armour. She would face them down.

The cough of an engine called her to her upstairs window in time to see the black car swerve up the road in a cloud of summer dust. She went down to meet them, stood tall in the open doorway. This time there would be no pounding of fists against the door of her sanctuary.

Two men unfolded themselves from the car. Dietsz, looking grim, and another, shorter man, in a black leather trench coat despite the summer sun. His eyes were small and bright, set among the folds of a fleshy face. His hair was dark, barely hiding a small scar that jagged across his forehead.

"*Bonjour*, Madame Aubin. I believe you know the Kommandantur from Avallon. I am Hauptsturmführer Eber, stationed at Château-Chinon. If you could spare a few moments of your time?"

Gabrielle stood to the side and they entered her cottage. Dietsz's presence disconcerted her. Would he keep to his part of the bargain? She had already broken hers. For some reason, she was uneasy that he would be there, watching her lie. She tried to catch his eye as he followed Eber into the room, but his profile was rigid, and he did not look toward her.

She sat them at the table, but offered them nothing. To do so would be a mistake, a departure from the unspoken French vow to be inhospitable to the invaders. It was a passive-aggressive gesture that Eber would recognize. He glanced around the room.

"You have a comfortable home, Madame. No doubt your husband was a good provider."

"Yes."

"But you are now working in the *boulangerie?*"

"Madame Pascal is a dear friend, and elderly now. Besides, I needed the money."

"*Quel dommage.* It's a shame a beautiful woman like you must work. Had your husband thought more of you and less of the Resistance, you might still have led an easy life, *non?*"

Gabrielle raised her chin, but said nothing, letting the disdain in her eyes show her rejection of his sleazy compliment and his self-serving version of Jean's execution.

"Now it seems the Resistance has struck again." He slammed the ugly coffin onto the table, hoping to shock her. "You recognize this? It is their calling card."

"I've never seen it before." She kept her eyes on Eber, dared not a glance at Dietsz.

"Kommandantur Dietsz found it on the body of your friend. She was stabbed several times, the body found in close proximity to this cottage late last night. So, I must ask, where were you last evening?"

"I was here. I went for a short walk in the late afternoon, in the forest, as I do on most days. Then I returned home and went to bed."

"You heard and saw nothing? No screams in the night?"

"Nothing."

"I see. And why was this friend of yours so close to your home? You didn't perhaps lure her here under false pretences, then coldly abandon her to the revenge of terrorists?"

"That's ridiculous. Marie-Claire was my friend."

"Ah, yes. You villagers are all friends, we know. And yet, your husband thought nothing of the reprisals that might have befallen his neighbours for killing a German soldier. And now a young woman dies because the villagers were jealous of her lover. We have to consider all the possibilities, do we not?"

"You may. But I don't, and that's one possibility I refuse to think about. It's just not possible."

"Ach, you French. You like the world to be simple, eh? Black and white. Good guys and bad guys. Well, if you want to pretend, so be it. You want to kill each other, it's — how do you say? *Rien?* — it's nothing to me. But the Resistance is something else. My business. What did your husband do for them?"

"Nothing."

"Oh, come now. He killed a German soldier for fun?"

She sensed rather than saw Dietsz's ice-blue stare. If she defended Jean again, as she was wont to do, Dietsz's mission to find Meyer's killer, and her own attempts to clear Jean's name, would be jeopardized.

"He told me nothing."

"Really? Not even any pillow talk, snuggling up in bed?"

She risked a quick glance at Dietsz, caught his fleeting expression of disgust. *He despises them,* she thought, *despises Eber.* The realization gave her strength. She looked at Eber coldly, wondered what was going on behind the wide, fleshy face and the deep buried eyes.

He flashed a thin, sinister smile. "You and your husband seem fond of the woods?"

"Yes, we played there often as children."

"And as lovers, no doubt?"

She ignored the repeated salacious hints. She spoke unashamedly, with dignity. "Of course."

He licked his lips. "The Resistance, as you no doubt know, use the Morvan to hide, to plan their sabotage against us. Are you even now working for them, Madame Aubin?"

"I am not."

"Very well. But let me warn you. If you are ever caught in the forest, day or night, from this moment forward, you will be arrested immediately. In prison, your beauty will not help you — rather the opposite, I fear."

She ignored the threat. "Am I under house arrest?"

Eber slammed down his fist. "The forest is forbidden to you. You may continue to come and go into the town, to your workplace. Do I make myself clear?"

"Eminently."

He rose to leave. "This stabbing case will be turned over to the local *gendarmes.* They will no doubt want to question you. I advise you to tell them the truth."

Eber stomped out, impatient now to return to the car. Dietsz lingered, seemed about to speak. He reached a hand toward her cheek, only inches away from the softness of her skin, then dropped it. Instead he raised a finger to his lips, and smiled. *You did well to be silent,* his eyes said. *Be careful.*

The instant they were gone, Gabrielle mounted her bicycle and rode after them into town. She nodded at Madame Pascal, and smoothly took over serving the bread queue.

Marie-Claire's murder was foremost on everyone's mind, the news having spread quickly. There was an unsettling mix of ghoulish curiosity and the acrid smell of fear in the air. The coffin had done its malicious work. The villagers looked sidelong at each other. Who among them had taken vengeance on the *horizontale?* Gabrielle could not help but hear the muttering.

No less than what she deserved.

Who would have been so bold, eh? Under the noses of the Germans.

This is what collaborators can expect.

Gabrielle lost her temper.

"What's happened to you? Can't you see that this is what the Germans want? All of us turning against each other. Have you no pity in your hearts for Marie-Claire? She was one of us, a victim of the war, nothing less. You should be mourning for her."

The shop fell silent. A few people scurried out, a few others had the decency to look ashamed. At noon, Gabrielle closed up. Madame Pascal raised an eyebrow. "A pretty speech. I'm going to take some provisions to Marie-Claire's parents. You want to join me?"

"Of course."

"The Gestapo officer came looking for you here. I trust they found you at home?"

"They did. The message was delivered. Yves was there. But I'm forbidden to enter the forest. Eber ordered it."

"I see. Then we must find some other task for Amélie's talents."

Gabrielle prepared a cold supper and sat down alone to eat it, pushing the food in desultory circles around her plate. The visit to Marie-Claire's parents had gone badly, the old couple bewildered by their loss, barely in touch with reality. One moment, they would be talking of her death; the next, they would speak as if it was all a misunderstanding and she was simply late home. It was heartbreaking. Madame Pascal offered to take over the funeral arrangements, and Gabrielle prayed that the villagers would forgive enough to attend. ·

She picked up a book and tried to read, but the words blurred on the page. She felt guilty that she had not been home when Marie-Claire had come. She couldn't help thinking that had she been there, her presence might have altered her friend's fate. She imagined how Marie-Claire would have entered the cottage calling out for her, how a stealthy figure would have followed her inside.

Suddenly Gabrielle closed the book. Suppose Marie-Claire had not been followed. Suppose instead that she had interrupted someone already here, already searching the cottage. She remembered the note she'd found at the graveside. It was more than possible that the coffin had been meant for her.

Gabrielle shivered with a dreadful certainty. She did not believe that the Resistance had killed either Meyer or Marie-Claire. But now she had lost all hope of finding the murderer, a man who might yet kill again if he believed she knew his identity. The irony that she could be in danger for knowledge she didn't have, but wanted desperately, made her feel small and vulnerable.

She locked the door. Upstairs, she changed into a long white cotton nightgown, combed out her hair, felt again the ache of climbing into bed alone. What use was she now to anyone? If she couldn't go into the forest, even her minor role as the courier known as Amélie was over.

She lay awake for a long time, listening to the sounds of the night, struggling against her fear and the greyness of the days to come.

September 13

The funeral was subdued and solemn. The villagers, Gabrielle among them, had walked behind the plumed horses from the church to the cemetery, every footstep watched at a careful distance by the soldiers from Avallon sent to replace Meyer and Klaus. Gabrielle saw no sign of Dietsz. His debt to her had been repaid, and she supposed he would no longer feel the need to watch over her.

As a sign of respect, Madame Pascal had kept the *boulangerie* closed, but Gabrielle suspected a second motive. Unable to buy their daily bread, the villagers would be sure to attend the small reception at Marie-Claire's home if for no other reason than the funeral meats. Their resentment, evident still in a few sullen faces, did not run as deep as their hunger. Their presence, however secured, comforted the shaken parents.

As people began to trail away, Madame Pascal pulled Gabrielle aside.

"You will visit Jean's grave on your way home?"

Gabrielle shook her head. "I've had enough of graves today."

"Amélie would not think so."

Gabrielle smiled, her spirits lifting.

When she reached the churchyard, Jean's grave looked undisturbed. She knelt beside it, ran her fingers over the stones she had fashioned into a cross. Beneath one, she found a note and read it hurriedly before hiding it in the pocket of her black dress. Later, she would burn it as she waited for her visitor.

Yves came just after midnight, not to the front door, but to one of the back windows facing the field and the forest that was forbidden to her. Even though she'd watched for him, she'd seen no sign of movement, had heard nothing, until the rumble of thunder. The sky flickered. In that moment, she saw him at the window. She opened it, helped him inside. He was drenched, caught in the suddenness of the storm. She brought him wine to warm him, and a dry sweater of Jean's.

Across the room, she glanced up as he was changing clothes, saw the scars fanning across the muscles of his back. She gasped.

"What happened to you?"

His dark eyes met hers, the hurt buried deep inside. "I was arrested in Paris, tortured. It doesn't matter. It was a long time ago. Another life. I'm sorry about your friend, Amélie."

She nodded, but said nothing.

He reached for her hand, gave it a reassuring squeeze. "The Gestapo questioned you?"

"Yes, a man named Eber. He has forbidden me to go into the forest. How can I help you now?"

"I'll come to you. We'll change the drop site to Jean's grave. Many people come and go to the village church. The graveside is safe, I think."

Gabrielle hesitated. Should she tell him someone else had already left a note at the graveside? And if she did, would he still consider her an ally and not a liability? She settled on a half-measure. "But the cottage isn't safe. I'm sure I'll be watched, at least for a week or so. You mustn't come here again."

"Oh, we'll wait. We'll watch, too. But when the Gestapo lose interest, we may call upon you. We need the cottage, Amélie."

"I don't understand."

"Some of the people we're helping are injured or weak. They won't last long in the caves of the Morvan. Until the St-Léger escape line is up and running again smoothly, we need a safe house, close to the forest. Are you able to do this? If you're frightened, Amélie, we'll understand. You know the risks."

She knew. The cottage was small. There was no convenient attic, no false wall. If the Germans decided to search the place, she would be caught in an instant. No one would blame her, or think less of her, if she said no. No one but herself.

"Come," she beckoned. "I'll show you what space I have."

Yves followed her up the stairs. She stood at the door of the room she had shared with Jean, empty now but for the cold bed and the wardrobe that held what remained of his clothes.

Yves scanned the room. Then he touched her elbow gently and she half turned, gesturing to the other bedroom and small bathroom. When he returned from inspecting the rooms, her head was bent forward, her features screened by her hair. He took a step toward her, then slowly moved away.

"This will do," he murmured, "I must go now."

Downstairs at the window, Gabrielle reached out, touched his arm.

"Wait. You know who I am. Won't you tell me who the tailor's son is?"

"You know my face. Of all the people in the St-Léger line, even Madame Pascal, only Amélie knows that. Is it not enough?"

She smiled, but he saw the disappointment in her eyes, the loneliness. Perhaps the human need to trust was as deep as the need to hide.

He leaned forward, kissed her cheek. "In another life," he whispered, "I was Luc. Luc Garnier."

She placed her hand over her cheek, watched while he melted into the night.

September 16

The *gendarme*, Étienne Fougères, entered the shop just before the two o'clock closing. He waited patiently until the last of the customers was served and then approached her. "Madame Aubin, I've questions I must ask about Marie-Claire."

"Of course." She led him to the backroom, waved him to a chair. "What can I do to help?"

"She was found, as you know, close to your home. Do you know why?" His moon-face was innocent, not a trace of guile.

"I'd invited her to supper, but I didn't think she would come. I expect she decided to, after all. Had I known, I would have looked for her."

"Oh, it's good you didn't. You might have put yourself in harm's way." He spoke earnestly, and then blushed to the roots of his hair. "I mean, you were kind to her, everyone knows that. Some might have resented it. The Gestapo man, Eber, seems to think the Resistance was involved in her death."

"I see, but still you've been asked to investigate?"

"Only to determine if she may have been killed because of, um, her relationship —"

"With the German Klaus. Tell me, how long have you been stationed here in St-Léger?"

"Just over a year now."

"And what do you think of us? Do you think the villagers would have done such a thing?"

Étienne smiled shyly. "I think not. I'm filling up my notebook with all the usual — who she talked to that day, where she went. But the truth is, no one would talk to her, except you and the priest. She went to confession. Several people saw her enter the church. Eber won't approve that she was atoning for her sins with a German. But that is all I have for my final report."

"Was Père Albert in St-Léger that day?" Gabrielle knew that his duties were spread over several of the smaller hamlets. She, herself, had last seen him in Dun-les-Places on the very night of Marie-Claire's murder.

"Yes. Apparently she asked him to come. Her telephone call was overheard by customers in the Café du Sport. Perhaps she found some peace in the end, *hein?*"

When he was gone, Gabrielle returned to the backroom and placed a call of her own. Though Marie-Claire had not had time to tell her anything, perhaps she would have confided in a priest. Whatever had passed between them, she knew it wasn't atonement. Marie-Claire hadn't believed she'd done anything wrong.

Père Albert sat in one of the armchairs next to the fireplace, Gabrielle in the other beside him. How often had she sat like this with Jean, the two of them reading or talking over their day? She listened to the fire crackle and spit, the flames licking away the coolness of the evening. The priest looked wrung out, she thought. For the first time, he seemed old to her. She studied his bent head, the thick silver hair, the elegant hands with their long fingers that had traced the sign of the cross on the foreheads of so many of the faithful over the years.

She had told him absolutely everything, all about Meyer's secret and Marie-Claire's knowledge of who had been meeting with him. He had told her nothing.

"*Mon Père*," she sighed. "You must see that whoever killed Hans Meyer also killed her."

"That seems likely, yes."

"Did she give you a name?"

"She spoke to me in the confessional, Gabrielle. You know what that means. I will say this. Until tonight, may God forgive me, I thought a great deal of what she said was nonsense. Now ... You must leave this in my hands."

"I don't think I can. Dietsz thinks I may be in danger. If you know something, or even suspect something, it's only fair you tell me."

Père Albert raised his head and looked at her sternly. "Fair is a word for children waiting their turn in a game. It has no meaning in a country overrun by Nazis." He saw the flush of her shame on her neck and cheeks, and reached for her hand. "I will say this much. Marie-Claire believed in your goodness. She wanted to say goodbye to you."

"Goodbye? She was leaving?"

"I've said too much."

"But where would she go? She wouldn't leave her parents alone, and she had no money."

"And yet, as you've told me tonight, there is talk of Meyer the *voleur*, the looting in Paris, the hidden fortune no one has found. He didn't strike me as a clever man."

Gabrielle was astounded. "Are you saying Marie-Claire knew where it was?"

"I'm only speculating. I wonder about this poor man Klaus, whom everyone skips over. I wonder what a man would do on the eve of being sent to Russia. Now, I must go, *ma petite*. Leave things to me."

"But Père Albert —"

"No, Gabrielle. Others are depending on you. Be quiet. Attract no notice. Give up this hunt for a murderer. If Dietsz is trying to find this man, let him do his job."

She hung her head in frustration, and he reached out to lift up her chin. "You're not alone. Remember that. We'll watch over you."

*

J

September, October

A week went by. Two. A month. Autumn crept over the land, long mellow afternoons drenched with light from a sun low in the sky, and smoky bonfires of fallen leaves and pruned vines, the bitter-sweet smoke that smelled of the dying summer. The night air grew chilly.

Juliette grew more and more anxious with the passing of time. During the day, she exhausted herself polishing, sweeping and scrubbing, even working in the vineyard. But at night, while she listened to Sophie's breathing, her fear surfaced. Soon, she knew, there would be snow in the mountain passes. Sleep, when it came, was haunted by imaginary blizzards that made escape more and more improbable.

She found little comfort in Laurette, who was taciturn and brusque. She found even less in Sylvie Lamy, who seldom spoke to her and avoided her questions. During the nights when Madame Lamy entertained well-heeled visitors from Toulouse, Juliette kept out of sight in the cottage, listening to the laughter leaking out from the dining room. It began to seem as if the war didn't exist for the Villa Lamy, as if it floated above it, as if she and Sophie were trapped in some other dimension.

By early October, the grapes were heavy on the vines. Laurette woke her one day at sunrise.

"The harvesters are coming," she said. "You'll have to sleep somewhere else for a few days."

Their suitcase of shabby clothes was quickly packed and moved to the loft of the old stable. Juliette and Laurette hauled two mattresses up the wooden ladder and put them on the floor, then left Sophie to play with Jacques while they went to the kitchen to begin preparing food for the pickers.

The truck arrived just after nine with a dozen workers. Juliette watched them working, while she helped set up a long table for lunch on the terrace. The older men went along the rows of vines, clipping the grapes until their woven baskets were full. Then they would call out for one of the younger men roaming the field with canvas sacks over their backs. As the small baskets emptied, the sacks grew fuller and heavier and the young men would haul them to a horse-drawn wagon. There was a rhythm to the work that Juliette sensed was centuries old. As the morning wore on, the mound of grapes grew larger, the air fragrant with their heavy scent.

At noon, the harvesters stopped to eat. Juliette was moving down one side of the table pouring out glasses of water when she recognized the gypsy features of a young man, the man she knew only as the Wolf. Her hand shook slightly. Water sloshed over the side of his glass and he turned to look at her. Laurette had bobbed her hair and turned it the colour of toasted almonds, but when Juliette looked into his eyes she saw that he knew her, saw also a momentary expression of alarm. She moved on, saying nothing.

All afternoon, she tried to figure out that look in his eyes. Was he afraid that she would give him away? Or was he surprised to see her still here? She thought about all the work she'd been doing, willingly, in exchange for food and a place to hide. Suddenly, it dawned on her: she was a prisoner here, doing forced servitude. With her realization came the first flutter of panic. Was Laurette watching her? Had she seen the look exchanged with the Wolf? Everything seemed to have hidden meaning, secrets like shadows behind every action. She had to speak to him.

She waited for Laurette to leave the kitchen, then slipped into the courtyard. She climbed the low wall behind the cottage and crouched in its shadow until he neared, a sack slung over his shoulders. She knew she was putting them both at risk but she had no choice — she stepped forward.

"Why are you still here?" he hissed.

"I don't know. They tell me nothing. I'm sure something's wrong."

"Where are they keeping you?"

"The loft of the stable."

"Wait for me. I'll come tonight," he said, continuing on down the row of vines.

She turned, ran back to the kitchen. Laurette was standing in the doorway, watching for her.

"Where were you? What are you up to?"

"Nothing. Just checking on Sophie." The moment she spoke, Juliette felt uneasy. She realized she hadn't seen the child in the courtyard, nor had she been in the kitchen all day. "Where is she?" she demanded.

"Madame took her into town. She needed new clothes."

Her eyes slid away from Juliette.

She was lying.

A cold crawling sensation spread over Juliette's scalp. Sophie was gone. She had failed to protect her.

The white heat of rage overcame her sense of helplessness and she roughly grabbed Laurette's arm.

"Where is she? What have you done to her?" she screamed.

Laurette's slap stunned her and she staggered sideways, one hand pressed to her burning cheek.

"You're all the same," Laurette shouted. "You come here and put us at risk. You care only about yourselves. Madame will speak to you when she comes back. Now get to work."

Juliette backed up, leaned against the kitchen wall and folded her arms over her chest.

"I'll do nothing until I know where Sophie is."

The two women glared at each other. Then Laurette shrugged. "Suit yourself, bitch." She turned her back and resumed her chores as if nothing had happened.

Juliette was so angry she was shaking. What an idiot she'd been to trust Sylvie Lamy! She thought it would be easier here, where there were no German patrols, but she'd been careless. All the little signs she'd ignored — the conspicuous consumption, the parties, the repeated delays. But she fought against her self-recrimination. She had to stay strong. She had to get Sophie back.

She rushed across the front courtyard through the gate, and hurried down the road toward Toulouse.

She heard the car chugging along before she saw it, and positioned herself in the middle of the road. Madame Lamy pulled up, her face through the windscreen perfectly composed. Juliette kicked the driver's side of the car.

"Where have you taken her?"

"There's no need for a scene, dear. She's perfectly safe. Get in."

They rode back to the villa in silence, Jacques whimpering in the back seat. Juliette was sure Madame Lamy had used the dog to coax Sophie into the car.

Madame Lamy led the way into the sitting room, and called out for Laurette.

"I think we need some tea. Renée and I are going to have a little chat."

"I'll not serve the likes of her."

"Now, now Laurette. Don't be churlish. She's still a guest."

Juliette sat with her hands in her lap, her back rigid, hoping against hope that Sophie was merely hidden, and not turned over to the authorities.

The tea came. Madame Lamy poured, nudged a cup toward her. Juliette ignored it.

"It's time you moved on, I think. Some of the pickers may mention your presence. It's why I took the little girl away, you know, so she wouldn't be noticed."

Juliette glanced up, surprised. She studied Sylvie Lamy's face, the arched brows, the blue veins pulsing at the temple. "I'll go immediately, if you return Sophie to me."

"Go where? You still need me. I'm sure we can work something out. I have a *passeur* ready to guide you, but I require something in exchange for my trouble."

"I've already told you I have no money to speak of. You're welcome to the little I have."

"I don't think it would go far, do you? The villa is so expensive to keep up. But perhaps you have something else to give?"

Juliette stared at her, let the question hang in the air.

"Come, now, you're not a stupid girl. I need names, a lead on the people who sent you here. Something I can trade with my friends in the Milice. You've already helped a great deal by mentioning the Wolf. Remember? There's a line called Noah's Ark. We know they take the names of animals. Have you ever met a man named Hedgehog?"

"You've made a mistake. I've already told you all I know."

Madame Lamy waved her hand impatiently. "Perhaps you're the one who's making a mistake. Come on, give me something, a description even, and we'll remain friends."

"You and I are not friends."

"Yes, we are, though you don't seem to realize it yet. Look, I'm offering you a way out. But I have to give the Milice something. Otherwise — such a pretty child. There are quotas to be met here in the South, you know, for Jews." Her voice held a faint distaste, as if the child had a contagious disease.

Juliette's stomach clenched. She remained perfectly still, though the knuckles of her clasped hands were now white. Madame Lamy had no idea she'd hired the Wolf to work in her fields. He was steps away. Should she, could she, trade him for Sophie?

Silence. Then cold as a sliver of ice, "What exactly do you want to know?"

Sylvie Lamy smiled. "That's better. We want your contact in Toulouse, but most of all, we want Hedgehog. Have you ever seen him?"

Juliette pinned her hopes on the incorrect pronoun. "I saw him once. I can describe him." The words seemed to burn her mouth. "But I'll say nothing until I see Sophie. How do I know you haven't already turned her over?"

"This is foolish. You're not in a position to make demands. I could simply report you, let the Milice do their own questioning."

"I don't think so. First, you'd have to explain why you've kept us here so long. But then perhaps they've known all along? In which case you'd lose your usefulness to them and your profits from future travellers. That would be a shame, given that the villa is so costly to keep up."

Juliette's guess was accurate. How many others before her had believed the villa was a safe house, only to find themselves blackmailed for money or information? Madame Lamy kept up the false smile, but Juliette could sense that greed, and her need for self-importance, were weaknesses she could exploit. The one thing she didn't know was how long she could keep up her own part in this deadly game.

"Very well. I'll fetch Sophie tomorrow. But she'll stay inside, with Laurette, until your information checks out. And you must work in the kitchen until the harvest is in. You'd best not do anything to upset Laurette. She has a temper."

Juliette stood up and walked away, through the kitchen, across the courtyard and into the stable. She held her head high, but her heart was pounding. They hadn't handed over Sophie yet. If only she could get the child safely into the hands of the Wolf, she didn't care what they would do to her.

"Renée? Are you there?"

She reached down, grasped his hand and helped him into the loft. She was glad for the darkness. He could not see the wreckage of her face, strained with worry and stained with tears.

"They've taken Sophie," she whispered.

"What?"

"It's a trap. They want information in exchange for Sophie." Slowly, in a voice as brittle as glass, she told the Wolf all that had happened. "If Lamy brings her back to the villa tomorrow, you have to get her away."

She could see the outline of his body as he moved away and slumped down on one of the mattresses against the wall. She knelt down beside him, took his hand. He was only a boy, after all. "We'll need help."

He squeezed her hand. "I'll go tonight. You still have your bicycle?"

"In the courtyard."

He stood up. "I can be back before dawn."

"And then?"

"If Lamy brings Sophie back, trade me."

Juliette's breath stopped. She couldn't speak.

"No, listen to me. Stall for time. Tell her you'll lead her to the Wolf, but get her away from the villa. She'll make you leave Sophie behind with the housemaid, but at least we'll split them up. Tell her I'll be at the chapel. Do you know where it is?"

"I think so. I've seen it in the distance."

She remembered. The chapel with the scallop shells and the gun. "When?" The single word fell from her mouth like a death knell.

"I'll give you a signal. You'll know. But bring her at night."

He left her alone in the darkness, with the acid knowledge that she was prepared to sacrifice one child for the life of another.

October 18

Sylvie Lamy brought Sophie back just after four o'clock in the afternoon.

Juliette had counted every minute of every hour of that interminable day. She rushed to the courtyard when she heard the car, but Jacques had beaten her there. Sophie's face was buried in his fur. She looked up and smiled at Juliette.

Her clothes were ragged, her face was dirty. She was beautiful.

Juliette started toward her, but Sylvie intervened. She hadn't returned alone. The man accompanying her was well-fed, his sandy hair slick with brilliantine. He wore a grey suit, immaculately pressed. He held out a manicured hand. His grey eyes were cold.

"Let me present Monsieur Marin."

Juliette nodded, her fingers barely grazing his hand. She was repulsed at the touch of his skin. She moved to avoid him, looked beyond him toward Sophie. He took a step to the side to block her path, the slightest of movements, filled with menace.

As if on cue, Sylvie Lamy's voice floated over the courtyard. "Come along, Sophie. It's time for a bath. Would you like to bring Jacques? Yes?"

Juliette smiled as she passed by, looked into the black eyes for a moment. *She isn't frightened,* she thought. *She doesn't know what's happening.* She felt her muscles relax slightly. Wherever they had hidden Sophie, she hadn't been mistreated.

Her eyes swung back to Marin, who was studying her closely.

"I look forward to our conversation, *mam'zelle*. I know you'll do your best for the little girl." A flat, even voice, without edge, without colour, it gave nothing away.

Juliette turned, walked back to the villa, so he would not see how he filled her with dread.

Inside, Laurette had vanished from the kitchen, leaving Juliette to cope with the evening meal for the harvesters on her own. The old woman, no doubt guarding Sophie, would be certain to keep them from each other. But Sophie was here at least, so close. And the Wolf was in the field again, his midnight ride to Toulouse and back apparently unnoticed. All she had to do was play her part. She thought of the young boy's courage, his willingness to face the enemy in the chapel. She prayed that she could match him in her test with Marin.

After several hours of rushing to and fro in the kitchen, her stomach tightening into a knot, she heard the harvesters singing in the field, a signal that their work was done for the day. They lined up on either side of the long table set in the courtyard, the gold of twilight burnishing the weathered faces. Juliette began moving down the line, ladling a thick chicken stew into their bowls. She stopped by the gypsy boy, wearing a red neckerchief, served him, moved on. Was this the signal? She hadn't seen him wearing it before, but many of the harvesters wore neckerchiefs. What if she were wrong? She longed to approach him, knew she mustn't. On the opposite side of the table from him now, she glanced over, raised a hand to her neck, a question in her eyes. He didn't look at her.

She moved back and forth, from the kitchen to the table, back and forth in her mind. Was this the signal, or not? She felt like screaming. The meal dragged on. Then, with the suddenness of an autumn night, the men were gone. She rushed to the kitchen window, watched them joking and laughing as they crossed the yard to the harvester's cabin. Someone handed the gypsy a bottle of wine. He swung it up, took a long swallow and disappeared from her view into the cabin.

She heard a growl from behind her. "You'd best clean up. There's still work to be done."

Laurette mocked Juliette's posture from the day before, arms crossed over her chest, refusing to help.

Juliette pushed past her, gathering empty dishes onto a serving tray.

And then she found it, a single scallop shell, nestled against the Wolf's empty bowl. Quickly, she slipped it into the pocket of her skirt. It weighed nothing, but to her it felt like a piece of armour, armour she would wear when she faced Marin.

Sylvie Lamy called her to the living room at ten o'clock. Juliette had had to serve dinner to her and Marin an hour earlier, a task made to demean her while they chatted idly of a reinvigorated France, the wisdom of Pétain, a cleansed and pious future.

Their hypocrisy fed her anger, reshaping her fear into steely determination. She kept her contempt for them from her eyes, crossed the room to the chair that had been left for her, deliberately placed under a lamp. She transformed herself as she bowed her head, became what they wanted to see. She let her hands tremble nervously over her skirt, glanced up meekly.

Across the room, Sylvie Lamy preened in a dress of blue satin, while Marin wore a wolfish grimace and took the lead, as she knew he would.

"I understand you've met the man who goes by the name of Hedgehog."

"Y-yes."

"Where?"

"In Lyon. He met my train."

"Why are you so important? I find it hard to believe you would warrant such attention."

"I wasn't alone. There were others."

"Other Jews? Escapees?"

"Yes. And a man. An agent I think. I don't know his name. He and Hedgehog went off together. I stayed behind to meet my contact."

"How do you know this man was Hedgehog?"

"My contact. He was excited to see him, he let the name slip."

"You're lying."

"No." Tears came to her eyes.

"Perhaps you are the agent, *non?* How did you manage to cross the demarcation line into Lyon?"

"I have papers, an *Ausweis.*"

"Worthless. We already know you're not who you claim to be. Do you think Madame Lamy has not already searched your room, checked your papers?"

"Check again. The papers are stamped in Lyon."

A laugh, quickly strangled. "Well done, Renée. Perhaps you're not the milksop you seem. Who are you, really?"

"This is not about me. The deal is Sophie in exchange for whatever I can tell you. You must let some people go, otherwise the Wolf would never have trusted you. Let us go, and I'll give you the Wolf."

Marin hesitated, only for a second. But in that second, Juliette knew as clearly as if he'd spoken aloud that he'd never planned to release them. She was fighting for Sophie's life.

"Very well. Describe this Hedgehog."

"I can do better than that. I can draw him, if you bring me paper and pencil."

Marin nodded at Sylvie. She disappeared without a word, a column of blue satin, and came back with the drawing materials. Juliette moved to a side table, dropped to her knees, the pencil moving slowly across the page. She took her time, controlled her breathing. When she was finished, she handed Marin a sketch that captured as best she could the features of the *gardien* from rue des Beaux-Arts in Paris.

"Give this picture to the Wolf. He'll know at once that you can identify Hedgehog."

Marin studied the image greedily, his brows raised.

"Such a plain man? We've reports that he is tall and blond, a man with a powerful build. This is some trick."

"You've heard what people want you to hear. He is indistinguishable, a man of small stature easily melting into a crowd. But if you show this to the Wolf, in that moment of recognition, you'll know I'm telling you the truth."

"*Eh bien.* Who is this Wolf?"

"A young man, here in Toulouse."

"Name?"

"I know him only as the Wolf." Juliette held her breath. The easy part was over.

"Draw him. We'll pick him up. If your story is true, we'll let you go."

"No. I don't trust you, Monsieur Marin. Once you have the

Wolf, you could arrest me. But I'll lead you to him, just you, me and Sophie. Tonight. Once you have him, Sophie and I will go."

"I could arrest you now."

"You could. But then you won't get the Wolf as easily. Prisoners talk. The news always gets out. Hedgehog will never use this safe house again. But this way, quietly, you have the chance that the Wolf could lead you to others, perhaps eventually to the Hedgehog's door. Your choice."

"And is this what you would choose for the child? Arrest and imprisonment?"

"I've done my best for her. Either we leave, or we're arrested. Our fates are intertwined. She could scarcely hope to survive on her own without me in any case."

"That's certainly true. Perhaps the only truth you've spoken. You expect me to take you into Toulouse tonight, after curfew?"

"I've said nothing about meeting him in Toulouse."

The room fell silent, but for the whisper of her own breathing. Somewhere close, behind a closed door, Sophie lay sleeping. Juliette had never gambled anything more precious.

"If not Toulouse, then where?" Marin's voice was as cold as his eyes.

"Close by. We can walk there in twenty minutes or so."

"*C'est impossible*," protested Sylvie. "I know the people who live nearby."

"Did I say he lived here? We have a meeting place. Last night I left him a note. The Wolf is waiting for me as we speak; for how much longer I can't say."

"It's a trap. Don't listen to her."

Marin held up a hand. Sylvie shut up instantly.

"Your little game intrigues me, *mam'zelle*. You are not the desperate young woman that Madame Lamy described. In my experience, people sometimes tell a foolish lie to cover up some deeper, more dangerous one. Perhaps you yourself are the prize, more valuable to us than the Wolf. I'm curious. Let's see where you might lead me in the countryside. But, if it is an ambush," he paused long enough to remove a pistol from his jacket and laid it on the table, "you will be the first to die. And the child stays here, my insurance."

"How do I know you will let her go?"

"It seems we must both make a leap of faith."

Juliette looked away. The Wolf had been right. She would have to leave Sophie behind, put her faith in a boy, a chapel she hoped she could find in the darkness, a gun hidden behind a statue of St. James. From here forward, every step would be improvised. She had no idea what her ally planned, only that she must lead this dreadful man to him.

The night was cold and clear, the fields silvered by the moon. Juliette struck a path through the vines, Marin close behind her carrying a torch. Every step took her further away from Sophie, closer to the unknown.

They came to a narrow road, a pale river of dirt stretching away from the villa, curving slowly uphill to disappear in a rocky tor. If she remembered correctly, the chapel was just beyond the rocks where the land dipped into a gentle hollow with grass and fir trees.

She could hear Marin behind her, his breath labouring as they climbed. At the crest, she stood silhouetted in the moonlight, the chapel below, looking abandoned and desolate. "There," she said, pointing a finger. "He'll be waiting in the chapel."

"Keep moving."

They picked their way down the hillside, sliding on loose stones. A breeze fingered the limbs of the trees in the hollow.

Juliette stopped. "Give me the torch."

"Why?" Suspiciously.

"He's waiting for my signal."

He thrust it toward her. "Remember, you still have a gun at your back."

She flicked the torch on and off, on and off, three times.

Nothing. The chapel slumbered on, buried in decades of neglect.

She tried again, this time sweeping the torch to and fro, like a searchlight.

She clicked off the torch, waited. The darkness thickened around her. She felt desolate. It had been a mistake to improvise a signal. A sudden agitation seized her, the sense of something broken loose, veering out of control inside her. Marin was stirring behind her, impatient.

She closed her eyes. Opened them to a flicker of light, a candle burning behind a grimy window.

"There, he's there." Her words were spoken in an exhalation of breath.

Marin prodded her forward, wrenching the torch from her hand. She walked stiffly, reached for the door, saw that someone before her had crushed the grass and weeds crowding the entry. She pushed.

Inside, the chapel swam in a murky light, a single votive candle playing over the features of the small statue of St. James raised on a pedestal. The air smelled dank, like brackish water.

She heard a voice, a harsh whisper. "Renée?"

It was not the Wolf's voice.

Marin raised his pistol to Juliette's temple at the same moment as he flooded the small room with blinding light from his torch, catching a startled face coming toward them in its beam.

By the time Marin noticed the gun in the man's right hand, he was barely two metres away. Juliette lunged to the floor as Marin opened his mouth to scream. The first shot blew off his lower jaw. He fell to his knees, shooting blindly, a bullet crashing into the wall just inches from Juliette's head. She cringed, terrified, as a second shot caught Marin in the chest, spinning him around. He fell, lifeless, at her elbow.

For a ghastly moment, the torch rolled across the floor, circles of light rolling over the stone, casting bizarre shadows on the walls. The man leaned forward and picked it up.

"Are you all right?"

She raised herself to her knees, looked up into his face, about to speak when, without warning, another shot rang out from the direction of the open door. The impact of the bullet, like the muffled blow of a hammer, caught the man in the back and threw him against her. Staggering with the force of his weight, she twisted away, dove to the foot of St. James, and pulled herself up behind the statue where the Wolf had hidden the gun.

"You'll hang for this," a voice hissed from the chapel doorway. *Sylvie Lamy. She'd followed them.*

Juliette picked up the gun. She didn't think, just felt the resistance of the trigger as her finger tightened around it, her hand steady, her aim sure. She fired, the explosion ringing in her ears.

Lamy crumpled in the doorway.

Juliette walked in a daze to where her fallen rescuer lay unmoving. She searched for a pulse, but could feel not even a flicker.

She swallowed a sob, put the gun in her skirt pocket, crossed the chapel floor and stepped over the body of Sylvie Lamy, red blood on blue satin.

Then she ran.

She ran until she saw two figures outlined on the hillside where she had stood with Marin minutes before. The taller one waved.

She scrambled up the hill, hugged Sophie to her breast.

"Laurette is dead," the Wolf said. "We have to disappear."

WINTER

1942–1943

G

November 27

Gabrielle obeyed the priest. It was not so much a conscious decision as an inevitability. She had no leads, no one to turn to for
help. Several times, she saw Dietsz at the *boulangerie*, where he
was stiffly courteous, nothing more. She felt he had abandoned his
search for Meyer's killer, his debt to her repaid. Étienne Fougères
filed his report. Somewhere in a drawer, it gathered dust.

She puzzled over what Père Albert had said to her. Perhaps
Klaus had found the money — the simplest explanation, after all
— and given it to Marie-Claire. Perhaps she had been killed for it.
If the priest was trying to trace any names Marie-Claire might have
given him, he was taking his time.

She felt split in two again. Gabrielle during the day, over and
over again the same dull routine, the ache of loneliness, the fear of
drifting, of making a mistake. At night, Amélie. Countless times,
she had answered a midnight knock on her window. Once, Yves
had brought two children, a brother and sister; another time, three
men, downed pilots, one of them with a smashed leg. The children
had terrified her. Three days they had stayed, and each night they
had nightmares and cried out and would not stay in the bedroom.
She'd taken them into her own bed to keep them quiet, to muffle
their screams. The men were easier. They shared her certainty that
the slightest accident — a figure glimpsed through a window by
someone walking along the road, a sound out of place, a jealous
eye noticing extra rations — could bring a German to the door.
They spoke little, sensing that their interlude with her was fragile,
that anything at anytime could shatter it. The injured pilot had
been delirious with pain and told her rumours of concentration

camps that made her skin crawl. Being sent east to Germany was to be sent into a fog, a terrible, thick fog in which no one was ever recognized and from which no one seemed to return.

The faces that came and went were always thanking her and it made her feel ashamed. They thought she was being kind, taking risks for them, and she didn't know how to tell them it wasn't true. She was empty at the core. Their coming filled her up. The tight, unnatural beating of her heart when they were hidden in her home made her feel alive. She thought of the forest animals, how they lived purely instinctually, how a cat, in a sudden burst of animal frenzy, climbed the bark of a tree, gloriously alive in the moment, in every fibre of its being. Being Amélie was like that.

Then the morning would come, or the people would move on, and she would coax herself into becoming Gabrielle again, disciplining herself to carry on with a life that had lost its meaning. Madame Pascal noticed, but for once misread the signs of strain.

"We're patching up the escape line," she said. "Soon we'll have new routes. We'll not have to put you in such danger."

Gabrielle smiled, feeling false and flat.

That afternoon she found a message from Yves at Jean's grave, and wondered if it would be the last.

Long after sunset, she wrapped herself in a thick shawl and waited outside for Yves, leaning against the wall of her cottage until he stepped forward, his head a mass of short, dark curls, rumpled trousers sagging on slim hips.

"I've brought you something."

"Not someone?"

"Not tonight." He pointed to the sack he carried and grinned.

Inside the cottage, he made her close her eyes, like a boy playing a game. When she opened them, a radio was sitting on the kitchen table. She could hardly believe it, reached a tentative hand toward it.

"Go on," he laughed. "It won't bite."

She unwound the thick brown cord and plugged it in. Yves reached out to turn it on. The sudden static shocked them and they both jumped. Quickly, he turned down the volume. She leaned over his shoulder, barely able to read the tiny dial in the moonlight, as he scrolled through the transmission frequencies. She listened in a kind of wonder as the wider world she had almost forgotten whispered to her. Parisian French, Flemish, Dutch, Danish.

"Listen," he said. "English. The BBC."

She nodded, recognizing the sound of the language but not its meaning. "Can you translate?"

"Sure. I'm the radio contact for my unit. There are still bombs in London … British flyers are winning the war in the air. Wait a moment. The best part is coming."

She listened to the announcer, saw Yves' face light up. "What?" she asked impatiently.

"Aunt Mabel is visiting her niece tomorrow. The man who ate rabbit cooked in white wine wishes to thank his hosts."

She laughed. "You're crazy. What did he really say?"

"No, it's code."

"Code?"

"A way of sending information in case the Germans are listening in. It sounds like nonsense, but it means something to someone. The man who ate rabbit, for example, names his last meal at a safe house. That way, the escape network knows he's made it home."

"And the ones who stayed here, did they send codes like this?"

"Some of them."

She nodded. She didn't ask who had made it, who hadn't. There would always be a part of the story untold.

The announcer stopped talking, his voice replaced by a jaunty tune.

"Irving Berlin," Yves said. He leaned back in his chair so that his face was in darkness beyond the reach of the moonlight. Softly, he began to hum along with the music. "Do you like to dance, Amélie?"

She stood up, executed a graceful pirouette, stumbling out of it at the last moment, laughing. "I used to be good at it. My body's forgotten. You?"

"I like jazz and swing, though I couldn't dance like the *Zazous* in Paris. They slicked back their hair, wore suit coats with wide lapels. The Nazis hated them, called them degenerates."

"In Paris. Was Luc Garnier born there?"

He was silent. The music played on. Aaron Copland. Glenn Miller. He knew them all. He leaned forward, took her hand. "You must forget that name, Amélie, as I have forgotten that life."

She nodded, felt she had strayed too close. Inside this room, they were Amélie and Yves, two people without a past and with an uncertain future. He gathered her into his arms and they danced in the moonlight, their bodies swaying in unison to the rhythm of the music.

"You'd better go," she said. "It's dangerous to have the radio on."

At the back window, he leaned forward, kissed her on the cheek. She looked into the dark eyes, at his lips, almost trembling. It seemed to her that they parted a little, and that his fingers were reaching for her face. She moved away abruptly and looked down. "It's too soon," she whispered.

They stood motionless, the silence heavy around them. Then, in a husky voice, "I'll come again, Amélie. Perhaps we'll dance again."

She smiled, and watched him go.

Christmas Day

Bells. Gabrielle walked to the church, meeting neighbours along the way, faces lit with joy from the glorious, rippling sound. The bells were a gift from Dietsz, a rare concession. Nobody wanted to think of the war today. She wore a navy woollen dress under her black coat, a small departure from her mourning clothes, a gesture to happier memories.

The church was decorated with boughs of pine from the forest and swirls of red ribbon. Gabrielle hesitated at the threshold, remembering the sea of white flowers she had knelt among in July. She shivered, stepped forward reluctantly. Beneath the wreaths and the ribbon, the church interior looked shabby and unloved. She wondered how many others had lost their faith; how many, like her, bowed their heads to words that had lost their meaning, clinging to the familiarity of ritual. She closed her eyes, listened to the rich, sonorous tones of Père Albert's voice, sang the *cantiques de Noël*. She didn't line up to take communion, caught the stern glance of the priest and shrugged.

She heard rustling and whispers from the back of the church and looked around. She saw Dietsz standing just inside the door, the unwelcome guest at the party. Their eyes met and he nodded. She flushed and turned away. Did Kommandanturs believe in God? Did they go to confession? Did they think they could be forgiven? She wondered how he felt about the villagers of St-Léger. Mouths that wished him *bonjour, bonne nuit.* Eyes that wished him dead. She crushed the stirring of compassion she felt for him. It was too dangerous, too complicated to think of Dietsz as an ordinary outsider. His authority prevented it.

When the mass ended, there were presents for the children, wrapped in newspaper and tied with string: mittens and hats knit from unravelled blankets and worn-out sweaters, toy animals carved from wood, boiled candy made from long-saved stores of sugar. Gabrielle laughed along with the children, and felt lighter.

When she left the church with Madame Pascal, she looked back once, saw Dietsz deep in conversation with Père Albert, the silver head and the blond head almost touching. She nudged her companion.

"What's that about?"

"I'm not sure. The priest has been troubled lately. He's been spending a lot of time in Dun-les-Places, and has been to the Abbaye de la Pierre-qui-Vire several times."

"You don't think Dietsz suspects him?"

"No, the Père is too clever for that. But Dietsz is a strange one. Not even I can read him. It's Eber we must watch out for. That one would arrest his own shadow if he thought it had stretched too far. But enough of this. I have a chicken to roast and a cake in the oven."

The meal was as festive as the old woman and plenty of local wine could make it. The doctor brought his pretty wife and two young children. Joseph told the little boys stories and bounced them like feathers on his thick knees. When he'd drunk enough wine, he tapped his glass and offered a simple toast to Jean. Gabrielle hugged him for it, glad to have the invisible presence acknowledged.

Afterwards, she walked across the square with Madame Pascal to visit Marie-Claire's parents. Their home was quiet and dim. A candle had been lit beside a photograph of their daughter, a smile forever frozen on her lips. It was difficult to look at it.

Gabrielle was in the kitchen brewing an herbal tea when Marie-Claire's mother approached her with a package wrapped in wrinkled tissue paper.

"She would want you to have this. You were her only true friends, you and Jean. Please, take it. There's a letter inside, too, from Klaus. It came after ... well, we couldn't bear to open it."

Gabrielle kissed her. Her hands trembled when she took the parcel.

They stayed for an hour, the minutes crawling by.

At dusk, she said her goodbyes to Madame Pascal and hurried along the road to her cottage. In the distance, the forest was silver, brushed with frost. Dark wings flashed against the lavender sky as a flock of birds plunged and swept upward in tight formation, finally disappearing amid the trees.

A familiar figure waited at her door.

"*Joyeux Noël,*" said Père Albert.

"*Et toi,*" Gabrielle smiled. Though glad of his friendship, she had to fight to hide her impatience. All she wanted to do was rip open Klaus' letter.

She invited the priest inside, and busied herself making tea. The parcel she'd placed on the table was like a magnet. Her eyes kept straying to it. She barely listened as her old friend rambled on about his day.

Finally, she could stand the waiting no longer.

"*Excusez-moi,*" she interrupted. She picked up the parcel and climbed the stairs, leaving Père Albert to stare after her.

She closed her bedroom door and tore off the parcel's brown paper wrapping. Inside was a wooden box. She opened its carved lid. The unopened letter lay on top of a jumble of cheap trinkets and costume jewellery.

She slid a finger under the seal, unfolded the single page. Her eyes scanned the writing. A few love phrases in broken French, but mostly German. She almost cried in frustration. The characters meant nothing to her. She couldn't read them. She caught only names — Meyer, Dietsz, Gabrielle. What could it mean? Why and how had Klaus linked the three names? She knew only one person who spoke the language, yet she hesitated, uncertain whether to trust him, or whether she already trusted him too much.

Her need to know what the letter said overwhelmed her. She marched back to the kitchen and thrust the page at the priest. "I'm sorry, *mon père*, I can't think of anything else right now. This is a letter from Klaus to Marie-Claire. Her parents gave it to me."

Startled, Père Albert took the page and scanned it. "My German is poor, but I have friends who could translate this. You think it so important?"

"I think it might tell us the name of the killer."

"And it might be only a sad farewell, a private matter. Calm yourself, Gabrielle. I see you've not given up your pursuit, despite my warnings."

"I've tried."

"You must try harder. It is the season of forgiveness and peace, despite the war, *non?*"

Gabrielle nodded, but she couldn't believe in the priest's words. She felt no peace.

Later, after Père Albert had left, she sat alone in the dark, then sighed and went up to bed. She wondered if she was still in danger, and if she were, what direction it would come from. She curled her knees to her chest and whispered, "I miss you, Jean. I'm so afraid." ,

January 15, 1943

Gabrielle was sleepy and clumsy. Yves had come in the pale grey just before dawn to take away the last pilot. The line was mended. They wouldn't need her cottage any longer. She'd been glad to see the pilot go — he'd asked too many questions, had even asked her name. He was only frightened, she told herself, bewildered by where he was and where he might next be taken, but the questions made her uneasy. Yves had warned her that the Germans sometimes fed their own airmen into the escape lines, men who pretended to be English or Canadian or American. They'd be sheltered, passed through the network, only to expose, at the end, all those who'd taken them in.

By nine o'clock at the *boulangerie*, the queue for bread was at its longest. She'd had no time to glance out the window, hadn't seen the sleek black car glide into the square. When the bell rang yet again above the shop door, she didn't bother to look up, not until she noticed the hush in the room, a palpable shift in the atmosphere. Eber. Her heart skipped.

He strode to the front of the line, the villagers shrinking away from him.

"You will come with me, Madame Aubin." The voice was flat, the face menacing.

She stared at the scar on his forehead, avoiding his eyes, unable to move. Madame Pascal was suddenly at her side. "What is this? What's going on?"

He ignored her, his eyes never wavering from Gabrielle's face. "Now, unless you want me to arrest everyone in the shop."

Madame Pascal sputtered a protest. He cut it off with one glance.

Gabrielle removed her apron, her hands shaking and clumsy. She walked like a robot to the backroom and fetched her coat. With every ounce of strength she had, she smiled at her old friend. "It's all right. I'm sure it's some mistake."

She walked to the door, her back stiff, Eber behind her. She felt the gaze of the villagers, those in the shop, those outside in the square. People stopped, almost in mid-step. The wind blew up and her eyes stung. She dipped her head, slid into the back seat of the car, Eber climbing in beside her. He grunted something to the driver and as they pulled away from the square, she saw Joseph. Their eyes met for an instant before he turned away, walking quickly toward the *mairie*.

The car began to gain speed. She felt close to panic when she realized Eber was not taking her to the *gendarmerie*.

"Where are we going?" She was sorry to hear how small her voice sounded to her own ears, a child's voice.

His head turned slowly and a smile crossed his fleshy face.

She looked away, sorry she'd spoken and betrayed her fear. They were travelling south, on one of the roads that twisted through the Morvan. She saw the turnoff to Dun-les-Places and thought about Yves. Perhaps he had been caught. Perhaps the last pilot had betrayed them. When they passed Lac des Settons, with its wooded islands, she knew with a cold certainty that Eber was taking her to the garrison at Château-Chinon, Gestapo headquarters.

It was raining by the time they reached the garrison. She played a game with herself, tried to match her breathing to the rhythm of the windshield wipers, anything to keep her heart from racing out of control. But her mind kept flipping back to Jean's face, how it had looked after they had beaten him. The thought of physical pain made her feel sick. She realized she was a coward, and the brutal knowledge stunned her. She was afraid to open her mouth, afraid that words would pour from her throat like blood.

She was ordered from the car, and almost slipped on the cobblestones of the courtyard. She tried to tell herself that they were slippery from the rain, but she knew her legs were trembling.

Eber flicked a finger and an armed soldier pushed her forward. He steered her inside, down a long hallway. She could hear typing and German voices behind a series of closed doors. They made a turn to the right down another hallway, paused before a low, thick door.

Eber shouted something over his shoulder in German, and the soldier turned her around to retrace their steps back around the corner. They entered an office. The soldier pushed her into a chair and stood behind her. There was a desk across from her, and there was Eber behind the desk, a second door to his rear.

Slowly, he removed his gloves, tugging on each finger, one at a time. When he was finished, he walked around the desk and leaned toward her. His hand moved so quickly, she didn't see the blow coming. Stunned by the burning sting of leather across her cheek, she clutched the arms of the chair.

"You and your friends in the Resistance have been busy, *non?*"

She said nothing, body clenched for another assault. *How much did he know?* She thought of Madame Pascal, remembered she would have to last forty-eight hours, knew in a flash of certainty that she couldn't.

This time, she caught the movement of his hand as he removed it from his pocket, opened his clenched fist over her lap. She scrabbled backwards, her hands brushing at the object on her skirt. A miniature carved coffin fell to the floor. She stared at it, astonished. *What was he doing? Why this?*

"You are a dangerous woman to know, Madame Aubin. Your friends die. First your husband, then the woman Marie-Claire, now the priest."

The priest?

"Ah, you look so surprised. But I am used to the art of liars. What happened? Did he stumble onto your secret?"

"I don't know what you're talking about." The words came out as a whisper.

"Very well. We will play your little game. I prefer it that way."

She closed her eyes, certain he would strike her again, but he stepped away. When she glanced up, he was smiling again, his tongue running over his lips.

She felt a violent push from behind and her chair crashed forward, her arms and legs splaying instinctively to break her fall. She had forgotten the other soldier. She staggered to her knees, then froze as the muzzle of a pistol pressed against her cheek.

"Now, let us begin again. How long have you worked for the Resistance?"

If she let herself say anything, she would say everything. She clamped her lips shut.

"When was the last time you saw the priest?"

Nothing. The gun dug harder against her cheek.

"You may as well confirm what the priest already told us. It's why you killed him, is it not?"

He's lying. Père Albert was strong. Not like me.

She heard the click as the soldier drew back the hammer. The sound flicked a switch in her head. Animal instinct took over, the instinct of a hunted animal in the forest that turns to meet its death when it's hopelessly cornered. She let go of Gabrielle, and found Amélie. She lifted her head and looked straight into the eyes of the soldier.

"Do it."

His eyes widened in surprise.

The moment was broken by shouting in the hallway, a commotion of voices. The door to the office burst open.

Dietsz.

In two strides, he was pushing the soldier aside and pulling her up from her knees. The room swirled around her, a cacophony of angry German bouncing back and forth between Dietsz and Eber.

Then she was simply walking away, down the hall. Dazed, she risked a glance at Dietsz, striding along beside her. His profile was like a stone carving.

Cold air on her face, rain. Across the courtyard stood a woman, tall and thin, beside a Gestapo car, watching her. Her short brown hair was drenched, wide brown eyes alert, watchful. Gabrielle stared at her, her heart wrenching. How lucky she was to walk away from the place this stranger was about to enter. With a look, she willed the woman courage. Then she ducked into Dietsz's car and he pulled away. When she twisted around to look back, the woman was holding out her hands to the rain. She didn't look afraid. Not like Gabrielle.

*

J

November 3

Martres-Tolosane, St-Martory, Lannemezan — the market villages were small and sleepy all the way to Pau. Their nights and days were inverted. They walked mostly at night, skirting the roads, the Wolf often carrying Sophie. During the days, they slept when they could in fields, woods, even barns when they were lucky enough to find a friendly face that asked no questions. Once, they scrambled over the high wall of a cemetery and slept among the tombstones. When they neared the villages, they braved the daytime and were sometimes able to hitch rides on horse-drawn farm wagons filled with sweet hay. At Tarbes, they met a salesman who drove them into the heart of Pau, leaving them on the boulevard des Pyrénées, the horizon crowded with snow-capped mountains.

Even the days were chilly now, the nights cold. The sidewalk tables had packed up for the season, retreating into the smoky interiors of cafés and bistros. It was here in one of these cafés, as they sat counting out the last of their money to see what they could afford to eat, that Sophie saw the first poster. She tugged at Juliette's arm and pointed.

It was a crude sketch, pasted to the wall behind the cash register, two barely recognizable faces. Renée Lachaisse and Serge Degrave, wanted for the murder of three citizens in Toulouse. They gathered up their francs and left quickly.

Outside, the Wolf turned to her. "No one would recognize us. Don't worry. When we reach Oloron-Ste-Marie, Javier will help us."

Oloron-Ste-Marie and Javier, the two magic words that had kept her going, kept her hope alive. The Wolf's contacts in Toulouse had set up a meeting with Javier, a guide they could trust.

She lifted her eyes to the snowy peaks. Another barrier, one she could scarcely imagine. She took Sophie's hand. She realized as they began walking that her memories of Luc were dissolving. There'd been too many tightropes to walk, too many days of hiding. Sadly, she no longer dreamed of him. She dreamed of food and warm clothes, and sometimes of blood, red poppies bursting open on a blue dress.

November 8

Oloron-Ste-Marie, an ancient town, stood at the mouth of the Aspe valley at the confluence of the *gaves*, the mountain rivers of d'Aspe and d'Ossau. Even this late in the year, the vista was mesmerizing, the soft contours of the valley floor contrasting with the jutting angles of the mountains, emerald green foliage spilling into dark blue, almost purple water, against a background of crystal snow.

Juliette watched their breath making plumes in the air, Sophie leaning against her thigh for warmth. Hollowed out by exhaustion, Juliette filled her lungs with the fresh, chilled air, letting the beauty fill her up, trying to take strength from the land as she had since she was a child. She knew that treachery lay on the other side of the valley, the treachery of the climb, but she hoped the memory of this landscape, seemingly untouched by the devious, nebulous war of Unoccupied France, would feed her courage.

The Wolf touched her arm, and they turned away reluctantly, back toward the town which suddenly seemed dwarfed and insignificant. They climbed through narrow streets, past a twelfth-century church, finally stopping before a large stone house with green shutters, now an improvised lodging for hikers and skiers. The Wolf knocked on the door.

"We'll take rooms," he said. "Javier will meet us here."

"But we have no money left. How can we —"

A woman of indeterminate age, somewhere between forty and sixty, opened the door, her hair invisible beneath a white kerchief knotted behind her neck in the Basque fashion, her hands flapping.

"Come in, come in. My son expects you." She was like a large bird, fluttering around them, hands lighting for a moment on Sophie's head, then waving them along a corridor and up a flight of stairs, her nose like a sharp beak, her eyes glittering. "In here," she chirped.

She pushed Juliette and Sophie forward into a small room with a sloped roof and pine plank walls, a large bed covered with a thick white eiderdown under a high window, a copper bath in the corner. A bath. Juliette's knees weakened. She heard a gurgle of laughter from the Wolf as the door closed behind her.

Half an hour later, two pairs of bent knees touching, she regarded Sophie at the opposite end of the bath, water dripping from her drenched corkscrew curls. Their skin was warm and soapy, rosy from scrubbing and steam.

"I like baths," the child said.

"Mmm."

"Wolf says we'll climb the mountain. Will he come, too?"

"I don't know. I hope so."

"Do we need money? My papa has some."

Juliette stayed very still. It was rare for Sophie to speak of her lost family.

"They've been gone a long time," Sophie continued. "I know the bad people took them away."

"I'm afraid so."

A long pause. Then, "What's on the other side of the mountain?"

"Spain. Do you remember Frère Jean-Claude? Remember we talked about the kind family that is waiting for you in Scotland? You'll be safe there. Once you get to Spain, someone will take you to the family."

"I don't want to go. I want to stay with you."

It was the inevitable moment Juliette had dreaded. She felt her bones softening, her heart coming to a standstill.

"It's what I want too, *ma chérie*. More than anything. But I'll make you a promise, like I made Mathilde. When the war is over, and it will be over someday, I'll find you and we'll be together always." *If I'm still alive, if we both don't die on the mountain.* "You must be brave, Sophie. Brave like the Wolf."

She climbed out of the bath, lifted Sophie up. They dried themselves on thick towels, pulled on clean cotton shirts they found folded on the bed. She caught Sophie up in a hug.

There were no tears, but something in the child's face had closed, her full lips set in a serious expression. They climbed under the lavender-scented eiderdown, Sophie's arms clinging to her tightly. Gradually, the arms relaxed. Sophie rolled over, one cheek pressed against the battered rag doll, and slept. Juliette closed her eyes, the little girl's face tugging at her heart.

The dining space of the lodge was not crowded. The three fugitives ate hungrily, scooping up the gravy from the stew with slabs of bread. Across the room, two men lit up cigarettes, the smoke curling up to the ceiling in lazy arabesques. A wet dog slept under their table.

A man in his mid-thirties, slim and sombre-looking, emerged from the direction of the kitchen. He placed two brandies on their table, and with his back toward the smokers, raised a finger to his lips. Sophie, her head propped on her hand, watched him with cat's eyes. He winked at her, a hand disappearing into his pocket then placing a square of chocolate on the table beside her. She grinned at him before he disappeared back to the kitchen.

Javier.

Eventually, the two men rose to leave, the dog following behind them, swinging his heavy head from side to side. As they opened the door, Juliette heard the bells of the church outside, a pure crystal sound rolling across the quiet valley.

The brandy slid down Juliette's throat, and her body relaxed. She allowed herself the luxury of living fully in the moment — safe, warm, clean. The past was a blank, the future on hold. She felt she was floating in another world.

She almost resented the Wolf's interruption.

"What are you thinking?"

"Blissfully, nothing."

"What do you think of Javier?"

"Too soon to tell."

"His wife was killed by the Germans."

"What?" It was like a slap, the intrusion of the reality of a shattered world.

"Javier's wife. She was killed in the civil war. German planes strafed the roads leading into Barcelona."

"You know him?"

"I know *of* him. French mother, Spanish father — he died, too, fighting the Fascists."

She leaned back, resting her head against the wall, closing her eyes. So many stories of pain and loss, she wondered if the world would ever heal from them. She wondered how some people could stagger on, how they could ever mend the gaping holes left in them by missing loved ones. Would Sophie mend? Would she?

She opened her eyes when she heard Javier's footsteps and rose to greet him. He took her hand in his own. Beautiful, strong hands, and old, old eyes. His skin was darkened and leathered by a life of work out-of-doors, a web of wrinkles around deep-set hazel eyes. Black wavy hair swept back from his forehead, a peasant's shirt, a leather vest, thick flannel pants. A mountain man.

He greeted the Wolf, then pulled out a chair and straddled it.

His voice when he spoke was deeper and softer than Juliette had imagined. "How old is the child?"

"Ask her," the Wolf said.

Javier looked at the little girl and raised his eyebrows. She held up seven fingers.

"Ah, that old? I have a son your age. He crosses the mountains with me sometimes, but in the summer." He glanced at the Wolf and Juliette. "It would be better to wait. *C'est possible?*" He read their faces. "*D'accord.* No one can wait these days. Which of you is coming with Sophie?"

The Wolf took Sophie's hand. "All three of us are crossing, if you can manage it."

"Very well. We'll follow the path of the pilgrims, through the pass of Col du Somport, 1,632 metres. It will take thirty stages, perhaps as many as thirty-five with Sophie, some stretches as long as thirty kilometres. I won't lie to you. The French side of the mountains is wet. There will be rain, and higher up, snow. You'll wish you hadn't come. If you stop halfway up the mountain at this time of year, you'll die."

Juliette leaned forward to stop him talking. He was too harsh, too much for Sophie.

He sensed her movement, and turned to the child.

"Don't worry, little one. I've done this a thousand times with smaller ones than you. On the Spanish side of the mountains, a bright sun shines. We'll hire you a mountain pony for the lower slopes." He glanced toward the Wolf. "You'll need warm clothes and proper boots. Do you have money?"

"Papa has," Sophie piped up.

Javier looked at Juliette. She shook her head.

He shrugged. "I have a little put by. More would be useful. It's always easier if you can bribe the guards at the border. I'll see what I can do. We leave in five days. You can stay here until then, rest."

Upstairs, Juliette and Sophie were undressing for bed.

"The Wolf is coming," Sophie whispered. "I knew he would."

The little girl almost danced around the room. She was happy. Juliette realized she didn't fully understand Javier's dire warnings, only that she didn't have to face another parting. Her spirit was contagious and Juliette laughed with her. With the Wolf to help, they would carry Sophie over the mountain if they had to. She picked her up now, swung her in the air. They collapsed onto the bed.

Sophie rolled over onto her stomach, suddenly serious, clutching her doll.

"No one listens to me, Juliette."

"What do you mean? Of course we listen."

"Not about Papa's money. Here." She pushed the doll toward her. "Mathilde sewed it inside. Javier needs it to buy a pony."

Juliette was astonished. She stared at the grimy rag doll, counting all the times it could have been lost or left behind.

She pulled her dress back on. "Wait here," she whispered. She ran down the hall in her bare feet, knocked on the Wolf's door. "Do you have a knife?" she asked when he opened the door. "Come with me."

He followed her without a word, and picked up Sophie who ran to greet him. Her hands shaking, Juliette held the doll under the lamp and ran the Wolf's knife gently down the inside seam of one cloth leg.

She wiggled a finger inside and felt something hard hidden in the stuffing. She enlarged the opening, reached in again. She was holding a diamond, a chip of chiselled sunlight in the palm of her hand. She held it out to the Wolf. "Look!"

He laughed. "Keep going."

When she was finished, she had laid seven diamonds in a line on the night table. Long ago, Papa had had a small jewellery shop. Now Sophie had money enough to bribe a border guard and buy her passage to Scotland.

Juliette kissed the top of her head. "Clever girl," she murmured.

"Clever Papa." She picked up one of the diamonds and handed it to the Wolf. "Give this to Javier. Tell him Sophie wants a pony."

It was mid-afternoon and Juliette was reading a storybook to Sophie when the Wolf burst into the room.

"Hurry. We leave in an hour." He tossed a knapsack toward her, and two pairs of boots. His face was flushed, his chest heaving.

Juliette sprang to her feet. "What's happened? What's wrong? We weren't supposed to leave for two more days."

"The Germans are pouring over the demarcation line. In a few hours, all of France will be occupied. Javier's ready to go. Hurry."

November 11, 1942. The pretence of Pétain's France was over. The mountain was waiting.

After their initial scramble through the valley, their days settled into an inexorable pattern, one exhausting day following another, and another.

Sophie had her pony, shaggy and sure-footed. They travelled in the mornings when the mist kept them safe, rested in the afternoons, then pressed on in the grey smudge of twilight until darkness made their sinuous trail invisible. Their anoraks gave them a modicum of protection from the veils of rain, their thick woollen sweaters and flannel pants, smeared with lanolin and stinking of sheep, kept them almost warm. As they climbed, beech forests gave way to evergreens, Norfolk pine, larch and balsam, the wet air spicy from their scent.

Sometimes, when they stopped to rest, Juliette would look back at the white and green mountain villages in the distance, circles of land Javier called *cirques*, hollowed out thousands of years ago by the grinding of glaciers, stretches of rough pasture and tumbling cascades. She did her best not to look up at what still lay ahead. "Not far," the Wolf would pretend. *The other side of the world*, she would think. The distance between safety and danger couldn't be measured in kilometres.

At night, while Sophie slept, Juliette's body curled around her like a spoon, the adults would whisper together before fatigue silenced them. They were ghostly conversations, Juliette thought, words borne by voices that seemed disembodied in the dark.

Once, a week or so into the journey, the Wolf's voice floated across to her. "We'll have to cross into Spain. It's too risky for us to stay behind now that the Germans have crossed the line."

Yes, she thought. Yes. It would be foolish to stay now. She would be free. She would keep Sophie close. The thought gave her courage, and she almost believed in it.

Two days later, the first snow fell — fat, lazy flakes, but by the time they stopped for food, their footsteps were leaving prints. Javier led them away from the path, looking for shelter. Juliette borrowed his axe, began cutting boughs from the trees.

"What are you doing?" Javier asked.

"You know about mountains. I know about snow. I know how to build a lean-to."

He smiled, but said nothing. There was something ancient about Javier, some quiet centre, eyes that saw much more than they gave away. By morning, the snow had thickened. The Wolf unfastened their packs from the pony, and Javier slapped its rear. "She knows her way home. We'll have to share the weight."

They'd brought very little, mostly food and blankets. Juliette knew the weight was Sophie.

The Wolf opened his arms to the child, but she shook her head, determined to walk, her little face hard, her mouth pressed together.

Up and up they climbed, the snow now topping their boots,

halfway up Sophie's legs. Javier and the Wolf paused, looked back at Juliette and Sophie trailing behind. They were too slow. The men waited for them, watched while Sophie slipped, struggled to her feet and slipped again, this time her face coming up covered in snow. Javier knelt beside her, brushing her cheeks with a mitten, pretending not to notice her tears. "Little goat," he called her, "climb up and keep me warm." She straddled his back, hugged her arms around his neck. "Come on, Juliette," he laughed. "Keep up."

The days blurred together, endless stretches of burning muscles and aching feet. They stepped outside of time and beyond caring, four ants crawling up the face of unflinching granite, hidden among hostile trees in an unpopulated world. Once, at midday, the wind blew clouds, swift and violent shadows across the sky, blocking out all light, freezing the snow into icy pellets. The climbers huddled together like forest animals. When the storm abated, there was an eerie silence on the mountainside.

"We're almost there," Javier whispered. "Another day, perhaps two. We'll leave the trail now. There's another route only the *passeurs* know. But keep quiet. We don't know what lies ahead, or where the Germans may be."

His words fell like stones. Juliette was too exhausted to speak, too numb even to feel fear. She looked at the Wolf, his face pale with strain. He trudged ahead, while she fell further behind.

Sophie was heavy, so heavy, a dead weight across her back. How could she be so small and weigh so much? Juliette wanted to lie down in the snow, burrow into it. It would keep her warm, for a while, just long enough for her to sleep. Just drift, just for a moment. Her eyelids fluttered.

Suddenly Javier was there, shaking her roughly. "Stop it. Don't go there. I need you."

She stared at him. She was angry, angry at the mountain, angry at him. She pushed back.

He grabbed her arms, hands like vices on her wrists. "That's better." There was an expression in his eyes she couldn't read. He leaned forward, brushed his lips against her cold face. "Fight back. Ready?"

She nodded. He shifted Sophie onto his back, and they moved again, one foot in front of another. One step at a time.

Javier left them about a kilometre south of the border patrol station, insisting on approaching the guards alone. Saying prayers under her breath, she watched him lope off into the distance. He had money to bribe the guards. It would be all right.

She wanted to feel relief that they were so close, but she only felt conflicted and confused. She held Sophie in her arms, feeling jealously protective of her. Her presence, her needs, were immediate. But what of Luc, Céleste? Henri and Bernard? They were far away, she told herself, perhaps already lost to her. More than anything, she wanted to cross into Spain with Sophie. Why did that feel like a failure of courage? The Wolf was right, she always wanted too much. If she stayed, she would be hunted down as a murderess, a danger to everyone she knew, everyone who had helped her. She could do no more good here in France. She swallowed, her resolve hardening. Her allegiance was to one child now, no one else. If she could save her, she would at least have done one fine thing, sheltered one precious soul from a monstrous fate.

Between the tangle of branches that protected them, the sky was a patch of smoky blue, the sun a yellow smudge. Javier had promised them that the sun shone in Spain. She lay back, listened for his return.

The Wolf whispered to her. "When I get to England, I'll join the Free French."

"You'd risk coming back to France?"

"With a new identity, a new name. Yes."

"Somehow it doesn't seem real that this war will end for me just a few hours from now."

"You have to believe."

"I'm trying." She reached for his hand, squeezed it. "Javier will be back soon."

But he didn't come. They watched as the light began to fade, tried not to think about what his delay might mean, tried not to think about being cold and hungry and afraid, stranded on the top of a mountain. Sophie slept, curled up in a fetal position. Juliette heard the crunch of footsteps in the snow and bent instinctively to shelter Sophie's body with her own.

"It's all right," the Wolf whispered. "He's back."

She swung around. Javier's face was grim.

"There are Germans at the station. Six of them, with rifles."

"How did they get there so quickly?"

He shrugged. "Up the Spanish side? Probably drove partway."

"I thought you said Spain was neutral."

"Officially neutral, not necessarily impartial. But you'll still be safe, once we cross the border. They won't bother with us then."

"But how —"

He held up a hand. "We'll wait until it's completely dark." He swung down his pack, pulled out a pair of wire cutters. "We'll crawl."

They lay on their stomachs, inching forward, cold granite beneath them, no trees for cover. The rolls of coiled wire were twenty metres away, a mass of jagged barbs glinting in the icy moonlight. They timed the silhouette of the German walking the line, his rifle slung across his back. He turned, began to retrace his steps to the patrol station. Javier had maybe eight minutes to cut the wire.

He ran forward, bent at the waist, dropped to the ground at the wire. Juliette couldn't watch. She pressed the side of her face against the rock, fastened her attention on Sophie's black eyes, wide with terror. She pulled her closer until she could feel her panting breath on her neck, the shuddering of her small frame as she struggled not to cry.

"*Je t'aime*, Sophie, *je t'aime,*" she shushed, grateful for the gift of the howling wind which would help keep other sounds from the guards' ears. She groped for the Wolf's hand and squeezed it hard.

Javier skidded across the rock and slid onto the ground beside her. She didn't stir a muscle, concentrating on the rock beneath her, trying to become part of it. She counted in her head, waited for the German to make his turn. Adrenalin surged through Juliette's blood, her body impatient to move.

"Now." Javier whispered. "Wolf first. Pull Sophie through."

The Wolf swung Sophie onto his back and was off in a half crouch, running across the gap.

She lifted her head. Javier pushed it down again.

She focused her entire being on the sense of sound. The wind, the thudding of her heart, Javier's breath. She strained her ears, thought she heard footsteps, heard them blown away again in the wind. No shouts, no rifle shots. Surely they were across by now. She felt a second of wild jubilation.

"Go."

She was running, no pain, no fear, running toward Sophie, Javier pounding behind her.

"Keep down," he hissed.

She dropped to the ground, saw the gap in the barbed wire, crawled toward it, began to wriggle through.

The first yell came from a distance. She ignored it. She was almost through.

The second shout was closer. Her body jerked involuntarily. She felt the barbs sink into her thigh. She heaved herself forward. The barbs bit deeper. She couldn't move. Something slammed into the ground inches from her head. A split second later she heard the whine of the bullet. She raised her head, trying to catch a glimpse of Sophie.

"Stay down, you idiot."

Hands clamped around her ankles. She felt a mighty pull, the barbs ripping her flesh up to her waist, saw Javier's bare hand curl around them and yank them free. Then she was running again, half stumbling, half dragged across the rock. She tried to keep up, but her leg wouldn't work properly. Javier swung her across his shoulders. She thought the shouts were growing more distant now, but she couldn't be sure. Then they disappeared completely.

Juliette opened her eyes, every breath a soft groan. The darkness was too thick to penetrate. She waited for her eyes to adjust, turned her head and listened. Everything was still, oddly still. The wind had disappeared. She sensed hard ground beneath her, put out a hand. She felt packed earth, not rock. Her hand was bare, her arm was bare. Where were her clothes? She shifted her weight, touched her body. She was naked under a pile of sheepskins and blankets. Almost naked. She felt thick socks on her feet, strips of cloth binding her upper thigh, hips and waist. She touched the bandage and winced. She glanced up. The sky had disappeared. There was a roof. She was inside some kind of building. It felt strange, after so many nights in the open.

Alarm flooded her senses. *Inside? Where was she?* She raised herself on her elbows, looked about frantically. *Sophie? The Wolf?*

"They're safe. They made it." Javier's voice.

She turned toward him. He was sitting on the floor, legs splayed out, his back resting against a closed door.

"You're sure? You saw them?"

"I'm sure."

She laid her head back. Relief, joy, loss washed over her. Sophie was safe. Sophie was gone.

She thought maybe she'd drifted asleep again, but when she spoke, it was as if Javier had been waiting only a moment.

"What is this place?"

"A shepherd's hut. They're scattered across the mountain, usually abandoned at this time of year."

"You broke in?"

"They're never locked. *Mi casa, su casa,* as the Spanish say."

"And the Germans —"

"Haven't found us yet. In a day or two, once your wound has begun to heal, we'll try again."

"No, Javier. Take me back down." A long silence. "You don't seem surprised."

"No."

"My only regret is that I never had a chance to say goodbye to her."

"You did, a thousand times. I saw it in your eyes. So did she."

"I had a crazy fantasy that I'd be able to watch her go until she disappeared from view."

"Not so crazy. Close your eyes, and I'll tell you where she is." He waited until her eyelids flickered. "My people were watching for them," he began. "They gave them warm clothes and baths, and food for their bellies. The slopes are gentler on the Spanish side. There's a donkey for Sophie to ride. They'll head south, to the Mediterranean, to a beautiful fishing village called Cadaques. The little houses cluster on a hillside around a church painted white, everything is white. When the sun shines, the reflected light almost hurts the eyes. The royal blue sea laps against the curving shoreline and the bay is dotted with fishing boats. When Sophie and the Wolf are rested, a friend will take them by train into Portugal. No one asks questions in Lisbon. It is the haven of refugees from all over Europe. They will welcome her diamonds. She and the Wolf will buy tickets and fly to England where your friend's family will meet her and take her to Scotland where there are no bombs and no enemy soldiers, and she'll tell them stories of the brave woman who carried her over a mountain."

How was it possible that going down would be more treacherous than going up? The muscles in Juliette's legs throbbed. The joints in her ankles and knees strained to keep her weight balanced. Her injury made her clumsy. Twice she fell backwards, flinging her arms out as she slid out of control, desperate to find a hold that would slow her momentum.

Her clothing was drenched from the snow. At night, it stiffened in the cold. She would have frozen to death had it not been for Javier. She pressed against his body, hungry for its warmth. She had no idea where she was, how far they had come or how far they had still to go. They had long ago left the marked trails, mindful that the Germans could be anywhere.

When they reached the second shepherd's hut, they found a half-empty bottle of brandy, and finished it off greedily. They risked a fire and undressed, hoping to dry out their clothes. Juliette was neither embarrassed nor self-conscious. The demands of her body, the fierce need to survive, pushed all modesty aside. She studied the contours of Javier's face as he knelt to change the dressing on her left side. He soaked the strips of blanket in water, removed them gently. She felt the pulling of her skin and cried out, but only once.

"It looks like hell, but there's no infection," Javier said. He cut fresh strips of blanket and rebound the cut. They made a game of counting the bruises from her free-fall slides down the mountain.

She clasped her hands around his neck, searched for his lips. She felt his body tremble for an instant before they melted together in the shelter of darkness. She wanted to think of Luc, but the fire of

Javier's hands on her breasts stole away all her grief and fear. She abandoned herself to them, set her own body free, until they were both exhausted and slick with sweat.

Afterwards, they lay in the stillness, holding on, the rhythm of their breathing in perfect unison.

They slept in snatches, their minds long since trained to listen for any treacherous sound. More than once, half awake, half asleep, she rubbed against him, his body responding. Yet no matter how fiercely they tried, they could not slow the passing of the night.

Juliette opened her eyes to the thinning darkness.

Soon she would let him go.

She thought how danger sometimes closes the heart down, but more often opens it wide. She wanted to know, and keep safe, one small part of Javier.

"Tell me," she murmured. "Did your wife come from Cadaques? You spoke of it in such detail. What happened to her?"

"She grew up in that beautiful place, it was part of her. She left the village to visit her sister in Barcelona, who was about to give birth. She was so happy that day. A new life even in the midst of that bloody war. On her way, German planes strafed the road, bullets flying at random. She was struck in the neck and bled to death six kilometres from her sister's home."

She touched his face, felt the tears, waited.

"I remember the last time I kissed her," he continued. "She'd just washed her hair and it smelled like flowers. I lifted its weight, so thick and shiny in my hands, and kissed her on the cheek. Just a peck. I took for granted that I would kiss her again many times to come. I was wrong."

He sighed, while Juliette remained still. Eventually, he spoke again. "I'm sorry now ... We must go."

Sorry that chance had been so cruel, or that the dawn had come? She couldn't be certain. They dressed, gathered together the blankets and the last of their food. She had an unwelcome fear that putting on their clothes would be like placing a barrier between them. But before he opened the door, he took her face in his hands.

"And what of you? There must be some man you left behind, perhaps in that exotic country I heard you tell stories of to Sophie.

What was your last kiss like?"

"I can't remember. I didn't know it would be the last. I didn't pay attention."

"Then remember this one. Just in case."

A long moment later, they stepped out into the misty dawn. On the other side of the pasture, the trees closed around them, protecting them. They made good progress. Juliette felt renewed, as if her body had regained its strength and balance. Fifteen or so kilometres down the slope, she almost crashed into Javier, who had stopped abruptly before her.

She peered over his shoulder. Bodies in the clearing. Three men. No, two men, and a boy. They lay lined up with bloody faces to the sky, their torsos torn apart by bullets. They had no packs, no belongings. One of the men was barefoot. His boots had been stolen.

A dreadful silence enveloped the scene. Nothing moved, no birds, no animals; even the air was still and steely cold. Juliette was paralyzed, her eyes fixed on the boy, against her will: the vacant, dirty face, the shattered chest.

Javier moved to block her view, and she turned her back on the godforsaken trio and mutely followed him away. They had cheated the war for one precious night, but now its taste was bitter again in her mouth.

At dusk, twelve days later, they reached Oloron-Ste-Marie and crept through the quiet streets to the lodge. On the threshold, Juliette stopped and looked back once at the mountain, its pinnacle bathed in pearly blue light. It was appallingly beautiful.

Christmas Day, 1942

Javier rolled toward her.

"Where will you go?" he murmured, his breath warm against the hollow of her throat.

"Back to Beaune, eventually back to Paris. My friends there will know if Sophie and the Wolf made it."

"Not if, when. I have a present for you."

He slipped some papers out from under the pillow and laid them on her stomach. She read them quickly. Rosa Aldaya.

Twenty-three years old, wife of Javier Aldaya. Born in Spain, resident of Oloron-Ste-Marie. The face in the photograph that stared back at her was her own.

She was speechless.

He stroked her hair. "Your old papers were worthless, but I used the photo. Rosa's identity is safe, they won't be able to trace it. She'd approve, I know. She'd have wanted to help."

Juliette's eyes shone. "I don't know what to say."

"Those who really love, love in silence, with deeds and not with words."

She laughed aloud, and wrapped her body around him.

Later, they knelt by the window and watched the people in the square below. The men wore thick sweaters and berets, the women had abandoned their scarves for jauntier hats, some of them even fashionable. Children darted in and out among the groups of adults, calling out to each other joyously.

"Look," Juliette pointed to the old men behind the plate glass windows of the café. Every day they'd see them there sipping brandy or wine and sharing out cigarettes, their faces wreathed in a smoky fog. "Nothing breaks their routine, not even Christmas."

They laughed together, but then Javier grew serious. "When will you go?"

"Soon. I'm a multinational fugitive — Canadian, Swiss, French and Spanish. And you?"

He kissed her, but his eyes strayed toward the mountains.

January 3, 1943

She was walking toward the square at mid-morning, carrying a small sack of bread, cheese and potatoes, when suddenly she felt uneasy. She stopped, took a few wary steps back to the wall of a corner building.

The hairs on the back of her neck were rigid, but she felt coolly detached. She leaned forward slightly to see what had unsettled her.

The square was quiet, too quiet. She glanced over at the café, squinting through the sunlight reflected off its windows. No trio of old men, no smoke. She turned her head slowly toward the lodge.

In an upstairs window, a curtain was swaying, as if it had been pulled back, then released to swing back to its original position.

There was nothing to be done. She walked away from the square without once looking back.

January 11

Ironically, travel was easier now that the Germans had spread themselves out over the whole of France. There was no longer a demarcation line intensively guarded. She had the money Javier hadn't been able to use to bribe the Spanish patrol. With it, she bought her way back to Vichy and eventually onto a barge, ploughing through the narrow waters of the Canal du Centre.

The barge rode low in the water, heavy with its load of gravel, its stern engine hammering away in a haze of blue smoke. She kept out of sight during the days, but the Germans paid them only cursory attention at the checkpoints. They needed the gravel, the captain had told her, for fortifications along the Channel coast, and were anxious to hurry them along.

At night, she stood on the deck as she had once before with Sophie, wrapped in mist, wrapped in memories, allowing herself to drift. She had to believe the child was safe now. She would try to find Henri or Bernard. Perhaps the smuggling line to Switzerland had been restored. There would be other children needing help. With her new identity as Rosa Aldaya, she could still be of use.

The canal brought her close to Beaune, close enough for her to walk the remainder of the way over several nights. She timed her arrival carefully, choosing a market day when there would be plenty of people. With her new papers, she was able to take a hotel room. She took a bath, water sluicing down her body. With her fingertips, she traced the path the barbed wire had made across her skin. She was almost glad of it. It anchored her, made tangible a time that was already beginning to seem surreal.

Her first task was to find suitable clothing and shoes. She needed to blend in, but could hardly do so in hiking boots and a mountain skirt and vest. But she had no ration tickets, and the stalls of cheap clothing on market days had long since disappeared. She would have to find the Château Dumais and pin her hopes on the housekeeper Lucette. She hoped she'd remember her.

Her plan, sketchy enough, was to approach the wine Co-operative on the edge of town and ask directions. She would say she was looking for work, or that she had once helped with the harvest. If that didn't work, she would think of something else. Already, as she walked through the streets, people were noticing her. She began to feel conspicuous. Ahead of her, lounging against the wall of the Co-operative, two soldiers glanced up. She began to feel afraid. Her papers had not yet been tested.

Don't look at them. Keep walking.

She drew closer, her pace steady. She glimpsed a man leaving the Co-operative. He stopped, held open the door for her. The soldiers straightened up, one of them took a step toward her.

"Hold on. I know you. You're —"

The voice startled her. She swung her head up. It was old Marcel, Lucette's husband. Her words rushed from her, before he could make a mistake. "I'm Rosa. I helped with the harvest last year."

The soldier lost interest, turned back to his conversation.

"Ah, yes. I remember. Come along. Lucette will be glad to see you."

She followed him toward the Dumais van. When she looked back, the soldiers were lounging against the wall again.

The danger passed, she began to tremble.

Marcel drove, pretended not to see. "We thought we'd lost you."

"Very nearly."

"Henri will be glad to see you."

"He's here?"

Marcel grinned. She couldn't believe her luck.

He looked older, thinner, a hint of lines around the mouth. But the boyish haircut and the glasses still gave him the look of a student dressed up in a business suit. His blue eyes were as keen as ever. He picked her up, swung her in the air. They laughed and hugged, both tried to speak at the same time, and laughed again.

"Sophie?"

He nodded. "You did it. She's safe in Scotland. Who on earth is the Wolf?"

"I'll tell you. Oh, I want to tell you everything, but first, what of Céleste?"

"Insouciant, unstoppable. Taking too many risks. They've no idea how well she can understand German. She passes us valuable information. But come." He tucked her arm under his. "We've so much to catch up on and I've only a few hours before I must leave."

They talked until the sun was scarlet on the horizon, the clouds wispy streaks of wild rose. She would have loved to return with Henri to Paris to stay with Céleste again. But for now, Marcel would drive her back to Beaune, and then tomorrow take her to Autun, on the edge of the Morvan, where she would meet with Bernard. The Resistance was building there. More and more people needed hiding. She felt light, the weight of her story relieved by its sharing. She was ready to begin again.

There'd been no news of Luc. In her heart, she'd expected none. She'd said goodbye to him, just as she had to Sophie, in the mountains. Javier had been a dream, a gift she'd never been meant to keep.

She'd learned that Hedgehog had been arrested, but escaped, and was in England, itching to return. More and more, she thought of their brief meeting in Vichy, of that aristocratic face and the quiet courage within the frail body. She hoped that the Wolf would finally meet the elusive Hedgehog in England.

Marcel dropped her off in the central square in Beaune and she headed off in the direction of her hotel, anonymous now in her new clothes and shoes. As she walked, she practiced holding each bright memory like one of Sophie's diamonds in her hand.

She didn't notice the stranger who was observing her. He wore a dark suit, right hand buried in the pocket of his jacket, eyes two pinpricks of light in the glow of his cigarette. Limping slightly, he followed after her.

The night clerk lifted his eyebrows when he saw her, no doubt at her change of clothing. He handed her the key with a gruff good night. Across the street, the stranger ground out his cigarette and disappeared into the shadows.

January 15

Snug behind its ancient Roman ramparts, Autun was a pleasant country town of sombre grey stone, red tiles and peeling paint, in a pretty setting — farmland and pasture on one side, the beginning of the great forests of the Morvan on the other. Juliette wandered around the main square, Champ de Mars, and then ordered what passed for coffee these days in a small bistro where she would wait for Bernard in his disguise as Frère Jean-Claude. The day was as grey as the town, the air heavy with a threatening storm.

She took a table by a window so she could watch the square. The bistro was quiet in mid-morning. Two white-haired men, heavy sweaters under their jackets, were playing cards. A farmer in rubber boots, drinking *pastis*. A couple of old ladies in another corner. She sipped her coffee, hot but tasteless. A man, limping slightly in a shabby-looking suit, took a table two down from hers, ignored her.

She had ration tickets now, she could eat. She called to the waitress and ordered bread and soup. The girl was nervous, her eyes kept flicking toward the newcomer who was now reading a newspaper. When the bread came, it was stale. Juliette dipped it into the broth to soften it. Twenty minutes went by, a half-hour. Jean-Claude would be coming soon. As she glanced up to check the clock again, she caught a slight movement, almost imperceptible, from the man reading the newspaper. He had lifted a hand, as if signalling someone outside.

She felt she was just being paranoid, but she scanned the square nonetheless. The usual bustle, she thought, people lined up in queues for supplies, a few small groups of shoppers stopping for a morning gossip. Then she saw them. Two tall men, blond, hands buried deep in the pockets of their overcoats, studying the display in a shop window across the street. *Come on,* she chided herself, *not all blonds are German.* One of the men looked over his shoulder, caught her watching, and looked away quickly.

Her heart began to pound. Had she been followed? She signalled to the waitress who came to clear her dishes away. When she picked up the plate, Juliette could see her hand was shaking. She looked at her face. This time there could be no mistake —

her eyes darted right, in the direction of the newspaper man. Then she scurried away like a frightened rabbit.

At that moment, Frère Jean-Claude in his monk's robes entered the far side of the square. It was a trap. Three men, two outside, one inside, were waiting to see whom she would meet.

She didn't think. She didn't breathe. She had to stop Bernard from coming any closer. She threw a couple of francs on the table and rushed to the door, turned to walk quickly in the opposite direction from her old friend.

"Halt!"

She broke into a run.

"Halt!"

She changed direction, skidded on the cobblestones, darted into a side alley. Her heart stopped. The end of the alley was blocked by a stone wall too high to climb, part of the town's old ramparts. She stopped, panting, turned around slowly. The two men from the square blocked the mouth of the alley. She stood tall, motionless, staring at them. One was older with cropped hair and a wide flat nose that spoke of street fights. The other was hardly more than a boy. His was the palest face she had ever seen, pale hair, pale eyes, pale skin, almost translucent. He walked right up to her, his expression a mix of anger and triumph. An icy ripple of revulsion crossed her face.

He swung his fist.

Pain flared at the back of her eye, her cheek burned.

"*Maudit bâtard,*" she whispered.

The second punch caught her in the stomach, and she sagged forward.

They dragged her across the square like Sophie's rag doll. She didn't look up, couldn't look up. She sensed rather than saw the emptiness of the square, the fear-filled silence, broken only by the bustle of people disappearing quickly behind closed doors. Surely Bernard had slipped away. She'd steered them away from him.

They pushed her into the back of a car. No one spoke to her. It began to rain, the sound drumming on the roof of the car. She recognized the driver as the newspaper man. He talked to the others in rapid German she couldn't understand. She caught a few syllables here and there — "Kommandantur," she thought she heard, and more ominously "Hauptsturmführer Eber." The car climbed up, through narrow twisting streets, then left the town behind. *Where were they taking her? What did they know?*

They stopped in a courtyard in a place called Château-Chinon, before a large building. *The mairie?* No, something larger. German flags were everywhere. *Maybe a garrison, or a prison? German headquarters?*

They pulled her out, left her standing in the rain in the courtyard while they went inside. There was nowhere for her to go. Armed soldiers milled about, some of them nudging each other and pointing at her, one or two smirking, others looking away. A tall man in uniform — not Gestapo — came out of the building and walked toward a parked car. He was followed by a woman, black hair, black dress, black coat. She paused before entering the car, turned her face toward Juliette. Their eyes met across the distance. For a long moment, the woman's serious green eyes studied her, as though learning her by heart. Juliette felt a wave of compassion from the stranger like an electric current, almost as if she'd been touched. Then the moment was broken. The woman ducked into the car and Juliette was alone again. As the car left the courtyard, she turned her palms upwards to the sky, threw back her face to meet the driving rain. She would not flinch.

The pale boy-man came back for her. He grabbed her roughly by the arm and jerked her forward. They walked along a hallway with polished wooden floors, the sounds of typing and telephones, of people working in offices.

The door to the cellar was halfway along another hallway leading to the back of the building. He opened it, pushed her again toward winding stone stairs, suffused in an eerie blue light from overhead electric bulbs. The first thing that hit her was the stink — sharply, eye-wateringly ammoniac, mixed with damp and mould. She started down into it, the grunting breath of the boy-man behind her. At the bottom, they continued along a poorly lit corridor, passing a series of closed doors with heavy locks.

He stopped before one, opened the lock, the thick door scraping across cement. She felt his hands slam flat against her back, the shove pitching her forward. She tried to brace herself against the fall, the skin of her palms tearing, her chin crashing against the rough hard floor. Her teeth bit into her lip. She swayed on all fours, tasting her blood.

She heard as if from a great distance the slam of the door, the heavy clunk of the lock as a million tiny pinpoints of light faded into darkness.

The world returned as stars in a black sky glimpsed between bars. When she moved, her body was stiff from lying on the cold floor. She stood on tiptoes beneath the bars and strained upwards toward the narrow rectangular opening, but it was too high. Back against the wall, she surveyed the cell, faintly illuminated by the starlight. She made out the shape of a mattress and bent to touch it. It was thin and lumpy, but reasonably dry. She picked up the rough, scratchy blanket and pulled it around her shoulders to stop her shivering. Over by the door, she found a washbasin of stale water and a rag that smelled of mould. The toilet was nothing more than a drain in the floor.

She tried to calculate how long she'd been here — ten, maybe twelve hours? She knew why they had left her alone. They were giving her time to imagine what could be done to her. Her mind veered away from that track. She counted the stars instead. Ten. Thirty. A hundred and three, four? She couldn't see more than that through the narrow window. *Start over. A hundred and three.*

She heard a door open noisily and then shut, the tread of boot heels, two pairs, and the slow sweep of a body being dragged along the stone floor. The metallic clatter of keys echoed throughout the cellar. A door opened and shut. Another door, closer, opened. Someone began to scream, man or woman, she couldn't tell, the screams near madness. More boot heels, receding now. She heard groaning, someone crying. Then silence.

That was the end of the first day.

The next time she opened her eyes, the slice of sky was grey and sodden. No stars. Murmuring voices, smart footsteps, the hum of cars from the courtyard. And wind. It was blowing in gusts through the barred window. The cell was icy, the damp walls striped with frost.

Loud footsteps approached along the corridor. She held her breath. A circular trap in the door to her cell slid open. A cup of broth, a slice of black bread. She snatched the food from the tray and backed away. She remembered the offices she'd passed. They would not question her during the daytime. The screams would be distracting.

The broth was cold and smelled foul. She swallowed it quickly, gagging on bits of what might have been cabbage. The bread was more palatable, heavy enough to keep the soup down. She chewed it slowly.

The solitary confinement did not unsettle her. She immersed herself in the landscapes she and Sophie had imagined on the barge, the stories she had told her. She thought about Henri and Bernard. They would know she'd been taken. She had to believe they were safe, that her being here had saved them, given them time to get away. She mustn't, must never, let go of that. She walked up and down to keep warm. Five steps across, ten steps from the door to the back wall.

Stretched out on the mattress, the blanket tucked around her, she weighed the pros and cons of sleeping. It would be an escape. It would eat up the empty hours. But she wanted to be alert when they came, didn't want them to find her disoriented. And would she have nightmares? Finally, she decided she would sleep in the daytime and wait for the soldiers in the night. She closed her eyes.

When the boots came, she was standing at attention, counting. How many steps from the cellar door to her cell? A sudden harsh light, hands reaching roughly for her. She blinked, tried to adjust her eyes to the glare. She counted three other locked doors before the stairs. The pale boy-man prodded her unnecessarily. She judged him the crueller of the two guards and moved slightly closer to the one with the mashed nose.

Their footsteps echoed in the empty corridor, the offices silent now. She saw no one else. They ushered her into a room, sat her on the single chair. She studied the back of a shortish man with dark hair. SS, she could tell by the uniform. She stared at his boots. They were polished to such a reflective shine, it seemed impossible that they were made of leather. Black glass, rather. She thought if she were close enough she would see her own ghostly face peering back at her.

He turned around, small eyes in a pudgy face sliding over her from head to toe. He raised a thin eyebrow.

"You are tall for a Spanish woman." His voice was flat. He moved closer, pushed up her skirt slightly above her knee. "Strong legs, from the mountains, eh? They will not break easily. There will be much pain."

Words, just words. She tried to keep the fear from her eyes, still her mind.

"So what is your name?"

"Rosa Aldaya."

"Your real name, please."

"Rosa Aldaya."

He sighed, raised a finger. The man with the mashed nose first forced her arms back to bind her hands with rope, then punched her in the stomach. The chair rocked. Between gasps, she decided she'd been wrong about him.

The SS man stepped forward again.

"What is your relationship with the Dumais family?"

"I worked for them, during the harvest."

"And you work for them now in the Resistance, yes?"

"No."

"Come now. You were followed from Beaune to Autun. You were to meet someone in the café. I want his name, and details of the escape line. We've shut it down once. We'll shut it down again. It's only a matter of time."

"But I know nothing. I live in Oloron-Ste-Marie. You can check. I only came to look for work. I was waiting to meet a wine dealer. I don't know his name. He was to find me."

"So you bolted from the café beforehand? Do you take me for an idiot?"

"No. The time to meet had passed. I thought I'd gotten mixed up, chosen the wrong café. I left in a hurry to see if I could find him in the other café, and then the soldiers shouted at me and I was frightened. That's all."

"I will give you one last chance. Tell me your name."

"Rosa Aldaya."

He walked to the door. His hand on the knob, he suddenly turned back and leaned into her face, peering into her eyes.

"Gabrielle Aubin has betrayed you," he whispered.

She stared back at him. The name meant nothing to her. She saw her lack of reaction register in his face, saw a moment of disappointment in his eyes. He ran a finger across her cheek. "Perhaps you will be more co-operative another time."

The door slammed behind him, and she was alone with the two soldiers.

Then the beating began.

That was the end of the second, third, fourth day.

Her eyes could hardly open. The only piece of day left was a faint orange glow. The sun was setting. She touched her face. Blood had trickled from her nose, crusting a path across her swollen lips to her chin.

They would be back, they would come for her again. Sometime between the fists and the pain, the names had tumbled out. Juliette Benoit. Renée Benoit. Renée Lachaisse. Bernard Levy. Luc Garnier. The Wolf. They all swirled together muddily. Old names, discarded names. It wasn't enough. They wanted more.

Fear pulled at her during the empty times. She felt empty, hollowed out. Bernard and Henri must be safe. She hammered that fact into her brain. She shut down, went numb, tried to fill the emptiness with faces. *No. No faces, no memories. Go back farther. Go to Chapleau. No war. No one to betray. So empty.* She feared she would vanish from the inside out. She felt death coil around her senses. Deep shadows, darkness.

Heavy steps. Her senses snapped alert.

The door opened. A woman screamed, and her anguish cut through the night like a diamond cutting through glass.

She recognized her own cry with a shock. She hadn't vanished. Instead she was here in this terrible place.

They dragged her to a different room. *A bathtub?* Shiny Boots was there. Opaque eyes. More questions. The rope. Hands at the back of her head.

The water was icy. She gasped, swallowed water, couldn't breathe. She was bursting apart. Blood rushed past her ears, roaring like a tide.

They pulled her head back out. On her knees, she retched repeatedly until her throat hurt. More questions.

Sophie, Sophie. I promise to find you.

Water again. Her body convulsed, legs kicking. She was drowning. A ghastly image from her childhood flashed briefly through her mind — drowning kittens floating away in burlap sacks, still alive, desperately clawing at the cloth and fighting to breathe.

Suddenly there was air. She coughed, tried to fill her lungs with oxygen before they forced her head under again. Hands in her hair, yanking her head back, pushing it forward. Up and down, again and again. Then fog.

When consciousness returned, she staggered to her knees. The revolting sensation of fluid rose to fill her pharynx. The taste of iron and acid. She leaned forward, gagging.

She was delirious. She saw the face of the child she loved, felt her near. Her voice cracked, coming back to her from a great distance. *Once upon a time, there was a beautiful snow queen with hair as black as ebony . . .*

*

G

January 15, 1943

Dietsz kept his eyes trained on the twisting forest road. The drumming of the rain and the slap of the windshield wipers were the only sounds in the car. The relief she felt at escaping Eber was overwhelming, the force of it shaking her body, and she was afraid to speak, even to murmur her thanks, in case her voice should break. The shame she felt at her cowardice was an anvil dragging her head to her chest.

Finally, he spoke. "Breathe, Gabrielle."

She lifted her head. It was the first time he had used her given name. Still, he kept his eyes turned away from her.

"Listen to me. I am taking you to the *gendarmerie*. Père Albert has been murdered, in the same fashion as Marie-Claire."

"I didn't —"

"Stop. I am taking you there as my prisoner for questioning in the murder. This is how I was able to force Eber's hand. You understand? The murder, should it have nothing to do with the Resistance, is not a Gestapo matter. You will stay in the *gendarmerie* until I can convince Eber of that fact."

Tears welled and spilled down her cheeks, whether for herself or for Père Albert, she wasn't sure. "There was another carved coffin," she said, her voice husky. "He showed it to me. He'll never believe you."

"He will when I tell him about Meyer. He was a German soldier. His actions before his death reflect badly on the honour of the Wehrmacht. It is my duty to solve these murders. My agenda will take precedence over Eber's."

He spoke the words with a stiff dignity. She didn't blame him for retreating to formality. He had risked a great deal for her. She studied his profile, saw the jaw muscle clench.

"How did you know where I was?"

"Joseph told me."

"And Père Albert?" she asked. "Where was he? Who would kill a priest?"

"A farmer found him in the church at Dun-les-Places. He was killed because he knew the identity of his murderer. Somehow, he knew who had killed Meyer and Marie-Claire."

She stiffened, her mind racing to put the pieces together: Marie-Claire's confession, the letter from Klaus she had given to him on Christmas Day. "You know this for certain?"

"I do, Madame Aubin. He told me so two days ago."

"What? If he knew, why wouldn't —"

"Why wouldn't he tell you? Why choose to tell a *boche* instead? Because he wanted me to know I had made a mistake about Jean Aubin." He spoke the words with bitterness, a reminder of his own failure.

"But who? Who is it?"

Dietsz shook his head. "I think perhaps he knew the person. He was very troubled. I cannot be sure, but I believe he was torn, trying to protect two people. In the end, he asked for time and did not give me a name."

"I don't understand."

"He believed you to be in great danger. And yet, he would not, or could not tell me a name. Perhaps it was the seal of the confessional that stopped him, or perhaps concern for another parishioner. He asked me to be patient, to protect you."

She felt cold. She turned away from him, stared blankly out the window of the car, seeing nothing. The person who had done these terrible things, the person responsible for the deaths of three innocent people she loved, was someone who knew her, perhaps someone who talked to her, greeted her on the street, smiled at her.

She felt the car slow, saw the familiar square, the shops, people scurrying through the rain. The shapes blurred in her vision, suddenly sinister. Her birthplace seemed alien. What did she know of these people, of anyone?

"Of course, there is another explanation." He stopped the car in front of the *gendarmerie*, and turned toward her.

Something in the chilling mildness of his voice alarmed her and she met his solemn gaze, her own eyes widening.

"Eber could be right, in his own fashion. The motive may have nothing to do with the Resistance, though the murderer might. That would explain Père Albert's reluctance, would it not? Someone involved, someone whose arrest would put other lives in peril?"

She refused to blink. She was balancing on a knife's edge with Dietsz, one minute her rescuer, the next her interrogator. Had she survived threatened brutality only to slip up on assumed gentleness?

"Is it worth it, Gabrielle? Is it worth your life? Trust me," he urged.

Amélie stared back at him, her face chiselled by determination to a cold marble beauty.

He sighed and shook his head. "I will tell you something, Madame Aubin, something I have told no one else. Germany will lose this war, but not for some time. Eber, and those like him, will become increasingly desperate. There will be no rules. *Résistants* will be shot. People whose houses are used by *résistants* will be shot. The relatives of those executed will be arrested and tortured. In the end, there will only be one life you can save. Choose the right one."

January 18

She spent three days in a cell in the *gendarmerie*. The rain that had begun falling on the day she was arrested had chilled to snow. Étienne Fougères was awkward in her presence, but kind to her, bringing her extra blankets at night and books to read during the day. She stared at the words, unable to make sense of them, unable to think of anything but Dietsz and, like a menacing shadow lurking behind him, Eber. She was heartsick about Père Albert. She should not have confided in him. She should not have passed the letter to him. Perhaps, if she'd faced her fears alone, he would still be alive.

On the morning of the fourth day, Dietsz questioned her in a perfunctory way about her relationship with Père Albert — when she had last seen him, whether he had told her anything. They both knew the questioning was a charade, put on for Étienne's benefit. She searched his face for some hint of real news, but he had withdrawn from her again, spoke to her as if she were a stranger, or worse, a burden.

"You look tired," she whispered, in an effort to close the gap between them.

He stiffened as if she had insulted him, and stood up abruptly.

"You may go, Madame Aubin. Père Albert's funeral is this afternoon at the *abbaye*. Madame Pascal is waiting for you outside."

"I can go into the forest?"

"You may go to the funeral. That is all." He turned his back and strode away.

The Benedictine monastery was nestled deep in the Morvan behind high walls of pale grey stone. Though the rectory buildings and dormitories were forbidden to the public, the monks had long made their chapel open to the community. If not gregarious, the Brothers were not excessively austere either, and they had taken to heart the Benedictine rule that strangers and searchers of God would not be turned away. They welcomed the villagers to mass on special feast days, and it was rumoured that more than one family had turned to them for food during harsh times. Père Albert had had many friends among them.

On this day, there was no joy. Many people from the surrounding villages had walked or ridden in horse-drawn carts along the snow-packed roads to the front entrance of the *abbaye* where the brethren, in their long brown robes, had greeted them solemnly. Gabrielle knelt in the chapel among them, a black shawl covering her hair. She listened to the prayers recited in singsong Latin: *Benedicat vos omnipotens Deus: Pater, et Filius et Spiritus Sanctus.* Women wept openly, but her eyes were dry. She wondered if the Père's murderer was even now on his knees, crossing himself, hidden behind a false contrition.

She felt very alone. Several villagers looked at her suspiciously.

Whispers stopped when she approached. They knew Eber had come for her, and that Dietsz had kept her in the *gendarmerie.* Eyes that met hers were filled with questions. Even Madame Pascal, though she had hugged her and fussed over her, had seemed wary.

Head bowed, she lifted her eyes, her face screened by the shawl, and scanned the crowd. There was the doctor and his family, Joseph's shaggy head, Madame Sorel and Guillaume, faces she saw almost every day. She felt the weight of someone staring and caught the glance of one of the monks. It was the man she had seen in the church at Dun-les-Places, the man she had seen the night the parachutes had floated down from the sky. He nodded, ever so slightly.

With a final prayer, the Mass ended. As people began to shuffle away, Madame Pascal and Gabrielle walked outside the walls of the monastery to the marble statue of the Madonna with child. She stood with her head in the trees, atop a tall carved pillar, precariously balanced on a huge slab of rock — the rocking stone from which the Abbaye de la Pierre-qui-Vire took its name.

"It's a miracle, eh?" Madame Pascal leaned toward her friend. "How she keeps her balance. You must learn to do the same."

A minute passed. The wind tossed the branches of the fir trees, making them dance around the Madonna's head.

"I would have told them everything if Dietsz hadn't come. I wanted them to shoot me."

"So would we all."

"I don't think so. There was a woman prisoner in the courtyard as I was leaving. She was not like me. I could tell she would be strong."

"You saw a woman?" Madame Pascal asked. "Young? Old?"

"Young, about my age. Why?"

"We're looking for someone. Wait here."

Before Gabrielle could speak, Madame Pascal was hurrying back to the chapel. She watched her go, dumbfounded. Several monks appeared on the path, their shadows merging with the wall to disappear into the secret interior. She waited. An arched wooden door set into the stone opened and Madame Pascal emerged, waving her forward. She stepped through the door into a cloistered garden, dry fallen leaves underfoot, and beds of denuded flower stalks stiff with frost. The tall man from earlier stepped out from the shadows.

"I am Frère Jean-Claude. We have met before."

She nodded.

"A friend, a very dear friend, was taken by the Gestapo in Autun five days ago. Please, can you describe for me the woman you saw in Château-Chinon?"

"She was tall, very short hair. I'm not sure of the colour. It was raining and her hair was wet. Dark blonde, I think, or brown. Brown eyes. She looked straight at me. She was wearing a trench coat, a dress underneath. That's all I can remember. It was only a moment."

She watched mixed emotions cross his face — joy that he had found his friend, pain that he had found her there, in the garrison of Château-Chinon.

"How many soldiers?"

She read his thoughts. "It's hopeless. Too many."

"What do you remember of the inside?"

"A long hallway as you first come in. The doors were closed, but I could hear people and telephones. Offices, I'm sure. No, wait. The soldier took me first down a second hallway, to the right. There was a wooden door, not like the other doors. He stopped in front of it and I was sure he was going to open it, but Eber called him back."

"That must be it then. The door to the cells. We must act quickly."

"I'm truly sorry for your friend, but I'm telling you it's hopeless."

He arched a dark eyebrow and shook his head. "There's always hope. You walked away."

"Only because of Dietsz."

She saw a glance pass between Madame Pascal and the monk. "It's not what you think," she flared. "He only helped me because of Jean, because he knows Jean was innocent. I've told him nothing of the escape line. But I don't blame you for your doubts. I've learned that I can't be trusted."

"No one is blaming you, Gabrielle," the monk said softly. "You think Eber doesn't frighten me, that the thought of torture doesn't paralyze me? You've lost a husband. Perhaps you believed you had nothing to live for, and that gave you a kind of freedom. There's nothing more they could do to you, you thought. Eber took away that freedom, not your courage. You've discovered that you want to live. That is all."

Gabrielle was silent for a moment. She wanted to believe him. "And you? You would risk impossible odds, risk torture and death for this woman?"

"Ah, *how* we live our lives is another question, is it not? I could say that if you refuse to fight evil, you're complicit, but that's not enough. Empathy is the soul of courage. My friend's name is Juliette, though she's had many other names. She willingly took my place in that cell. Without her, I would surely have been arrested. Twice, in fact, she has saved me, once long ago in Paris. If she's still alive, I'm her only hope. You understand now that I must try?"

"Yes. But how?"

Madame Pascal cleared her throat. "I can get inside. Nobody ever watches old women. We can use that against them. If there are offices, there'll be cleaners. Find one, and she can easily be bribed to let me take her place. Do you know what the Germans call us? *Alte schwarze Krähen* — old black crows."

"It's not enough," the monk said. "You couldn't get her out by yourself."

"Forgive me, Frère, but she may not even be alive. We need information first. If I have access to the offices, I may be able to find out something. The Nazis keep impeccable records."

"All right. Leave the cleaner to me. Be ready to leave at a moment's notice. I'll arrange transportation."

They both looked at Gabrielle.

"Yes," she said. "I can take over the shop."

That night, Gabrielle sat alone before the fire, mesmerized by the flames, feeling the iciness inside her melt. She thought about Dietsz and the monk. A strange coupling, and yet, in their own fashion, they had both given her the same advice. Choose life. She thought how reckless she'd been as Amélie, how she needed the balance of the Madonna in the forest. She needed to be whole again, one person.

She heard the tapping at the window and rose to meet it with a lightness she had not felt for a long time. In a moment Yves was beside her, his skin cold from the night, smelling of the forest, damp earth and pine needles. His hair fell across his eyes, his cheeks were unshaven. He ran his hands along the length of her back, buried his face in her hair.

"I've been so worried," he murmured, his breath against her neck. "Desperate. Then we heard Dietsz had you locked up in the *gendarmerie*. I've been watching the cottage. I saw the smoke from the fire. Amélie, I could not stay away."

She held his face in her hands. "It's a long story. I'll tell you one day, but not tonight."

"You're safe?"

"Are any of us safe?"

She leaned toward him then, opened her mouth, tasted the salt of his skin, the softness of his lips.

He held her tightly, led her to the fire. His hands trembled as he lifted her nightgown, found the smoothness of her thighs. Then the night closed around them, and the glow of the flames flickered across their bodies. He murmured her name: "Amélie, Amélie."

"No," she whispered. "Call me Gabrielle."

January 19

The monk was as good as his word. The telephone rang midway through the morning, and then Gabrielle saw Madame Pascal hurrying out the back door in lumpy layers of black wool.

Time crawled. She kept busy, serving the customers, answering their questions. *Madame Pascal?* She lifted her eyes to the ceiling, *Upstairs in bed. The long walk to the abbaye, you know, she must have caught a chill.*

She scrubbed the shop from top to bottom, meticulously followed directions for making the next day's bread. At night, when the blackout curtains were drawn, she crept up to Madame Pascal's flat and lay exhausted on her bed, snatching a few hours of restless sleep before it was time to fire the oven.

Just before dawn on the third day, Madame Pascal returned. She stood in the doorway of the kitchen, laughing at Gabrielle whose face and clothes were dusted with flour. She tested the hot bread, tapping the crust with her finger. "You've done well, *ma chérie.*"

"And you?"

The black eyes filled with sadness and she shrugged. "I can't say. I found documents, saw the name *Juliette* and memorized what was written, but can't decipher it. I think the monk will come for bread today. Now I must try to get this down on paper before it leaks from my old head."

"Is she alive? Do you know?"

The old woman seemed to shrink before her eyes. She shuddered slightly. "I heard sounds, Gabrielle. Terrible sounds. Pray for her."

While Madame Pascal locked herself up in the office and tried to write down words in a language she couldn't understand, Gabrielle stumbled through the rest of the day in a fog of remembered terror, her hands clumsy, her heart leaden. She felt great compassion for the monk whose friend was surely lost to the cruelty she had so narrowly escaped herself.

He entered the shop just before closing. The hope in his eyes made her throat tighten and she waved him toward the side room without a word. She reached for her coat, thinking she would slip away quietly, leaving him to mourn in privacy.

But Madame Pascal called out to her. "Come, Gabrielle. Lock up the shop and join us."

Reluctantly, she entered the little sitting room with its ragged chairs. Jean-Claude was sitting at the desk, his head bowed over the page of writing. She saw his shoulders stiffen. Her eyes flew to Madame Pascal who had the courage to speak.

"What does it say? Is she alive, my friend?"

His face was ashen. He thrust the papers aside and murmured what seemed a prayer, strange syllables in a language unknown to Gabrielle. *Baruch Atah Adonai ...* She held her breath.

His voice was raspy. "It says *Nacht und Nebel*, night and fog, German orders that mean they're shipping her out to Ravensbrück, no return required."

The name sounded ugly. Unbidden, Gabrielle's mind filled with images of blackbirds trapped inside a closed room, flinging themselves against windows and walls.

"What is that?" she asked in a small voice.

"A concentration camp for women. Under interrogation, a polite word for torture, she gave them the name of Renée Lachaisse. That was one of her identities. She's wanted for murder in Toulouse."

The room fell silent, a heavy foreboding gloom.

"But she must be alive. They would not transport a corpse," he added caustically. "And when they move her, we'll be ready. They leave tomorrow, at two o'clock."

"I want to help," Gabrielle blurted out, the words surprising even her. She closed her eyes and thought about what she was saying. She saw the woman's face in the rain, Eber's opaque eyes. *If he could be forgiven,* she thought, *hell must be empty.* "I do," she said more slowly, clearly. "I want to help."

"Child," Madame Pascal whispered. "Do you know what you're saying? If, by some miracle, we get Juliette away from them, Eber will be all over you. You'll have to leave St-Léger."

"Eber will come for me anyway. Dietsz won't be able to put him off for long. Our friendship already puts you in danger. No, you must stay, and I'll go. Even though I'll miss you." *And Yves, too,* she thought but didn't say. She turned to Jean-Claude who had listened to the two women in silence. "What must we do?"

Abruptly, Madame Pascal left the room. Gabrielle knew why. Whether they failed or succeeded, Madame Pascal would eventually be questioned. It was safer to know nothing of the details of the plan.

When Gabrielle emerged from the sitting room, Madame Pascal helped her on with her coat, and hugged her before she strode away in the fading light. At the top of the square, Gabrielle turned toward the churchyard for one last visit to Jean's grave.

Hours later, Gabrielle leaned against the back window of her cottage. The starlight was mostly blue, reflected by the snow. She waited, but Yves didn't come.

The next morning on the outskirts of Autun, three Frenchmen in workman's clothes erected a barrier and a sign that read *"Déviation."* The detour swung away from the town, along a gravelled road that skirted the edge of the Morvan for ten kilometres or so before linking up again with the main road on the east side of the town. Their caps pulled low, the men worked quickly, for they had no papers. They hoped traffic would be light, hoped the barrier was far enough away from the centre of town to escape the notice of the *gendarmes*.

Their boots crunched on the gravel as they walked the detour for three kilometres, stopping at a curve in the road. They took turns sawing at the trunk of a tall pine, a hard, bright sun reflecting off its frost-whitened branches. After an hour or so, they pushed, heard the tearing and snapping of wood, saw the tree bounce once as it hit the road, then settle onto the ground as if heaving a great sigh.

The three workmen slipped behind the screen of trees and waited. At their feet lay coils of rope. They didn't speak, listened instead to the music of the wind in the branches that sheltered them, ears straining beyond it for sounds from the road.

They heard a low rumble, and their eyes searched each other's faces. One of the workmen looked at his watch and shook his head. It was too soon. A delivery truck pulled up before the barrier of the fallen tree. Its driver saw a man emerge from the woods, waving his arms frantically.

"Get out of here. Turn around. Hurry."

The driver was startled, then frightened. They heard him curse as he maneuvered the difficult turn, gears grinding, gravel spitting out from under the tires. The truck slewed sideways, then straightened out and pulled away.

The wind moaned. They tried not to think of all that could go wrong. The driver might report them. The *déviation* sign might be removed. There might be two soldiers accompanying the transport, or twenty — they had no way of knowing. The stillness of the woods was only slightly less menacing than the Germans.

An hour passed. Two. Their nerves were as taut as the wood that had snapped.

At two o'clock, they left the trees and walked into the road. Two of them began chopping at the tree with axes, while the third kept watch, clutching a sack. They'd calculated the distance and the time. It wouldn't be long now. *If they came, if she was still alive.*

Over the sound of splintering wood, Gabrielle heard the smooth hum of an engine and signalled the others. They bent to their task, their backs to the road, while she sat on a part of the felled tree and pulled an apple from her sack, facing straight ahead. The sound of the engine grew closer.

"This is it," she murmured. "An army truck. Two soldiers in the front."

She stood up and waved. The truck pulled to a halt ten metres from the tree. The two soldiers spoke briefly to each other, then the driver got out, lit a cigarette. He was tall and bulky, a crooked nose in a placid face.

Gabrielle approached him, playing the part of a French peasant in baggy pants. She ducked her head, a gesture of respect for the uniform, and a smile lit her grubby face. "You gotta wait," she said in her lowest voice. "Should be cleared soon."

The driver reacted with surprise, seeing a boy, a pretty boy beneath the dirt, a voice not fully broken. He drew on his cigarette, blew out smoke.

Gabrielle's grin turned wolfish. "Got cigarettes?" she asked hungrily, inching sideways toward the truck. "*Für Apfel, ja*? Cigarettes for apples?"

The soldier laughed, turned toward his companion in the cab and spoke in German.

In an instant, Gabrielle dropped from sight and rolled under the truck, shouting.

The soldier whirled around. The cigarette fell from his lips. He was staring into the blunt snout of a pistol. At the same moment, the door of the cab was wrenched open, a gun pressed to the temple of his mate. Already pale, the man's blood drained from his face. He was prodded forward and stood beside the driver like a ghost. Disarmed, they were herded to the edge of the road.

One of the workmen cautiously approached the back of the truck. With a knife, he cut the ties lashing down the tarpaulin. He knelt down, reached a hand under the truck. Gabrielle crawled forward from her hiding place under the chassis and put an apple in the outstretched hand.

Standing to the side of the truck now, the workman hurled the apple against the canvas.

Instantly, a burst of machine-gunfire from inside the truck

ripped across the sky.

The workman at the side of the truck cried out as if he'd been struck.

The ruse worked. Two black boots dropped from the back of the truck to the gravel. On her stomach, Gabrielle stretched forward and grasped a boot, yanked on it with all her might. The weight of the soldier lurched forward, slammed to the ground.

It was all over. Two workmen disappeared into the trees with three soldiers.

Gabrielle crawled out from under the truck, her black braid falling to her waist as she pulled off her cap. She lifted up the canvas, hoisted herself into the back.

Juliette was lying on her side, her eyes wide with confusion. Her lips were ashen and swollen, her hair matted and the colour of weak tea. Through the holes in her torn and filthy clothing, Gabrielle saw livid purple bruises. She dropped to her knees, placed an open hand as gently as she could against Juliette's face, trying to ignore the stench. Her skin was ice.

Quickly, she peeled off her jacket and threw it over the woman's shoulders. Staring at Gabrielle, Juliette tried to speak but her words became a swampy cough convulsing her body.

"Hush," Gabrielle whispered. "Jean-Claude is here. He's come for you."

The brown eyes searched her face for a moment, then became unfocused, turning back slightly before fluttering shut. Desperately, Gabrielle searched for a pulse. She felt Jean-Claude kneel beside her.

"Is she alive?" he whispered.

"Barely. We must get her warm."

He picked her up as if she were a child, hugging her to his breast, and carried her to the waiting van.

They sped along the narrow dirt roads that criss-crossed the vineyards just north of Beaune. Henri, still in workman's clothes, helped Jean-Claude carry Juliette into the *cave*, Gabrielle following. Together, they laid her on a makeshift bed and wrapped her in blankets.

Gabrielle faced the two men and shook her head. "She won't survive here for long. It's too damp. She needs a doctor, hot water, warmth."

For a moment, they stared down at the ruined face, listened to the laboured breathing.

"Our best chance is the convent at the Hôtel-Dieu," Henri said. "We can move her tonight."

None of them spoke what all of them were thinking: *Will she last that long?*

"I've an idea," Gabrielle said. She knelt down, removed her own boots and socks. "Put these socks on her."

While the two men bent to their task, she slipped under the blankets, maneuvered her body as best she could around Juliette's, and held her in her arms, trying not to put too much pressure on the bruised limbs. "An emergency hot water bottle," she smiled. "Now go, do what you have to do. You won't keep her alive by staring at her."

When they were gone, Gabrielle lay in the darkness of the *cave*, feeling Juliette's chest heave spasmodically, working hard for air. She couldn't explain it, but she felt indebted to her, as if Juliette had taken her place in prison, taken the punishment that Eber had meant for her. She thought about the ambush and the three soldiers tied up in the Morvan. Briefly, she thought how just it would be if they froze to death, but she knew they would be found soon enough, and the hunt would be on.

The woman stirred briefly, but did not regain consciousness.

"Juliette, whoever you are," she whispered. "Don't stop fighting yet. Cheat them. Cheat Eber."

It was Henri who returned hours later, accompanied by a doctor, young and bearded, his face grave and strained. Gabrielle released her patient and stood beside the bed, while the doctor began his examination.

Henri touched her arm. "Put these on, please. Just in case the ambulance is stopped."

She stepped away to the back of the *cave* and undressed. The bundle of clothing was a nun's habit and wimple. It took her some time to figure out how to put it on. When she was ready, she picked up her sack. It held only a few clothes, a picture of Jean, and her wedding ring tucked inside the box from Marie-Claire, the only possessions she had taken from her cottage in St-Léger. She waited, feeling the tension of the doctor's silence.

Finally, he stood up. "Pneumonia," he said. "You did well to keep her warm."

She stepped through the door of the *cave* and looked up at the sky. The night was windless, but snow was falling, so fine and weightless it filled the air like fog or smoke. While the others loaded Juliette into the back, she climbed up into the front of the ambulance without hesitation. She realized her life would be different now, lived among people she didn't know, in places she'd never before seen. She felt surprisingly content. Meyer's killer would not find her now; nor, she thought, she him.

The doctor slid in behind the wheel, and Henri rapped on her window. She lowered it as the ambulance pulled away and heard him say, "Thank you. Take care of her."

She could see very little in the hooded beams of the ambulance — denuded vines in silver rows, then the buildings of the town, blocks of darkness and, here and there, a chink of light behind blackout curtains. The ambulance slowed for a patrol, and her heart beat a little faster, but they were waved through without having to stop.

When they reached what she assumed was the back entrance to the Hôtel-Dieu, she saw Jean-Claude and several nuns. While hands reached out for the patient, Jean-Claude pulled Gabrielle aside.

"Will you stay with her, until she's settled? I'll wait down-stairs."

She nodded and followed the stretcher into the hospital. They turned away from the wards to a private room. The nuns worked gently and efficiently under the doctor's orders. When they removed her clothes, Gabrielle turned away, aghast. She heard Juliette moan.

"She needs a bath," someone said.

"No," the doctor spoke harshly, "not that. Use a basin of hot water and cloths."

Gabrielle thought she heard someone whisper, *la baignoire*, and the nun beside her drew in a sharp breath. She knew, without having to ask, that it was a name for some kind of water torture.

Finally, the doctor turned to her. "Tell the Frère if she makes it through the night, she has a chance."

She retraced her steps, found him pacing in the vestibule, his face expectant and worried at the same time.

"I'll stay with her," she said. "I won't let her die."

It was thirty-seven hours before Juliette regained consciousness. During that time, Gabrielle had watched her eyes move beneath the veined lids, watched her body quiver and twitch, as if in dreams she were still fighting the darkness.

Then, suddenly, her body grew still and her brown eyes opened wide, flecked with gold and full of depth.

Gabrielle held her hand, "Welcome back."

Juliette blinked, struggled to form words, her voice low and raspy, "Soeur Hélène?"

Gabrielle realized she still wore the nun's habit. She reached up and unfastened the wimple, her hair floating long and loose. "No, but a friend. You're safe here. Jean-Claude and Henri will be overjoyed."

The patient tried to smile then, and with the barest movement of her lips, asked for water.

Gabrielle helped her raise her head, held a glass of water to her lips. She drank greedily, then fell back, exhausted by the effort. She drifted into a deep sleep, so deep that Gabrielle could not rouse her again, not even to give her more water. She had an image of Juliette sleeping for the rest of the winter, like a forest animal, rising finally when the warmth came in late March or April.

Over the next few days, fever gripped Juliette and she grew delirious. Her skin was shockingly hot to the touch. Gabrielle stripped off the blankets and discovered that her shift and the bedding were soaked. She called out to the Sisters, and together they moved her to another bed and put on fresh nightclothes. One of the nuns pressed a towel soaked in cold water to her forehead.

"Please," Gabrielle asked, "let me." She took the cloth and wrapped it around Juliette's head and face. She felt the need to protect her. When her body began to shake violently, she held her down, amazed at Juliette's strength. Her eyes opened again, but they were as unfocused and meaningless as her speech. Gabrielle strained to follow the mangled phrases, to understand, but she couldn't. When she was sleeping peacefully again, the doctor pronounced she was through the worst. The swelling was going down. There were cheekbones now, almost normal lips. The doctor had plastered a deep cut above the right eyebrow. They moved her from the hospital to the convent to a bare room with two beds, and Gabrielle, dizzy and heavy with fatigue, finally collapsed.

She slept sporadically, ears still attuned to the slightest noise. In dreams, Juliette still called out and Gabrielle could recognize names. *Sophie.* She murmured the name over and over, like a kind of incantation. Once, she stirred, and cried out, *Luc!*

Gabrielle heard the name with a kind of shock, and then relaxed. There must be a thousand men named Luc in France. She felt a slight stirring of desire and wondered if he missed her.

In the morning, Gabrielle fed Juliette hot chicken broth with a spoon, and bits of soaked bread.

In between mouthfuls, Juliette asked questions. "You're not a Sister?

"No. My name is Gabrielle Aubin. The convent is hiding us."

"Then we'll have to move soon."

"Why?"

"We always do. New places, new names. I'm sorry to lose my last name. It was a present."

Gabrielle smiled encouragingly, not at all understanding what Juliette was talking about. "Jean-Claude and Henri ask about you every day."

"Do you see them?"

"Jean-Claude sometimes. Henri sends messages. Someone named Céleste sends her love and wishes you were back in Paris."

"Paris — a lifetime ago."

Gabrielle thought how the words echoed something Yves had once said. "Come, let's see if you can walk a few steps."

They circled the room slowly, Juliette leaning heavily on Gabrielle's shoulder. When she was settled back on the bed, Juliette took her hand and squeezed it.

"Thank you. I've seen you before, haven't I? I mean, before coming here?"

"Yes. In the courtyard in Château-Chinon."

"I remember now. You were with a German officer. You looked at me with compassion. You were the only one who did."

Gabrielle turned away, still ashamed of that day.

"No, wait. I have to tell you something. Eber, the Gestapo man called Eber, he told me you'd betrayed me. I didn't know who you were then, but I knew it was a lie. Is that why you're hiding?"

She knew nothing of the ambush. She'd been too ill.

"Yes." Gabrielle answered. "Now try to rest."

SUMMER

1943

J

⌒

May 5, 1943

The weeks passed in a blur. The convent room became Juliette's world, one she shared with Gabrielle, who was both nurse and companion. The breezes through the window grew warmer and birdsong woke her in the morning. In the courtyard, the fruit trees slowly turned pink and white with blossom. She grew stronger every day and walked the hallways at night with Gabrielle by her side.

One day, as the light was fading, they crept outside to smell the coming of spring. Once they had found a bench to settle on, Juliette drank in the perfume from the trees. She sat as she often did, back straight, hands folded neatly in her lap, watching from the corner of her eye as Gabrielle fidgeted.

"How do I look?" she asked. "Should I be afraid of mirrors? I think my nose will never be quite straight again."

Juliette's question seemed to startle Gabrielle, as if she'd read her mind.

"No," she laughed. "You look fine. Your face is, well … interesting."

"And yours is beautiful. Why is it always sad? Do you mind my asking why you wear black?"

"My husband was executed. His name was Jean."

There was nothing adequate to say, nothing that would come close to mending the loss. Juliette lifted a hand to her breast in a mute gesture of sympathy, and let it drop again to her lap.

Gabrielle filled the silence. "Who is Sophie?"

"A little girl. She's safe now."

"Your little girl?"

Juliette smiled. "Yes, in a manner of speaking. I'm her family now. Her real family, her parents and her sister, were taken by the Nazis in Paris."

"They were *résistants?*"

"They were Jews. That was enough for the Nazis, and many French, too."

"What happened to them? I've heard stories, terrible stories."

Juliette felt dizzy, remembering the squalor of Drancy. She shivered. "It's getting cold. We'd best go inside."

But later that same night, Juliette lay awake for a long time, haunted by her memories. She stirred in the darkness, longing to speak of what the daylight seemed to forbid.

"Gabrielle," she whispered. "Are you sleeping?"

"No."

"I think you should know that some people fought back. The monk, Frère Jean-Claude. His real name's Bernard Levy. He started an escape route, helped me rescue Sophie."

"I think I guessed that. Oh, not about Sophie or his true name, but there's an escape line that operates through the Morvan. That's where I met him."

"And your husband, Jean? Was he captured?"

"Not exactly."

Hesitantly at first, then in a rush of intimacy, Gabrielle told her the story of Jean and the murders that had blighted St-Léger.

"So the priest knew the killer?" Juliette asked.

"Dietsz thinks so."

"And you trust him? He's not just saying so to gain your confidence?"

"Dietsz saved me from Eber."

"But don't you see, Gabrielle? If Jean had told you the killer's identity, you'd have revealed it immediately. The killer knows that. He *wants* you alive. It could still be Dietsz, he could still be looking for Meyer's money, believing you hold the clue to where it is."

"No," Gabrielle insisted. "It can't be Dietsz."

Juliette was silent for a long time, wondering at Gabrielle's conviction. It all fit together — Dietsz's search of Gabrielle's cottage, his presence on the night of Marie-Claire's murder, his knowledge of the carved coffins, even her rescue. And yet, Gabrielle seemed reluctant to even suspect him.

"Why do you trust him so?" Juliette dared to ask.

"I couldn't have endured what you suffered," Gabrielle whispered. "If not for Dietsz ... tell me, Juliette, tell me if you can how to be that strong."

It was an impossible request. Juliette had no words for what had been done to her. She closed her eyes, and her ordeal rushed back with the disorienting liquidity of a nightmare. But Gabrielle's question hung in the air, and after a long pause, she began to verbalize her experience for the first time, her voice almost a whisper.

"It's not about strength. It's not about courage, either. What they did to me was a kind of rape. One by one, they severed the connections that tethered me to reality. Each name I gave them, and I did give them names, was another thread cut. But after a while, the pain protected me, numbed me. I went someplace else. I found the tie they couldn't sever."

Speaking the words was like breaking a malevolent spell. Juliette felt the tightness buried deep inside her begin to ease.

"Sophie? Was she the tie?"

"Yes. Not simply because I love her, but because she lives, beyond their grasp. We stole her from them — my friends and people whose real names I'll never know."

"These were all people you knew in Paris?"

"Some of them. Others were like angels who interceded along the way."

"And Luc?" Gabrielle breathed out, "You said his name when you were delirious."

"Luc Garnier. My first love. They can't reach him either anymore. He died in Paris."

Juliette heard a sharp intake of breath from Gabrielle, felt an instant shift in the atmosphere. She shifted her weight onto her elbows and, propping herself up, stared through the darkness.

"What is it? What's wrong?"

She heard Gabrielle rise, then caught a glimpse of her face as she stooped to light a candle. Her sea-green eyes were startling in the pale face. She crossed the room and sat on the edge of Juliette's bed.

"Listen to me, just listen. I know a man, a good man who came from Paris. He was arrested there. I've seen the scars on his back. Did your Luc have a code name?"

Juliette sat up, feeling Gabrielle's tension.

"Please. Did Luc have a code name?"

"Yes. It was silly, really. We used to go to the cabarets, before the Germans came. Yves Montand and Edith Piaf would sing together. He took the name Yves."

Gabrielle spoke, as if to herself. "Then it must be him. There's too many coincidences — Paris, the code name."

Suddenly, she reached for Juliette's hand. "I think your Luc is alive. He gave me his real name for safekeeping, as a sign of trust between us. But it doesn't belong to me. He doesn't belong to me. I can take you to him."

Juliette felt the room spin around her. "It can't be. He's dead. I believed him dead."

Juliette held Gabrielle's hand and listened into the night as Gabrielle told of the tailor's son hiding in the Morvan, who had sworn Amélie to secrecy.

In the morning, the Sister who brought breakfast found Juliette still asleep.

"*Vite, vite.* The Frère is here to speak with you. He's waiting in the courtyard."

Juliette roused herself, surprised to see Gabrielle already dressed and sitting quietly on her bed across the room. As she ate, Juliette felt slightly shy of Gabrielle, not certain what to say, for the long night of confidences they'd shared had put their relationship on a new footing. She struggled to find daylight words, to sort out her mixed emotions. Her world had shifted again. She owed a great deal to Gabrielle, not just for her convalescence, but for her revelation about Luc, one she suspected had cost her new friend a great deal. She risked a glance at her and was rewarded with a smile.

"Would you like to see a picture?" Gabrielle asked. "Of Jean."

Juliette nodded and watched while Gabrielle reached for her bag and turned its contents onto her bed. She opened a carved box and sorted through its glittering trinkets.

"Look, here's my wedding band. I can wear it again now that I'm no longer pretending to be a Sister." Then she held out the photo. "I couldn't bear to leave it behind. But I don't really need it. His face is always with me."

Juliette glanced at it — an open, trusting smile, eyes full of laughter.

"It's not the same for me. Sometimes I forget the details of Luc's face, the sound of his voice. What happened between us happened long ago, in space if not in time."

"Do you love him?"

"A part of me, always. I'm overjoyed that he's alive. But he has become a memory. I hardly know what I would feel if I saw him, flesh and blood."

"Then we must find out."

"Yes. I want to, Gabrielle. But I'm quite prepared for the fact that he may no longer love me, except as someone in a dream we shared in Paris before the war. I understand that. I'm trying to say I understand if he … if you …"

Gabrielle turned away, began braiding her hair. "It was only a moment, nothing more." But her voice wavered slightly. She walked to the window, and pulled the curtain aside. "Look. Frère Jean-Claude is already pacing."

He rose to meet them as they entered the courtyard, holding out his arms to Juliette. "Ah, you look well. Céleste will be pleased."

"I've had good care," she responded, nodding to Gabrielle. "You have news for us?"

"Please, sit. A great deal has changed. First, I must tell you that the Vichy stooge, Laval, signed a law in February that makes clear the extent of his collaboration. *Service du travail obligatoire*, it's called. It means that every French person of reasonable health and workable age must make themselves available to go and work in Germany. All pretence of volunteerism is off. The effect has been immediate."

"Deportations?" Gabrielle asked.

"On the contrary, it seems the Resistance is the popular alternative. Young men from villages all over the Morvan —

Montsauche, Planchez, Dun-les-Places, Manlay and Clamecy — are swarming into the forest to join the *maquis*."

Gabrielle wrinkled her nose. "*Napthalines?*"

Juliette looked puzzled at this, and Jean-Claude explained. "It's the French word for mothballs, and yes, it's being said that the latecomers smell of them, having been hiding in their cupboards for so long." He shrugged. "But are we to turn away Laval's accidental gift? I think not. For whatever reason, priorities have shifted. You must've realized that Henri is already in the Morvan. He blames himself, Juliette, for leading you into a trap."

"How could he have known?"

"Nonetheless. Eber has shut down the escape line once again. The focus now is on subversion and sabotage. There's more outside help too, from de Gaulle's Free French and from Churchill's SOE."

"SOE?" Gabrielle asked.

"Special Operations Executive, a group dedicated to putting agents behind enemy lines to disrupt the Germans and, more significantly, to arm the *maquis* in preparation for an Allied landing. The key is to organize and train our disparate bands into a united force."

Juliette felt a rush of excitement. "A landing? When?"

"We don't know yet. And as you might imagine, patience is not a virtue of the *maquis*."

Juliette could see that Gabrielle was fidgeting again. She interceded on her friend's behalf. "And St-Léger? What has Eber done?"

"Your cottage, Gabrielle, was the first he visited. You can imagine his rage to find you gone. But Joseph and Guillaume Sorel have eluded him and joined the *maquis*. Madame Pascal, I'm afraid, is vulnerable. He has not yet arrested her, but her home and shop have been searched. She is under surveillance. I think you'll agree we must get her out."

"But?" Gabrielle prompted.

"She refuses to go without you."

"You could bring her here, couldn't you?"

He looked away, and Juliette answered for him.

"No. It's time to leave, isn't it? I'm well enough. The Sisters have already risked too much. To stay would be to put the convent in danger, and Eber is widening his search even as we speak. Where shall we go? To the Château Dumais?"

Jean-Claude shook his head. "It's been requisitioned. Those doors are closed to us. No, you must go to Paris. Céleste will find safe houses."

Juliette looked at Gabrielle, who was already shaking her head. There was no need to tell Jean-Claude that she and Gabrielle had a strong reason for staying in the Morvan.

"No, Jean-Claude. We refuse," Juliette insisted. "You must send Madame Pascal to Céleste. But our presence would only increase the danger for both of them. Gabrielle and I will join the *maquis*."

"Are you strong enough for that, Juliette? These are rough men, living in rougher conditions. And there'll be armed combat. Oh, I'm not talking about full-scale confrontations with the Germans, but certainly ambushes, skirmishes. They're not likely to accept two women."

"Then they'd better learn." Juliette raised a hand to silence Jean-Claude's protests. "No, listen to me. I've survived a mountain and Eber. Living rough is nothing to that. I'm probably a better shot than most of the men, and Gabrielle has known the Morvan since childhood. They'll be lucky to have us. When do we leave? Surely it's easier to find clothes for us than new sets of papers."

Jean-Claude turned to Gabrielle. "You agree with this madness?"

"Absolutely. You'll take Madame Pascal to Paris? I know I can convince her to go."

He bowed his head for a minute, working out the details. "All right. Be ready to leave tonight. I'll meet you tomorrow in Madame Pascal's shop, at midnight."

The old produce truck bumped and bounced along the dark side roads of the French countryside, the moonlight glinting now and then on the church spires of sleepy villages. By daylight, Juliette and Gabrielle were skirting the southern edge of the forests of the Morvan. Leaving the truck and hoisting their backpacks, Gabrielle led them north along invisible trails toward St-Léger. Juliette was sure that anyone noticing them through the shreds of morning fog might have thought they were two schoolgirls, thin as willow wands, their hair in braids.

They stopped to eat by a small lake, the warm air teasing them with hints of spring.

"It's not far to go now. About ten kilometres," Gabrielle said. "Tell me about Céleste."

"She's smart and generous. Brave to the point of recklessness. With a face that looks seductive for no reason whatsoever, like half the women in Paris before the war." Juliette smiled. "She has a fine temper."

"Then she'll find a boon companion in Madame. How long did you live in Paris? In your fever you talked about a place called Chapleau."

"I was born there, in Canada. I grew up with street French in northern Ontario. I expect you can still hear traces of it, but it's good enough for the Germans."

"Luc has an accent too. Parisian French, I suppose. I've never been to Paris."

"It sounds like music, like running water."

"When we meet up with the *maquis*, I'll find him."

"Yes."

"I've been thinking we might also meet up with Meyer's killer. He could be any one of those men, and I'd never suspect."

"I'll help you, Gabrielle. It's the least I can do. We should tell Henri, in case there's a traitor in their midst."

They sat for a moment longer, enjoying the gentle breeze on their skin and the smell of the new grass, glad to be in the open air, glad to be alive. Then Gabrielle rose, and Juliette followed her back to the trail.

*

G

When the time for the rendezvous with Jean-Claude approached, Gabrielle left Juliette in the shelter of the forest and entered the fringes of St-Léger alone, guided by starlight and memory. Moving swiftly and silently from shadow to shadow, she began cutting in toward the town centre, ducking beneath windows and keeping close to the walls of houses. It felt odd to be a fugitive in her own birthplace. She could name the inhabitants behind every wall she touched, and yet she felt remote from them, like a ghost trapped in another dimension.

She was sure the square would be patrolled if the shop was under surveillance, so she crept toward the alley, took a breath and leaned forward.

The path was clear.

In an instant, she was knocking at the door. The rattle of a chain. The next moment she was in Madame Pascal's arms.

She'd thought they would have so much to say to each other. She had marshalled her arguments, ready to bully the older woman, if need be, into leaving the only place she had ever known. Now, she gazed into the kind face of her dear friend, and words would not come.

Jean-Claude stood patiently by the door as Madame Pascal held Gabrielle close and whispered, "It's all right. I only wanted to see you once more. Paris, *hein?* I can do some damage there. The monk will travel with me. Our train leaves in the morning from Beaune."

She looked over to Jean-Claude and nodded. They were ready. He opened the door and the three figures stepped across the threshold and into the night. When the moment came for their paths to separate, Madame Pascal leaned forward to kiss Gabrielle and murmured in her ear. "I meant to tell you — Dietsz was relieved, I would almost say glad, that you'd vanished. I don't think he could have stared Eber down a second time. Be safe in your forest."

Gabrielle merely touched her hand. Madame had never needed words to read the human heart.

*

J

≈

Jean-Claude had told them they would be met at sunrise at the old logging cabin. Juliette's stomach fluttered, remembering that that was where Gabrielle had first seen Yves, wondering if he would be their contact, but it was Henri who was waiting for them. She flew into his arms, but caught sight of Gabrielle's face, read the disappointment there.

"Henri," she said, pushing him away. "You remember Gabrielle?"

"Remember you?" He reached out a hand. "I am indebted to you. I can't say I'm returning the favour by leading you to the camp."

They headed off in single file, climbed up a rock face, across a grassy plateau, and deep into the thickest part of the Morvan.

It was still cold in the forest, the sun's pale light revealing patches of snow here and there among the twisted roots of trees. Juliette shivered, but not from the damp. The *maquis* camp that lay before her was a crude assembly of tents and lean-tos made of fir branches, the charred remains of several campfires and silent bands of unwashed, haggard men who regarded her and Gabrielle with hostile eyes and frowns of disbelief. Juliette held her head high and stared back. *This,* she thought, *is the Secret Army?* She thought of the might and venom of the German war machine, regarded the underfed, bedraggled and slightly hunted demeanour of the boys and men in front of her, and almost laughed. Here and there, a *résistant* wore a belt that carried a pistol, but most were unarmed. Their only weapon was one of concealment, the forest itself with its terrain of rocky fissures, caves and twisting paths. She looked up at two silhouettes at the top of an outcropping of rock.

Sentries, she supposed. No doubt, the camp had been warned of their arrival.

Henri stepped forward. "This is Renée and Amélie," he said. "They'll be joining my squadron."

A few men scoffed openly. Another whistled. "You need two cooks?" someone else snorted. "There's barely enough food for one. Or maybe you need warming up at night, *hein?*"

Henri stepped forward, but Juliette stopped him. "They'll learn," she said. "Leave it."

They walked away from the centre of the camp to a racing stream, one of the many tributaries of the Cousin River, Henri said, edged with reeds, cattails and rushes.

"You'll need to build some sort of shelter," Henri advised.

"Up there," Gabrielle pointed. "The ground will be drier."

Henri left them and went to hunt down the SOE commander, a man called Laurent, whose seemingly hopeless job it was to train this motley crew.

"It's not that I'm competitive," Juliette murmured. "But this'll be the best damn shelter in the camp. Agreed?"

"Agreed," Gabrielle laughed. "Follow me."

They cut down the slender trunks of saplings and the supple branches of firs, dug out rocks and hauled them back to the site. Fixing their saplings upright with the rocks, they wove the branches through them. No one offered to help them, but everyone watched stealthily. By late afternoon, their wooden tent was large enough for them to stand up in, and wide enough for two makeshift beds of pine boughs wrapped tightly in blankets. Juliette stood back to admire their work. The entrance was merely a gap, affording little privacy. "It needs a final touch. What can we find to screen the entry?"

"Come on. I've an idea."

They walked downstream a kilometre or so until Gabrielle found what she was looking for — the long trailing tendrils of a weeping willow. In another hour, they had woven together a feathery curtain that closed them off from the curious eyes of the *maquis.* Inside, Juliette grinned triumphantly. "Round one to us."

Round two came when Henri fetched them to meet with Laurent. Even in the darkness, Juliette could feel eyes following them. Henri left them in front of a large, army-issue tent, wishing them luck. When she pulled back the flap and entered, she saw a blond man with shaggy hair and a reddish beard poring over a map. He raised his head, his cool, grey-blue eyes assessing them. He looked to be in his mid-thirties, a thin aristocratic nose, skin chafed by the roughness of living outdoors. He was not handsome so much as imposing. Even when he was still, he exuded energy and an intensity of focus.

"*Bienvenue.* Welcome, Henri has vouched for you." He waved them to a seat on his cot and sat across from them, straddling a wooden chair. "You'll take some getting used to," he went on, his glance lingering on Gabrielle for a moment, "but eventually the men will accept you. They're a good bunch — farmers, *garagistes,* engineers, students, shopkeepers, even a hairdresser. We've a host of leaders who pick the best men from each local band in the area for weapons and sabotage training. We use code names, of course: the separate bands take the name of their leader — Serge, Camille, Vauban, Socrate, Bernard, Louis, and so on. You'll be with Bernard. You can help with the parachute drops. Sometimes we have as many as two or three a month."

"I've helped already," Gabrielle interrupted. "You still use the same plateau?" He nodded. "I know of others you can use too."

"You know the Morvan well?"

"Is that the map you were studying? May I see?" Gabrielle stood and entered the circle of light, bending forward over the map, the tip of her long plait just brushing the paper. "Ah, I see what's missing. With a little help, I can give you the topography. There's no indication here of the elevations and valleys, no indication of the conditions of the logging roads. Is Joseph here? Together we could manage something better."

Laurent smiled, his eyebrows raised in surprise. "Henri will arrange it. You can start tomorrow."

"Will the drops include weapons?" Juliette asked. "The men seem ill-prepared. I saw a few pistols, some hunting rifles, nothing else."

"We also have half a dozen horses we stole from the Germans. Perhaps you'd agree to take over their care?"

Juliette became very still, her back straight, hands folded in her lap. When she spoke, her voice was determined and her brown eyes flashed. "Tell me about the guns."

"Machine pistols called Stens, light machine guns called Brens, Lugers and Walthers stolen from the enemy, various English and American pistols."

"Teach me how they work."

"You can't expect me to arm a woman. There's little enough to go around for the men."

"Then you're wasting your talent."

Laurent stared at her. "You seem sure of yourself."

"I am."

"Care to put that to the test?"

"Name the place and time."

"All right. Roches des Fées, at ten tomorrow." He turned to Gabrielle. "You know it?"

Before Gabrielle could answer, a man, wiry and short with curly hair, entered the tent. He was carrying what looked like a suitcase, but Juliette had seen something like it before, something she'd carried across a moonlit vineyard in Burgundy. It was a field radio.

"Ah, Danard. Meet Amélie and Renée."

The stranger beamed at them, and extended his hand. "*Enchanté, mesdemoiselles*. It seems life in the backwoods is improving. Time to check in with London," he said, opening the case and fiddling with knobs.

Juliette caught Gabrielle looking puzzled.

"But where is Yves?" she blurted out. "I thought he was the radio operator ..." Her words trailed off as Juliette and the two men stared at her.

"You know him?" Laurent asked.

"I was his courier, for a short time. With the escape line."

Laurent and Danard exchanged glances.

"What is it? He's not hurt, is he?"

Danard answered, his voice cool. "Not that we'd know. He took off, went to the Free French, further south near Autun. I don't mind saying, he left his unit high and dry. That's why I'm here, transferred from Paris so we could contact London again. He put us back several weeks."

Juliette saw Gabrielle's cheeks flush. Danard's answer had sounded like a recrimination directed at her. She stood up and walked to Gabrielle's side, glaring at Danard as she passed him.

"Good night, ladies." Laurent was dismissing them.

Outside, they picked their way in the darkness past several well-banked campfires, glowing embers instead of more telltale flames. In the strange orange light, Juliette looked at Gabrielle's pinched face, sensing that she was troubled by Yves' disappearance.

"There must be some explanation," she consoled.

"I don't understand. I was sure he'd be here."

Juliette said nothing, kept walking toward their shelter.

"I can't imagine why he would leave." Gabrielle tried again. "His messages came from London. He never mentioned the Free French."

When they entered their makeshift home and began undressing, Juliette spoke across the darkness. "I can imagine why he left. Didn't you say the ambush that freed me was near Autun? Don't you see, Gabrielle? He's looking for you."

She lay down on her bed silently, remembering the confidences shared in the dark nights of the convent, listening for Gabrielle's breathing. She was so close that if she had stretched out a hand, she would have touched Gabrielle's. She wondered at the way their two lives had intersected, and realized that, no matter how much she had once loved Luc, she did not want the possibility that he was alive to come between them.

"I was a different person then, Gabrielle. It was Paris. You *have* to be in love to appreciate Paris. I remember that Luc used to call me Jules. I miss that."

"Jean called me Gaby, except when he was annoyed with me. You can too, if you like."

"Jules and Gaby it is then."

"Can you really shoot?"

"When I have to. I learned that from an eighteen-year-old boy."

When Juliette spoke again, she changed the subject. "I wonder if Laurent's Bernard is our Bernard?"

"Who knows, with all these shifting identities. But I hope so. It would be good to have him here. By the way, do you think Danard is French?"

"Oh, I don't think so. English I'd say. Why?"

"I'm not sure. Something in the way he spoke made me feel uneasy."

"He'd no right to make you feel uncomfortable just because you knew Yves."

Juliette lay awake for a long time, wondering if Gabrielle had fallen in love with the tailor's son, but couldn't bring herself to ask. Eventually, she drifted off to sleep.

The meeting at Roches des Fées was not what Juliette had expected. She'd feared a western-style showdown, some kind of target practice to test her skill, but instead Laurent had taken her at her word. He was there to teach, not to waste ammunition. Together with roughly twenty others, Juliette was handed a Sten gun and set about learning how to strip, clean and reassemble it. She found a single friendly face in Henri and took up a place beside him, working with concentration, determined to prove herself. After an initial failed attempt, she managed to work through the cycle. Laurent wandered among the group, and stopped by her side. "Do it again," he said. "Over and over. Do it until it can be done with your eyes closed."

Between repetitions, Juliette leaned toward Henri. "Laurent mentioned a Bernard. Our Bernard?"

"Yes, he'll join us after returning from Paris. He fears the monastery is coming under the scrutiny of the Gestapo. These weapons were hidden for months in the chapel organ."

For a moment, she studied the serious profile as he bent over his task, his glasses sliding forward over the bridge of his nose.

"Henri, did you ever meet the radio operator named Yves?"

"No, he'd left before I arrived."

"What about Bernard? Did he know him?"

"I don't think so. Yves operated out of Dun-les-Places. I know they helped out with transport once when the line was broken in Beaune, but you know how these things work. One person only ever knows the next in line, never the whole network. With the line already in jeopardy, Bernard would've been even stricter about security. Why do you ask?"

"He told Gaby his real name. Henri, listen. He told her he was Luc Garnier."

His hands slipped on the gun. He stared at her.

"There could be any number of reasons why he didn't try to find us," she insisted. "Don't you remember Pierre, how ashamed he was when the Gestapo broke him? Perhaps Luc was forced to give our names in Paris, when we first had to flee."

"Luc betray you and Sophie? I'm sorry, Juliette, but you know better than that."

"I thought I did. But you don't know what it's like. How you fight for breath after agonizing breath, hating each moment of pain when you inhale, but desperate for the next gasp of air. I gave Eber his name, in the end."

"Stop this, Juliette. You gave Eber the name of a dead man."

Her heart rebelled, but she bit down what she might have said, and the silence grew heavy between them. After several more hours of mind-numbing repetition manipulating the Sten guns, Laurent finally called a halt to the day's lessons and Juliette walked with Henri through the trees' long purple shadows back to the camp.

When they reached the stream, they stopped to wash the gun oil from their hands. Henri sat on his haunches and spoke to the reflection of Juliette's face in the water.

"I *do* understand. I know what it's like to lose someone you love."

"Céleste."

"You knew?"

"I've known for a long time, ever since the night in the vineyard when you introduced us to Max and the Jewish monk. But you're glad she's alive, and I think that's what I feel, too. Just that I want Luc to be alive, for Gaby's sake as much as for my own, because I think they may have fallen in love, and she's already lost so much. She has a story to tell. Will you listen to her? Perhaps you can help."

They were resting on the bank of the river, when Juliette saw Gabrielle walking toward the tent and waved her over.

Gabrielle plopped down beside her and Henri, rubbing her neck. "Whew. I've been poring over maps all day. How did the shooting go?"

"It didn't. Just mind-numbing exercises putting the guns together. Listen, Gaby. I think you should tell Henri about Meyer and the murders. We've a better chance of finding the killer if we all work together."

So as the last light of the day faded into pale gold, Gabrielle told once again the story of Meyer, Marie-Claire and Père Albert. Henri looked at Gabrielle, her eyes luminescent with the green of the pines and the stream and the thick fringe of reeds growing on the water's edge, and made her a promise.

"We'll get word to Bernard before he leaves Paris. Perhaps he and Céleste can trace what Meyer was up to before being transferred here. Maybe the story begins there. I have one question," he said as he rose to his feet in a fluid movement. "What happened to the letter you gave the priest?"

"I don't know."

"I'd love to know what it said about Dietsz."

Through most of May and into June, the weather was warm and showery, the forest floor growing lushly green and thick with wild-flowers. The creek widened into a deep pool carpeted with water lilies, and when Juliette could coax the men to look the other way, she would wade into the water to bathe, shaded by the long heavy branches of a giant weeping beech. When she entered the water behind the curtain of beech branches, she felt like she was entering the apse of a church glazed in green and yellow glass, dappled with leaf-shadow and light. She grew to love the Morvan, tamer than the woods of Chapleau, but dense enough to protect them from German eyes.

Laurent's training intensified. Besides teaching how to use the guns that dropped from the sky in cylinders on moonlit nights, he showed the *maquis* how to use explosives. Juliette and Gabrielle were good students, eager to prove themselves. The best thing, they were told, was to derail a goods train in a cutting — that way, it would be blocking the line for a long time, as it couldn't easily be moved aside. They learned where best to place explosives to blow up a bridge, and how to disable a car with a handful of sand. Cause as much damage to the Germans as possible, Laurent urged, and as little as possible to the villagers. When the time to mobilize came, victory would lie partly in having the local population behind them.

Juliette sensed it was for this last reason that Laurent forbade the men to pillage food and animals from the surrounding farms. They ate only what grew in the woods and what could be hunted there. Occasionally, under strict guidelines, a small band of men would be allowed to enter a village at night to gather bread, cheese, turnips and wine from families who were willing to help them.

One hungry night, Gabrielle turned to Juliette as they lay resting in their tent. "Jules, I left wine in my cottage. A bottle of brandy, jars of preserved pears and tomatoes. Soap."

"You had me with the wine. How far is it?"

"About eight kilometres. We could borrow one of the horses."

"Laurent will skin us alive."

"Only if he catches us. And he's not here tonight. Danard told me there's a meeting of all the leaders."

Juliette smiled in the shadows of the tent. What she loved about Gaby was how she leaned into life, never away from it.

A group of men down the slope of the hill were drinking around a low fire. Their gruff conversation gave the women cover as they circled toward the tethered horses behind the men. Gently, Gabrielle slipped a farm horse free, whispering into its ear, patting its grey muzzle, and they disappeared with it into the darkness.

Once they were well clear of the camp, Gabrielle swung herself up and reached down a hand for Juliette. At first, the horse picked its way along the thin trails, then managed a trot as they reached a wide logging road. A half-dozen kilometres down the road, Gabrielle steered the horse back into the trees, and they threaded their way to the field behind her cottage.

Dismounting, Juliette stared for a few minutes at the home Gabrielle had shared with Jean. She imagined how it would look in the daylight, bright green patchwork fields bordered by flowering hedges and screens of tall elms and copper beeches. But the colour was bleached from the scene now, leaving an abstract of black angular shapes, and swathes of grey and silver. Juliette thought the cottage looked forlorn, abandoned, but she kept her thought to herself.

They crept along the hedgerows, Gabrielle leading the way. When she reached the back window, she gave it a push. It slid open easily and she tumbled inside, only to cry out.

Juliette scrambled over the windowsill to stand beside her. As her eyes adjusted to the darkness, she discerned the ruin that lay before them. Furniture had been overturned, curtains torn down, dishes and glasses shattered. Gabrielle stood like a statue, her face hardened to marble.

"Oh, Gaby, I'm sorry. This looks like Eber's work. He must've been in a rage to find you gone."

Gabrielle said nothing. After a moment, she crossed the kitchen floor, shards of pottery and glass crunching beneath her boots. She found a broom and began sweeping automatically. Her face was blank, but Juliette sensed she was struggling to keep her emotions at bay. Silently, Juliette stayed her hand. They must leave things as they were.

Gaby turned her back on the room and climbed the stairs. Juliette watched her go, and then crossed the kitchen floor. Behind gaping doors, the cupboards were bare. The treasures Gabrielle had been so excited to look for only hours before had been looted. She turned to the pantry. There, pushed to the back of the bottom shelf, she found one jar of pears resting on its side. Carefully, she wrapped it up in a worn kitchen towel, tying a knot at the top to make a sack.

There was no sound from upstairs, and she began to worry. Slowly she mounted the stairs. In the doorway of a plain bedroom, she stood and looked down at Gaby, curled like a child on a bare mattress, clutching a black cardigan to her breast. Her long lashes were wet, her face shining with tears. Juliette stepped forward and ran her hand over the soft black hair.

"Gaby? It's time to go."

The green eyes opened, staring up at Juliette. "I'll never have your strength," she said. "Nothing has been right since he died. I'll just stay here."

Her words chilled Juliette, for she had seen this glassy look before during her early days with Sophie when the child seemed lost in perpetual silence and shadows.

She reached for the white marble hand holding the sweater and tugged on it. "No. I won't leave you, and I need you to guide me back."

"Everything is broken, Jules."

"Not everything. Not us."

"I've failed Jean. I couldn't even find his killer."

"You know I'll help you, as you helped me."

"Everyone who tried to help is dead. Just go." Gabrielle turned her face away and closed her eyes.

Juliette lay down on the bed, crossed her arms over her chest, and stared at the ceiling. She waited.

Finally, Gabrielle stirred. "What are you doing?"

"I'm not leaving without you. If you're staying, then so am I."

"*Merde.*"

Slowly Gabrielle rose from the bed, and slipped on the cardigan as if she were strapping on armour. Without a backward glance, she left the room and led the way downstairs to the back window.

"Wait," Juliette said, retrieving the small bundle from the kitchen. "I found one jar of pears. Not the treasure we came for, but something."

The night felt cool as they headed off across the field to the tethered horse. When they were almost at the end of the logging road, they heard the low rumble of a truck, its gears grinding over the rough ground. Quickly they dismounted and ducked into the dense woods, Juliette patting the horse to keep it quiet.

As the truck heaved into view, rocking from side to side, it looked like some strange forest animal, its hooded headlamps like two great eyes. From behind the trees, they could make out the silhouette of a half-dozen German soldiers riding in the open back. Beside her, Gabrielle gasped, and Juliette peered into the cab to see what had alarmed her.

It was a German officer, riding beside the driver. For an instant, his face was turned toward them as he scanned the edges of the wood, maybe looking for some fugitive shape flitting between the trees. Juliette saw that his chiselled face was haggard, smudges beneath his eyes, as if grown weary by the hour and the war that had ransacked all their lives. The moment passed, and she realized, with a kind of shock, that she had looked at him as if he were not a German, not a person of power, but just a man. It was only an illusion, she realized, a distortion caused by the moon and the dusty glass of the windscreen.

When the truck was out of hearing, they headed back to the camp as quickly as the treacherous ground allowed. The circle of drinking men were sleeping now, so they kept silent as they wiped down the horse before sneaking back to the safety of their tent.

Unwrapping the pears seemed to cheer Gabrielle up, but she was still unnaturally quiet.

"Do you want to talk, Gaby?"

"Dietsz was riding in that truck. That was him. For a moment, he seemed … almost vulnerable."

"So that was Dietsz. He looked —" Juliette shook her head. "But it's dangerous for us to believe that."

"And something else. Ever since you mentioned treasure, I've been thinking. Dietsz was going to tell Eber about Meyer and the murders. I think when he destroyed the cottage, Eber was searching for Meyer's stash. Everyone seems to think I must have it, but I've no idea where it is, Jules."

June 22

The morning brought them Bernard and news. Gone were the monk's robes, cast aside in favour of a woodsman's sweater, logging pants and boots. Still, Juliette saw he'd lost none of his authority, and his presence in the camp was a comfort.

She and Gaby shared breakfast with him by the edge of the stream, a thin band of pink from the rising sun appearing above the sentry hill, enough to light up the blue-grey clouds as if from inside. When Gaby brought out the preserved pears, his black brows rose in surprise, but Juliette only laughed mysteriously, and pressed him for details of Paris.

"You had no trouble on the journey?"

"None. We borrowed a habit from the convent. Madame Pascal made a formidable nun. She's now Céleste's aunt, visiting from the country. She's already printing and distributing butterflies. But there's a great need to get accurate information out of France to the Allies, especially about troop movements and fortifications on the northern coast."

"The invasion is close?"

Bernard shook his head. "Probably a year away."

"A year?" Gabrielle said. "The men here are already restless."

"Yes, that's what the meeting was about last night. We're stepping up the sabotage missions. Several of the bands are leaving tonight to hit the railroad lines. Telephone lines will also be cut."

"The Germans will fix them as soon as they're down."

"True, but in the interim, they will have to depend on radio communication, which can be intercepted. Everything helps, however small it seems. And though there are no factories in the Morvan that might be disabled, we're close to one vital part of the German plan."

"The canals," Juliette exclaimed. "Of course. I travelled from Vichy on a barge loaded with gravel."

Bernard nodded. "They need it to build bunkers all along the channel coast. We're blowing the lock at Pouilly-en-Auxois, north of Beaune, tonight. Anything we can do to slow construction of the fortifications helps."

"We?"

"You and Gabrielle, Henri and I, if you're willing."

Juliette glanced over at Gaby and they both nodded their assent.

"Good. Be ready to leave in an hour. Laurent is finding street clothes for us. We'll take the horses most of the way, then change outside of the town and walk in. There's a port, so there should be lots of people in the cafés."

"And lots of Germans, too?" Gabrielle asked.

"Around the port, yes, but the Free French group from Autun is planning a distraction for us. There's a metal bridge a kilometre or two from the lock. They'll blow it at midnight. Then we'll have ten minutes to set our charges. Our lock is the last before the great tunnel at the summit of the canal. If we're successful, it will take the Germans some time to repair the damage. I needn't tell you this is our only chance. Once the Germans know we're targeting the canal system, there'll probably be infantry stationed at every lock on the inland waterways."

Once the foursome left the shelter of the Morvan, they clung to copses wherever they could, but there was nothing like the wild thickness of trees they were leaving behind. They had no papers. Juliette reached down to touch the pistol she was carrying in her belt. She, Henri and Bernard were armed, but she worried for Gabrielle. Not knowing how to shoot, she had only her horse and her wits to save her should they run into trouble.

In the early evening, they tied the horses in a small thicket and changed their clothes: travelling suits for Henri and Bernard, a little worse for wear but presentable enough. For her and Gabrielle, Laurent had found summer dresses, each with a fiddly row of buttons, and a pair each of wooden-soled shoes. Given their respective heights, Gabrielle's dress was a shade too long, her own too short. They each carried two packets of explosive in their shoulder pads, grateful for the 1940s women's fashion which made them unnoticeable. They masked the strong almond smell of the explosive with a dousing of flowery perfume, and the four of them walked the last kilometre to the port, holding hands to look like strolling couples.

They passed the lock and slowed their steps. There were two heavy gates on either end of a long *barrage*, a dam of dry-masoned stone that measured several hundred metres from end to end, large enough to hold twenty barges.

"Bernard, there are people on the barges," Juliette whispered. She could smell smoke from cooking fires. Somewhere somebody laughed and a woman called out to a friend.

"We'll be lucky to punch a hole in the gates. They should be unharmed, and they can easily scramble to shore."

"And the guards?"

"Laurent says four sleepy *gendarmes* in the lockkeeper's hut. They'll not argue with Henri's pistol."

They avoided mention of the two powerful searchlights that would turn night into day in the area immediately next to the lock, all aware that they would have to count on the band from

Autun for that window of confusion.

They drifted into a café around nine o'clock and ordered a meal, eating slowly. It was a fine summer night, the light lingering and the curfew lenient as people wandered around the port and travelled to and from the barges waiting to cross the lock in the morning.

"I think we should try to be gay," Juliette said. "We don't look much like spooning couples."

They began to chatter, Juliette and Gabrielle gamely trying to fill the silence with meaningless dialogue. Toward the end of this charade, Bernard turned to Gabrielle.

"Oh, by the way, Henri said you were interested in a German called Meyer? Céleste couldn't find out much, except that he was a bit of a blackguard. For a while, he was stationed at rue des Saussaies, Gestapo headquarters, but they discovered he was taking bribes and shipped him out, back to his infantry unit. I'm sorry we couldn't —"

He stopped in mid-sentence. Two German soldiers were walking down the sidewalk in front of the café, stopping here and there at random tables to ask for papers.

"C'mon Henri," Juliette said, grabbing his hand.

With Henri in tow, she threaded a line through the tables, stopping not fifty metres from the soldiers. Then she swung her arms around Henri's neck and kissed him passionately. He leaned into her, his hands running up and down her back, her skirt sliding up slightly. Several men at nearby tables whistled. The Germans grinned, and shook their heads, as if there was no accounting for the immodesty of the French. They moved on.

Watching from their table, Bernard laughed and turned to Gabrielle. "Céleste always said Juliette had great legs. Let's go."

He tapped Henri on the shoulder as he passed, and the four of them walked toward the lock.

"Sorry, Henri." Juliette giggled.

"Don't be," he smiled, though Juliette could see that his face was scarlet.

The searchlights were on, two powerful beams bathing the area around the lock in an eerie, electric-blue light. Just beyond the beams, the darkness thickened.

They crouched alongside the bank beneath the trees, and Juliette and Gabrielle slipped their hands inside their dresses to remove the explosives. Henri and Bernard attached the fuses and wires and packed the explosives into two large cans. Then they waited. Juliette silently prayed, wishing luck to the sabotage group from Autun.

At two minutes past midnight, the sky exploded.

The searchlights flared brilliant white, then swung in a wild arc toward the explosion and away from the gates of the lock. Juliette crouched, tense, poised to run. Above her, the night was red, orange and black with fire and billowing smoke. Around her, soldiers shouted and cursed and ran toward the ruined bridge. Somewhere a siren began its mournful wailing.

"Now!" Bernard hissed.

Henri disappeared in the direction of the lockkeeper's hut, and with Bernard keeping watch, Juliette and Gabrielle slipped noiselessly into the canal.

The water was cold, currentless. Juliette kicked against the slimy pull of broad bladed grass, long tentacles that reached up from the bottom of the canal, pulling at her bare legs. She flipped onto her back, saw Gabrielle do the same. Together, using only their legs, they inched toward the centre of the lock, their hands holding the crude bombs above the surface. When they reached the exact point where the gates of the lock met, Juliette helped Gabrielle brace herself against the gates and carefully slid her bomb into Gabrielle's arms. Leaving her, she swam back to Bernard for the two slender logs that would keep the explosives in place.

The logs seemed weightless as she guided them through the water toward Gaby, whose teeth were chattering as she hung from the gates, cradling in one arm enough Ammonal to blow her to bits.

"Steady," Juliette whispered. "It's almost over."

She turned one log on end, disappeared below the surface to root it into the muck at the bottom of the canal. The water was opaque and she swam blindly. She began to count. One, two. Ten. Thirty seconds. *How long could she stay under?* Finally, her hands sank into the muck at the bottom of the canal. She shoved the end of the log into it, and shot to the surface. When her head broke through the water, she gulped air, grabbed the second log and disappeared again.

When she surfaced again, she heard feet pounding along the bank.

"Hurry," Gaby gasped. "Someone's coming."

She helped jam the bombs between the lock and the logs, and swam frantically for shore, trailing a fuse in her hand, Gabrielle keeping pace beside her. She treaded water as Gaby scrambled up the bank. Then Bernard was pulling at her arms. A German, unseen in the darkness, called out, the raucous syllables abruptly cut off by a single pistol shot.

Henri lowered his gun, and Juliette ran for the trees, knowing the shot would alert others. She could still hear commotion in the area of the bridge, the eerie whine of bullets, the louder bursts of machine guns. *Were the bullets coming closer?*

She looked back in time to see Bernard's face in the brief flare of the lit fuses. Mesmerized, she watched the light travel like two twisting snakes skimming across the water, heard shouting and a splash as a soldier dove in, frantically trying to reach the fuses.

The explosion vaulted him into the air like a great bird, arms and legs flailing in an eruption of water and woodchips and smoke. People on the barges began to scream and leap for the embankment. Juliette grabbed Gaby's hand. Bernard was suddenly beside them. The hole in the gates was only three feet wide to begin with, but the force of the water gushing through pried loose one piece of cracked wood, then another.

She felt a tug from Gaby and they ran for the horses, Henri and Bernard at their heels. The animals were nervous, alarmed by the smell of smoke and the sound of gunfire still coming from the site of the blown bridge downstream. There was no time to change clothes. Juliette boosted herself onto her horse, and, single file, the foursome moved through the trees, skirting the area of the gun battle.

In the lead, Bernard came to an abrupt halt, and Juliette reined her horse to the side, her heart pounding. She peered through the shadows.

A lone man confronted them, his face so blackened his voice seemed disembodied. "I'm with the band from Autun, the Free French. Help us. The Germans have five men pinned down."

"Gaby, you stay here. Mind the horses." Bernard said. He turned to Juliette and Henri. "Hurry!"

Quickly Juliette dismounted, her hand grasping her pistol. She turned to Gaby, who looked shocked, and handed her the reins. She had no time to comfort her. She turned and sped after Bernard and Henri.

*

G

Alone, Gabrielle pressed her hand to her mouth. She had recognized the voice of the man from Autun.

In an instant, she slid from her horse.

"Yves?" she whispered into the darkness.

She shivered in her wet dress, jumped when the shadowy form reached a hand to her neck.

"Amélie, where have you been? I've searched everywhere."

"There's no time. Take my horse. Get help."

He shook his head. "I can't leave you here."

The barrage of gunfire intensified.

"Go. I'll leave a message for you in the oak tree. I promise."

His eyes were bright in the dark face, his hair dishevelled. He stared at her wordlessly. Behind him, she heard people crashing through the underbrush of the thicket. Yves whirled around, caught up a comrade who emerged from the bushes, wounded in the leg, and hefted him onto the horse. Then he swung up behind him, and kicked hard.

Gabrielle rushed to help Bernard and Henri, each man half-carrying, half-dragging two wounded saboteurs, their faces streaked with blood and smoke.

"The others didn't make it," Juliette gasped, scrambling up onto her horse. "C'mon. Double up."

Gabrielle swung up behind Juliette and leaned against her back. She tried to distinguish the sound of Yves' horse, but it was soon swallowed up in the madness of the cross-country dash.

By the time they reached the camp, the sun was rising, streaks of pale rose and yellow behind milk-white clouds. Henri and Bernard shouted out for help for the wounded. Dazed and exhausted, Gaby and Jules left the horses with the *maquis* and walked toward their temporary home. Some of the men congratulated them, others nodded. She and Jules were accepted now. They had proven themselves.

Gabrielle fell onto her bed. She closed her eyes, and a vision of Yves' haggard face bloomed in the darkness. She turned toward Jules to tell her Luc was found, but her friend was already asleep. Her news would have to wait.

When she awoke, Jules' bed was empty. Still in her dirty street dress, Gabrielle gathered up a fresh set of clothes and some soap and waded into the stream. Behind the curtain of willow branches, the pool was almost warm. She stripped off the dress, soaped her body and her hair, the water silky against her skin. Her muscles ached, and her thighs were chafed where they'd rubbed against the horse, but she didn't care. She felt clean and new. She floated on her back, swaying in the ripples she made with the movement of her hands. She thought about Yves' voice, how in the darkness it had seemed to come from nowhere, how she had recognized it instantly.

She stood up abruptly, accidentally swallowing water, coughing, scrambling onto the bank. *Yves' voice.* She suddenly realized what it was about Danard that had made her feel uneasy when she'd first met him. She dressed quickly, the realization filling her with a sense of urgency. She had to find Jules.

The camp had never seemed so large. Everyone wanted to talk about the previous night's exploits. Two railway lines had been sabotaged, one near Dijon, one near Beaune. Besides the lock at Pouilly-en-Auxois, another, near Joigny, had been destroyed. The *maquis* were pleased, but edgy, wondering how the Germans would retaliate. The sentries were doubled. Gabrielle hurried from group to group, inquiring after Juliette. One group thought they'd seen her with Bernard, another thought she was with Henri.

Finally, Gabrielle found her, sitting on the ground amid a circle of pines, writing on a page spread upon a block of wood.

"What are you writing?"

"It's a letter to Sophie. I'm hoping Bernard can smuggle it out.

Henri brought me the paper from Laurent's tent." Juliette glanced up and smiled, then laid down her pen. "What is it, Gaby? Your cheeks are flushed."

"I'm not sure. Tell me, when the man from Autun asked us for help last night, did you recognize his voice?"

"No, I don't think so. But I was frightened, eager to get away. I didn't pay much attention."

"Try to remember. Did the voice remind you of *anyone?*"

"Hmm. Maybe a bit like Danard. There was a slight accent."

Gabrielle dropped to her knees and stared directly into Juliette's eyes.

"That's what I think, too. When I first met Danard, something about him upset me. But it wasn't *what* he said, it was how he spoke. I recognized the accent because I'd heard one like it before. Jules, the man in the path was Yves."

Juliette stared at her, unable and unwilling to believe her ears.

Gaby took Juliette's hands in her own. "He can't be your Luc Garnier. Not with that accent. I'm so sorry."

Juliette turned her face away abruptly. "But why?" she whispered. "Why would Yves use his name? Who is he?"

"I don't know. But I think we should find out."

"How?"

Gabrielle looked down at the unfinished letter. "Give me some paper. We'll leave a message. I told him I would."

*

J

⌒

June 26

Juliette had slept fitfully, hoping that Gaby wouldn't hear her toss-
ing and turning. She hadn't realized how much she had clung to
the sliver of belief that Luc might yet have been found. She felt as
if Luc had been killed twice.

She'd risen to a late morning that was soft and blue, with no
trace of wind. Cicadas trilled in the bark of the trees, the humming
chorus making the day seem drowsy, hotter than it really was. She
lazed against a willow tree, knee bent and bare foot resting against
the smooth bark. Through half-closed eyes, she watched Henri
shave in a mirror he'd tied to a branch by the stream, the sun
reflecting off its surface and playing across the water. Even among
the rough men of the *maquis,* she thought, he had the air of a
gentleman, a good, kind man. She wondered how he felt about
Germans now living in the Château Dumais, sleeping in his bed,
eating in the courtyard where once, long ago, they'd shared a magic
evening under the spell of Céleste.

"What are you thinking?" Henri asked between strokes of the
razor.

Juliette slid to the ground, settling down on a cushion of grass. "I
was thinking of your family, of the château." His face darkened.

"They're collaborators. They're lost to me."

"They're not evil, Henri. They tried. They helped me, tried to
help Pierre. Perhaps even now it's not as it seems. Perhaps they're
pretending for your sake, should you be arrested. If they had
influence with the Germans, they might convince them to release
you."

Henri wiped the shaving soap from his face and sat down beside her. The bare skin of his shoulders and arms was warm as he leaned toward her.

"Sweet Juliette," he teased. "You still see goodness even now. But they wanted to keep their fancy apartment, their status, at any price, even collaboration. So be it. I have the grass and the forest now, and sometimes a kiss from a lady with explosives in her shoulder pads."

Juliette smiled at him, pulled at the grass underneath her fingers.

"I was thinking," he continued. "Maybe I could go with you when you look for Sophie."

"Maybe. But what of Céleste?"

He shrugged. "A dream. Bernard is a better man than I."

She reached out and touched his cheek. "Not better, just different."

For a moment, they sat in silence, shoulder to shoulder, feeling an intense friendship, a quiet peace between them.

Juliette sighed. "What are you up to today?"

"Joseph and I are taking the wounded men from the FFI to Dun-les-Places. There's a doctor there who'll see to them."

He stood, reached for Juliette's hand and pulled her up, kissing her on the forehead. "Thanks for understanding," he murmured, then strode away.

She watched him head back to the camp, feeling guilty that she hadn't told him where she would be that day, and what she was planning.

She met Gabrielle at three o'clock and they struck through the woods for the logging shed. The forest paths were overgrown with buttercups and cornflowers and all sorts of other wildflowers that Juliette couldn't name. They gleamed in the sun like tiny gems.

When they reached the hut with its sagging roof, Juliette waited under the trees while Gaby stepped into the long grass that brushed against her knees. No one had been here for a long time. The clearing was wild and overgrown, undisturbed. Juliette lifted her head and listened, but heard only the chatter of birds. She kept watch as, warily, Gaby walked to the oak tree, stretched up to the hollow and tucked in the message. It read simply, *Meet me tonight in the cottage.*

"It's done," she said when she returned to Jules. "I'm going now."

Jules grasped her hands. "Are you sure? You could wait with me. It's you he wants to see."

"No, it's better this way, as we planned. The memory of Luc Garnier belongs to you. Yves trusted me with the name. I don't want to see his face when he knows I've told you, however innocently. If he still trusts me afterwards, he'll come to the cottage."

They embraced, Gaby's lips grazing Jules' cheek. *"Bonne chance, ma chérie."*

Juliette watched her go, listening to her retreating footsteps, still smelling the scent of soap from the beautiful black hair.

Perhaps a half-hour passed, no more. Juliette crouched in the shade of the woods, her eyes dazzled by the sun in the clearing.

At first she thought it was a trick of the light, a twist of her imagination. She gripped the side of a tree to steady herself. She shook her head as if to clear it. For the first time in her life, she doubted the evidence of her own senses. She must have made a sound, for the face swung momentarily toward her. There could be no doubt. She watched from her hiding place as the man reached for the note in the oak tree. *But he was dead. He'd been arrested, and they'd said he was dead. He had betrayed them, betrayed Sophie. What had happened? What had he done?*

Already, he was moving away, striding quickly to the opposite side of the clearing.

She followed him, her mind whirling with questions. Instinctively, she hugged the shadows of the trees, keeping the distance between them, matching his pace, ducking down when he stopped.

Once he called out, "Who's there?" but she couldn't speak. She had no reason to fear him, and yet she hung back. *Why had he lied to Gaby? Why had he hidden himself from her, from Henri and Bernard?*

On they went through the forest along a maze of paths, the distance between them gradually increasing. Juliette's heart was hammering.

Suddenly, he was out of sight. She peered through the dappled light, realized she could no longer hear him. She began to run, heedless of the snapping of branches and the pounding of her boots on the rough ground.

Almost without warning, the forest came to an end. There was no thinning of the trees, no change in the green light, but as if she had crossed some invisible line, Juliette found herself at the edge of a smooth lawn leading to the back of a stone church, stained gold by the sun.

He was gone. She'd lost him. She cursed herself for her hesitation. Now she wished she'd called out immediately, let him see her state of shock, demanded answers. She circled cautiously to the front of the church.

She read the sign on the front: "Dun-les-Places." She pushed against the heavy wooden doors, remembering Gaby's story of coming here once to bring clothes to the priest for one of the es-capees. It was a simple and beautiful place, the air cool and sweet, not musty, as if someone had opened a window to heaven. She sat down in one of the pews, the wood polished to a shine. Light streaming through the panes of stained glass painted the squat pil-lars and floor with splashes of pale red and yellow, the pattern of interlaced vines and leaves creating a dark tracery of shadows.

She closed her eyes, felt rather than saw the figure sliding into the pew next to her. For a moment longer, she clung to the tranquility of the church, then she turned and looked straight at him.

"Hello, Max." She spoke in English.

"Juliette, isn't it? So you remember me."

"I remember everything — the night we met, that was the night I made my choice to join the Resistance, though I scarcely realized at the time what that would mean. What happened to you?"

He shrugged. "What happens to most radio operators in Paris. I was captured, taken to the rue des Saussaies."

"And you escaped? From the prisons of the Gestapo?"

"They were moving a group of us. There was an air raid, some confusion. I managed to slip away in the darkness. Lucky, I've always been lucky."

Juliette stiffened. She might almost have believed him once, he sounded so sincere, had it not been for the long nights she had lain awake listening to Gaby's soft voice telling of terrible deeds. And she knew so much, had learned about Hans Meyer being stationed once at the rue des Saussaies, about the blackmail and the stealing of Luc's name. And remembering little Sophie's diamonds and Gabrielle's wooden box, the final piece of the puzzle clicked into place in her mind.

"No, Max," she sighed. "You're not lucky. I'll tell you what I think happened. You were arrested. I understand what happens when they arrest you. We would've forgiven you for giving them our names. But promising to work for them? Infiltrating the escape line? You delivered the identity papers to Mathilde and Luc, didn't you? What happened that night, Max? Please don't lie. It doesn't matter anymore."

"You don't understand. I didn't have a choice. I felt sick about what I was doing. I took the papers, but it was almost dawn when I reached the flat. All hell broke loose when the roundup started. They were looking for Jews. We were trapped. We tried to hide, but they found Mathilde first, dragged her from under the bed by her hair. She was screaming. Luc tried to help her, and fought them. They killed him on the spot. There was nothing I could do."

Juliette turned her face away from him. *Yes,* she thought, *Luc would have done that, would have died trying to protect Mathilde, while this coward remained hidden.* Her contempt for him was so deep she couldn't speak. She felt the silence between them thicken. From outside the stone walls of the church, she heard a low rumbling sound like thunder.

Max started to his feet. "Listen. Do you hear that?"

She grabbed him by the sleeve of his jacket, pulled him down. "Tell me what happened next. Tell me how you stole Luc's identity. That's how you got away from them, isn't it? You switched the identity papers. Did you beat his face so no one would recognize him? Was he still alive when you did that?"

He pushed her hands away. "You're crazy. He was dead."

"What else did you steal, Max? Where had Mathilde hidden

the jewellery from her father's store?"

He froze. The muted rumbling outside grew louder.

"There was no jewellery."

"Stop it Max. I've seen it. Gaby has it. You took it and ran back to the Morvan. But Hans Meyer recognized you, didn't he? He bled you dry and you killed him."

Juliette jumped to her feet, her legs quaking. From beyond the walls, she could hear running, screaming. A pistol shot, then the unmistakable rattle of a Bren gun. She whirled around, but Max was already running, not to the doors, but toward the back of the church. Instinctively, she followed him.

Behind the altar, there was a curtained doorway leading to a small vestibule, where the priests donned their robes for mass. Beyond that, an archway led to stairs that twisted upwards. She followed him up and up the worn stone steps. At the top, boards had been nailed crookedly across an open archway. She waited while he wriggled his body through one of the gaps. He disappeared into the darkness beyond, without a backward glance or an offer to help.

She waited, listened. She could hear boots striding across the stones of the church floor, angry shouts, sharp cries of pain. She ducked between the boards and entered the shadows.

She felt along the dusty walls to keep her balance in the dark. This must be the way to the church steeple, fallen into disrepair and boarded off. The stairs took a last twist, beyond which she could see light again streaming across an open floor through the gaps of a wooden railing. She looked up into the open mouth of a huge silent bell.

Across the floor, Max was lying on his stomach, his head covered by his arms. She crept toward him on her hands and knees and peered through the railing.

From high above, she had a long view of countryside, the village and the square in front of the church. A field had been set on fire. Above it, a large bird hovered, a black silhouette with a golden wing, and the sky glowed red. Below, villagers had been driven from their houses to huddle in terrified groups. There were Germans everywhere, ordinary soldiers and SS. She gasped when she spied among them a hated face. Eber. He strutted toward the church, shouting orders as he went.

Frantically, she scanned the groups of villagers. *Where were the young men?* There were women crying, children with their faces pressed into their mother's skirts, a grandfather who could barely stand, but no young men. She turned her attention back to the racket of boots and voices below her and realized what was happening. The soldiers had driven them all inside the church. They had arrested a whole village of men.

Like a knife, the memory of Henri's voice cut through her panic, cutting her to the bone: *Joseph and I are taking the wounded men from the FFI to Dun-les-Places.* She squirmed closer to Max and shook him.

"Do you have a gun? We have to do something. We have to try to get help."

He rolled over onto his back and stared into the space above him, avoiding her eyes. "You're as reckless as Luc. There's nothing we can do except stay quiet and hope they don't find us."

For a moment, her anger was worse than her fear, a blind rage that threatened to suffocate her. She wouldn't hide like this, like a rat in a corner, doing nothing to help the men trapped below. She refused to lie passively on the floor beside Max. She got to her feet, crossed to the top of the stairs. Perhaps she could surprise a German, get his gun.

Then she saw it — the coil of rope attached to a pulley at the edge of the archway. She gave a little cry and leapt forward. She could ring the bell, ring it and ring it and the *maquis* would hear.

The rope was thick and heavy in her hands. She was pulling at it with all her strength when she staggered forward, pain ripping through her skull from a blow to the back of her head. Dizzy, she swayed for a moment and then was swallowed in a dark fog.

She lifted her head slowly, her vision blurred. She touched her fingers to the throbbing at the back of her head. It was swollen where Max had struck her, probably with the butt of his pistol, but there was no blood. He had vanished.

She crawled over to the coil of rope, only to see that he had cut it, the loose end dangling high in the rafters where she couldn't reach it. She felt a wave of helplessness, for herself, for the men in the church below.

Were they still there? She had no idea how long she had been unconscious. As her strength gradually returned, she sensed an unearthly silence surrounding her. Perhaps the Germans had left, she prayed. She crept across the floor to the railing and looked down upon the square.

It was still light, a golden, late afternoon light. A house was burning, flames licking slowly up its sides. The villagers watched the fire in stony silence, except for one woman who sobbed in the arms of an old man. Beneath Juliette, inside the church, was a terrible stillness.

Suddenly, a window exploded in the burning house, and the fire roared, surged upward, racing for the roof. She could hear its rushing now, like a greedy, destructive wind. Its heat shimmered across the square, the fear-stricken faces of those who watched bathed in an eerie orange glow.

She heard shouting below, and the doors of the church opened outward with a bang, boots crunching on the gravelled path. The prisoners were herded forward, hands tied behind their backs. She counted. Two, five, twelve. So many, and still more coming. Light glinted off a pair of spectacles and Juliette stopped counting, stopped breathing. Henri. Beside him, a burly man with a shaggy beard. Joseph.

Heedless of her own safety, she forced herself to stand and leaned over the railing, willing Henri with all her might to glance up, to see her.

The guards prodded him forward with the others, jabbing between their shoulder blades with the butts of their machine guns. Some prisoners were dragged, dust from the square rising and settling on their trousers.

With growing comprehension and horror, Juliette watched as the men were lined up in front of the church. The lowering sun illuminated the black and purple swellings on their faces, the bloodstains on their torn clothing. One man fell to his knees and couldn't, or wouldn't, rise. Henri stood at attention, one arm supporting Joseph. His face was defiant as he stared forward at the guards.

The villagers began to panic, screaming and pressing forward, calling out names of fathers, husbands, sons. They were met by a line of gun barrels, angry warnings in German.

Then suddenly a silence fell, profound and sorrowful, the silence of breath withheld and a thousand prayers rising into the radiant, indifferent sky.

Eber's brutal voice cried out in absolute command, shattering the stillness. Almost simultaneously, the Bren guns erupted and the square spun out of control.

Juliette sank to her knees, her hands gripping the railing.

As the bullets sprayed across the line of men, their bodies jerked and twisted. One man, still miraculously standing, began to run. A burst of bullets nearly severed his body in half.

But Juliette's horrified eyes were fixed on the terrible spray of blood erupting from Henri's chest. He shuddered once, slid sideways to the ground, his body falling across Joseph's as if to protect it.

In the eternity of the few seconds that followed, Juliette knelt utterly still, numb. She opened her mouth, but could make no sound. She tried to stand but her body wouldn't move. The slaughter was imprinted on her gaze, her soul, a blur of images she would never forget. Then, involuntarily, her body did move, shaking uncontrollably. She knotted her hands in her lap, tried to breathe as ice spread through her veins.

The air reeked of blood. She stared down at the faces of the villagers, slack with shock, their eyes dull and expressionless.

Juliette forced herself to count, though she shrank from the sight of the bodies. Twenty-one. They'd executed twenty-one men in sixty endless seconds. She felt a trembling right down to the bone, an unbearable tension and nausea in her stomach. Henri had died without seeing her, without knowing she was there. She lay down on the wooden floor, closed her eyes and waited to be found. There was no way back, no way forward. No way out.

When Juliette lifted her head again, she was still alone. The night was filled with smoke. She crawled forward and saw that the entire village was ablaze. Barns, houses, stores, all were burning.

She watched motionless as the roof of someone's home collapsed, sparks spraying across the sky. A terrified plough horse galloped across the square, eyes rolling wildly. There was a cacophony of dogs barking, pigs squealing.

Madness. How glad she was that she had gotten Sophie away from this cursed country, this senseless cruelty. Then she remembered with a jolt Henri and Joseph and the others whose names she didn't know, and all feeling drained away. She thought she might never move, might never speak again. Except to bear witness to the horror still playing itself out beneath her.

She heard a single pistol shot and her eyes flew to a figure moving in front of the church. A soldier was wandering among the heap of bodies, casually finishing off those who were still stirring, with a gun pressed against the head.

The sight sickened her, but then she thought of Max, and her anger saved her. He'd had a gun. At the very least, there would have been one bullet for Eber. Gabrielle would have applauded her for that shot.

Gaby. She'd told Max she had the jewels. He had a gun.

She felt adrenalin surge through her body, warming her limbs. She cursed herself for her idiocy, crept back to the archway and through the boarded door. Silently, she descended the twisting stairs, fully aware that around each turn she might meet a German.

There was not a sound in the church. She stood in the vestibule, taking in deep breaths. She remembered how sweet the air had been when she'd sat in the pews with Max. She scanned the interior for an open window. Nothing.

She dropped to her knees and crawled behind the altar to the opposite wall of the church. There, in a little cloakroom, she found a window, its glass shattered. She vaulted herself up and over the stone sill, dropping onto the soft grass behind the church.

The huge shadow of the forest beckoned to her. She put her head down and ran.

*

G

Gabrielle had waited all day in the woods behind her cottage for Jules to return. She'd imagined likely scenarios, then increasingly frightening and wild ones until her head ached. Once, she almost decided to return to the camp where she knew Laurent and Bernard would already be missing her, but she couldn't move. She had to know if Yves had forgiven her for revealing his secret identity, if he still cared enough to keep their rendezvous.

It was a tender June night, the moon the colour of honey and the air perfumed with wild roses and strawberries as she crossed the field to her cottage. She tugged at the window and slipped inside, crossed the living room, bathed in soft, pearl-grey shadows, to curl up in one of the armchairs before the cold fireplace. It was almost a year since Jean had been executed. She could scarcely believe the woman she'd become.

She stared at the floor where she and Yves had made love. What had that meant? Was it just two lonely people living intensely in the midst of so much death? Was it daring fate? She didn't know. She couldn't know who he really was, what had happened in his past, why he'd lied to her. But he was good, he'd saved lives, those of the pilots and the children who'd hidden in her bedroom. Everyone lied. Except Jules. She trusted Jules.

She heard the low, smooth sound of an engine, and stepped to the window. Glimpsing hooded headlights, she ducked back into the shadows, listening intently. The car slowed, but then moved on and she breathed again.

She crossed the room, returned to the window that overlooked the field and the forest beyond, and leaned her forehead against the glass. She would watch for him, for his low, loping shadow against the hedgerows. She didn't feel sad. She had learned to accept the vagaries of war, the people it snatched from you and the unexpected blessings of strangers who became dear to you.

She caught a slight movement from the corner of her eye, and stepped back quickly from the window. It came from the side of the cottage, not from the field. Her eyes widened as the figure stood for a moment outside the window, then slowly pushed up the sash.

Paralyzed, she watched him swing a leg across the sill and stop halfway through the window when he saw her, saying nothing, only looking at her.

She gazed back at Dietsz, and all her fear drained away. She realized now that only Jean had ever looked at her that way before — as if he knew everything there was to know about her in an instant, and still thought there was more to reach for.

"Gabrielle. Why have you come back?"

The high cheekbones were more pronounced now in the thinner face, the mouth still chiselled, but less proud.

Instinctively, she reached out, grasped his hands. "What are you doing here? You look ill. Are you unwell?"

He laughed, a harsh, grating sound. "If only that were all. I tried to stop them, Gabrielle. They would not listen. Eber would not listen."

"*Mon Dieu*. What has he done?" Dietsz shook his head, as if trying to shake away a nightmare.

"Reprisals. Villages all over the Morvan. Three columns of soldiers, Gestapo and SD from Château-Chinon and Chalon-sur-Saône."

She pulled her hands away. "I must go then, I have to warn them."

"It's too late. All is done. Stay here with me."

She heard a longing in his voice she had never heard before. He took a tentative step toward her, reached out, buried his hands in her hair.

She placed her hands flat against his chest, pushed him away gently.

"Gerhardt," she whispered, and shook her head.

He released her instantly, stood with his head averted. "Forgive me."

"I do. I did, a long time ago."

"Where will you go?"

"Back to the camp."

"You are with the *maquis?* I see. Then we are still enemies, after all. I hope never to find you in your forest."

"Then you'll let me go now?"

"From here, yes."

She stood on tiptoe, kissed his cheek. "*Adieu,* Gerhardt."

He held her hand for a moment. "Before you go, there is one last promise to you I must keep. I know who killed Hans Meyer. He must also have killed Marie-Claire and the priest."

She stared at him, then led him back to the living room, gesturing to a chair.

"Please, sit. Tell me everything." She sat in front of him, leaning toward him.

"It was as I thought. Père Albert knew this person, but felt the need to protect him. We searched the Père's rooms and found a letter, written by Klaus to Marie-Claire. I do not know how the priest came to have it."

"He got it from me," Gabrielle blurted out. "Marie-Claire's parents gave it to me. It was in German. I couldn't understand it so I gave it to Père Albert. He might have lived, if I had —"

"If you had trusted me. But no matter. I did not always trust you."

"What did the letter say?"

"Klaus found Meyer's stash, jewels supposedly, and gave them to Marie-Claire the night before he was sent to the Russian Front. Then he must have feared that I would guess the truth and follow them to her. He sent her the letter to warn her against me ... What is it, Gabrielle?"

She was sitting straight up, her back rigid.

"The jewels, the damn jewels. I've had them all this time, but I didn't know. Marie-Claire's parents gave them to me with the letter. I thought they were just gaudy trinkets."

"Klaus told Marie-Claire to flee, take the jewels and leave the area. She must have stayed to warn you. She and Klaus had already worked out the identity of the man Meyer was blackmailing. The letter only confirms it. Klaus told her to beware of me, and someone called the tailor's son, someone Meyer recognized from his days in Paris."

"What did you say?" Gabrielle whispered.

"The tailor's son. It must be someone in the Resistance. A code name." He leaned forward, a sense of urgency in his voice. "You know this man?"

Gabrielle felt a wave of revulsion. She had cared for him, danced with him, laid with him before the fire, the man who had left the ugly note at the graveside, the man responsible for Jean's death. *It couldn't be.* She felt ashamed, confused, wanting to push away what she had learned from Dietsz. *It must be some trick,* she thought, *some ruse to trap him.*

She stood and faced Dietsz, feigning a calmness she didn't feel.

"I must go now. People will be looking for me, and they can't find us here together."

For a moment, he said nothing, only looking up at her from the chair, his eyes filled with sadness, revealing his last secret.

The words resounded in Gabrielle's head as if he had spoken them aloud. *He couldn't look at me with such love and still hurt me. He's telling the truth.*

With an effort, he turned his face away. "Do not do this, Gabrielle. The priest tried to protect him, and he died for his trouble."

They both heard the sound at the same time, the sliding of the window, like a sigh in the darkness.

Dietsz was on his feet in an instant, his hand on the holster of his gun.

Gabrielle swivelled around, saw a dark shape lunge toward her. Yves' left arm encircled her shoulder, his right hand pointed a gun at Dietsz.

"No, Yves. Don't be foolish. He's the Kommandantur." She stepped away from him, saw that the lines around his mouth were deeper, the circles under his eyes darker.

"Take his gun, Amélie."

She hesitated, and his eyes widened in disbelief.

"You trust him? You trust a German? What have you told him? What have you done?"

"You should ask instead what he's told me, about the tailor's son."

Yves' face hardened. He crossed to Dietsz in one easy step, snapping open his holster and removing the pistol. He tossed it across the floor. "Sit down, both of you. Tell me what I'm being accused of."

"You killed Hans Meyer." Gabrielle said.

"I did. He was hiding near the logging camp, waiting for the courier. Had I not killed him, Jean would have been captured. I did it for Jean, and the Resistance. How was I to know they would execute Jean?"

"But Jean was deliberately framed, they found personal items from Meyer hidden in his desk in the *mairie*."

"So ask yourself, Amélie, how would I have access to the *mairie*? Who had better access than the Kommandantur?"

Dietsz's eyes darkened from blue-grey to slate. "Tell her what your cover was in Dun-les-Places. Were you not a postman? It will be easy enough to check. A postman, or a deliveryman. It would not be difficult to gain access to the *mairie*. There was time, before the body was found."

Gabrielle swung her face from one man to the other, the first seeds of doubt blossoming into confusion. "But what of the others, Marie-Claire and Père Albert? Why did they have to die?"

"Think, Amélie. Who was Marie-Claire most afraid of? She confessed to the priest and he died too. He killed them. Dietsz killed them for the jewels."

Gabrielle felt the tension inside her suddenly release.

You killed my husband, you bastard.

She stood up, smiled at Yves. "All right. I believe you. Let's get out of here. Leave him."

She took a step toward him, then another, saw his eyes harden.

"I'll not leave him alive. Stand up, Kommandantur."

Yves raised his gun.

Gabrielle stepped in front of it.

"Yves, listen to me. Dietsz told me there were reprisals tonight. They will only be worse if you kill him. You'll put the whole village in danger, my village. Tie him up. Leave him. We can slip back to the camp, get the jewels and be gone before morning."

Yves hesitated, and Gabrielle saw her chance. She strode over to the window, gathered up the curtains that had been torn down during Eber's search of the cottage, and twisted the material in her hands. "This will do for rope. Help me. Put him in the kitchen."

Gabrielle gripped the twisted curtains with all her strength to keep her hands from trembling. Her heart flipped and veered in her chest. She dared not look at Dietsz.

She waited an eternity, breathless, before Yves waved Dietsz forward with his gun, then pushed him down onto a kitchen chair.

Swiftly, she knelt behind Dietsz, pulled his hands behind him. She squeezed them once, winding the cloth around his wrists, forming a knot. As she stood, she feigned a mighty pull on the cloth, shielding the loose binding with her body.

"Let's go."

Yves took a step forward, raising the gun to strike a blow across Dietsz's temple.

Gabrielle tensed, saw his arm freeze in mid-air, his eyes lit with panic.

She swivelled around. A figure had materialized in the doorway.

Juliette.

Turning back to Yves, she caught the glint of moonlight on metal as he aimed the gun at Juliette.

"No!" she screamed, diving forward.

She felt no pain, no fire. The impact of the bullet threw her backward and she collapsed into Juliette's arms. As she slipped to the floor, she felt an intense cold creeping down her throat. She saw Juliette's face, like a distant moon filling her sky, briefly. As she turned her head for the last time, she saw Dietsz's body slam into Yves, heard a second shot reverberate through the night.

*

J

Juliette bit down on her lip, tasted the blood. A sob wracked her body; her bones shuddered.

The German officer knelt beside her, searching Gaby's neck frantically for a pulse. She heard him moan as he gathered her into his arms, cradling her face, her hair a dark pool around him.

"You're Dietsz?" she asked softly.

He looked up, his face stricken.

Juliette leaned forward, her heart cracking open as she felt Gaby's cool, pale cheek beneath her hand.

She turned away, saw the dark shape of Max, limbs splayed, motionless. "He's dead?"

"Too late."

"Did Gaby know?"

"He tried to confuse her, but he made one mistake. When he mentioned the jewels, she knew." His voice broke.

Juliette reached for his hands and tugged at them gently. "Let her go now. We must let her go."

He touched Gaby's face, a soft tracing with his fingertips, and lowered her head to the floor. When he moved away, Juliette saw the dark stain covering the breast of his uniform where he had held her to him.

He stood with his back to Juliette, staring at the tailor's son.

"Who was he?" he asked.

"I knew him as Max. Once I helped him get to Paris. He stole the jewels from a Jewish girl, and an identity from someone I loved. He must've come back here because it was the only place he knew."

"Meyer recognized him, and blackmailed him. You know about Meyer, about the murders? He put coffins around his victim's necks to shift blame onto the Resistance."

"Gaby told me. She was my friend."

"So you also are a *résistante?*"

"Yes. Will you arrest me?"

"For tonight, I am not German."

"Then help me."

"How? What are you asking?"

"I can't leave her here alone with him. And I don't want soldiers to bury her." She did not say *German* soldiers, but she saw the pain in his face when he turned around.

"Very well. I will carry her."

"You loved her?"

He stooped over her body, lifting her gently.

"How could that be?" he puzzled, his eyes blurring with tears. "She was my enemy. I barely knew her."

JULIETTE BENOIT

OCTOBER 1944

October 1, 1944

Today I found this journal I was forced to abandon two years ago in Paris. It was still there, hidden in the hallway outside of the apartment I shared with Céleste in the rue des Beaux-Arts. I have read it, page by page, wondering at the voice of the woman who wrote it, and sometimes missing her.

I left the Morvan, Gaby's forest, ten days ago, with Bernard at my side, just as he was in mid-September when we marched through the main square of St-Léger, once again a free village. The war rages on across the Rhine, but for me it's finished. Others will mark the final days of cataclysmic events, while I try to pull together the little threads of individual lives.

I was numb for months after the deaths of Henri and Gaby, after witnessing the horrifying events in the martyred village of Dun-les-Places. I must have seemed a spectre as I walked among the men in the camp. I felt burdened with unspeakable secrets and the weight of testimony. I could feel at ease only with Bernard. He read to me, talked to me about Sophie, told me stories about Henri I had never known.

One day, when it was safe, we rode horses, black stallions with glossy coats captured from the Germans, back to Dun-les-Places. Even among the gutted buildings it looked out upon, the church, with its smooth lawns and golden stone, exuded a profound sense of peace. It was a perfect day under a dazzling sky. I couldn't make nature and history coincide when I knelt there. It was as if the church had risen above the violence of that night to something higher, something healing, as if its serenity made the memory of those who died there incarnate and inviolate.

My heart began to beat again that day.

I sorely miss Gaby, especially at night when I can almost hear her voice as it was in the convent, when we would lie awake for hours and whisper our secrets like schoolgirls. I feel the weight of living, while she lies cold and still. Logically, war should change everything, but it didn't change enough for Gaby. It didn't change Max's greed, or prevent him from committing murder. Amongst so many anonymous deaths caused by the war, I think of hers as personal, a private matter between her, the husband she mourned, the man who betrayed them and the German who loved her.

There were acts of sabotage and skirmishes with the Germans after she died, but I never saw Dietsz again. I know I shall never forget that moonlit tableau as we stood over her grave, locked together, unable to move. The small cross we erected in the forest is almost invisible now with trailers of ivy and bright weeds.

Then on June the fourth, almost a year after Gaby's death, Bernard and I crouched over a radio in Laurent's tent and heard the words on the BBC that signalled the invasion. Amid a flurry of coded messages, we heard the first line of Verlaine's poem, *Chanson d'Automne*. We'd been hearing it for several weeks. We held our breath, and waited. This time, the pattern was altered and the first line of the poem was followed by the second. The Allies would land within forty-eight hours. The news rocked us. In that moment, we knew — the Resistance knew — the fight for France was on.

My period of mourning was over.

Within months, the Germans began to retreat, almost as quickly as they had come and, in some cases, just as painfully. They left behind them ashes that were once villages, graveyards that were once fields of grain.

When our role in the fighting was finished, Bernard and I leaned into each other on the deck of a barge on the Burgundy canal and watched the great forest of the Morvan slowly disappear, each lost in our own memories. When we could no longer see even its green shadow on the horizon, we turned away, toward the future. We boarded a train in Joigny and reached Paris at dawn.

The platform was crowded, but I spotted Céleste and the proud, dignified figure beside her immediately. Madame Pascal, Bernard told me, who'd cried like a mother burying a daughter when she'd learned of Gaby's death. We were showered with kisses and flowers, bottles of champagne and fruit. The second liberation, Céleste teased, recalling how on Liberation Day the streets of Paris were ankle-deep in flowers.

Now as I walk these streets alone, the winding cobblestone lanes and the sweeping boulevards and the bridges over the Seine where Luc and I kissed, I realize that the Paris I knew will never exist again. But this new city is exquisite, too. It bears its scars well. The old women in the bird market are beautiful with their weathered skin and shy smiles. Some of them wear black armbands for the sons they have lost. The young women are tanned and lean, as stylish as ever in their patchwork dresses and tricolour scarves. And the light is still intoxicating, the palest gold of champagne, the deepest pink of a rose.

Amid the lingering jubilance of Liberation, there are murmurs, too, of shame. While many young women leapt onto the running boards of their liberators' trucks, and vaulted over the treads of their tanks to flood the soldiers in a deluge of kisses and tears, other women felt the sharp bite of scissors as their hair was cut and their heads shaved. Young Monique from the brothel was shorn before her father could save her. A final, cruel injustice. Other suspected collaborators ducked for cover, and those not quick or slippery enough met a brutal retribution.

There are long shadows in the narrow streets of the Marais. Drancy yawns empty in the moonlight. This, too, is part of the City of Light.

On my last night in Paris, Céleste coaxed my shoulder-length hair, emphatically plain brown again, into an elegant roll, and Madame Pascal fitted me with a fine dress, white with thin stripes of green, long hidden in a cupboard. We packed a basket with cheese and purple grapes, a bottle of Dumais wine and chocolate, and joined a street party.

Madame Pascal watched Céleste dancing with Bernard. "*Ravissante,*" she sighed, and it was true. Céleste was ravishing, radiantly in love.

Later, Bernard danced with me, and whispered that I mustn't stay away too long.

I leave in the morning for England and from there for Scotland and Sophie. My arms ache to hold her again, to run my fingers through her curls, to feel her arms around my neck. In my suitcase is a carved wooden box enclosing a jumble of necklaces and brooches that seem to dance in the light. I'm bringing them home to be part of Sophie's future and to cleanse them of the past. The photograph of a handsome young man named Jean Aubin is mine alone.

Someday, perhaps, I will write again of the people who touched my life, so deeply, so unexpectedly. Someday perhaps, but not now. Not yet.

MORE FINE MYSTERY FICTION
FROM SUMACH PRESS ...

* SLANDEROUS TONGUE
by Jill Culiner

* BOTTOM BRACKET
by Vivian Meyer

* GRIZZLY LIES
by Eileen Coughlan

* JUST MURDER
2004 ARTHUR ELLIS AWARD
FOR BEST FIRST CRIME NOVEL
by Jan Rehner

* MASTERPIECE OF DECEPTION
by Judy Lester

* HATING GLADYS
by Leona Gom

THE VICKY BAUER MYSTERIES
by Leona Gom —

* AFTER IMAGE
* FREEZE FRAME
* DOUBLE NEGATIVE

www.sumachpress.com

— Arthur Haberman

JAN REHNER has published poetry, literary criticism,
a feminist analysis of infertility and a text on critical
thinking. Her first mystery novel, *Just Murder* (Sumach
Press) was the winner of the 2004 Arthur Ellis Award for
Best First Crime novel. Jan lives in Toronto and teaches
humanities and writing at York University.